THE WEAVER CONSPIRACY

A Novel By Ken Blaisdell

D1521176

Outskirts Press, Inc.
Denver, Colorado

The Weaver Conspiracy

Outskirts Press, Inc.
http://www.outskirtspress.com

Paperback ISBN: 978-1-4327-1570-0
Hardback ISBN: 978-1-4327-0971-6

Outskirts Press and the "OP" logo are trademarks belonging to Outskirts Press, Inc.

PRINTED IN THE UNITED STATES OF AMERICA

Dedicated to my loving wife, Diane, without whose support, encouragement, and unending patience, this book could never have become a reality.

To MARY,
BEST WISHES!

Prologue

Henri Marchaund focused his telescope on the naked woman sunbathing on the deck of the sailboat as it cruised serenely in front of his Mediterranean villa. At eighty-two, Henri no longer became aroused while watching the young women on the boats, but he would be damned if he'd give up looking.

Hearing the new-mail "bing" from his computer, Henri looked up from the eyepiece to see who had sent the message. It was from the Bank of Zurich.

Picking up his cane, he crossed the few steps to his desk, and dropped down heavily into his old leather chair. The message was a confirmation of the transfer of funds into one of his numerous accounts.

No sooner had he read the communication when a second e-mail popped up.

My dear Henri:

I hope this note finds you well and enjoying your splendid view of the sea. I wish that I could be there with you, but alas, business before pleasure. As you are probably aware by now, the funds have been moved into your account, and the wheels on this end are in motion. I apologize for the delay in getting the project started, but I only recently received confirmation regarding the date and location where the action must take place. As we speculated, our best opportunity will come during his class-reunion trip at the end of October. I realize that that does not allow much time to bring the pieces of such a project together, but that is why I have turned to you, old friend. If anyone can do it, that person is you! I know that you will have much to do, so I won't keep you any longer.

Yours faithfully,
Leland

Henri smiled at Leland's flattery, but it was true. Few people in the world had the connections and resources that Henri Marchaund had culled together over his many years in the business. But it was also true that this project—perhaps his last—would be more complex, higher risk, and unlike anything he had ever orchestrated before. And if he managed to make it all come together, it would be a fitting end to his career; his *pièce de résistance*.

As with all such projects, Henri needed to give this one a simple, nondescript name to make communication on the matter easier, and somewhat secure. He settled on the name "Weaver," after one of his mother's favorite sayings; "Oh, what a tangled web we weave when first we practice to deceive."

O, what a tangled web we weave,
when first we practice to deceive!
                    Sir Walter Scott (1771–1832)

But when we've practiced quite a while,
how vastly we improve our style.
                    J. R. Pope (1909–1991)

Chapter 1

Tuesday, October 14
Laurel, MD

The President's armored limousine was parked with its left side as close to the hotel door as it could get without being on the sidewalk. Black Secret Service Suburbans were parked directly in front and back. A pair of police motorcycles waited at each end of the line. The engines of all seven vehicles were running and their drivers were ready.

The hotel door opened, and two Secret Service agents emerged into the cool October morning. They quickly, but thoroughly, surveyed the area, and then one of them spoke into the miniature microphone attached to his wrist. A moment later a phalanx of agents came out of the hotel moving nearly as one, closely surrounding their boss, the President of the United States. Onlookers had been kept well back from the hotel door; a lesson painfully learned when President Reagan was shot in 1981 while leaving the Washington Hilton Hotel.

Just as the lead agent, Aaron Powell, got the back door of the limo open, the *crack!* from a high-powered rifle split the air, and he dropped lifelessly, half inside and half outside of the car. Almost instantly, Claire Bradley, the agent to the President's right grabbed him by the back of the head and pushed him down and forward into the car while shielding him with her body. But the President stumbled over Powell's legs and fell to

1

the sidewalk, out of Bradley's grasp. No longer in a position to help push him into the car, she jumped up and used her torso like a tent to fill the open area between the roof of the car and the open door.

A second shot echoed between the buildings, and Bradley was hit in the back. It was a glancing blow across her vest that deflected the shot, causing it to strike her in her unprotected left arm. Letting out an oath, she held her position, and the agent behind the President, Dan Burger, shoved him head-long into the limo, over the top of Powell's body and under Bradley's. Scrambling in on top of the President, shielding him with his body, Burger yelled for Bradley to get in. But Bradley, her left arm limp by her side, took hold of the fallen Powell's belt, and with all of her might, heaved him deeper into the car. She then grabbed hold of his legs, and with a shove, rolled him inside, head on the floor, and legs on the seat. She yelled, "Go! Go! Go!" as she pushed the heavy door closed. The car was screeching away from the curb as another shot hit Bradley. She collapsed to the sidewalk, as lifeless as her friend Powell had been.

Two agents rushed forward to carry Bradley back into the hotel as the others took up covering positions, scrutinizing the building from which the shots were fired, aiming machine pistols at the upper windows.

Suddenly, at the end of the block, the President's limousine came to a stop. It hesitated just a moment, and then came back toward the hotel in reverse, nearly as fast as it had driven away. It stopped in the middle of the road, and its back doors opened. Agent Burger, the recently-deceased Powell, and the President got out. The "President", a solidly built man who belied his 67 years by a decade, placed his fingers into the corners of his mouth and let out a shrill whistle. All of the agents, including the mortally-wounded Bradley, got up and began walking toward him.

"Well done," said James Gants, the presidential stand-in, and the agent's immediate boss. "Two casualties, but the President got out un-scathed. Good reactions, and good execution from the play book." He looked at Bradley, and added, "And good improv. Throwing yourself over the top of the door probably kept me from getting hit. How long have you had that move up your sleeve?"

"Just came to me as you fell over Powell's body, sir," she said.

"On the other hand," he went on, "you left yourself in the open far too long after I was in the car, and you delayed closing the door and the pull-away."

"Begging your pardon, sir," she replied as she removed her laser-tag vest, "My body was blocking the open door the whole time, and I think I got Powell into the car pretty quickly, considering he was dead weight and control told me I was *wounded* so I only had one arm."

"My point, exactly," Gants replied as he handed his own vest to another agent. "Powell would have been dead. It was a head shot from a thirty-aught-six; there wouldn't have been much left, and you'd have seen that. We could have been rolling probably three or four seconds sooner if you'd pulled him out of the car rather than pushing him in. I applaud your loyalty to your fellow agents, but our mantra, *cover and evacuate*, refers to the President, not to us.

Claire began to challenge Gants' contention that all head wounds were fatal, citing Jim Brady during President Reagan's shooting, but Gants held up his hand to stop her. "I'm not dinging you for it, Bradley, and I'm sure Powell enjoyed the wedgy he got as you heaved him into the car, but the bottom line is, this isn't about us; it's about the President. Anyway, let's get to the debriefing room, and we'll go over everything there."

As the other agents pulled their vests off, and loaded them into the limo's trunk, Gants walked over to the sidewalk where three men and a woman onlooker were standing. The tallest of the men, and the oldest of the group was Jim Whitherspoon, Director of the US Secret Service. Addressing the distinguished man next to him, Whitherspoon said, "Senator, I'd like to introduce my senior supervisor of security personnel, James Gants. Mr. Gants, Senator Evans."

Gants shook the senator's hand and said, "It's a pleasure, Senator. I hope you enjoyed our training exercise."

"Very much," he replied. "I have to admit, when I heard the shot and saw that first agent go down, I forgot for a moment that this whole city block is just a big training facility, and I looked for a place to take cover. So, who comes up with these scripts? Who decides which agents die and which live?"

"There's no script, sir. None of the agent's know what's going to happen during a given exercise. You hear the rifle, and then if you've been hit in one of the laser sensors on the vest, you hear a tone in your earpiece. Different tones tell you how badly you've been hit, and you have to act accordingly. Sometimes the exercise-controller will communicate and add detail. You may have noticed the female agent, Agent Bradley, lost the use of her left arm before she was killed. That was an add-in to make her job just a little tougher.

"The goal of the agent assigned as the sniper is to tag whoever is playing the President, and if he can do that by taking out an agent or two first, then that's what he'll do. That's what you saw here today. Only he didn't get his second shot off quickly enough. The other agents got the President into the car and out of harm's way, just as they're supposed to do."

"Well, as expensive as this facility and all your toys are," the Senator said, "I suppose if it keeps the President safe—and those of us *running* for President—then it's a worthwhile investment, aye Mr. Gants?"

Extending his hand once again, Gants said, "I couldn't agree more, sir. Now, if you'll excuse me, we have the classroom part of the exercise to do. It was a pleasure meeting you, Senator."

"Then I can count on your vote, Mr. Gants?" the Senator said with a practiced chuckle.

"You can count on me voting, Senator," Gants replied with a return chuckle.

As Gants walked away, Director Whitherspoon led the Senator, his secretary, and his aide back to the standard-issue limo that had brought them out to the Service's training facility. As they walked, Evans looked over his shoulder at the car that had been used in the exercise. "That's a real presidential limousine, isn't it?" he asked Whitherspoon.

"Yes, sir. Realism is the name of the game out here," Whitherspoon answered. "That's one of the 2001 Caddy's that President Bush used during his first term. They're building a set to replace the current 2006s, now, but they haven't told us if they'll be ready for inauguration day."

"I certainly hope so," the Senator replied. "I'd hate to ride down Pennsylvania Avenue, next January, in a used car."

Chapter 2

Wednesday, October 15
Washington DC

At 0800 sharp, the following morning, the lights in the Secret Service briefing room dimmed, and James Gants began the final update before the President's class-reunion-slash-campaign trip to Newburyport, Massachusetts. He stood behind a podium at the front corner of the briefing room, and brought up a map on the projected computer screen, beside him.. The map showed the area where south-east New Hampshire, and north-east Massachusetts bordered, and he moved his mouse, positioning the cursor over the icon of an airplane and double-clicked. A text box opened to display a description of the airport that the icon represented.

"Air Force One will land at Pease International at 0900," he began. "Transport will have arrived twenty-four hours earlier to set up the vehicles, and make check runs to the local hospitals and alternate airports."

He looked over his glasses at the heavy-set man in the front row, and the tall man sitting next to him. "Pollard," he said, "you'll have primary transport, and Kittery you'll have secondary."

The two men nodded in unison.

"Calypso will be rolling at 0930 Saturday morning," Gants went on, using the Secret Service code name for the President's limousine, "with the President and First Lady aboard."

With a click of his mouse, the primary route down I-95 from the airport to the President's destination, Newburyport High School, lit up in green. An alternate route using myriad surface streets showed in yellow, and the evacuation route to Logan Airport in Boston, was displayed in red.

Without looking up he said aloud what he knew was on everyone's mind. "And yes, this twenty-four mile jaunt from Pease to the school would be a lot simpler if the President didn't dislike helicopters so much."

Though it made their job more difficult at times, the agents understood their boss's phobia. During his time in the Army, the future President had survived three separate helicopter crashes, one in which, he was the sole survivor.

"Regardless of his aversion to Marine One, however," Gants went on, referring to the presidential helicopter, "it will be nearby for evacuation, as always."

Next, Gants brought up a satellite photo of the high school and the surrounding area. He centered his cursor on an area to the west of the school's open-air football stadium, and zoomed in. "There are three big old houses and a hospital on a long gradual hill that all provide vantage points from which one can look down onto the field where the President will be speaking," he said. "The homeowners have agreed to let our people seal their houses during the President's address, in return for passes *to* the address.

"The hospital—where, by the way, the President was born—is nearly two miles away to the west, but is high enough to also offer an unobstructed view down into the stadium. It's too far for a rifle shot, but someone with a shoulder-launched missile and a grudge would love it. Peters and Madden; you'll be on the roof.

"The hospital will allow agents to inspect each room that has a view of the school, and to be on duty in the hallway outside those rooms to make sure nothing changes after the inspection. As I said, the hospital is too far away to be an issue, but as always, we're going to err on the side of caution. Plus, the roof will make a good observation deck for us. You can literally see for miles from there."

He took off his glasses and looked around the room. "I know you all agree with me in thinking that an outdoor speech in a high school football stadium is highly inadvisable, but it's coming down to the wire for his reelection, it's his hometown, and it's his thirtieth class reunion. It's not our job to like the decisions he makes—just to make sure he's safe while he carries them out. About the only thing we can do, is to pray for rain. If it rains, the whole thing will get moved indoors to the school's auditorium."

Aaron Powell raised his hand. "What's the forecast?" he asked.

"Sunny and mild through Tuesday, so pray hard," Gants replied. For the next forty-five minutes he went over the President's itinerary, from his arrival at his alma mater, to his speech in the stadium. From his luncheon with local Democrats at the Elks Lodge, to the reunion dance in the high school gymnasium on Saturday night.

Getting to the final item of the briefing, Gants announced, "Assignments," as he pressed a button, turning off the computer projector and bringing up the lights.

"Most of you know where you're going to be, but I've got a couple of changes. Bradley, you're with the First Lady on this trip. Levine, you'll switch with Bradley and take her spot with the President."

Claire looked across at Levine, and then up at Gants. "Is this about trying to save Powell's life yesterday? You're *reassigning* me because of that? I thought we agreed that it was an agent's-call. No harm, no foul."

Levine, who had been "with the missus" since inauguration day, was equally puzzled. "Why pull me from the First Lady?" he asked. "If you need a sub for Bradley, why not bring up Bryant or Salter?"

"I don't have those answers, because I didn't make the decision," Gants said. "I got a memo directly from Mrs. McClure this morning, specifically requesting that you two swap jobs. I don't know any more about it than that."

"Is this permanent?" asked Levine.

"She didn't say in her memo, Paul. Let's call it 'Till further notice,' for now."

His fellow agents looked at Levine, clearly wondering what he had done or said to account for the switch. Being on the wrong side of the First Lady, inaffectionately known as *The Dragon Lady*, was no laughing matter.

When the other agents filed out, Levine remained in his chair, staring at the floor, trying to recall what he might or might *not* have done to warrant reassignment. Nothing came to mind.

When he rose, he saw Bradley waiting for him by the door.

"I don't know if *congratulations* are in order," he said extending his hand, "but good luck."

She returned the shake with a firm grip. "Thanks, Paul. And just so you know, I'm as surprised about this as you are. I have no idea why she'd ask for me specifically. I've never even had a conversation with her."

Paul shrugged, still trying to make sense of it. "I don't remember saying or doing anything that might have ticked her off. I don't get it." He looked at her and said, "I'm two-years-and-change away from retirement—I don't need something like this!"

"You don't know that it's anything bad, Paul," Claire countered. "Maybe it doesn't have anything to do with you, at all. At least with anything you've done. Maybe she just wants another woman with the family, now that Melissa's a teenager."

"Why? What am I, some old pervert who can't be trusted around young girls?"

"I'm sure that's not it!" Claire said. "That's not what I meant. Maybe she just wants someone around who understands—who's been there; thirteen is a weird age for a girl. It takes some understanding. Believe me, I know!"

"Yeah, that's probably it," Paul said with very little conviction. "So, I guess I'll be covering your spot in the circle, huh? Where were you?"

"Two o'clock," she told him, referring to the position that she occupied when the agents formed a ring around the President as he walked through crowds. "So, help me out, Paul," she said, changing subjects. "What's she really like? Is her *Dragon Lady* reputation deserved? I think I said 'Good morning, ma'am' to her, once, and I don't recall that she even replied. So the extent of my contact with her is exactly three words."

"She's not that bad once you get to know her, I guess. As long as you don't screw up. I've never met anyone with less tolerance for mistakes than she has. I just wish I could figure out what the hell I did." Without another word he turned and left the room.

"Mrs. McClure would like to meet with you, Claire," Gants said from behind her as he clipped his cell phone back onto his belt, having just ended the call from the First lady.

"Now?" she asked, seeing things going from bad to worse.

"Twenty-hundred hours tonight … in the family dining room," he said. "And try not to embarrass us, Claire. No boardinghouse reach; no slurping your soup; remember to say please and thank you, those kinds of things." He couldn't help but smile at the expression of dismay that came across her face.

"You're kidding, right?" she said. "I don't want to dine with the Family."

"Well, this must be your lucky day!" he replied. He enjoyed bantering with Claire. She was quick-witted and had a wry sense of humor. "The President's in a cabinet meeting, and Melissa is in Phoenix visiting her grandmother. It will just be you and the missus."

"Oh yeah, what luck! I should go buy a lottery ticket!" she said, sardonically. "Mr. Gants, what's going on? Why did Paul suddenly get canned? Why me? Why *dinner* for God's sake? Have *you* ever had dinner with her?"

Gants held up his hand like a traffic cop to stop the rapid-fire string of questions—a habit that Bradley had. "Taking your questions in order," he said, 'I don't know, I don't know, I don't know, and no."

She rolled her eyes at what she took to be a dismissive non-answer.

"Claire," he said seriously, "I really don't know what's going on. If Paul had done anything wrong, I'd know it, believe me. Mrs. McClure is not the least bit shy about pointing out the faults of my people—or anyone else for that matter. All I can guess is that she wants to have a young woman around now that the kid's a teenager. Anyway, you should go change. Mrs. McClure said 'casual.' Did I mention that?"

"Casual to me is pajamas," she said wryly. "Think that'll be okay?"

"I think jeans might be more what she had in mind."

"Don't own any."

"You don't own a pair of *jeans*?" he asked incredulously.

"When would I wear them? I've got a closet full of dark business suits, and dresser full of pajamas. Work and sleep—that's my life."

"Maybe you could at least lose the jacket?"

Claire pulled it open to reveal a 9mm semi-automatic in a black nylon holster on her hip. "Are my accessories okay?" she said. "Or is black too formal? Should I go with a silver Smith & Wesson? Pearl grips perhaps?"

"Perhaps you could just go with a simple 'ankle bracelet'," he said, referring to the .38 snub-nose that agents wore in ankle holsters as a back-up piece.

Claire lifted her pant leg to reveal the smaller weapon exactly where he had predicted it would be. "What the well-dressed agent is wearing this fall," she said, striking a fashion model pose. "How about if I just let my hair down?" she offered. She reached up and pulled the clip from the bun at the back of her head, and her hair tumbled to past her shoulders. She shook it out, and then added a pouty-lipped, magazine-cover facial expression to her pose. "Casual enough?" she asked.

Gants chuckled, happy that she was loosening up again.

Then in a little more serious tone he said, "Just go and play it by ear,

Claire. But be careful with that wit of yours. Not everybody gets you, and I don't recall any of Mrs. M's biographies mentioning a great sense of humor. I don't know that anyone's ever recovered from being on her bad side. On the other hand ..." he added, "if she *likes* you, you're golden!"

She smiled at him. She and Gants had developed an unusual bond almost from the day they had met. Clearly seeing special potential in her, he had taken her under his wing, becoming her mentor, drawing everything that he could from her, helping her to exploit that potential.

"Thanks, Mr. Gants," she said as she opened her arms and stepped forward to give him a hug. After a couple of seconds, they stepped apart, and Gants handed Claire the 9mm pistol he had deftly lifted from her holster, and she returned his wallet. Bradley and Gants' pickpocket embraces were an odd game that the two played, but as well as being good practice for close-quarters crowd assessment, it was also something of an excuse to demonstrate the almost father/daughter bond that existed between them. Though he never said as much, if Gants had had a daughter, he would want her to be just like Claire Bradley. And similarly, part of her connection to him was that he reminded her so much of her late father, the one man in her life against whom all other men were measured.

As they put their respective items away, Gants said, "Relax, Claire. It's just a Wednesday night like any other. It's just going to include a one-on-one dinner with the wife of the most powerful man on the planet. What's to worry?"

"Yeah, maybe I'll get lucky and her husband will launch a nuclear strike somewhere so we'll have something to chat about."

"That's what I like about you, Claire," he said with a laugh, "you can always find a silver lining."

The kidding with Gants did serve to relax her, but later on, as she left her apartment for the White House, she couldn't shake the feeling of foreboding that had come over her. And it wasn't just nervousness about meeting the First Lady. Her *voice* was warning her that something was going to happen. But, her *voice*, unlike a fortune-teller's prediction, never told her *what* was going to happen, or when. All she could do was to be on her guard.

Chapter 3

Wednesday evening, October 15
Washington DC

At seven forty-five, Claire arrived at the White House and was admitted through the security offices in the west wing.

Kevin Henderson was the agent on duty, and Claire knew him from having worked with him while on the campaign trail four years ago. Though they both worked protecting the same man, neither had spoken since Inauguration Day. Their paths simply never crossed. Claire was assigned to the President when he traveled, while Kevin was with him when he stayed at home.

"Cover for me, will you Dale?" Kevin said, pressing the intercom button on his phone. "I'm going to escort Agent Bradley over to the kitchen."

"The kitchen?" Claire said. "Gants told me the dining room."

"Nope," Kevin replied as he led the way down the carpeted hallway. "The missus called down about an hour ago, and said to show you to the kitchen when you arrived. We turn right here, then left and down the stairs."

"So, is this pretty common?" Claire asked. "Agents having dinner in the kitchen with the missus, that is?"

"If by common you mean twice in four years, then yes," Kevin

11

teased. "Well, technically only once so far—you'll be number two, once we get there. Paul Levine was the other one. The kitchen is usually just for family and close friends—nothing formal."

Claire stopped in her tracks and Kevin took a couple of steps before realizing he was walking alone.

"What?" he asked as he stopped and turned back toward her.

"What do you mean, '*What*'? What the hell is going on, Kevin!? I've never even spoken to the woman, and now all of a sudden, I'm in some inner circle, and Paul Levine—who's known her for what, four years or more—is out on his ass! And worried about his pension I might add! I don't get it! Why me? If she just wanted to replace Levine, why not move up one of the agents that've been with the family all along? Why not Karen Horner if she's looking for a *woman*? Doesn't this seem odd to anyone but me?"

"Mrs. M. doesn't confide in *me*, Claire," Kevin replied. "I heard through the grapevine that you and Levine were switching, but I didn't hear why. But, if she's going to make a change, why *not* you?" he said. "You're an excellent agent, or you wouldn't be at two-o'clock with the President. You're a woman—if that really is a factor, here. You're intelligent—the Missus doesn't take to stupid very well. You're articulate—when she does talk to you, she expects complete sentences in return. And aren't you from around Newburyport? Maybe that's got something to do with it."

"Why would *that* make any difference?"

"Maybe she thinks she'll need an interpreter for the foreign language up there. *Pahk the cah in Hahvid yahd*," he joked, exaggerating her Bostonian accent.

"I don't talk like that!" she said defensively. Then with a bit less defiance, she added, "Do I?"

"No, Claire," he said with a laugh as he started walking again. "Not *that* bad, anyway. I'm just teasing. You need to loosen up. Look at it this way. You have two options here. Turn around, and go home and write out your resignation, or stay and have dinner with Mrs. McClure. At least with the second option, you get a free meal."

"The last supper?"

"Nah," he replied with a grin, "That was just with Christ and a bunch of the guys. *This* is with the First Lady! *This* is serious!"

"Oh, thanks, I feel *much* better now!" she replied as Kevin rapped on the kitchen door.

The First Lady was standing at the kitchen counter, and turned as they entered the room. She wore jeans and a light V-neck sweater that flattered her trim figure. Claire couldn't recall ever seeing her in anything but a conservative suit, before.

"Mrs. McClure," Kevin said, "Agent Bradley, as requested."

The First Lady appraised Claire with a raised eyebrow. "Not exactly *as requested*," she said coolly. "I'm sure that I told Mr. Gants that the attire was to be *casual*."

The knot in Claire's stomach grew to twice its size. This was *not* starting well.

"Thank you, Kevin. That's all," Mrs. McClure said, and he turned and left without a word.

"Sorry, ma'am," Claire said, tugging at her crisply pleated navy blue slacks. "Mr. Gants *did* tell me 'casual.' It's just that I don't have a lot of casual clothes—unless you wanted me to show up in pajamas." Immediately, Gants' warning about her wit came back to her, and she wanted to bite her tongue. What was she *thinking*, wisecracking to The Dragon Lady?

To her complete surprise, the First Lady laughed. "I wish you'd have suggested that before coming over," she replied. "Pajamas *would* be more comfortable."

Claire didn't know how to respond to the First Lady's reaction. She'd expected a reprimand or at least a glare in return for her flippant reply.

"Relax, Miss Bradley," the First Lady said. "I'm not nearly the ogre I'm made out to be. I have a sense of humor and everything—just like a real person. And I sure-as-hell like to be comfortable. It's nice to meet you, Clarice," she said, extending her hand.

Claire shook her hand, and was impressed by the firm, but not intimidating grip of the First Lady. "The pleasure is mine, ma'am," she replied. "And it's just Claire—not Clarice. Claire with an 'E'."

"Good, good!" Mrs. McClure said with a smile. "I wondered if you'd correct me right away, or if you'd just let me go on calling you Clarice all night. I'm so glad my instincts about you were right."

"You were *testing* me to see if I'd correct you? Why?" She quickly added the formality of, "If I may ask, ma'am."

"I needed to see what your tolerance for incompetence was. Apparently it's about as low as mine."

"Incompetence, ma'am?" Claire repeated. "I wouldn't exactly classify getting my name wrong as *incompetence*. That's a pretty simple mistake. You'd hardly be the first."

"Addressing you as Clarice instead of Claire is a small thing," Mrs. McClure explained, "so a lot of people would just let it go rather than contradict a superior—especially on first meeting. Believe me, *that* happens all the time, too. Your correcting me indicates that you have little tolerance for even small mistakes, and that you're not easily intimidated. Both prized qualities in my book."

"Well, I'm glad I passed the test, ma'am, but I'd be happy to just *tell* you anything you'd like to know about me," Claire said, smiling.

"Fair enough," the First Lady replied, "but there isn't much about you that I don't already know." She motioned for Claire to sit at the island counter as she returned to the salad that she had been preparing. "Aside from all of your excellent credentials as an agent, the thing that interested me most about you is that you grew up in Newburyport, Mass."

"Technically, ma'am, I grew up in the *Newbury* section of *Plum Island*, Mass.," Claire told her. "I went to *school* in Newburyport, but I *lived* in Newbury on Plum Island. Maybe you *should* ask me what you want to know. Whatever your source is, it seems a bit short on accuracy." Claire's hand went up to her mouth. She couldn't believe she had said that to Katherine McClure! For some reason, Claire felt strangely comfortable talking to the First Lady as if they were old friends sitting in Starbucks. And she was sure she was going to get herself *fired* because of it! She now wished that she *had* bitten her tongue earlier to remind her of her place. "Sorry, ma'am. I didn't mean any disrespect. It's all one and the same to most people, anyway."

"Don't apologize for being correct, Claire. Certainly not with me. And please try to relax, will you? In fact, while we're in private, I want you to call me Katherine, okay? 'Ma'am' is too formal for the kitchen, and it makes me feel old. Deal?"

"Okay, ma'am ... um, Katherine," Claire replied, seeing that that was going to take some getting used to. But as the evening went on, Claire was surprised at how easily she *did* get used to it. It was amazing how at ease she felt with this woman whose reputation for unpleasantness was legendary within the Service.

"Anyway," Katherine said, getting back to the subject at hand, "I know that you didn't actually grow up in Newburyport, I was just condensing information to get to the meat of the matter. *Technically*," she repeated with special emphasis on the word, "you were *born* in Newburyport—in the same hospital as my husband, coincidentally. You attended K through eight in Newbury, and only attended *high school* in

Newburyport. Shortly after graduation you moved to Phoenix Arizona with your parents. I can go on, but it's not very relevant to why you're here."

"I stand corrected," Claire said, with a slight bow of her head. "Sorry I doubted you. But why, exactly, *am* I here?"

"In a nutshell, you're here because you went to the same high school that my husband did," Katherine replied as she began tossing the salad in a big wooden bowl. "A couple of months ago, before we officially announced that my husband would attend his class reunion, I had some information sent to me about Newburyport. It was your typical touristy Chamber-of-Commerce stuff. Pictures of old colonial houses with widow's walks, the waterfront, three-hundred-year-old churches, and all those quaint little downtown shops." She stopped tossing for a moment and looked at Claire. "It was seeing those shops that made me realize how much I miss a normal life. I can go shopping anywhere in the world, Claire, but always with half a dozen men in dark jackets that bulge in the most unnatural places. And always with at least that many cameras clicking and whirring away."

Claire knew exactly what she was talking about; she was *part* of it.

"That sleepy little New England town made me realize how much I miss just being able to walk down the sidewalk, window shopping and chatting with a friend, or sitting on a park bench eating an ice cream cone and people-watching, without being the center of attention.

"Well, I happened to mention that longing-for-a-normal-life to Mr. McClure one evening, and he said, 'If you want a tour guide for Newburyport, you should talk to Claire Bradley. She went to school there, too. *She* could show you around.' As usual, he had completely missed my point."

Claire laughed and said, "Men!"

Katherine chuckled in agreement as she got two salad bowls from the cupboard. "But I said to myself, 'What the heck. Maybe a personal tour guide could take the edge off the Men In Black syndrome.' So I got hold of your files, to see what I could see about Special Agent Claire Lynn Bradley from Newbury-slash-Plum Island, Mass."

"So, that's the only reason you asked to have me and Paul reassigned?" Claire asked. "You wanted a tour guide?" The explanation seemed almost too simple, but it was a great relief to hear it.

"Pretty much," the First Lady replied, walking to the refrigerator. "Ranch, Thousand Island, or Italian?"

"Ranch, please. So this is just a temporary reassignment for us then?

After I lead you and your entourage around Newburyport we go back whence we came?" Claire said.

"There won't be an entourage," the First Lady answered, sidestepping the question adeptly. "My plot has just two characters—you and me."

"Your *plot*?" repeated Claire, intrigued by that choice of words, but mentally noting the sidestep.

"It has everything. Danger, intrigue, false identities ..."

"Romance?" Claire inquired, not taking the whole thing too seriously.

Katherine pursed her lips and thought for a moment. "Okay, no romance. But it has everything else!"

Claire blew a dismissive, "*Pffft*" and rolled her eyes. "It'll never sell without romance," she said, serving herself a generous portion of salad. "Okay, so what's this romantically-challenged plot all about, if I may be so bold?"

"Simply put, I want to go shopping like a normal person and I want you to take me," Katherine replied flatly.

"Just you and me?" Claire said frowning, as if Katherine were pulling her leg.

"Yup. Just you and me. A couple of gals on the loose shopping in downtown Newburyport."

"Have you talked this over with Mr. Gants?" she asked, not believing for a second that he would agree to such a thing.

"Oh, he'll come around," Katherine said. "In the end, I can assure you that I'll get my way with James. It's *your* approval I need. Certainly, I can't go up there shopping all by myself."

"*My* approval?" Claire replied with a laugh. "I'm a lot further down the totem pole than Mr. Gants is. If he doesn't have a choice, do I?"

"Absolutely!" Katherine answered seriously. "I'm asking a lot of you, Claire, I know that. That's why I needed to know everything about you before I even brought it up. I needed to know that I could feel comfortable with you personally and that your professional reviews and appraisals are so good that Mr. Gants can't shoot me down because you're not qualified for the assignment. But, if *you* don't feel this is something that you can do—or if you can see some reason that it's an impossibly bad idea, just say so and it's back to the Men In Black. I mean that. I trust your judgment, Claire."

"Thank you. I'm flattered," Claire told her. "Well, assuming that when you mentioned 'false identities' you meant that you'd be incognito, no *impossible* problems leap to mind. Beyond Mr. Gants, of course. If nobody knows you're the First Lady, protecting you shouldn't be that difficult."

"Is that what your 'sixth sense' is saying?" Katherine inquired.

"Sixth sense?" Claire repeated, a bit surprised. "Who told you I had a sixth sense?"

"It was in your latest personality assessment," Katherine answered. "Mr. Gants wrote something to the effect that you seem to have a sixth-sense about imminent danger. Even in training exercises, he wrote, that you seem to be able to be in the right place at the right time, doing the right thing. He said that he wished that the trait was teachable. So tell me, are you really clair-voyant, Claire-Bradley?"

Claire laughed politely at the play on words. "I don't know. I never thought about it as clairvoyance, I guess. I just *listen to the voice*, if you will."

"Have you always heard these *voices*?" Katherine teased. In fact, she was very intrigued.

"You make it sound like I'm loopy," Claire replied. "Technically, it's not an actual voice. I just call it that for want of a better description. It's really just kind of a thought that pops up." Claire rarely tried to explain her *voice*, but for some reason, she felt it was important for Katherine to understand.

"My mother used to say that it was my guardian angel looking out for me, and that I really made her earn her wings. There was this one time when I was twelve, I was at a friend's house and we found a gun in her dad's desk—a revolver. I'd never held a gun before, and just the feel of it in my hand fascinated me. I was aiming it at different things and I was about to pull the trigger and say '*Bang!*' when something told me not to. I turned the gun around and looked at the front of it, and I nearly fainted. Her dad was a cop, so I figured he'd never leave a loaded gun lying around. You guessed it, it was loaded … all six rounds. You know what I was aiming at when my *voice* told me not to pull the trigger? The back of my friend's head. Aside from learning to respect firearms from that, I began respecting that little voice a lot more, too."

"Is your 'voice' always right?" Katherine asked, as she took two mugs bearing the presidential seal from the cupboard. "Coffee?"

"Yes, please. It's right more often than not, I think. The trick is understanding what it's trying to convey. There are no actual words involved; I just get a feeling that I should do a certain thing. Most of the time it doesn't even make sense until later." She took the mug of coffee from Katherine, and went on, "We were out at the training center yesterday, and the President—Mr. Gants—came under fire from a sniper as we approached his car. As his two-o'clock, my job is to get his head down and shield him on his right side while his six-o'clock pushes him into the car and covers his tail. Well, yesterday, my *voice* told me to leap up on top of the car, and shield him from above after I got his head down. That's something we've never done or even discussed before. A split-second later, I took a hit in the back that probably would have taken out Mr. Gants, if I wasn't there."

"Some guardian angel!" Katherine said. "It tells you to jump in front of, not away from flying bullets?"

Claire laughed. "Good point. Maybe it knew it was just laser tag. But I think that, especially in real situations, it knows more of the big picture than I could comprehend. Maybe my sacrifice would save the world from destruction, somehow. I don't even try to figure out what it all means, any more."

"Well, loaded revolvers and saving the world, aside," Katherine said, "what does your voice say about my shopping plot?"

"It says, 'Don't be around when the First Lady springs this on Mr. Gants!'" Claire said with a grin.

It was nearing eleven o'clock when Katherine walked Claire back through the corridors to the west-wing entrance. As they walked, Claire reflected on the surprising closeness that she felt to Katherine—like she'd known her for years. Katherine was having similar thoughts about Claire.

Breaking the silence, Katherine said, "You asked earlier if this assignment was temporary. Frankly, before this evening I wasn't sure. Everything I found out about you said you could help me with this little *project* of mine, but in all honesty, I wasn't sure if you and I were going to click. Now, though, I have to tell you that I haven't met anyone in a very long time with whom I feel as comfortable as I do with you."

"Thank you, ma'am," Claire replied, having switched back into the formality of employer/employee as soon as they had left the kitchen. "I feel the same way. If I may speak frankly, ma'am, you're not at all the person I expected to meet tonight."

"Not as much breathing of fire as you expected, huh?"

"And a lot more laughing," Claire added. "I enjoyed myself—and I hadn't expected to."

"I enjoyed it, too," Katherine said. "Answering your question, Claire, I *would* like to bring you over permanently. But I'll leave it up to you. You can give me your answer after the trip, if you'd like."

"What about Paul?" Claire asked. "Where does that leave him?"

Katherine smiled at her. "I *do* like your loyalty! You're just not going to let that go, are you?" She stopped midway down the last corridor, and looked around conspiratorially. "Okay, this is strictly between you and me—even Mr. Gants doesn't know this yet. But Paul Levine is in line for a promotion—as is Mr. Gants, himself. It's all going through after the trip. Trust me, Paul's going to be okay."

When they reached the inner door to the security lobby where Claire had signed in, Claire extended her hand, and said, "Mrs. McClure, it's been a real pleasure meeting you—the *real* you. I look forward to working with you."

"Believe me, Claire, the pleasure is mine," the First Lady said. "I think we can actually have some fun together. Do me a favor, though? Take some time tomorrow and go buy some casual clothes, will you? I don't want people to think my little sister doesn't know how to relax!"

As Claire was signing out, she realized that she had *not* felt this relaxed in quite some time.

Dale, who had taken over the shift from Kevin, looked back to be sure the door was closed, and said to Claire, "Well, you survived anyway. That must have been hell! One-on-one with *The Dragon Lady* for a whole evening!"

"You can't even imagine, Dale!" she replied. "You just can't imagine!"

Chapter 4

Friday, October 17
Near Washington DC

At twenty minutes before six, Friday morning, Claire pulled her Jeep to a stop at the Andrews Air Force Base outer-perimeter guard shack. A combat-armed Air Force MP checked her ID, while his partner looked at that of her passenger, Katherine McClure. After checking their names against the day's roster, they saluted and waving them through.

Ten minutes later, they were climbing the fold-down stairs into one of the largest airplanes in the world, the C5 "Galaxy". Nearly 250 feet long, and taller than a six-story building, it could carry nearly a quarter of a million pounds in its cargo hold, and with midair refueling, could carry that load anywhere in the world.

Today, its cargo bay held two presidential limousines—a primary and a backup—and the rest of the myriad vehicles that would make up the president's motorcade the next day. It also carried the Secret Service advance teams for transportation, communications, and site security.

Seating in "Vehicle Transport-1", known to air-traffic controllers as VT-1, was not as austere as a troop transport—which consisted of web-belt seats hanging from the sides of the cargo bay—but it was still a far cry from the ultra first-class seating in the presidential jumbo-jet.

20

Though she normally flew with the President in Air Force One, Claire had occasionally traveled in VT-1, as part of an advance team. But this was a first for a First Lady. No other presidential wife had ever been inside the "flying parking lot" before.

As Katherine was shown to her front-row aisle seat, she was offered a soft drink, which she declined as she sat and buckled her seatbelt. One of about thirty agents on board, Claire took a seat a row behind and across the aisle from the First Lady.

As the plane lumbered down the taxiway, headed for the end of the runway, the flight-deck door opened and James Gants appeared, almost directly in front of the First Lady. "Good morning, Mr. Gants," she said cheerfully. "Thank you for finding a couple of extra seats on such short notice."

When she'd phoned him and informed him that she and agent Bradley would be traveling with the transportation team a day ahead of the President, she'd said that she would explain *why* when they were in the air. Gants had protested, of course, but ultimately Katherine had gotten what she'd wanted—as always.

"Good morning, ma'am. Welcome aboard," he said, taking the seat beside her, while glancing over at Claire. Claire could see that he was not happy. Mr. Gants did not like surprises.

Gants was about to speak when the captain announced that they were cleared for takeoff. The roar of the engines and the rattle of the plane as they picked up speed, quickly made conversation impossible.

When the pilots finally cut power after reaching cruising altitude, Gants said to Katherine, "You know, Mrs. McClure, if I'm going to do my job as it should be done—as your husband would want me to do it— then I'm going to have to know what you have planned after we land in New Hampshire. I'm going to have to make the proper arrangements to guarantee your safety. But perhaps we ought to talk about this in private. And I think Agent Bradley should join us, since she seems to be involved somehow." Gants looked over at Claire, who was watching them, and he crooked his finger in a "come here" gesture. The expression he wore made it clear that it was not a casual invitation—it was an order. Gants led the two women to the metal-basket elevator that was located against the forward bulkhead, and closed the gate behind them. He pressed a button and the elevator began its decent. "Please keep your hands inside," he added, sounding like a museum tour guide.

The elevator stopped at the sleeping quarters on the lower deck and they made their way through the back door of the bunk-lined room and into the cargo bay.

At over a hundred feet in length, nearly twenty feet wide, and twenty feet high, the Wright Brothers could have completed their historic first-ever powered flight within this aircraft.

For military operations, this area could transport two fully equipped M1 main battle tanks, six Apache helicopters, or the army's 74-ton mobile bridge. Today, however, it looked like a parking garage.

Parked side by side, facing the rear ramp of the plane, and strapped to the deck, were two Chevy Suburbans, one full of communications gear, and the other loaded with SWAT team equipment. In front of those were two identical limousines, code named *Calypso I* and *Calypso II*. Referred to by the Secret Service as "Parade Cars," the vehicles appeared to be Cadillac DTS limos, and were also identical to a third in the set, which was parked in the White House garage. Aside from outward appearance, however, they were quite unlike any other limousines in the world, in terms of protection for their occupants, instantaneous world-wide communications—and cost.

In front of the limos were four more Suburbans used to transport Secret Service personnel, and at the front of the line was a Ford 1-ton van with banks of TV monitors, padded boxes of video equipment, and a virtual forest of antennae on its roof. Next to the van was the only non-black vehicle in the cargo bay. The fully equipped ambulance was armored, rode on run-flat tires—as did all the vehicles—and was outfitted to handle any emergency from a gunshot wound to a heart attack. Inside, six pints of the President's own blood sat in a special refrigeration unit. In addition to the usual ambulance markings, it also had the presidential seal on each door.

As Gants, Katherine, and Claire stepped into the dim light of the cargo bay, they quickly realized how well insulated the passenger compartment had been, both against the cold and the noise. Gants led them between the rows of cars until he got to the rear door of the left limo. He opened it and gestured for the two women to get in.

Inside there was instant and complete silence. The hand-built cars were so thick with bulletproof glass, armor, and insulation that there was actually a reverse public-address system that allowed the President to hear the cheers of the crowds over speakers inside the car.

As Gants settled opposite them on a rear-facing jump-seat he said, "This is about as private as it gets. And now, ma'am, if you don't mind, will you please tell me what's going on?"

Gants' tone with the First Lady made Claire feel even more uncomfortable than she had before. This was shaping up to be a battle of the Titans in which Claire felt *very* out of place.

"Agent Bradley and I would like to go shopping in Newburyport and we'd rather not have a battalion of your agents surrounding us—calling attention to us."

Claire's heart almost stopped. *Oh great*! she thought, *She's making it sound like this is something we cooked up together*!

Gants shot Claire a look that would have sent a rookie looking for a parachute. A look that was not lost on the First Lady.

"Mr. Gants," she began in an almost reproachful tone, "This is *my* idea. Agent Bradley had nothing to do with it. She is here only because I feel that she will be the best agent you have to act as my single bodyguard, and ..."

"Single bodyguard!" Gants interrupted. "Absolutely not! I'm sorry, Mrs. McClure, but the answer is no!"

"It wasn't a request, Mr. Gants," Katherine replied calmly. "I'm explaining what we're going to do when we get to New Hampshire. That *is* what you wanted to know, isn't it?"

Gants took a deep breath. "Mrs. McClure, please," he said. "There will be thousands of people on those streets, some local, many of them in town because of your husband's visit tomorrow. How can I keep you safe in crowds like that with just one agent—no matter *who* she may be?"

He accompanied his last remark with a chilling look at Claire. She could tell that he was now certain that the two women had conspired against him, despite the First Lady's assurance to the contrary.

"I intend to be incognito, Mr. Gants," Katherine told him. "No one will know the First Lady is even among them, so I won't be in any danger at all."

"Incognito?" he repeated doubtfully.

"Yes. You know, disguised. Made up to not look like one's self," Katherine teased him, fully aware that he knew the meaning of the word. "Besides, no one knows I'm even going to be *in* Newburyport today. Everyone thinks I'll be arriving with my husband, tomorrow. So if there were some sinister plot to assassinate the First Lady—for God knows what reason—they wouldn't be planning to do it until tomorrow. They certainly wouldn't be planning to shoot some tourist walking down the street with her sister just for target practice."

"Her sister?" Gants repeated. And from his tone, Claire knew that he was rapidly losing patience with both of them. Though the First Lady was undoubtedly used to getting her way, Claire wasn't sure that Gants didn't actually have the last word here. He *was* in charge of security. He could certainly stop *her* from doing this.

"Mrs. McClure," he said, trying logic, "this is not a good idea. A shopping trip was never on the agenda. We haven't done sweeps in those shops, haven't checked backgrounds on store keepers … This kind of thing takes time to set up, ma'am. I just can't allow it on a moment's notice."

"Perhaps you weren't listening, Mr. Gants," Katherine replied with a tone that Claire was glad wasn't directed at *her*. "No one is going to know it's me."

"Yours is one of the most recognizable faces on the *planet*, Mrs. McClure! I don't believe that putting on a wig and sun glasses is going to make you disappear! I'm afraid I just can't let this happen, ma'am. If I have to go higher, I will. But I can't let you out on the streets with just a single agent."

Katherine stared at him, accepting his challenge. Without looking, she lifted the armrest beside her and picked up the telephone that was cradled inside. "Shall I dial the Oval Office?" she said. "I believe this has service even up here."

Claire had been thinking about how this exchange might go ever since she had left the White House Wednesday night, and since this was remarkably close to one of the scenarios she had imagined, she was prepared with an option.

"Sir? Ma'am?" Claire interrupted what was clearly about to become a test of monumental wills. "I wonder if I might offer a compromise. If there were two more agents, sir—your choice—would that make you feel better?"

"Claire!" Katherine said as if she had been betrayed by her best friend.

Swell! thought Claire. *First-name basis! Now he's sure we're in cahoots*!

"They'd have to be plainclothes and in the background," she continued quickly before Gants could cut her off. "And no closer than a hundred feet to Mrs. McClure and me."

Katherine suddenly realized that this was not spur-of-the-moment, and waited to see where Claire was going.

"Not that I'm *agreeing* to anything," Gants said, "but a hundred feet would be out of the question. Fifty feet would be the maximum—and constant radio contact."

Claire felt a glimmer of hope. She knew that Gants had confidence in her instincts and her skills, but she knew his temperament wouldn't allow him to just cave in. She had expected him to make her defend whatever plan she had in mind.

"I'll give you the fifty," Claire said as if haggling over a used car, "but having a wire running out of my ear isn't going to be very *inconspicuous*. I'll keep a Tac radio in my pocket, and I'll have my cell phone on."

He just stared at Claire for several seconds before saying, "I don't know ..."

Claire could see that he was on the edge of being persuaded, but needed a little more convincing. And she was prepared for that.

"You're still thinking that people are going to recognize her, aren't you?" Claire said. "Then how about this? I'll check into the Water Street Motel, under my own name, and I'll slip Mrs. McClure in without anyone seeing her. The other two agents can check into the adjoining rooms, but after they do, they'll wait for us in the lobby. Mrs. McClure and I will transform her into someone else, and she'll walk out through the lobby, right in front of the other agents. If either of them recognizes her, then the whole thing is off. How's that?"

Katherine was surprised at the bravado with which Claire had thrown her cards on the table, but she saw the logic in the plan, and she also saw that her boss was being all but forced to take the challenge.

"Why some little motel?" Gants asked. "Why not the Hyatt where the whole floor is reserved, and we've swept?" He knew what Claire was probably thinking, but he wanted to hear it from her.

"Because if anyone *is* looking for Mrs. McClure," she said, knowing that he was just testing her, "the Hyatt is where they'd be looking. Not in some little motel that could be *bought* for the cost of a weekend in the presidential suite at the Hyatt."

"And what makes you think you're going to be able to get a room— or *three*—with all the people in town for the President's visit," he pressed.

"It's already done. Three adjoining rooms." Claire replied, seeing this one coming as well. "I know the family who owns the motel; I used to baby-sit their son."

Gants was feeling a little better. He could see that, despite the First Lady's claim that Claire was not a coconspirator, that she had done her homework, and he trusted her attention to detail. Besides, they still had to pass the incognito-test—a feat that he found difficult to imagine, given the alertness of his agents.

"Okay," he said begrudgingly. "You've got a deal."

Claire smiled at her victory, but Katherine quickly added, "Do we have your word, Mr. Gants, that you won't tell your agents to be on the lookout for an incognito First Lady? That they'll have to spot me on their own like anyone on the street would?"

Claire had thought of that, but had forgotten to mention it. She was surprised—and pleased—at what a good team she and Katherine were making.

"Agreed," Gants said. "And do I have *your* word that *you* won't tip them off to the game?" he said to Claire.

"Scouts honor!" she said, holding up her right hand with three fingers extended.

Gants selected Aaron Powell and Dan Burger to be Claire's backups, and they were coincidentally exactly who Claire would have picked. Then, for the next hour, the four of them sat around a table in the galley, discussing the details of the shopping trip. Claire had agreed to tell them that the First Lady would be incognito, because it was necessary to plan strategies. But they were not told about the "test" they would unknowingly be taking. Deep inside, Gants had little doubt that his agents would be able to pick her out, and he felt sure that the whole thing would be over before it began.

They agreed that in order to make conversation about the First Lady a little less cryptic-sounding to anyone who might overhear, they would not use her usual code name of "Capricorn," but would refer to her as "Cousin".

The final topic of discussion was weapons. Each agent would wear an ankle holster with a .38 snub-nose revolver, loaded with close-range hollow-point ammunition.

Reluctantly, in the name of keeping a low profile, Gants agreed that none of the agents would wear a shoulder or belt-holster, but would instead wear a hip-pack holster that held a 9mm semi-automatic pistol just behind the front flap. The wearer could slip his hand in the side of the pouch, and fire the gun right through the canvas, or with a twist of the wrist, the fasteners on the cover would release, and the gun was out in the open. It was effective concealment for their weapons, but it limited how quickly an agent could draw his weapon and have it on target.

As they were wrapping up their briefing, the PA announced that they were on final approach to Pease International Airport, but when they headed for the elevator to go up to their seats, Gants asked Claire to stay behind.

As the elevator passed the floor above them, taking Powell and Burger out of earshot, Gants spoke. "I like your hair that way. It's cute. And practical, too."

She ran a hand through her almost boyishly-short hair, still a bit self-conscious about the change, and wondering if she had made the right decision last night to have it cut so short.

"You held me back to tell me you like my haircut?" She knew that that wasn't the reason, but she enjoyed teasing him.

"Yes!" he said defensively. "Can't a guy give a girl a compliment anymore?" Then he smiled, and confessed, "Actually, I wanted to tell you that even though I still don't like this, there isn't another agent that I would trust to do it, Claire. If you do manage to slip the missus past Powell and Burger, be careful, okay?"

"You mean like no running with scissors?" Claire quipped, a bit embarrassed by his compliment. Such a comment was downright *gushing*, for Gants.

"Yes, and look both ways before you cross the road with her, too," he replied, matching her dry wit. "I mean keep her safe, and keep a low profile. And if *anyone* recognizes her, you head for the barn, right away, got it? Get her off the street. If anything happens out there, neither one of our careers will survive it."

"I won't let you down," she said. "And thanks. I appreciate your confidence in me. But I've had a great mentor." She opened her arms and stepped forward. After hugging for a few seconds, they backed apart, empty-handed. Laughing, she said, "My pistol and cell phone are both topside in my carry-on."

"My wallet, too," he said. As they walked to the elevator basket that Powell had sent back down, Gants said, "I really do like your hair that way. What made you cut it?"

"I figured that I've shown up in enough photos of the President, that somebody might recognize *me*, and that might blow Mrs. McClure's cover."

"Good prediction. You've done your homework, and it shows."

"Just a Saturday morning of one-on-one shopping with the wife of the most powerful man on the planet ... in a crowd of unscreened strangers. What's to worry?" she kidded him. Outwardly, she was showing the confidence that she knew her boss needed to see, but inside, she still felt that tug of foreboding. She only hoped that her instincts, her training— and her *voice* could stave off whatever it was that was nagging at her.

Chapter 5

Friday, October 17
Newburyport, MA

Shortly after the C5 touched down at the airport in New Hampshire, Katherine, Claire, Powell, and Burger were on their way to downtown Newburyport in two rental cars, that Claire had also arranged. Thirty-five minutes later, Claire drove into the parking lot of the Water Street Motel and Diner, and Powell pulled in beside her, shielding the First Lady's side of the car.

Claire told them all to wait in the cars while she registered. As she walked to the lobby entrance, she looked all around her for anything or anyone that might seem out of place. She wasn't anticipating any danger, but after nine years with the Secret Service, *threat-assessment* was simply the way one looked at the world.

When she entered the lobby, the one thing that she had hoped wouldn't happen, did—she encountered someone she knew.

Bobby Bradshaw, the little boy that she used to baby-sit when she was in high school, whose parents owned the motel, was standing behind the registration desk. She recognized him immediately, as just a larger version of the boy she had helped to toilet train fifteen years ago. Under other circumstances, it would have been great to see him again, but having a reunion wasn't on the agenda this morning.

When she approached the counter, Bobby looked up and asked in a deeper voice than she expected, "Good morning, ma'am. Can I help you?"

"I have a reservation," she said as she slid her driver's license across the counter. "Under Bradley."

The boy looked at the license, then at Claire, and exclaimed, "*Claire Bradley*? Is that really you? Oh my God! *Oh my God*!"

Claire's single-syllable name came out as a two-syllable "Clay-ah", in the New England accent that Claire had tried so hard to lose all these years.

Patting himself on the chest, he said, "It's Bobby Bradshaw! You remember—you used to baby-sit for me!"

"Bobby Bradshaw!" Claire exclaimed, feigning sudden recognition. "I can't believe it! Look at you!"

She managed to keep the conversation that followed to a minimum by mentioning that she had an appointment to keep, and Bobby quickly processed her registration while eliciting a promise from her to get together again before she left town.

Outside the lobby doors, Claire made another look around, then gave a prearranged signal, and started walking to her left. As Powell and Burger watched, Mrs. McClure got out of her car, and joined Claire, who escorted her around to the side of the motel, and into their room. The two men then went inside, and registered, themselves. After dropping their carry-on bags in their rooms, they then returned to the lobby to wait for the First Lady and Claire to rejoin them.

Inside the spartan room, Claire did a quick, but thorough security sweep, and then, with exaggerated motions, she snapped a salute and reported, "Phase one of Project Shopping-trip complete, ma'am. Welcome to Newburyport!"

Opening one of the two carry-on's she had brought, Claire took out a wig of short blonde hair, and handed it to Katherine. "Are you ready for your new look?" Claire said.

"Do blondes really have more fun?" Katherine asked, taking it from her.

"If we can get you past Powell and Burger," Claire replied, "I think you're going to have more fun today than you've had in a long time—regardless of your hair color." Removing another item from her carry-on, Claire said, "And I think this is going to help."

Katherine took the padded push-up bra and held it up to her chest. Laughing, she said, "Going to help *what*? Get past Powell and Burger, or to have fun?"

"If we can do the former, the sky's the limit on the latter."

"You make it sound like we're going to be cruising for guys," Katherine said. "This *is* just a shopping trip, isn't it?"

"I guess we'll have to see how that plays out, won't we," Claire said with an impish grin. "But the real purpose of that little *enhancement* is just like the magician's art of misdirection; we want the audience—in this case the people on the street—to be looking the wrong way." Taking out her makeup kit, she went on, "Half the people in the world would recognize Katherine McClure's *face*, but how many do you think would be able to pick her *cleavage* out of a crowd?"

Katherine looked at Claire in surprise. "You know what you're doing here, don't you? I can't imagine that this is taught at the Secret Service Academy. Where did you come up with this little talent?"

"Ha!" Claire said. "I guess my file didn't tell you *everything* about my college days! But then, not too many people knew I was the girl-of-a-thousand-faces up at NAU."

"Master of disguise, were you?" Katherine asked.

"Yeah, but not my own," Claire answered. "I used to help my girl-friends—who were all under-age—get dolled up enough so that they wouldn't get carded in the clubs up there. I never cared much for drinking myself, so it was just something I did for a few close friends. If I say so myself, I got pretty good at it after a while, and it was a lot of fun. Of course, being a psych major and understanding how men's minds worked, helped."

"You're claiming that you understand how men's minds work?" Katherine said, skeptically.

"Well, for our purposes, we only need to understand the part that directs the instinctual urge to reproduce. The part that focuses on boobs and butts," Claire admitted. "But, fortunately, that's pretty much the whole brain for the first thirty-seconds or so."

Applying Katherine's makeup took longer than Claire expected because the two kept breaking into the fits of laughter as they shared college-days stories. Finally, and only after Katherine had wiggled into her snug, butt-hugging jeans, and slipped on her low-cut knit top, did Claire allow her to look in the full-length mirror on the bathroom door.

"Good Lord!" Katherine exclaimed. She turned back and forth, marveling at the size of her bust and the generous amount of exposed cleavage. She then turned around to look at her butt in the mirror, and was amazed at what a difference the jeans made to her fifty-something *derrière*. Katherine had to laugh at the transformation.

"If you've got it, flaunt it!" Claire teased. "At least for today. What do you think? Will Powell or Burger recognize you?"

"Hell, my *husband* wouldn't recognize me! But given this get-up, he probably wouldn't get as far up as the neck anyway."

"That's the whole point! And for those who do get further, the makeup and hair are insurance," Claire said, admiring her handiwork. She had highlighted Katherine's cheekbones and minimized her jaw, as well as shadowing the sides of her nose to give her face a narrower look. She had applied "seriously red" lipstick in such a way as to give her fuller lips, and had done some tricks with eyeliner and shadow that made Katherine's eyes look closer together, and at the same time, larger.

When Katherine added the short-sided, teased-on-top, wig that Claire had bought for her, the combined effect of wig and makeup was that her face not only looked narrower, but she also looked taller. And ten years younger. Certainly, she did not look like the President's wife.

Katherine was amused and thrilled with the transformation, and couldn't wait to get going. Slipping the strap of a small purse over her shoulder, she picked up a light windbreaker and draped it over her arm. She stuck a pair of fashionable sunglasses on top of her head, and she was ready.

As for Claire, she strapped her hip-pack around her waist, rotated the pouch to the front, and flipped open the front flap. She took out the Glock 22, popped the clip out of its handle, and inspected its load of 15 hollow-point rounds. She then verified that there was a round in the chamber, and pushed the clip back in place. As she slid the gun back into its pocket, the feeling of foreboding that had been coming and going crept back into her consciousness. It was disquieting, but it wasn't a feeling of imminent danger, so she decided, for now, not to bring it up to Katherine, nor to Powell and Burger. She would just make sure that all of her senses were on high alert.

Making one last inspection of the new Katherine, code-name, *Cousin Anna*, she noticed something out of place. "If we're going to be two single girls on the town," Claire said, "you should probably leave those here." She was pointing at the one and a half carat diamond engagement ring and the delicate gold wedding band on the First Lady's finger.

While Katherine removed her jewelry, Claire clipped the Tac radio to her belt, and picked up her jacket. Then, imitating Jim Carrey in *The Mask* she said, "It's show time!"

The motel had been constructed in the early 1950's, and typical of the era, there was no interior corridor connecting the rooms to the lobby. Guests had to go outside and then reenter through the front doors. In the 1960's, a restaurant had been added to the main building that had both an outside entrance, and access from the lobby. Claire guessed that her fellow agents would be expecting that she and Mrs. McClure would return to the lobby the way that Claire had left—through the front doors—so she decided to enter through the restaurant.

She also knew that they would be watching for the two to appear together, so Claire had Katherine enter the lobby ahead of her, instructing her to exaggerate the sway of her walk just a bit, to keep her lips slightly parted, as if she was saying, "Who," and to walk directly toward the front lobby door, no matter what went on around her.

Katherine was about ten paces into the lobby, heading for the door where the two other agents were standing, and wondering why they couldn't hear her heart pounding in her chest, when Claire came in from the restaurant at a fast walk. She looked quickly left and right, then back toward the restaurant.

Standing on either side of the front door, expecting Claire and the First Lady to enter that way, Powell and Burger were looking directly at Katherine as she strode toward them until they were suddenly distracted by Claire's entrance and peculiar behavior. Immediately, they left their posts, and, passing on either side of Katherine, hurried to Claire.

"What is it?" Powell asked, as he, too, began looking around and his hand slipped into his hip-pack.

"I thought she came this way!" Claire said excitedly. "Didn't she go by you?"

"You *lost* her?" Burger said. "How the hell did you lose her?"

Claire didn't answer him; she was busy dialing her phone while frantically looking around. "Where *are* you?" Claire said after a couple of seconds. Then, turning toward the lobby doors, she said, "Oh, thank God! Just stay right there."

"Where?" the two agents said in unison as they spun toward the door, seeing the woman who had just past them, but not the First lady. Then it dawned on both of them.

Claire gave a little finger-wiggling wave to Katherine. Katherine returned the wave and raised it a wink.

The two men just stared at Katherine with their mouths open. Claire let out a laugh, and poked her finger into Burger's side. "C'mon," she said, "let me introduce you to my cousin, Anna."

Chapter 6

Friday, October 17
Newburyport, MA

T hough she was thoroughly enjoying playing make-believe and the role of "Cousin Anna," it took Katherine a while to fully comprehend the idea that no one knew who she was.

She was so used to smiling and nodding at everyone, and responding to *How-are-you*'s and *We're-so-glad-you're-here*'s that she felt that something was wrong at first. Before too long, however, she was completely into her adopted persona.

At first the two women just walked down the street, "scoping the shops", with Claire pointing out all the changes that had taken place here since she was a kid. The big building on the north of the street, for instance, that now housed a dozen or more little shops and eateries, used to house the city's fire engines. The row of immaculately restored red-brick buildings at the east end of the square had been condemned and boarded up when she was twelve, but now housed an expensive clothing shop, a confectioner on the bottom floor, and an adorable restaurant with window-front tables up above.

"Let's have lunch there!" Katherine suggested.

Claire looked at her watch. It was nearly ten o'clock. "Hmm, I don't know," she said. "It might be a bit late to get a reservation for lunch."

Then, taking Katherine by the hand and setting off at a run, she said, "But let's give it a try!"

Almost immediately Claire's radio squawked. "What's going on? Why are you running?"

"Lunch reservations!" Claire replied into her radio as the two women darted across the street. "Try to keep up with us, will ya?" Both women were laughing as they reached the opposite sidewalk and started up the stairs.

At the top of the flight of steps, a short line had formed, consisting of half a dozen other visitors who either wanted to be seated for brunch, or who were also making reservations for later. As Claire and Katherine stood in the line waiting their turn, Powell and Burger came in and took up "defensive positions" with Powell standing beside the First Lady, and Burger behind her.

Leaning over and whispering into Claire's ear, Powell said, "Is this how the whole day is going to go? The four of us running through the streets playing follow the leader?"

"Sorry," she said with a guilty-as-charged grin. "I'll try to give you a little notice next time."

With reservations made for three o'clock, the four of them left the building, and headed back across the street at a more civilized pace where they separated to their fifty-foot range again, and Claire and Katherine began wandering in and out of the myriad shops. It didn't matter what they were selling, Claire noticed; toys, T-shirts, jewelry, or jelly; Katherine was thoroughly enjoying herself.

As Katherine browsed and chatted about this item or that, Claire kept a careful eye on whoever else was in the store. Outside, the two men, playing the part of bored husbands, continuously scanning the people in the square, and especially anyone entering the store where the "cousins" happened to be shopping.

At the end of the main square, separated from the row of connected buildings by a narrow alley, stood a three-story brick building. A sign hung above its wide wood and glass door that read, *The Brass Bell, Nautical Paraphernalia and Antiques.*

Stepping inside was like stepping back in time—or into one of the chamber of commerce brochures.

All around were items for sale that either *were* very old, or were made to *look* very old. Objects that would be typical in a colonial-American seaport town, or that were used on the great wooden tall-ships that were the lifeblood of the town two hundred years ago, were everywhere.

Large pieces, like a wooden-spoke ship's wheel or a Victorian baby carriage were arranged on the floor. Smaller goods, like brass and glass doorknobs, whale-bone thimbles, and polished brass telescopes were displayed on shelves, or in antique china cabinets with curved glass fronts. Still more interesting stuff of all sizes and shapes hung on wires and hooks, suspended from the ceiling.

As Katherine began looking at the varied *objects-de-old*, as Claire called them in mock French, Claire made her security scan of the establishment. From a vantage point at the far corner, Claire evaluated the people in the shop. There were six in all. A young couple—late twenties, two young men—probably also a couple, one elderly man, and the shop keeper.

The shopkeeper appeared to be doing some paperwork, but looked up frequently to see if anyone looked like they needed help. As Katherine stretched to reach an object on a high shelf, Claire watched the young man's eyes travel from her hand as she picked up the scrimshaw letter opener, all the way down her exaggerated figure, right to her feet. He nodded his head approvingly, but then he went back to his paperwork, and didn't look at her again. Claire smiled as she wondered what the young man would think if he knew that he had just been ogling the wife of the President of the United States.

A little bell jingled as the door opened, and the male/female couple left at the same time that a man in his early fifties entered.

The man immediately drew Claire's attention, because she had noticed him before. He had been in the restaurant when they were making reservations, and she had noticed him twice on the street. All three times, he appeared to be looking—staring, actually—at Katherine.

Claire had chalked up the man's admiration to Cousin Anna's *voluptuousness*, but now, as the man fixed his gaze on Katherine and walked directly toward her, she shifted into threat-assessment mode. Could this be what her *something's-wrong* feelings had been about? Had the man done what Powell and Burger hadn't—had he recognized "Anna" as the First Lady? If he had, what was he going to do?

Claire quickly sized the man up with regard to his threat-potential. He wore jeans and a casual cotton shirt that was loose-fitting and was not designed to be tucked in—classic concealment for a hand gun.

He carried a small bag with a drawing of a donut and cup of coffee on it in his left hand, the same hand on which he was wearing a gold watch. The watch on the left wrist meant that he was most likely right-handed, and his right hand—his *gun hand*—was free.

Though there was no credible reason to believe that this man *was* a threat to the First Lady, he sure was ripe with *potential*.

This was the type of profile they slipped into training exercises to see how an agent would respond. Under-reacting—missing the possible threat—was just as bad as over-reacting by pulling a weapon or tackling an innocent onlooker. The action taken needed to be decisive, but measured—appropriate to the situation.

Claire's heart rate went up as she fast-walked around the big ship's wheel in the middle of the room, and then had to wait for the elderly man to set a model ship back in its place before letting her by.

The man with the bag was now right next to Katherine, and Claire was still fifteen feet away. She wanted to run, but he had not given her a reason to do so—yet.

Katherine turned to face the man, and he smiled at her without speaking.

His right hand moved up his side, lifting his shirt.

Claire's hand went inside her hip-pack.

His hand went into his pocket.

Claire gripped the Glock and laid her finger across the trigger guard.

The man's hand came out with a small black object.

Claire's arm muscles tensed, but her movement to rip the gun from its pouch was held in check at the last split-second. Her *voice* was telling her not to pull the gun.

"It's beautiful, isn't it?" the man said to Katherine as he offered her a folding magnifying glass to more closely inspect the minute etching of the scrimshaw.

Claire let out a long breath that she didn't even realize she had been holding. She casually slipped her hand from the pouch and looked upward, and said to herself, "*Thank you, voice!*" Ripping the big black 9mm automatic out and aiming it at the old man in front of several witnesses would pretty much have ruined the rest of the day.

Claire relaxed, but did not lower her guard altogether. She was a bit surprised—although happy—that neither Katherine nor the man had noticed her hurried approach. She certainly would have caught their attention had she hauled out the Glock!

Though it was fairly clear that the man posed no threat, Claire decided to stay closer to Katherine, just the same.

"Are you a collector?" the man asked Katherine.

"A collector?" Katherine repeated in amused surprise. "Whatever would make you think that?"

"Most of these pieces here are fairly new," he said indicating the shelves of ivory or bone etchings. "Maybe ten years old—one or two only *six months*! That letter opener is the only piece here that was actually carved on a *real* whaling ship! Use the magnifying glass, and look closely. See the initials and the date; D.B. '81? That's *eighteen*-eighty-one, not *nineteen*!"

"It is beautiful," Katherine said, and proceeded to handle the piece a bit more delicately.

"I'm Martin," he said, with a slight bow and a wave of his hand, "welcome to my humble establishment."

"Anna," she said, shaking his hand. "It's very nice to meet you, Martin."

"Are you in town for the President's visit tomorrow? I don't recall seeing you around before," he asked, holding her hand a second or two longer than a handshake.

"No," she replied. "Actually, I'm just here visiting with someone."

"Anyone I might know?" he asked.

"Oh, I doubt it," Katherine answered. "I'm visiting my cousin. *She's* here for the President's visit. She's with the press. It's the first time we've been on the same coast, at the same time in a long while, so we thought we could kill two birds."

Claire was amazed at how smoothly Katherine lied; they hadn't rehearsed any of that. But then she remembered that she was the wife of a career politician; it *had* to rub off.

For the next ten minutes or so, Claire tried to catch as much of their conversation as she could without eavesdropping too obviously, while also trying to keep a close eye on them without openly staring. Though the risk was low, Martin *was* standing very close to Katherine, so any hint of threat would have to be acted upon quickly.

As she listened and watched, a certain pattern began to emerge, and as it did, a smile spread across Claire's face.

While they spoke, Katherine and Martin moved to the cashier's counter, and Claire followed. As Martin placed the antique letter opener in a narrow tissue-lined box, Claire saw something occur to Katherine that Claire had seen coming all morning. Katherine didn't have enough cash to pay for her purchase, and whipping out Katherine McClure's credit card was probably not a good idea.

Katherine turned to Claire, and said in nicely-acted embarrassment, "Um—sweetie? I'm a little short here—could you help me out?"

Claire decided to have a little fun with her "cousin" role, and said in an exasperated voice, "Again?" Claire shook her head as she handed Martin her credit card. "You know, for a girl who married well, and divorced even better, you never seem to carry much cash."

"The lawyers are the ones who got the cash, sweetie," Katherine replied, up to the game. "My money's tied up in that dumb trust! But don't worry, I'll write you a check as soon as I get home."

"Damned straight you will!" Claire said emphatically as she signed the slip. "Don't forget, I know where you live!"

"Anna," said Martin extending his hand, again, "it was *such* a pleasure to meet you! Perhaps if you're in town again you'll stop in and see if I have any more interesting pieces. Who knows, perhaps you'll become a collector after all."

"Oh, I doubt that I'll become a collector Martin," Katherine said with a wide smile, "but I promise that if I'm ever back in your lovely town, I *will* stop in and see you."

The little bell jingled as Claire opened the door, and with a little wave and a "Bye now," Katherine stepped out onto the sidewalk with Claire. Claire made eye contact with Powell and Burger and they all exchanged their silent "all okay" signal.

As Katherine and Claire walked from the store, Katherine looked into her bag at the little white box, and a contented smile spread across her lips. She looked up to find Claire staring at her with a thoroughly amused look.

"What?" Katherine asked.

In a sing-song voice, Claire said, "I'm telling the Pres-i-dent!".

Katherine couldn't help but laugh, but still didn't get it. "Tell him what? That I bought an antique letter opener? I'm *quite* sure that he won't mind."

"Probably not," Claire replied, with a grin, "But how about your flirting with the antique *dealer*?"

"Flirting?!" Katherine exclaimed. "I wasn't *flirting* with him!"

"Whatever you say, ma'am," Claire replied with a laugh as they continued down the sidewalk. "Whatever you say."

Claire watched as Katherine replayed the encounter with Martin in her head, preparing to mount a defense. She saw Katherine's expression slowly go from a defensive frown, to a look of puzzlement, and finally to a wide-eyed, open-mouthed look of surprise. Katherine brought her hand up to cover her open mouth, and exclaimed with a laugh, "Oh my God! I was *flirting*!"

"I think we can blame it on the cleavage," Claire suggested. "Maybe you should have to get a learner's permit for those things before you take them out in public. They're more dangerous than they appear."

Later on, when Claire bought them both ice cream cones and found a bench where they could sit and watch the people go by, she could tell from just her smile that Katherine was touched that Claire had remembered that that was one of the things she said she had longed for. But Katherine playfully backhanded her in the arm when she began to sing softly, "Katherine and Martin sittin' in a tree—K-I-S-S-I-N-G ..." They both laughed, and were both a bit surprised at what a genuinely good time they were having.

By a few minutes after three, Katherine and Claire were sitting at a small window table in the restaurant, overlooking the busy square. Powell and Burger were seated inside, near a rear wall, at a table that gave them a clear view of the entire dining room.

An hour later, the women were being poured a cup of coffee, and capping off a wonderful seafood combination with a desert called a "Mocha Cake" that Claire insisted that Katherine try. The pastry was as simple as it was tasty—a slice of raspberry jelly-roll on its side, topped with mocha icing and a maraschino cherry—and Claire had never been able to understand why this uncomplicated little treat had never made it beyond the north shore of Massachusetts. But it hadn't, so she never missed the opportunity to have one when she made it home.

As they returned to their cars, late in the afternoon, Claire sensed a melancholy come over Katherine that she would have to have been blind to miss. "Katherine, are you okay?" she asked.

"Huh? Oh, yeah. I'm fine," she answered, her mind clearly somewhere else, "I'm fine."

"Oh, that was convincing as all get-out!" Claire chided. "C'mon, what's wrong? If you're worried about me telling the President about you flirting with Martin, forget it—we really don't talk that much anyway, and when we do its always foreign policy—you know what he's like." Claire was trying to elicit at least a grin.

And Katherine *did* grin—if only for a moment.

Claire suspected that Katherine was feeling blue because her one day of freedom was coming to an end. Claire felt a bit sad about it herself.

She decided not press the issue.

They arrived at their car, climbed in, and watched Powell and Burger walk by. A few moments later Claire's radio announced that they were in and ready to go. As Claire started the engine, she looked at Katherine who was staring out the side window. "You ready to go?" Claire said, touching her lightly on the arm.

After a moment's pause, Katherine replied barely above a whisper, "I don't want to go back to the motel." Turning toward Claire, she continued, "Not just yet, okay?"

Claire was about to make some glib remark about shaking Powell and Burger, and cruising for guys when she noticed the wetness in Katherine's eyes.

"Of course," Claire said. For the first time she began to see how much this day of freedom must have meant to Katherine. It was obviously more than just an amusing diversion from everyday life. "What would you *like* to do?"

With the delay in getting moving, Powell radioed to see if everything was okay. "It's fine, Aaron—hang on just a minute, okay?"

"Can we drive out to Plum Island from here?" Katherine asked. "Would you show me where you lived?"

Claire was caught so completely off guard by the request, that it took her a few seconds to process whether it should be okay or not.

From a security standpoint, it wasn't real good that there was exactly one way on and off the island, but since no one had even hinted that they recognized Katherine all day—not even Martin—Claire decided the risk was minimal.

"Sure. I don't see why not," she said, and radioed Powell to tell them of the change in plans and to just follow her.

She took the winding road along the river, past the single-runway private airport, and around the wide expanse of salt marsh, finally crossing over a low drawbridge, and they were on Plum Island.

The island had changed little since Claire had left. It had changed little since Claire was born. It had changed little since Claire's *father* was born!

Claire loved this place. As she drove the narrow streets, she pointed out the house where she had grown up (now painted an *awful* blue!), her best friend's house (they'd added a dormer), the beach where she learned to surf ("You can surf?"), and the well-preserved lighthouse behind which Claire had tried her first (and last!) cigarette.

As the tour progressed, Katherine slowly, but surely, came out of her blue mood. Claire was surprised at how good she felt about that. In less than a day's time, Claire felt a closer friendship to the First Lady of the United States than many of the people she'd known for years. It was an amazing and wonderful feeling.

Chapter 7

Friday, October 17
Newburyport, MA

It was nearly eight-thirty at night when they arrived back at the motel. Claire phoned Gants to check in, and informed him that all had gone perfectly, that they were going to be in for the rest of the night, and that they'd see him at Pease at 0830, according to plan.

As long as Katherine was seeing how the other half lived, Claire suggested that they eat in the diner attached to the motel. Once again, the two women, and the two men sat at different tables. The meal was simple but satisfying. Katherine had meatloaf with mashed potatoes and green beans, and Claire had her favorite item from the menu; a fried clam plate with whole-bellied Ipswich clams. Claire had found that whole-bellied clams were almost as hard to come by outside of New England as were mocha cakes.

It was after ten when the four of them made it to their respective rooms. With great sighs of relief, Katherine stripped off her constricting "prosthetics", and, naked, scooted quickly past Claire saying, "Dibs on first shower!" Claire laughed as she felt as though she were back in her college dorm for a moment.

When she took her turn in the shower, the water felt good to Claire—even if the pressure was a bit low for her liking—and she luxuriated under the spray longer than she normally would.

When she finally came out of the bathroom toweling her short hair, and marveling at how easy it was to dry, she was surprised to see Katherine sitting on the edge of her bed, crying.

"Katherine! What is *wrong*?" Claire asked for the second time in a matter of hours—this time in an almost demanding tone. "And don't tell me '*nothing*'! I've *seen* 'nothing' before, and it's different than that!"

In spite of herself, Katherine let out a little laugh between sobs.

Claire felt relieved that it was apparently nothing life-threatening at least. "What is it Katherine?" she asked gently, sitting down beside her. "Talk to me—please?"

"I'm sorry, Claire," Katherine said. "With everything that's going on, I'm just an emotional basket-case, lately." She looked at Claire with a weak smile and added, "But it does feel good to be with someone who's just plain nice. Someone who doesn't have some political agenda or ulterior motive for wanting to be around the First Lady. In fact, you're *too* nice to be dumping *my* troubles on, Claire—that wouldn't be fair—you don't deserve that."

"Do you remember what my job is?" she asked as she took Katherine's hand. "I get paid to be here and take a bullet for you, if necessary. I think I can handle a little emotional dumping! Talk to me—please."

Katherine smiled, and shook her head. With a sniff, she said, "Claire Bradley, you are quite a person. Maybe *I'm* the one who doesn't deserve this."

"Talk to me," Claire urged her.

Katherine took a deep breath. "Don't say you didn't ask for it!" she said. "I guess it boils down to the fact that I miss having a real life. I just didn't remember how much until today. I've been a political wife all of my adult life. Virtually everything I've done—all the choices I've made—have been made with public-image in mind. I've spent years—literally most of my life—trying to become a public figure, because that was the best way I could help my husband's career. Now that I *am* a public figure, now that my husband's career has reached its zenith, I find myself longing for *normalcy*. But not for me, Claire. I don't regret the choices I've made. I long for normalcy for Melissa. I want to be able to do what we did today, with *Melissa*."

"You mean pick up guys in antique shops?" Claire interjected.

Katherine laughed. "*Especially* picking up guys in antique shops!" she replied emphatically. "How often do you think I can engage someone in simple, unguarded conversation like that in *my* life? And all I can think is that Melissa is going to grow up not even knowing what that type of exchange is *like*. Claire, that breaks my heart!"

Claire hesitated before asking her next question, as if it were something unthinkable. "What if he doesn't win?" she said. "What if you're *forced* into a normal life?"

Katherine gave a little laugh. "I doubt that being the wife of even *ex*-president Richard McClure would resemble normalcy. And here's one of the conflicts that's *made* me a basket case. Even if Richard's losing could bring my family normalcy—or some semblance thereof—I'd still want him to *win*. That conflict tears at my gut, Claire. As much as I want a normal life for my daughter, I think that Richard being president is more important. Not for me, not for Melissa, but for the country—for the *world*. I really believe that, Claire."

Claire looked deep into Katherine's eyes. Something told her that there was more that she wanted to talk about, but Katherine seemed to want to leave it at that. Claire was happy that she'd shared *that* much with her. Yesterday, she was little more than a complete stranger, now she felt as if she were an old friend.

With little more conversation, the two women readied themselves and crawled into their beds. Claire clicked off the light and they said their good nights.

Fifteen minutes later, still wide awake, Claire remembered that she hadn't taken her birth control pill. Not that she ever got much chance to *need* it, but she had to be consistent with it, just in case Mr. Right suddenly appeared. Without turning on a light, she fumbled her dial-a-pill from her purse and made her way to the bathroom.

As Claire returned to her bed, she heard Katherine whisper, "Can't sleep either, huh?"

"Kinda wound up," Claire replied, crawling under her covers. "It's been a heck of a day."

They lay there in the dark, in silence for several minutes. Finally, on a whim, Claire said, "Who was your first love, Katherine? Tell me about falling in love for the first time."

"My first *love* or my first *lover*?" Katherine replied.

"Let's start with your first love," Claire said with a laugh, "and we'll see where that takes us."

For the next two hours Katherine and Claire traded intimate insights into one another's lives. They shared touching, silly, and heartbreaking moments, and laughed and shed tears together. By the time they were ready to let sleep overtake them, both woman were more relaxed and more comfortable than either had been in a very long time.

But just as Claire was drifting off, her recurring feeling of apprehension struck her, and she was suddenly fully awake again. She didn't like this feeling at all. It wasn't like her typical *voice* warning that usually prodded some action on her part—like checking to see if a gun was loaded. This was simply an overwhelming sensation that something was very wrong, and there wasn't a damned thing she could do about it.

Chapter 8

Saturday, October 18
Newburyport, MA

At 0820 Saturday morning, Claire and Powell drove their respective sedans through the security check at Pease International Airport. They pulled the cars into the hangar where all of the vehicles from the Galaxy's belly were now parked. Gants opened the First Lady's door, and they exchanged good mornings.

"Did you have a good time, ma'am?" Gants asked her. "Did Agent Bradley live up to your expectations?"

"A wonderful time!" she replied cheerily. "And Agent Bradley even exceeded my expectations. Did you know she was a surfer? On the ocean, I mean, not the Internet."

He looked at Claire. "You went *surfing*?!" he blurted.

Both women laughed. "No, Mr. Gants," Katherine replied calmly. "Just shopping and sightseeing ... just as promised. You can ask Agents Powel and Burger."

Well within earshot to have heard the exchange, Gants looked over at them, and they both nodded.

"We're already planning a shopping trip for the next time we're in New York," Katherine said as she walked past him toward the President's parade car.

48

His mouth dropped open, and he began to protest, when, without looking back, Katherine raised her hand and said, "Juuust kidding."

Air Force One touched down at 0856; four minutes ahead of schedule. The F-16 escorts flew in a wide circle around the airport until the President's 747 had taxied to the apron, and its engines were shut down, and then they landed as well.

Calypso-I, with Katherine and Claire already inside, pulled up to the jumbo jet just as the door in its belly opened, and the internally stowed stairs extended to the tarmac. The few reporters who came to cover the landing were some distance away in the main terminal building, so their view of the stairs was blocked by the limousine. It would have taken a very sharp eye and a steady telephoto lens, to notice that the First Lady never got out of the plane.

The President came down the stairs first, returning the salute of the Air Force lieutenant who was standing at the bottom of the stairs. Following the President were his press secretary Diane Stevens, and his foreign affairs adviser, Matt O'Brian.

The three climbed into the car, and the President was startled to see his wife already in the car, sitting in the rear-facing seat. Then it came back to him … something about her coming to Newburyport to go shopping, or sightseeing, or something. Katherine and Claire smiled at his surprised expression. While they were waiting for him to come off the plane, Katherine had said to Claire, "Watch; he'll be surprised to even see me here. He'll be so wrapped up in something that he won't even notice that I wasn't on the plane." Then she added, "He is *so* predictable."

In typical Richard McClure style however, he recovered in a heart beat, and said, "Hi sweetheart! How was shopping?" Looking at Claire momentarily, he went on, "Did Miss Bradley show you the sights?"

"Hi honey," Katherine said as she leaned forward to give him a quick kiss. "We had a *great* time. I'm looking forward to doing it again sometime."

"Well, if we can't get our numbers up in the next month, you may have all the time in the world to go on shopping trips," he replied in a light, but not quite joking manner.

"Don't say that!" Katherine scolded. "You're going to win next month … don't even *think* otherwise."

He reached out and patted her on the knee. "No man succeeds without a good woman behind him," he said, acknowledging his appreciation for her unflagging support. Then, with the finality of turning off a light switch, his conversation with Katherine was over. He turned to his foreign affairs advisor and press secretary, and began talking about his upcoming speech.

With the on-ramps to I-95 temporarily closed for the President's motorcade, the string of cars made excellent time to the Newburyport exit. With the streets cleared and the State Police motorcycle units blocking all of the intersections, the vehicles could have made it all the way to the school without slowing below fifty. But as they got closer to the school, the President saw that more and more people were lining the streets, waiting to see him come by. He leaned over and spoke into the intercom to the driver. "How's our time Charlie? Can we drop down to waving speed for a while?"

"Sure thing, sir," he answered. "We're about 6-minutes ahead of schedule, and we have padding." Charlie pressed a button on the steering wheel, and spoke to the communications vehicle located four spots back in the motorcade. A few seconds later, all of the drivers, and all of the agents were informed of the change.

With nearly four years of practice behind them, the occupants in the passenger compartment of the limo smoothly traded places. When they were done, the President and Mrs. McClure were sitting together on the back seat, and the three guests were forward of them, a bit cramped, in the rear-facing seats. The President then opened the hinged top to his right armrest and rotated a small knob. As it rotated, the dark privacy shading on the rear windows faded until the windows were as clear as bullet-proof laminated-glass-and-polycarbonate can get. This was as close to riding in an open vehicle as any president got since Nixon used to stand up through the sun roof that he had put into his parade car. An option that hadn't appeared since.

McClure rotated another knob and the sound from outside the car came in over speakers in the headliner. Mostly, there was clapping mixed with the occasional whistle or whoop, as the President and First Lady waved to the supporters lining the streets. Shouts of the re-election campaign slogan, *"Four more for McClure"*, were punctuated sporadically by the anti-slogan, *"No more for McClure"*, and his opponent's *"Evans knows better."*

Listening to the crowd, it struck Claire that she heard Katherine's name being called out almost as often as the President's. She was a remarkably popular figure.

As they approached the school, where the crowds were naturally the heaviest, they slowed to parade speed, and agents from the follow-car jumped out, and trotted along with the limousine, one stationed at each of the four fenders.

From her position in the car, with her side window still darkened, Claire couldn't see the crowd very well until the car was actually past them. She paid little attention to them, because they posed no threat. There were numerous armed agents and police between them and the car, and the car was about the safest place they could be in case of trouble. It was often referred to as an armored-personnel-carrier disguised as a limousine. Claire should have been able to take these few last minutes to relax, but the nagging feeling she'd had for the past two days just wouldn't leave her alone.

Suddenly, Claire noticed a look of surprise came over Katherine's face. Then, she seemed to be smiling and waving at someone in particular in the crowd. Katherine turned her head following the person as the car idled past. Claire craned to look out at who it was, and saw Martin standing in the front row of the crowd, waving, and probably wondering why the First Lady appeared to be looking and waving directly at him. Seeing no hint of recognition, it suddenly occurred to Katherine that he *wouldn't* recognized her out of her Cousin Anna get-up. She turned to see if Claire had also noticed Martin standing there, and found Claire looking directly at her with a big smile. Claire gave her a wink, and rubbed her right index finger over the top of her left index finger in a "shame on you" gesture. Katherine stuck out her tongue.

Amid cheers, waving flags, and campaign posters, the President's motorcade pulled through the opening in the vine-covered brick wall that outlined the grounds of Newburyport High School. They snaked past the gymnasium, where the reunion dance would be held later tonight, and finally pulled into the secure area that had been set up behind the temporary stage at the east end of the football stadium.

A Secret Service agent opened the President's door, and as he stepped out, the agent said, "Welcome to Newburyport, sir—or, I guess I should say welcome *back.*"

For the next twenty minutes the President hugged and shook hands with former teachers, his varsity football coach, and the school's assistant principal during his years at Newburyport High. Sadly, the principal, who had encouraged Richard's interest in politics, had passed away five years ago—a year before the young man who had been elected class president was elected President of the United States.

While they were reminiscing, an aide came by, and gave the President a five-minute warning, and he, Katherine, and the dignitaries all made their way to the right wing of the stage. At ten twenty-nine, as the band finished playing Sousa's *Stars and Stripes Forever*, the principal walked to the podium. Standing behind the Presidential Seal, he tapped the microphone to be sure it was on, and then he began to speak. "Ladies and gentlemen, honored guests, welcome to Newburyport High School. Thirty years ago a class went forth into the world from this very field; a class challenged by their principal, the late William Gracey, to go into that world and make it a better place; for themselves; for their neighbors; for their children.

"Today I have the distinct honor of welcoming back a member of that class, who took that challenge to heart and who has *indeed* made the world a better place—for *all* the citizens of the world! Ladies and gentlemen, please join me in welcoming home Newburyport's favorite son, the President of the United States of America, *Mr. Richard M. McClure!*"

The band struck up *Hail to the Chief*, and the crowd rose as one, erupting in applause. President McClure strode to the podium, waving and smiling at the crowd. For the next five minutes the audience remained on its feet, clapping and cheering wildly, while the band played *Hail to the Chief* over and over.

Finally, after countless thank-you gestures from the President, the audience began to take their seats. As the stadium quieted down, he thanked the audience, one more time, for their stirring welcome, and then said, "Now that you've all taken your seats, will you please rise, and join me in singing our National Anthem?" Laughter spread through the stadium as the crowd rose, once again.

After the anthem, the band made its way off stage to the left, and as the stadium quieted, the President began speaking. "A few moments ago, Principal DePaul very generously credited me with having taken up Principal Gracey's challenge to make the world a better place. If I have succeeded in doing that in even a small way, I have not done it alone. Ladies and gentlemen would you please welcome my partner, my inspiration, the woman behind this man's success—the First Lady of the United States, *Katherine McClure!*"

During the seven minute standing ovation that the First Lady received (two minutes longer than her husband's), the President simply stood back and let his wife bask in the adoration of the American people.

Countless times, the popularity of Katherine McClure had been compared to that of Jacqueline Kennedy and Princess Diana, and her husband—wise politician that he was—took full advantage of that. But it was not simple exploitation. When he said that his wife was "... *the woman behind this man's success ...*" he was not exaggerating. He freely admitted that he would never have made it to the White House without Katherine by his side, or, more often, behind him and pushing.

After introducing his wife, it took twenty minutes for the President to introduce the rest of the people who would be sharing the stage with him. Unlike most Presidents before him, who were always introduced *last* among the guests, Richard McClure enjoyed introducing his fellow attendees himself.

With each introduction the President had some interesting comment or anecdote to tell about the guest, and he made each story sound like a personal memory, making each guest feel like a personal friend.

It had been said that if Richard McClure could talk one-on-one for five minutes with every voter in America, he would become the only president ever elected with a unanimous popular vote.

Finished with the introductions, the President asked the audience and his guests to stand and join him in the Pledge of Allegiance. Through his lapel microphone, his voice could be heard above the chorus of the crowd, and he spoke every word with such clarity and conviction, that the 31 words that most people just mumbled—if they said them at all—actually took on meaning. When they finished the pledge, the crowd applauded like they had never heard it before. Richard McClure was in his element.

While the president spoke, agents Bradley, Powell, and Burger were standing off stage to the President's right. Seated in the single row of chairs behind the President were his honored guests. In the chair at the far right, closest to where the agents stood, was Mrs. McClure.

As the President's speech went on, punctuated time and again by applause, Gants made a circuit of his agent's positions. He made his way through the passages below the concrete bleachers, touching base with the agent at each of the entrances, and eventually wound his way to the backstage area. He first appeared in the left wing, and then after talking briefly with those agents, he crossed behind the backdrop, and arrived at the right side, where Claire, Powell, and Burger were stationed.

Claire watched the crowd as the President moved back and forth across the stage in his trademark "evangelist" style. Claire wished, as did all the agents, that he would just stand behind the podium like a regular president. A frustrated agent once referred to his back and forth style as, *"One of them God-damned bears in a carnival shooting gallery!"*

The bulletproof sides and front of the presidential podium—which was transported everywhere the president went—were meant to provide protection to three-fourths of his body as he stood in front of a crowd. Additionally, its hollow interior provided a safe, if cramped, short-term sanctuary in case of trouble. And the big clear teleprompter screens that other presidents used also provided some protection. Although not bullet *proof*, they were highly bullet *resistant*, and offered bullet-deflecting protection. Of course that was a moot point, because Richard McClure never used teleprompters. Instead, as he moved from one side of the stage to the other, he relied on his remarkable ability to recall every detail of even the longest speech, and to ad lib even better than Jack Kennedy.

"How's it look?" Gants asked Claire quietly, as if someone might be able to hear him over the President's booming voice.

Claire didn't answer right away, but continued to scrutinize the crowd. Finally, without taking her eyes off the mass of people in the stands, she replied, "Fine, I guess. Fine."

"You guess?" Gants pressed, noticing her intensity and hearing a lack of conviction in her reply. "You see something?" He tried to follow her gaze as he spoke.

"No, no," Claire assured him, still not turning from the applauding crowd. "It's just ..." She really had no words to finish the sentence. Her *voice* continued to nag at her, but still it offered no *focus*. She had no grasp of what she should be looking at—looking *for*. The feeling had her so on edge that her palms were beginning to sweat.

The President was now making his way back across the stage, toward Claire's side. The intensity in his voice was building; he was obviously on his way to some important point. But Claire wasn't listening. She had long ago learned to tune out the words; they were a distraction she didn't need.

He had stopped at the right side of the stage, and with an imploring tone was saying, "I believe that the American people elected me four years ago to accomplish a certain number of things. We are, right now, about half way to that goal. Please trust in your judgment that you were right four years ago, and allow me to finish what we, together, have begun!"

The audience virtually exploded in applause. As the crowd cheered, and then eventually quieted, the President simply stood there, apparently deep in thought about what he was going to say next. Nothing could have been further from the truth, of course. Richard McClure knew *exactly* what he was going to say next, and knew *exactly* when to start saying it for the best effect. He was a *master* at working a crowd.

Claire turned her attention from the crowd for a moment and looked toward the rear of the stage to where Katherine was sitting.

Three days ago, and for the preceding four years, Claire had been part of the *President's* security detail. Three days ago, Claire had never even had a conversation with Katherine McClure. Three days ago, she was *afraid* of the woman that the agents referred to as *The Dragon Lady*. Now, Claire felt like they were sisters.

Partly because she was currently *assigned* to the First Lady, and partly because of the surprising personal bond they had formed over the past two days, Claire began to pick up on little things about Katherine that had gone unnoticed before.

She noticed, for instance, that when she retook her seat, she didn't lean back in a relaxed posture like the other guests, but rather sat erect, back straight, chin high, looking directly at her husband. Claire had never really noticed before what a *presence* she had. She certainly was the figure that she said she wanted to be for her husband.

As the President finally began to speak once again, he started off on his next excursion across the stage to his left. At the same instant, Claire's *voice* screamed at her like it never had before!

So emphatic was the *voice* that Claire's heart rate leapt because of it. So intense was her feeling that something was horribly wrong that, without even knowing why, she began moving toward the stage in Katherine's direction.

"What is it?" Gants shouted. "What?"

Before she could answer, Claire watched, as if in slow motion, as Katherine rocked violently back in her chair and threw her hand up to her chest. With a horrified expression on her face, she then began to topple sideways from her seat.

"Katherine!" Claire shouted as she launched herself in a dash toward her falling friend. "Shots fired! Shots fired!" Claire barked into the microphone at her wrist. She hadn't *heard* a shot, but it was a damned good assumption, and those two words would get the President evacuated immediately.

At a dead run, but still several feet away from Katherine, Claire made a diving lunge and was just able to get an outstretched hand under the First Lady's head before it cracked against the stage.

"Oh, God!" Katherine groaned through clinched teeth. "Oh, Christ!" Opening her eyes and seeing Claire's face, she said, "Jesus, Claire, it hurts so much!" She then closed her eyes, and became still in Claire's arms.

Claire pulled herself closer to her friend, using her own body as a shield against another shot, while, at the same time, half a dozen men rushed at the President. They surrounded him like a human cocoon, and hurried him off stage before he was even aware of the tragedy taking place behind him.

"Shots fired!" Claire barked into her microphone, again. "Capricorn is down!" she said, using the First Lady's code name.

"Where's she hit, Claire?" Gants said as he slid in beside her on his knees. "Can you tell? How bad is it?"

"Right upper chest, I think," she said, looking up and seeing Powell and Burger huddling down, as well. "She was talking a second ago, but she's unconscious, now. She's still breathing, though, I can feel it."

Gants moved aside as two agents, carrying a folding litter, appeared at his elbow. On their heels were two Secret Service EMTs and three more agents.

As she lay on her side, the agents positioned the stretcher against the First Lady's back while one of the EMTs carefully wrapped a cervical collar around her neck. Then, with many hands holding her against the stretched fabric of the litter, they gently rolled her onto her back. As they lifted her up, Claire rose, as well, keeping her body between the President's wife and where the shot seemed to have come from. Not until the knot of agents and EMTs were safely away from the open stage, did Claire allow herself to be separated from Katherine.

As two agents hurriedly bore the stretcher toward the ambulance that was parked backstage next to the President's limo, one of the EMTs broke a smelling-salts capsule and waved it under Katherine's nose. Instantly, she awoke, letting out a moan of pain. He then strapped an oxygen mask over her face.

Fast-walking beside the stretcher, the chief EMT, Bill Dow, opened Katherine's jacket and slit open the right side of her blood-soaked white blouse, exposing the bullet's ragged entrance wound. "Open pneumothorax," he called to his partner as he saw the tell-tale air bubbles gurgling up from the wound when Katherine exhaled. He pressed a gloved hand over the wound to stop air from being sucked back in and collapsing her lung. Once in the ambulance, he would get an occlusive self-burping dressing in place, but his hand would have to do for now.

"Tell Marine One we're coming," Dow told Gants. "I want to get her to Mass General in Boston."

"Boston?" Gants questioned. "The St. Jacques Hospital is two miles up the hill."

"They'll have a much better trauma team in Boston, and we can be there in ten minutes. And tell *them* we're coming, too."

Claire thought that Gants might argue the point, but it really wasn't his decision to make. It was a medical decision, not a security one. He called the helicopter and told them to get ready for an emergency evacuation to Mass General. The helicopter crew would alert the hospital immediately, and Dow would be in radio contact with them as soon as he was in Marine One.

As they came around the corner to the secured area where the President's limo and the ambulance were parked, Claire watched the President struggle free of his agents and rush to his wife.

"Oh my God, Kat!" he cried. "What have they done to you? I'm here, sweetheart. Don't worry. You're going to be okay, I promise. They're going to take care of you, Kat. It's going to be fine ..."

In that moment Claire saw a side of the President that she had never seen before—that few had. There was vulnerability where there had been only confidence. Fear where there had always been unflagging courage. Oddly, his lapse out of the presidency and into regular person and loving husband served to give Claire even more respect for the man than she already had.

As Katherine was transferred into the ambulance, both Claire and the President turned to Gants, and said at the same time, "I'm going with her."

"Mr. President, someone has just tried to kill you," Gants said, ignoring Claire's declaration, for the moment. "It's not a good idea for you to go to any unsecured place right now. I'd feel much better if you'd go back to Air Force One with us. We can get ..."

"I'm going *with* her, Mr. Gants," the President said in a tone that made it clear that the subject was not open to discussion. "My wife has just taken a bullet that was meant for *me*; I'm not going to just send her off with a get well wish, and go hide in some bunker. Look, I understand your concern, and my detail should come too, of course, but I *am* going with her." With that, he climbed into the back of the ambulance beside his wife.

"Sir, the First Lady is my assignment," Claire said to Gants, defending her request before he had even turned it down. He was not a man who was used to having his orders countermanded, and it had just happened twice. First by the EMT deciding to take Katherine to Boston, and then by the President deciding to go with her. Claire knew that she was pushing him, and of course, she couldn't simply override him like the others had. But she had to try. "Please, Mr. Gants? I feel responsible. I need to know if she's going to be okay."

It was the imploring look in Claire's eyes that convinced him more than her words. He could see that there was more than a professional feeling of responsibility there. She was deeply and genuinely concerned about Katherine.

"Go," he said, "but get your report to me, ASAP! You're a first-level witness; your recollection of events here is going to be critical."

"Yes sir!" she said wanting to give him a hug. But she didn't. Instead, she turned and ran to the passenger door of the ambulance.

As she leapt inside, she heard Dow say, "Shit! No exit wound. We're going to have to drain her." In the minute that Katherine had been in the ambulance, Dow and his partner had cut her jacket off, and rolled her, as gently as possible, onto her left side to look for an exit wound. An exit wound would have allowed some of the blood from her internal injuries to drain naturally, and reduce the need for a field invasive procedure. Without relief of some kind, the blood would collect inside her pleural cavity and cause her lung to collapse.

"Syringe or tube?" the other EMT said.

"I think a syringe will get us to Boston, and with a lot less added trauma." As the other EMT opened a drawer to retrieve a syringe, Dow swabbed Katherine's side with antiseptic.

Knowing that he wouldn't want to try to insert a needle into the patient's chest while they were moving, the driver called back to his partner, "Let me know when you're ready to roll, Bill."

Claire watched with relief as Dow inserted a rather small needle into Katherine's right side. Katherine made a little squeak of pain, and Claire winced, but was glad that they had decided to go with the syringe, and not the chest tube. She had watched videos of chest tube insertion as part of her training, and it looked very painful. Then Claire noticed that Dow was injecting something, not draining it. It was a local anesthetic, of course, she realized.

As Dow withdrew the needle, the President, holding his wife's hand, said, "It's okay, Kat. He's done."

Dow responded, as his partner handed him an instrument that looked to Claire like a fat-bladed ice pick, "I'm afraid not. This is going to hurt, ma'am, but try to stay still for me, okay?"

He felt for the correct spot between Katherine's ribs, and then pressed the tip of the pick against her skin. He pushed, and the skin broke and a trickle of blood leaked down her side. Katherine didn't flinch. As he pushed deeper, however, below the anesthetized tissue, Claire could see her tense, and then finally let out a long crying groan of pain. Claire gripped the arm of her seat and clinched her teeth in empathy. The President squeezed her hand and said, "It's okay. It's okay." Claire watched a tear roll down his cheek.

"Almost there," Dow said, delicately pressing the needle deeper and deeper. Finally, there was a dribble of blood near the handle, and Dow announced, "I'm in." He withdrew the "ice pick's" handle, which left a hollow catheter piercing Katherine's side. As soon as the pick was removed, blood spurted out of the tube. Dow quickly attached a large syringe to the tube, and pulled back the plunger, filling the syringe with bright red fluid. When it was full—which took only a few seconds—he removed it from the needle, handed it to his partner, and connected an empty one. As Dow filled the new syringe, his partner emptied the first into a bio-hazard bag.

"Let's roll!" Dow called out to the driver. As the ambulance sped down the maintenance road to the school's baseball diamond, where Marine One was ready for takeoff, Dow and his partner swapped syringes three more times. Each time, Dow would allow a little blood to escape and noted, with satisfaction, that the initial spurt was now just a trickle. He had managed to remove the blood that had built up inside her chest, and now only had to keep up with her actual bleeding.

As Dow managed the chest drain, his partner wrapped her in a blanket to help keep her from going into shock.

A minute after pulling along side the helicopter, Katherine's gurney had been lashed to the floor of the chopper, and the big five-bladed, three-engine AgustaWestland EH101 was lifting off the ground.

As soon as he was on board, Dow donned a headset and was talking with a member of the trauma team in Boston. "Subject is First Lady Katherine McClure. Penetrating thoracopulmonary wound, upper right anterior. Open pneumothorax; probable GSW. No apparent exit. Have inserted a drainage tube and observing new blood loss of approximately 300cc's per minute. IV of whole blood running; plasma at standby. Patient is conscious and on oxygen; she is breathing on her own, but we are prepared to intubate if necessary." Looking at the portable monitor, he reported to Boston, "BP: 100-over-80; pulse: 100, strong and regular; respiration: regular and shallow. Patient is stable." Dow was very pleased with the report, and attributed it to the First Lady's remarkable physical shape.

The President sat on the floor next to Katherine's gurney, holding her hand. "I'm so sorry, Kat," he said softly to her. "That should be me there, not you. I should be ..."

Katherine started to say something, but whatever it was was unintelligible from inside the oxygen mask, and speaking apparently caused her great pain, so she stopped abruptly. Instead, she conveyed her strong disagreement by scowling and shaking her head.

On a fold-down jump seat near the foot of Katherine's stretcher, Claire sat clutching Katherine's jacket. She had picked it up from where the EMTs had tossed in the ambulance, knowing it had to be kept as evidence. Now, however, she held it like a security blanket, unconsciously stroking it as if to comfort Katherine.

As she sat there, she couldn't help but overhear the President's comment about feeling that he should be on the stretcher, instead of her, and to see Katherine's reaction. Claire was startled to realize that she had been thinking the same thing. That it wasn't fair that Katherine was lying there in agony, possibly dying, because of the President's stupid *meandering*! Katherine's reaction brought her back to her professional reality, and she felt a bit guilty for thinking such a thing. Her prime objective, like all of the agents, was to protect the President. Everyone else was secondary.

She began replaying the last ten minutes in her mind, trying to figure out exactly what had happened. The shot had probably missed the President by just inches. Claire guessed that it missed only because *his* voice had told him to move at exactly the right moment to save his life. It was as if the President's *voice* and her *voice* had been in conflict. His trying to save him, and hers trying to save Katherine. Was that possible, Claire wondered? Was that why her feeling of dread had been so muddled?

Chapter 9

When Marine One touched down on the helipad at Mass General, four shock team members rushed forward to get the gurney. In less than a minute, Katherine was in the trauma-one emergency room.

In a blur of well-practiced activity, the tubes and wires that ran from the First Lady to the EMTs portable equipment and the drainage syringe were reconnected to the facilities of the trauma room, and the remainder of Katherine's clothes were cut off. A thorough search verified that the wound in her chest was her only external injury—that there was no exit wound. She was wrapped in a new warm blanket, and a series of front and lateral x-rays were shot of her chest.

Upstairs, an operating room was ready and waiting, but Dr. Kiel, the attending trauma surgeon, wanted to see her x-rays before he moved her from the ER.

"Holy shit!' he exclaimed as the first frontal image came up on the computer screen. Dr. Kiel rarely swore, so his expletive turned heads.

Instead of seeing a deformed slug, perhaps even fragments of bullet and a shattered rib, he saw scores of bright specks across Katherine's chest. It was an effect known as a "snowstorm." It was such a surprise, because a snowstorm was almost always caused by a bullet fired at close range, and striking a bone. He could see Katherine's fractured ribs, but he had been told that the shot came from a sniper's rifle that had been so far away that no one even heard it. He clicked to bring up a lateral shot, and just stared in disbelief. He had never seen fragmentation like this in any gun shot wound, before!

Without taking the time to count, he estimated that there must be over a hundred fragments! That was unheard of! Then a horrible thought struck him. He recalled a crime novel he had once read where an assassin used a mercury-filled bullet. Such a bullet would leave a pattern like that when it burst!

"Get her upstairs and prepped right now!" Kiel shouted as he pulled off his gloves, and headed for the doors. "Tell Dr. Ford he has two minutes to have her under or I'm starting to cut anyway!" Kiel knew how deadly even a small amount of mercury in the system could be, and the First lady had a whole lung full of it!

Standing outside the trauma room doors, looking in through the windows were the President and Claire. As Katherine was rolled from the trauma room to the elevator, her table was surrounded by four nurses, all working to get Katherine prepped even before she reached the operating room. Though they would like to have gone with Katherine, the President and Claire fell in on opposite sides of Dr. Kiel as he hurried to a different elevator.

"How bad is it, Doctor?" the President asked. "You seemed shocked when you saw her x-ray. She's going to be all right, isn't she?"

"We have a gunshot wound to the upper right thorax," the doctor began in a matter-of-fact tone. "Two ribs were shattered by the bullet, and I'm sure there is extensive tissue and muscle damage. All of that is pretty routine, though—I fix those things every day. What concerns me in this case, Mr. President, is that the bullet seems to have exploded into about a hundred pieces."

"Exploded?!" said Claire and the President, simultaneously.

The doctor was pleased at their reaction—he had their undivided attention.

"It appears that your wife was shot with a mercury-filled bullet that burst on impact," the doctor told them.

"Mercury?" repeated the President in horror.

"I'm afraid so. It's rare, but not unheard of. Apparently, whoever shot at you wanted to be very sure you died. If not from the wound itself, then from mercury poisoning. But I believe I can save your wife, Mr. President. I just might have to remove her entire lung to get ..."

"What size were the fragments, doctor?" Claire asked, cutting him off.

It was clear from Kiel's expression that he was not used to being interrupted. But since this woman seemed to be "with" the President in some regard, out of deference to him, he answered Claire.

"They varied," he said in a tone that he might have used in explaining something to a child. "Some were tiny—maybe half a millimeter. Others were perhaps eight or ten millimeters. I didn't ..."

"Were they rounded or did they have sharp edges," she interrupted again, not the least bit fazed by his condescending tone.

The question and her continued insolence caught Kiel off guard. People—especially young people—simply did not talk to him like that! "Unless you have a medical degree, Miss, I fail to see ..."

"Doctor, please," the President said impatiently. "Would you answer the question?" McClure sensed that Claire didn't think that the doctor's conclusion of a mercury-filled bullet was correct, and he had more faith in one of his agent's knowledge of weapons and bullets than the doctor's. He also *hoped* that the doctor was wrong.

"They were sharp," he snapped. "What else would one expect of a shattered bullet?"

"All of them?" Claire persisted.

"Well, I didn't examine them all *individually*," he replied, "but I would say the majority were. And what would ..."

"Thank God!" Claire said. "I don't know what caused the fragmentation, but it wasn't mercury. If it were mercury, there'd be only a few fragments with sharp edges from the bullet itself. The rest would be splattered liquid, globular, or possibly tear-drop shaped—but *definitely* not sharp."

The doctor said nothing at first, but the President was visibly relieved. "Well, let's hope you're right," Kiel said finally.

At that moment, the elevator doors opened and Kiel stepped on. "I'm sorry, Mr. President," he said, pushing the button, "you and your friend will have to wait here. I'll get word to you about your wife as quickly as I can."

Claire and the President stood in silence for a moment before the President turned to her and said, "What makes you think the doctor is wrong about the mercury? And I certainly hope he is, of course."

"The only place I've ever heard of a mercury-filled bullet was in a really bad crime novel. It's a stupid idea. If you're going to put something inside a bullet, there are a lot of faster acting poisons. Don't worry, sir. It's not mercury, and if it was something more sinister, she probably wouldn't have survived this long." She was 95 percent sure of that statement, but she felt that he needed an absolute to hang onto, so she said it with 100 percent conviction. As two of his other agents approached to take him to a more secure location in the hospital she said, "I have a good feeling about your wife, Mr. President—I think she's going to be okay. And I give you my personal promise you that we will never stop until we get whoever did this to her."

While the President was being ushered off by the other agents, Claire walked back toward the trauma rooms. As one of the nurses who had worked on Katherine approached, Claire said, "Thank you for the great job you did in there. You make it look routine—just another day of saving the First Lady's life."

The nurse gave a little laugh. "Unfortunately, gunshot wounds are far *too* routine around here. I'm just glad Dr. Kiel was on duty today. He's not exactly Mr. Warmth, but he's the best chest man the hospital has." Pointing to the jacket that Claire held in her hand, the nurse asked, "Will you be the one to collect the rest of her clothes? I'm sure you'll want everything kept as evidence. Would you like to put that in the same bag?"

Until that moment, Claire had not realized that she was still holding Katherine's jacket like a talisman for her friend. "Um—yes. That would be helpful. Thank you," she finally managed to reply.

They walked diagonally across the hall to the trauma room, where Katherine's bloody clothes still lay heaped in the pan where they had been tossed. A plastic bag had been pulled over the pan, and a red sticker that read "Evidence: Do Not Remove" had been used to seal it.

The nurse donned a pair of surgical gloves, removed the plastic, and with a practiced hand flicked each garment into a neat fold and slipped it into a new bag. She reached out for the jacket that Claire held, and Claire found herself reluctant to give it up.

The nurse smiled at her understandingly and patted her on the arm. "She'll be fine," the nurse said. She then reached into a drawer and took out a white tag with a string on the end of it. The word "EVIDENCE" was printed across the top, with lines for a date, inventory, and initials. She set the tag on top of the bag, and reminding Claire not to forget it, then she left her alone with her thoughts.

The adrenaline-rush that had been driving Claire up until then was finally beginning to wear off as other very capable people took over the situation. Replacing her calm professionalism were the natural human emotions that had been held in check since Claire darted out onto the stage. Fear for her friend's life, hope for her recovery, anguish for the pain she was in, and guilt over failing to prevent it, all swirled through her head as she carefully laid the jacket on the table to fold it. She ran her hand across its length to smooth it, and her hand ran over a bulge in the pocket. She reached in to see what it was, and discovered Katherine's cell phone.

Sadly admitting to herself that Katherine would, most likely, not be using the phone for some time, Claire decided to turn it off. But the buttons were located differently than on her phone, and she simply changed the display on the screen with her first try. The new screen showed "Received Calls," and Claire's number was at the top of the list. It was the call that Claire had made to "find" Katherine at the motel. She recalled, with a little smile, Katherine's almost child-like excitement at how they had fooled Powell and Burger with her disguise. But the smile quickly faded, and the number became a blur as Claire's eyes filled with tears.

Claire had always been prone to easy tears—an involuntary "girliness" that she found most annoying—but these tears were born of a deep emotional connection to Katherine that she was still finding hard to comprehend.

For the first time since the shooting, Claire allowed her emotions to have control, and she stood there, still holding the jacket and the cell phone, and cried for her friend.

Chapter 10

Saturday, October 18
Boston, MA

During the three hours and forty-one minutes that Katherine McClure was on the operating table, Dr. Kiel removed 121 fragments and chunks of what appeared to be ceramic material from her right lung and shoulder area. The pieces varied in size from an eyelash-sized sliver, to a cone-shaped piece as big as the end of his thumb.

Along with the ceramic fragments, Kiel was perplexed to find a piece of surgical tubing almost 8cm long—about three inches. At first, he thought that it could have been left over from a previous operation by an incompetent surgeon. But close examination revealed that one end of the tubing was attached to a small ring of ceramic, and he concluded that the tubing had actually been part of the mysterious exploding bullet.

What Kiel *didn't* find, however, was mercury. More than most, Dr. Kiel hated to be wrong, but this time he was forced to admit to himself that it was actually a blessing. Besides, no one on the hospital staff knew that he had misinterpreted the x-ray as showing an exploded mercury bullet. Only the President and that woman agent had heard his speculation, and that would be easy to deal with.

After he and his team found and removed all of the fragments, Dr. Kiel repaired the extensive damage caused by the bullet and by the surgical probing. Once that was accomplished—and it took a long while—he wired the First Lady's fractured ribs back together. Kiel then allowed his assisting surgeon to close the muscle tissue over the ribs.

After that, the plastic surgeon, a woman of about Katherine's age, took over, spending nearly an hour closing the incision that Kiel had made, and repairing the entrance wound on the upper curve of the First Lady's right breast.

Kiel's incision would be virtually invisible when it healed, but some of the tissue around the bullet's entrance wound had been mutilated by the bullet, rather than cut cleanly by a scalpel, so there would be some scarring.

The surgeon couldn't recall the First Lady ever wearing anything that showed cleavage, however, so she suspected that the scar wouldn't bother her too much. If it did, there was always makeup.

Chapter 11

Saturday, October 18
Boston, MA

During the time that Katherine was in surgery, the President's foreign affairs advisor, Matt O'Brian, and his press secretary, Diane Stevens, arrived in the police-escorted presidential limousine from Newburyport. Accompanying them was a Secret Service communications technician who had brought several padded cases full of communications equipment with him.

Those cases, now arrayed around the President's makeshift office, provided him with two secure phone lines, a secure fax, and secure link to his White House computer.

By the time the tech had the fax set up, there were more than forty messages in queue waiting to be printed. Most were relays of faxes sent to the White House from foreign heads of state, members of Congress, governors, mayors, and personal friends of the McClures, conveying prayers and best wishes for the First Lady. The President read them all, and drafted personal responses to many of them, asking Diane to handle the rest.

"The phones are up and working," the President heard the technician say quietly to Diane, so as not to interrupt him. Twenty seconds later, the President was speaking to James Gants who was still in Newburyport.

"No sir, we don't have a shooter yet," Gants replied to the President's first question. "But one of my teams did, just now, locate the gun inside the hospital. From what they've told me, it looks like it was fired by remote control. Apparently, there's a computer hooked up to the gun through a bunch of wires and motors, and a video camera with a telescopic lens."

"My God!"

"We do have a *person of interest*, though," Gants continued. "One of my agents on the roof yesterday had a conversation with a maintenance technician named Frances Dunham, who would have had access to the ventilation system where they found the gun. She's only been working here at the hospital for about three months, and she wasn't at work today. We have units on the way to her apartment here in Newburyport, right now."

"*Her* apartment?" the President asked incredulously. "The shooter is a *woman*?"

"Actually sir, we just want to ask her some questions, right now," Gants replied. "She could have just been in the wrong place at the wrong time, and have nothing to do with the gun or the shooting. After we talk to her, we'll know more. I'll keep you informed. Will you excuse me a moment, sir? I have another call. It could be about Dunham."

In a moment, Gants was back on the line. "I'm sorry, sir, but I'm going to have to sign off," he said. "I think we may need to evacuate the hospital. I've just been told that there's a bomb connected to the gun."

Chapter 12

Saturday, October 18
Newburyport, MA

Frances "Frankie" Dunham left her second-floor apartment on Dwight Street in Newburyport as the President was reciting the Pledge of Allegiance in the high school stadium. It was the last time she would ever leave her apartment. She carried a large box; taped and labeled for shipping. Had anyone noticed her leaving, they would have assumed that she was headed for the post office or a UPS drop-off somewhere. As she was putting the box into the back seat of her Ford Fiesta, a voice came from behind and above her. Mr. Dole, her next-door neighbor on the second floor, was on his porch watching the President's address on a small color TV with a rabbit-ear antenna. "Frances!" he called out. "How come you're not watching the President? I hear he's going to say something about gay rights—*that* oughta interest you." Mr. Dole refused to call Frances by her masculine nickname, and nearly always had some comment about her sexual orientation. At first, Frankie thought he was doing it just to be annoying; to get under her skin because he hated gays. Over time, however, she found out that it was just Mr. Dole's direct and blunt way. It was the way he was with the "negroes" on the first floor (whom he refused to call African American or even black), and the oriental postman, for whom he always had a comment about the current

70

tensions with China. (The postman had long ago stopped explaining that he was from Korea.)

Frankie turned and looked up at Mr. Dole. "Mornin' Mr. D," Frankie said. "Whatever he's got to say, I'm pretty sure I've heard it before. And if it's anything new, I'll hear it *ad nauseam* on the news tonight. Life goes on, Mr. D. I gotta get this to the post office before they close." She closed the back door of her car, gave Mr. Dole a wave, and slid behind the wheel without giving her neighbor a chance to further the conversation.

Rather than heading for the post office, however, Frankie drove out to the "mega" grocery store on the outskirts of town. She parked next to a white four-door Toyota, and then walked into the store. A few minutes later, after buying a few groceries and a copy of a tabloid newspaper, she was back at her car. She didn't really need these things; she just didn't want anyone to see her get out of her Ford, and immediately into the adjacent Toyota. Standing between the two cars, she quickly transferred the shipping box from the Ford to the Toyota, and then climbed into the front seat of the Toyota. As she backed out of the parking place, she pressed the button on her remote to lock the doors and set the alarm on the Ford. Several miles away, she pulled into a small strip-mall, and drove into the alley behind the buildings. Without stopping, she pulled along next to an open dumpster, and tossed in her key ring containing the alarm remote, the key to her now-abandoned Ford, and the keys to her also-abandoned apartment.

Frankie drove the Toyota north on Route-1A, until she crossed the Massachusetts border, and was in the town of Seabrook, New Hampshire. She could have tuned the radio to almost any station and listened to the breaking story of the events unfolding at the President's speech, but she preferred to hear about her projects only after the fact—after the media had had time to get at least some of their facts straight.

As she drove in silence, she took a baseball cap from her shoulder-bag purse. Around the band of the cap was sewn the lower half of a man's grey-hair wig. Driving with her knee holding the wheel, Frankie quickly twisted the long shank of her mullet hairdo into a knot on top of her head, and pulled the cap over it. Next, she swapped her stylish glasses for a pair of oversized "old man's" glasses with the same prescription. Finally, she took out a plastic box about the size of a pack of gum, and opened the lid. From inside, she peeled out what appeared to be a fuzzy grey caterpillar. She pressed it onto her upper lip. She checked the false mustache in the rear-view mirror, made one minor adjustment, and decided that her transformation from Frances Dunham into Lawrence Douglas was good enough.

Ten minutes later "Lawrence" turned onto a quiet tree-lined drive of middle-class single-family homes. Half-way down the block he pressed a remote door opener, and a neat two car garage opened to receive the Toyota. Lawrence pulled into the garage, and had the door closing before the Toyota's engine was off.

In the fictitious persona of Lawrence Douglas, Frankie had rented this house about three months ago, entirely over the Internet. Neither she nor "Larry" had ever met the rental agent. Larry had never met any of his neighbors face-to-face, either. Wearing the hair-hat, mustache, and glasses, the neighbors would see him come and go occasionally in the Toyota and he would wave at them, but that was the extent of his contact with the neighbors. He had even hired a landscaping service through the paper to keep the lawn and few shrubs neatly trimmed, so that he would not need to take part in the weekend ceremony of lawn-mowing that went on up and down the street.

Frankie carried the box that she had taken from her apartment into the big master bathroom, and stood it on the floor. She slit the packing tape with a pocket knife, and pulled out the wheeled carry-on. She took off the hat with its attached wig, peeled off the mustache, and set them both on the counter. She removed her "Larry" glasses, and dropped them into the box, and then with a practiced pinch in each eye, she removed the contact lenses that caused the nearsightedness that the glasses corrected, and tossed them in the box, as well. Finally, turning to the mirror, she used a pair of blunt tweezers to remove a small plastic cylinder from each nostril. Crafted to look exactly like the inside of her nose, including real nose hair, they enlarged each nostril, and broadened and flattened her nose. As she rubbed circulation back into her relieved proboscis, she threw the little tubes into the box.

After emptying her pockets, Frankie then took off her shirt and pants, roughly folded them, and dropped them into the shipping box, as well. Frankie stood wearing very curious undergarments, and she was glad to be getting out of them for the last time—ever.

Enclosing Frankie's torso from the waist up was a flesh-colored body suit with padding sewn into the sides, shoulders, and back to make her look bigger and heavier than she actually was. In the front were two cavities containing heavy plastic pouches filled with water to augment what nature had supplied in the way of breasts. Frankie peeled apart the Velcro strip located under her right arm, and shrugged the heavy garment off over her head.

Encasing Frankie's buttocks and hips was a flesh-colored girdle, of sorts. The opposite of most girdles, however, this garment *added* bulk to Frankie's natural physique. It had padding in the hips and thighs to make her look wider, but at the same time, was constructed so as to flatten her butt. Releasing the Velcro closure that ran from her crotch to her navel, Frankie wiggled the confining garment onto the floor. With a "free-at-last" sigh, Frankie reached down and rubbed his crotch getting the blood flow back into his penis and testicles. After hours of having them tucked tightly between his legs, the "metamorphosis" back into a man always felt wonderful! He unceremoniously dropped both garments into the box, happy in the thought that he would never again have to become the butch lesbian maintenance technician, Frances "Frankie" Dunham. For the moment, at least, he was his natural self, François "Frank" DeCarlo.

Naked, he picked up the carry-on bag and set it on the two-sink counter. He opened it and took out his shaving kit. For him the kit should actually have had a different name, for it contained no shaver. By odd genetic chance, he had no facial hair except eyebrows. Seen as a grievously unfair omission of nature as he was passing through adolescence, and his friends were growing scraggly mustaches, sideburns, and goatees, he now found it an invaluable asset, allowing him to take on the persona of a woman whenever the need arose.

From the shaving kit, he took a small plastic bottle, from which he removed an item that looked like a piece of white Chiclets gum, and a tiny tube of glue. Also from the kit he produced a pair of dental pliers. Watching himself in the mirror, he took hold of his chipped front tooth with the pliers, and slowly but forcefully twisted it back and forth. After a few twists he heard a light "snap", and the tooth came loose from its post. He applied a drop of the dental adhesive to the inside of the "Chiclet"—an un-chipped twin to the tooth he had just removed, and pressed it firmly onto the fang-like post in his mouth, biting down on it to make sure it was seated. He wiped his tongue over it, and gave himself a big forced smile in the mirror to check its look. Happy, he tossed Frankie's chipped tooth into the box.

In his final act of retransformation, he spread a bath towel over the sink and counter, and using a number-three shield on a pair of electric hair clippers, he gave himself a buzz-cut, letting the hair drop onto the towel, which would join the rest of the late Frances Dunham in the box.

Stepping into the shower, Frank let the water spray over his body for a good fifteen minutes before even picking up the bar of soap. He was in no hurry, and it simply felt *good*.

When he finally got out of the shower, he toweled off, enjoying how easily he could dry his short hair, and he turned on the bedroom TV. It was still too early, he thought, for any of the news teams or network analysts to be getting the story right, but the headline was really all he wanted. Had he succeeded or failed?

He flipped through the channels, and found that even those that had not preempted regular programming to televise the President's speech, had now interrupted everything to broadcast their special reports on the attempt on his life. Those that had been broadcasting the speech live had video tape of the shooting, of course, but the others were apparently still negotiating for broadcast rights to the footage, and so were stuck with news anchors describing what had happened; with after-the-fact footage of the orderly chaos of the crowd exiting the stadium through Secret Service screening points; and with eyewitness accounts from people who had seen virtually nothing until the Secret Service rushed the President. Several of them completely misunderstanding what they had seen, and described *that* as the attack on the President.

Frank settled on a station that had just begun replaying its tape of the shooting while an off-screen commentator pointed out the completely obvious in the video. He muted the volume and watched as the President began his walk across the stage following the standing ovation. As he moved to his left, the seated First Lady came into view behind him and to his right, at the edge of the screen. As the President—and camera—moved right, Mrs. McClure could be seen to rock back in her seat, and throw her left hand up to her right shoulder, as Frank's bullet missed the President and struck his wife. She then disappeared out of the shot, as the President walked on, oblivious to what had just happened.

"Shit," Frank said softly to the television. François DeCarlo rarely failed, and he had told them that what they were asking for—when and how they proposed that it be done—was very high risk. Though he had not guaranteed success, and he would get paid, nonetheless, it still bothered him to have failed. It was a matter of professional pride. But there was nothing he could do about it now, and there would certainly not be a second chance. His employers were just going to have to deal with it. Frank had already moved on to the exit phase of the project.

After dressing in a new set of clothes from his carry-on, Frank began getting the house ready for abandonment. This had been his safe-house and workshop. This is where he had created his "Frances" disguise, and where he came when he needed to leave Frances behind and to "morph" and be himself for awhile; it was where he had created or altered the programs that ran on the computer in the ductwork of the hospital; it was where he put together and debugged the mechanism that aimed the gun. The house and its few contents were now reaching the end of their usefulness, however.

After donning his "Larry" hat and mustache, and a pair of nonprescription sunglasses, he put his carry-on, and the box containing "Frances" into the car. He opened the garage door, and backed the car out into the driveway. He was immediately glad that he had taken the precaution to put on the Larry getup one last time. His next door neighbor, an elderly but energetic woman, was walking her dog in front of his house just as he pulled out. She gave him a big wave, and called out something that he didn't hear. He waved back and drove off.

As he drove south on I-95, toward Boston, he was equally glad that he had taken the precaution to make two flight reservations to Orlando, Florida; one out of Boston, and the other out of Hartford, Connecticut, 150 miles away. Listening to the radio while driving, he learned that the air traffic in and out of Logan was still screwed up even though the emergency flight of the President's helicopter was long over.

In the town of Danvers, 20 miles south of Newburyport, Frank stopped the car at a strip mall that contained a We-Ship-It package-mailing store. He put his "Larry" disguise into the box with Frances', sealed it, and went inside. Paying cash, he mailed the box to Thomas Beard—his *identity du jour*—at an address in Orlando.

Four hours later, from Bradley International Airport in Connecticut, Tom Beard was boarding a 757 for Florida.

Chapter 13

Saturday, October 18
Boston, MA

Dr. Kiel backed out through the operating room doors while Eva Pollard, the plastic surgeon, did her delicate work on the First Lady.

Kiel stripped off his gloves and surgical scrubs, and headed to the surgeon's locker room. Splashing water over his face and bald pate, he couldn't help but smile to himself. How could they possibly deny him the post of Chief of Thoracic Surgery, after this?

He almost laughed when he thought of how angry his rival for the post, Dr. Pelletier, was going to be when he got back from his fishing trip in Maine. He shook his head remembering that he had almost turned down Pelletier's request to cover for him this weekend.

He dressed in dark slacks and a sharply-pressed clean white shirt, and then tied a flawless Windsor knot in his blue and red striped tie. He knew there would be plenty of TV cameras and news photographers downstairs by now, and it wouldn't do to look rumpled on the cover of Newsweek.

Kiel rode down in the elevator, rehearsing the phrasing he was going to use to describe the peculiar bullet to the press. "A diabolical device that shattered like glass, spreading deadly fragments throughout the First

Lady's right lung." No, too dramatic. "A bullet unlike anything I have seen in my many years of practicing medicine." No, "... my many years of *saving lives* ... of *treating gunshot wounds*." No, "... my many years of *thoracic surgery*!" Yes! Deal with *that* Pelletier!

But instead of the elevator doors opening to a sea of reporters, Kiel was met only by Agent Levine, who escorted him to the President's temporary office. Kiel swore to himself when he saw that know-it-all female agent sitting in a chair across from the President's door.

"How is she, Doctor?" Claire said leaping to her feet. "Is she going to be all right?"

"I suspect the President will want to be the first to hear about his wife." he replied in a professional, but icy tone, conveniently forgetting that just moments earlier, he was ready to tell any journalist within earshot, anything they wanted to know.

Claire felt the color come up in her face as she struggled not to say anything to this pompous ass that she might regret later—as much as she'd enjoy it right now.

When Levine opened the door to the President's office, Claire was right on Kiel's heels.

In the small room with the President were his press secretary, Diane, his foreign affairs advisor, Matt O'Brien, the FBI special-agent-in-charge, Everett Cole, and the President's campaign manager, Chuck La-Costa.

As they entered, all eyes turned to Kiel—and he loved it. Ignoring the others, he walked directly to the President, and extended his hand. "How are you holding up, Mr. President?" he said.

You're not here for small talk, you ass! Clair thought to herself. *Tell us how Katherine is doing!*

The question even surprised the President. "How is my wife?" he asked in a tone that was more like an order than a question.

"Your wife was hurt very seriously, Mr. President," Kiel began in a compassionate tone that Claire thought was way too theatrical. "As you're aware, a bullet caused a massive trauma to the upper right thorax. The bullet fragmented upon ..."

"*Doctor!* I'm aware of what happened to her! How is she *now*?"

Claire saw the doctor flush at the President's brusqueness, but he had the good sense to finally answer. "After I located and removed 121 bullet fragments, I was able to repair the damage to her lung, her shoulder, and her fractured ribs. Thankfully, I was in the ER today, or the outcome might be quite different, but I expect your wife will make a full recovery.

We'll watch her closely for signs of infection, of course, but I don't foresee any complications."

Everyone in the room clapped and cheered. Watching the President, Claire could clearly see his relief, and it underscored the full extent of the emotional stress he had been enduring.

Amid the commotion of the room, Diane Stevens barely heard her cell phone ringing. "Stevens," she answered, and then listened intently for half a minute. "No. I haven't seen it, yet, but that would have to be Claire Bradley. Okay. Let us get a look, but I'm sure I'm right—can you get confirmation there? If you do, go ahead and release it. I'm going to put the TV on right now. Oh, wait. What channel?"

Snapping her phone shut, Diane caught Levine's attention, and said, "Turn the TV on to channel seven. Hurry."

As the picture came up, Tom Lawson, NBC's chief news anchor, was on-screen. "Our NBC technicians have just finished editing the two video clips that we've been showing you into a single continuous replay of this morning's dramatic events at the President's former high school in Newburyport Massachusetts," he said. "Once again, we'd like to warn you that this video graphically depicts a real life act of extreme violence, so viewer discretion is advised. Okay, Bob, can we roll the video?"

The recorded footage began with the President standing at the left side of the stage, accepting a standing ovation. Behind him, and slightly to his left, the First Lady could be seen clapping, as well. As the ovation ended, Katherine, along with the rest of the dignitaries, sat back down. As the President began his walk back across the stage, his wife disappeared from view behind him.

"Analysts here at NBC," Lawson said, "have determined that the shot that struck the First Lady missed the President by only inches, as depicted in these frames." The video advanced in slow motion and a graphic of a telescopic sight with a crosshairs was superimposed over the President's heart. As the President moved to his left the crosshairs remained still, and as Katherine came into view from behind him, now to his right, they lined up directly on her chest. "NBC has received an unconfirmed report that the weapon used to fire the shot at the President was triggered by remote control, indicating that it was probably fixed to a tripod, and was therefore incapable of tracking the President as he moved across the stage."

There was a collective gasp in the room as everyone suddenly understood how Katherine had gotten shot.

"Oh, dear God," the President said more to himself than anyone else as he saw that he, himself, was responsible for his wife being hit by the bullet meant for him.

"Right here," Lawson continued, "the First Lady is struck, and thrown back in her chair."

"Jesus!" exclaimed Diane as her hand flew to her mouth. Everyone there knew what had happened, of course, but none, save Claire, had actually *seen* it happen. And even Claire didn't remember it in this kind of detail. She was equally shocked.

The video, which all the networks had been showing, then showed Katherine's eyes go wide in shock, and her left hand come up to grab her chest. The footage continued in slow motion, showing Katherine tipping to her right, out of the camera's field of view, as her eyes closed and her face contorted in pain.

At that point, the NBC technicians had edited a second video clip onto the end of the first. This one, taken by a man in the fourth row using a hand-held digital camera was from a slightly different angle.

As Katherine continued to fall, suddenly, from the left of the screen, Claire appeared.

"In a head-long diving slide that you might expect to see in a sports clip," Lawson commented, "this unidentified member of the President's Secret Service detail tries valiantly to catch the stricken First Lady, and manages to prevent her head from cracking into the stage, possibly sustaining additional injuries."

There was a moment of stunned silence in the room. As close as many of them were when it happened, not one person in the room had actually *seen* what had taken place on stage. Even Claire was surprised. It seemed almost as though she was watching someone else.

"In these next few frames," Lawson went on, "the First Lady's lips can be seen to move as she apparently says something to her rescuer. This is the first indication we have that she was not killed instantly by the bullet meant for her husband. As you see, seconds later, her rescuer pulls the First Lady's head close to her body, and maneuvers her own body to shield the First Lady against the possibility of second shot."

As the clip showed Gants, Powell, and Burger appear at the First Lady's side, and block any further view of Katherine and Claire, all eyes in the room went to Claire.

"I guess I owe you even more than I thought, Agent Bradley!" the President said as he extended his hand, and then changed his mind and put his arms around Claire as the other's cheered. "Thank you so much! I had no idea what you'd done for Katherine back there."

The one person not cheering was Dr. Kiel. If there was anything he hated more than being proven wrong, it was having his thunder stolen. This Bradley woman had now done both in the same day.

On TV, the video continued until Katherine was taken off the stage on the stretcher, and disappeared into the wing area. When the station went back to the live shot of Lawson, he had just been handed a sheet of paper.

"NBC has just received confirmation," he said looking into the camera, "of the identity of the woman who, in the finest tradition of superheroes, appeared from nowhere and used her own body to protect the First Lady. She is Secret Service Special Agent Claire L. Bradley, on temporary assignment to the First Lady's security detail."

Another round of cheers went through the room, and people joked with Claire, asking, "Can we see your red cape?" and "Can you really leap tall buildings in a single bound?" and "Can you get Spiderman's autograph from me?" The President gave her another hug, and said, "Well, you're *my* hero, I can tell you that!"

"People! People! Listen up, please!" Diane Stevens called out as she flipped her phone shut, ending a call she had taken while watching the video. "The media folks downstairs have been hammering me for a statement, and I just told them we'd be ready in fifteen minutes, so let's get organized, okay?

"Mr. President, I don't think you should take part in this news briefing. We'll get your statement out separately. It will have a better impact that way. Right now, I think the media folks are going to want to know three things, and you really can't add much to them. One: They're going to want to know how the First Lady is—her prognosis, any complications, when she'll be released, etcetera, etcetera. Dr. Kiel, you'll be able to handle all that I assume?"

Kiel turned to the President, and began, "It would be my great honor to ..."

Diane cut him off. "Two: They're going to want to know about the investigation in Newburyport. So far, we haven't done any media briefings up there. This will be the first one—we'll give them some of the high points from *here* and then we'll give the go-ahead to the on-site people to give a briefing at the scene. Agent Levine, I believe you're senior agent here, will you take care of the Secret Service statement?"

Levine nodded his agreement.

"And three," she said with a smile, "they're going to want to meet the *super-hero*. Are you ready for your media debut, Claire?"

Chapter 14

Saturday, October 18
Orlando, FL

Frank sat in his Orlando motel room, where he'd registered as Tom Beard, watching the replay of the diving catch of the First Lady. He had first seen the clip before boarding the plane in Connecticut, but now they had a name to go with the so-called super-hero; Claire Bradley. Like most viewers, Frank had been impressed by the young woman's athleticism and obvious devotion to duty when he first saw the video, but he was also a bit amused by the media's lauding her as a super-hero. It seemed to him that she had done exactly what she was trained and paid to do, and aside from preventing a bump to the First Lady's head, had really failed to protect anyone. But there was also something that nagged at him about the feat, and it wasn't until he had seen the two video clips edited together by NBC that the incongruity dawned on him. She had gotten to the First Lady too quickly.

If this Bradley woman had been standing flat-footed when the First Lady was struck, she couldn't possibly have reacted and then run quickly enough to get to her—even with her dive—before she hit the stage. She had to have been in motion before the bullet hit. But how could she have known? And if she did know—or somehow suspected—why would she rush toward the First Lady, and not the President?

"Who, exactly, are you?" Frank asked the photo of Claire that the TV was showing.

He turned to his laptop and composed an e-mail in French.

My dear, Henri,

I trust this letter will find you in good health, old friend, prosperous as ever, and enjoying life.

I will make the assumption that you are, by now, fully aware of the latest details regarding the Weaver project, so I won't go into that. Suffice is to say that I regret the outcome, but your client had been warned of the possibility of failure. Regardless, we must now concentrate on the future and continue on our planned course.

If you have not already seen the video from the high school, please avail yourself, paying particular attention to the actions of the president's security agent, Claire Bradley. The footage is both interesting and disconcerting, and I believe it will explain the request that follows. As you will see, this Bradley woman seems to be reacting to events before they have taken place, which, I fear, suggests a security breach. If that is so, I will need to deal swiftly and definitively with those involved, and likely with Bradley, as well.

To that end, I wonder if you can obtain and provide me with more detailed information on Bradley. I remember her name from the project research, but as I recall, the only thing outstanding was that she was the solitary woman on the President's security detail. She was not seen by any of us as a threat to the project, at the time, but now, I am not so sure. You know my dislike of surprises, and Bradley's actions this morning were certainly that.

I look forward to your earliest reply.

Yours,
François

Frank checked that his encoding software was set to its highest level, and then sent the e-mail over his "skip" network. Skipping, which took its name from skipping a stone across the water, used hidden repeater programs hacked into thousands of poorly-secured computers all over the world to send and resend the e-mail hundreds of times before it finally reached its destination. Since the e-mail and the hidden "botnet" program were automatically deleted from their host computer after forwarding the message, it was virtually impossible to trace the e-mail to its true origin in any kind of practical time frame.

Three hours later, Frank received a skipped and encoded reply from Henri. Attached was a copy of Claire Bradley's Secret Service personnel folder. It was the entire file, including even her FBI background checks, assignment records, performance reviews, and a long list of friends, acquaintances, and family members. Frank marveled at its completeness. The contacts that Henri was able to tap into never failed to amaze Frank. It was the reason that he had agreed to become involved in "Weaver" in the first place. He would not have taken on a project like this one for anyone else in the world.

Chapter 15

Senator Thomas Evans sat in his hotel suite in Miami watching the recorded video of the press briefing that had been given an hour before from the First Lady's hospital in Boston. Because he had been attending a political rally, Evans had been unable to watch the briefing live. With him in the hotel room were his campaign manager Vince Gillis, his press secretary Jack Lane, an aide named Will Clark, and two speech writers.

"What the hell would have happened if they'd succeeded?" Clark wondered aloud. "I mean, if McClure had been killed, would they postpone the election, or what? Can they do that?"

"Good question," Gillis said, "It's not like there wouldn't be an incumbent president—Madden would be sworn in right away. *And* he'd be riding McClure's campaign, and probably get swept right in on a sympathy vote."

"I think that sympathy vote is going to be an issue for us, anyway," Lane said. "A lot of people, especially the undecideds, are likely to vote for McClure just to show their support for his wife. That's going to be a bitch to fight. It's not like he's making some *policy* stand that we can go after, and it's certainly not a character thing. Hell, it's not about him at all. It's pure emotion. There *is* no issue."

As if he weren't aware of the discourse going on around him, the Senator asked Gillis, "Did you ever meet her?—Katherine McClure?"

Having known Evans for many years, Gillis was well used to the Senator's seemingly out-of-the-blue questions, and went with the flow without missing a beat.

"I've shaken her hand," he said. "We exchanged a bit of small talk a few years ago at some fund raiser. Being from enemy camps, though, we don't travel in the same circles, too much."

"She's an incredible woman, Vince," Evans said thoughtfully. "If she were my wife, I'd have been in the White House twice already. By now, I'd be playing golf and negotiating an eight-figure deal for my memoirs."

"I didn't know you knew her that well," Clark said.

"I've been keeping an eye on Richard McClure for a long time. I told the party years ago to watch out for him. That's why I didn't run last time; the polls said a majority thought a Democrat should be in the White House for a change, and McClure was the cream of that crop.

"I'll give the devil his due," Evans went on as he stopped the replay on the TV, "Richard McClure is a damned good statesman. I first noticed him when he was running for state representative from Arizona. I watched one of his debates where he left the other guy in virtual shreds. He reminded me of Jack Kennedy. But his campaign manager sucked! He lost so badly, I thought he'd go back to teaching.

"But two years later, you know what? He's back—running for a seat in the US *Senate*! I thought maybe he just liked to throw money away. I mean, here's a Democrat in Arizona who's never won an election—even to the school board—and he's running against an incumbent Republican for a Senate seat in Washington. And the son-of-bitch wins! It's a squeaker, but he wins, damn it!" Evans laughed, thinking back at how shocked McClure's opponent, Tim Lowery, had been. "It had never even crossed Tim's mind that he could lose. I knew right then that this McClure was a guy to watch.

"But what really intrigued me was how much his campaign style had changed in two years. So I did some digging. Know what I found? The woman behind the throne,"

"Really?" Clark said. "I knew she was popular, in a Jackie Kennedy way, but I didn't think she was into the politics all that much. More like Rosalyn Carter, on that score."

"Exactly," Evans agreed. "Not many people see her political side, and that's just the way she wants it. She works behind the scenes pulling strings that you wouldn't even know existed. She has this way of getting people to do things, of changing their minds, and if you ask them later, they'd swear that whatever they did, it was completely their own idea. But you can take this to the bank; no matter what she does, who she manipulates, or what string she pulls, it shines some light just a bit brighter on her husband. She may be the most dedicated—and effective— political wife I've ever even heard of, let alone known."

He thought for a moment, and then said admiringly, "She is one hell of a woman. As much as she's a thorn in my side, I'm glad she's going to be all right."

Getting up from the couch, he said to the group, "Now, let's figure out how to beat her and her husband. Tonight's speech is going to need some rewriting, wouldn't you say?"

He pressed the "Play" button on the remote, and then fast-forwarded to the spot in the video where Diane Stevens was introducing Claire to the press corps.

"And how about seeing if we can get a little help from *Little Miss Super-Hero*?"

Chapter 16

Saturday, October 18
Boston, MA

By the time Senator Evans was taking the podium to give his revised speech in Miami, Katherine's daughter and mother had arrived at Mass General. They had been flown in a special Air Force Gulfstream-V executive jet from Luke Air Force Base just outside of Phoenix, Arizona, to Logan Airport, and then Marine One had ferried them to the hospital to keep vigil with the President at Katherine's bedside in the ICU.

Katherine had come out of anesthesia while the news briefing had been going on downstairs in the hospital. Understandably, she was in a great deal of pain, so, per Dr. Kiel's written instructions, her nurse added 1.5cc's of Meperidine to her IV drip, and she had spent most of the afternoon sleeping, waking only for brief incoherent periods.

As Katherine slept, Richard sat in a chair on one side of the bed, and Helen, a white-haired version of Katherine, twenty years older, sat on the other side lovingly stroking her daughter's hair. Melissa, whose facial features and lanky build favored her paternal side, sat on the end of the bed, legs folded Indian-style. It broke all of their hearts to see Katherine like this, her hair matted, her chest and shoulder all bandaged, her right arm immobilized so as not to irritate the broken ribs, and with an oxygen tube in her nose. But at least she was alive!

The President looked at his watch. "Hey, Lis," he said quietly to his daughter, "see if you can find NBC on the TV. Evans' speech is coming on and I want to see what he has to say about your Mom."

Keeping the volume low so as not to disturb Katherine, they listened to Tom Lawson and a political analyst discuss the importance of Evans' upcoming remarks, and their predictions as to what effect the day's events would have on both candidates. At six-thirty sharp, the network cut to the Marriot ballroom, just as the Senator was walking to the podium to a standing ovation.

Like everyone else, the President wondered what approach Evans was going to take to minimize McClure's "sympathy surge" that was already showing in polls. McClure had tried to think of what he would do if he were in Evans' shoes. He had some ideas, and was now anxious to see what his rival had come up with.

Before today, this stop on Evans' campaign trail, arranged and sponsored by the heads of the local fire and police unions, had been of relatively little importance in terms of swinging votes. It wasn't that Evans didn't feel that the support of those unions was important; it was just that he already *had* their support. Still, the photo ops of shaking hands with cops and firemen was today, what kissing babies was in the 1940's.

At best, Evans had expected one or two good stills to show up in newspapers, and ten to fifteen seconds of footage on the TV news shows. But that had been before this morning. Now, every network and local TV station had film crews here. All the political pundits knew that Senator Evans' reaction could win or lose him votes, and they couldn't wait to scrutinize, analyze, and criticize whatever he said.

"It is unusual, if not unheard of," Evans began after his applause quieted, "to start a campaign speech by talking about your opponent's wife. But the near-tragic events of this morning transcend any political rivalries and generate a sense of unity that, unfortunately, only tragedy seems to be able to do. I am sure that I speak for every American, regardless of party, when I say that our thoughts and prayers are with you, Mrs. McClure, and that every one of us wishes you a speedy and complete recovery."

In unison, the crowd was on its feet, and clapping in agreement. *So far so good*, Evans thought to himself. *But that was the easy part.*

"As is often the case when a tragedy strikes," Evans went on after the applause for the First Lady had subsided, "people who thought of themselves as ordinary, find themselves performing *extra*-ordinary acts—heroic acts. The men and women of the police and fire departments here tonight—and especially their families—know exactly what I'm talking about. Heroism is a daily occurrence to you.

"This morning," he continued, "during the attempt to assassinate President McClure, US Secret Service Agent Claire Bradley risked her life to protect the First Lady by using her own body as a shield. When asked about her actions at a press conference a few hours ago, she replied modestly, '*I was just doing my job*'." Evans shook his head and added with a practiced smile, "You heroes are all alike."

There was a round of laughter along with pockets of applause.

"Well, if that's the way you want it, so be it!" he went on. "But I'm going to make a pledge to you here and now, that if that's the way you're going to do your jobs, then by God *I'm* going to do whatever I can to help you!

"As president, the very first piece of legislation that I send to Congress will be what I am calling *The Heroes Bill*. A bill that will create a special federal fund for the education and training of emergency services personnel and first-responders in every state in the union!"

As the audience stood and applauded the Senator's proposal, it occurred to him that right then would be a great time to leave the stage. Nothing in the rest of his speech—the speech originally prepared for this evening—was going to elicit this kind of response or generate as much press for him.

In Katherine's hospital room, President McClure was nodding his head in grudging admiration. "*Money for heroes—that's good*," he said to himself. As he contemplated his opponent's new tack, he was startled by Katherine's voice.

"I hope that's his concession speech you're watching," she croaked.

They were the first coherent words that Richard had heard her say since before the shooting. "Kat!" he exclaimed. "I'm sorry you had to wake up to *that*. Senator Evans is trying to score points over you laying here all bandaged with tubes going everywhere! How are you feeling, honey?"

Looking at her husband, her daughter, and her mother, she said, "Lucky. Very, very lucky."

In the waiting room outside the ICU, Claire sat with Levine watching Evans' speech. "Look at that!" Levine said elbowing her. "Even the *op-*

position is calling you a hero! I'm telling you, you're going to be diving across a box of Wheaties before Election Day. Mark my words!"

She laughed, and added, "Yeah, and maybe they'll change their slogan from '*Wheaties; breakfast of champions*' to '*Wheaties; we're just doing our job!*'"

A few minutes later, an ICU nurse came out and told Claire that the First Lady was awake, and asking to see her.

Richard, Melissa, and Helen were all on the far side of the bed when Claire came into Katherine's room. Tears of joy were filling Claire's eyes as she smiled ear to ear, and reached out for Katherine's hand.

"I didn't think super-heroes were supposed to cry," Katherine teased, her own eyes glistening, and smiling a bit lopsided from the medication.

"They're not supposed to reveal their secret identity, either, but you certainly ruined *that*!" Claire retorted. Claire leaned down and gave Katherine an awkward, but wonderful embrace around the maze of wires and tubes that sprouted from her body.

"That was a very brave thing you did for my daughter, young lady," Helen said to Claire when they had been introduced. "I think Richard should give you a medal."

"Thank you, Mrs. Thornton," Claire replied. "But just having your daughter here with us is reward enough. Besides, that's what I get paid to do."

"Well, you don't get paid enough!" Helen responded and gave her son-in-law a meaningful look.

Katherine began to interject something, but was quickly cut off by a painful coughing spell.

"Well," her nurse said from the doorway, "it's nice to have you back with us, Mrs. McClure." She came in to check on her patient, and as she raised the back of her bed, she asked, "So, how are you feeling?"

Cautiously, so as not to trigger another coughing spell, Katherine answered, "Sore."

"I'll bet," the nurse said as she held her stethoscope to Katherine's chest. "Getting shot will do that. Tell you what; I'm going to ask your visitors to leave for a little while, and we're going to do a breathing treatment, okay? I can hear some fluid in your left lung, and we need to stay ahead of that."

The four visitors all hugged or kissed Katherine as they went out, with Claire being the last to leave. From the doorway, she looked back at her friend as the nurse helped her into an upright position, the pain of the ordeal obvious in Katherine's face. Claire was very happy that Katherine was alive, of course—a few hours ago, that wasn't such a sure bet—but she was angry as hell at whoever had done this to her. Claire wasn't sure how, yet, but she knew that she had to do something to be involved in catching this SOB. And the first thing to do would be to talk to Gants about a reassignment from security to the Service's investigative division. She began to mentally prepare her case for a transfer, knowing that Gants would make her defend the request as a logical, practical decision, not an emotional one. She would have to be very careful to keep the anger she was feeling out of her voice and her choice of words.

Chapter 17

Saturday, October 18
Boston, MA

As soon as Claire stepped into the corridor outside of the ICU, the elevator opened, and off stepped Gants and Powell.

"How is she?" Gants asked.

"She just woke up," Claire replied. "She's a little groggy from all the pain medication, but she was talking and even joking. Her doctors say she should recover completely. How about you? Anything new from the scene?"

Gants looked at his watch and replied, "Well, the gun should be off VT-1 by now, and on the road to Quantico. I left Easton in charge on-site to work with the FBI lab folks, but so far, nothing else earthshaking has turned up."

"How about the woman from the hospital?" she asked. "Anything on her?"

"Frances Dunham," Gants said. "She started at the hospital in the maintenance department about three months ago. That's just before the official announcement that the President would attend his reunion."

"Maintenance, huh?" Claire mused. "That's convenient if you want access to any place in a building."

"Including the air duct where we found the gun," Gants agreed.

"You think she's part of something bigger, or could she have acted alone?"

"If she is involved, I doubt she could have done it alone," he answered. "The whole set-up just seems too elaborate to be pulled off by some nut with a grudge. I think there's some serious planning and money behind this."

"A paid assassin or some unfriendly government?" Claire asked.

"No way to tell, yet. Maybe a closer look at the gun will shed some light," Gants said resignedly. "But Perkins made a good point when he said that that gun wasn't built in somebody's garage or ordered from the back of *Soldier of Fortune*. It's pretty sophisticated, which means expensive."

"Perkins?" Claire repeated. "Oh, yeah, he's the local cop who discovered the gun, isn't he? What the heck kind of gun is it, anyway? How could it fire a bullet nearly *two-miles* and put it on target? The thing must look like a small howitzer. How did it get inside an *air duct*?"

Gants smiled at Claire's typical multi-question run-on sentence. She was obviously keyed up about the subject. He knew she would be.

"Okay," he began, "in order, the answers are: Yes, he's the local cop who found the gun. Former Marine who actually worked at the hospital at one time. As for the gun; it's obviously an 'unconventional,' because it does *not* look like a small howitzer. It looks more like a long piece of pipe with hoses connected, which, I suspect, somehow accounts for why no one heard the shot. Also unconventional, is the fact that it was aimed with the help of electric motors, a camera with a telescopic lens, and a computer. At that range, even the best sniper couldn't be steady enough. And finally, the air duct probably isn't what you're imagining. I was told that that part of the ventilation system is called a *plenum chamber*; it's actually the size of a small room. This plenum chamber is located on what they call the facilities floor, which is the top floor of the hospital, above the last floor where patients are. The entire floor is taken up by electrical panels, plumbing, and the heating and ventilation system for the whole building."

Zeroing in on something that had been nagging at her, Claire said, "You said that this gun was aimed with the help of a computer, but it still missed. I'm wondering if it really did miss. What if the President wasn't the target? What if the shot was meant for the First Lady all along? Granted, I can't think of a motive—why anyone would go to such lengths and expense to kill *her* rather than *him*, but something feels out of place here."

"What makes you think the First Lady was the target?" Gants asked. The thought had naturally crossed his mind as well, but he wanted to see where Claire was coming from.

"Ballistics," she replied. "In the sniper training we took at Laurel we had a little plastic slide-calculator to give us the time of flight of a round after it left the barrel until it hit the target. I don't have the calculator with me, but if memory serves, on the 800-yard range we were allowing something like one or one-and-a-quarter seconds for the bullet to get to the target—you had to figure that in if you were leading a moving target.

"That was roughly a half mile," she went on. "So multiply that by four for a two-mile shot, plus add a little because the bullet is constantly slowing down, and you're at what? Six to eight seconds? *Six to eight seconds*!" she repeated for emphasis. "You can't hit a moving person that way! You'd be crazy to try. Hell, you'd be lucky to hit a moving *bus*. At least with a bus the speed is going to be relatively constant so you could anticipate when it would intersect your bullet's path, and fire accordingly. But a person walking can change speed, they can stop, they can even turn around and *leave* in the time it would take for the bullet to get to them after it leaves the gun!"

"Maybe the shooter didn't know that the President was going to be walking around," Gants said, playing his usual role as devil's advocate. "Maybe he—or she—just did the best they could when they found out he wasn't going to stand there behind the podium. They lined up and took the shot when he was standing at one end of his walks—hoping he'd stand still long enough for the bullet to get there."

Claire thought about that for a moment. "Sorry," she said finally. "I can't buy that this shooter is going to come up with some two-mile super-gun, is going to get it inside and set up in that hospital—obviously well before the day of the shooting—and is never going to take the time to watch the intended target give a speech. This person is a planner—or somebody in the loop is—he or she is not going to miss something like that. Sorry. Can't give you that one."

"That's a good point," Gants agreed. "Let's say they *did* do their homework, then. Let's say that they studied videos of every speech they could get their hands on. Maybe there's a pattern. Maybe the President stands still for a predictable amount of time at each end of his walks. Hey, how about this? The shot hit just after a standing ovation, remember? Maybe they *knew* the President would stand still for a long while if there was a standing ovation. Maybe *that's* the pattern they used."

Claire recalled the video she had seen earlier on the news, where the crosshairs remained still while the President moved away, leaving Katherine in front of the gun sight. The explanation made sense. It also fit with Claire's theory that the President's *voice* had saved his life by making him move at exactly the right time—*after* the shot was fired.

Intrigued by the uniqueness of weapons system that Gants was describing, she said to him, "I'd like to get down to Quantico and see the gun. Is that okay with you?"

"I don't know," he teased her. "The FBI isn't going to want tourists tromping through their lab."

"I'm hardly a *tourist*!" she countered as she set her feet apart and stuck her fists on her hips. "I'm a *super-hero*! Tom Lawson said so."

"Yes, I heard that," Gants said with a laugh. "I'm just glad it's not going to your head."

Just then Gants' cell phone rang. "Hello, Gants here. Hi, Diane. Claire? Yes, she's standing right in front of me. Okay, we'll be right down."

"I heard my name," Claire said when he had flipped his phone shut. "What was that about?"

"The President wants to see you and me downstairs."

As they walked to the elevator, Gants noticed the look of concern on Claire's face. "I don't know why the President wants to see us, Claire, but don't worry. There wasn't anything that you could have done differently to prevent this, and I will stand behind you all the way."

"Thanks, Mr. Gants," Claire said, "I'm glad you feel that way." In fact, Claire hadn't been worried about the President at all. He'd given her a hug and called her his personal hero. She was worried about Gants. She didn't want to offend him, but she had made up her mind to request a transfer so she could actively work the case. Her *voice*, however, was telling her not to broach the subject with him, and that concerned her. She felt that it meant that he either *would* be offended—and it might damage their relationship, or that he'd say no, and she would have to watch from the sidelines of the security detail as others went after the shooter. Neither prospect was the least bit appealing.

Chapter 18

Saturday, October 18
Boston, MA

The President's office had been moved from the waiting room, with its wall of windows, to an office in the basement that the Secret Service had determined was more easily secured. The switch had been made when the President made it clear that he was not going back to Washington as long as his wife was in Boston. Dr. Kiel had consulted with the First Lady's personal physician and they had both agreed that she would probably be okay to be transferred to George Washington Hospital in DC in about three days, so the hospital had agreed to the President's unusual request to take up temporary residency.

When Gants and Claire arrived at his office, they were shown in and introduced around the room. FBI Special Agent Cole had arrived just seconds before them. As SAC, or Special Agent in Charge, of the Boston field office, and therefore the Newburyport area, Gants had spoken with him, but had not met him before.

Also in the room were the President's press secretary, Diane Stevens, as well as Kent Klein, one of the President's aides. As Gants and Claire took seats, the President got right to the point.

"There are two very important things in front of me right now. One is winning an election in two weeks, but more important than that is bringing to justice whoever is responsible for trying to shoot me and for nearly killing my wife in the process. I want you all to know that if, by giving up the former, I could somehow undo the latter; I would not have one second's hesitation in doing so. Obviously, I can't do that. What I can do, however, regardless of the outcome of the upcoming election, is to issue an executive order, today, that will set up a joint-agency task force to put the best of the best from every branch of government and every law enforcement department to work on Katherine's case. It will be known simply as the Executive Task Force, or ETF, for short."

Claire's excitement grew. She found herself hoping for some opening, a call for volunteers, or anything that would get her onto the front lines of the President's task force.

"I've been in touch with Secretary Shepherd, Director Whitherspoon, and Director Coffey," the President went on, indicating the Secretary of Homeland Security, and the Directors of the Secret Service and FBI, respectively, "and they are all in complete agreement. They will be issuing their own orders to each of you, but in the meantime I'm taking the bull by the horns and getting things moving while I have you all in front of me.

"Out of this task force I want the FBI labs to find out where every nut and bolt of that gun came from. If any of it came from outside this country, I want the CIA to find the source. I want the National Security Agency to digest every bit and byte that's in that computer, and tell us things about the programmer that his mother doesn't know. I want Alcohol Tobacco and Firearms to tell me if any gun manufacturer in this country has even *heard* of a gun like this one. And I want every agency, every cop in this whole country looking for that Dunham woman.

"Right now," McClure continued, "because they were on-site when this started, the Secret Service is the federal agency in charge of the investigation. Typically, responsibility in a case like this would shift to the FBI, but I want the ETF to be a true joint-agency effort, and I want you, Agent Bradley, to head it up."

As the President was speaking, Claire had been mentally composing her request to be part of this new *ad hoc* agency, so she wasn't even sure she'd heard him correctly. "Head it up?" she said. "*Me?*"

"Yes, Agent Bradley. You."

"You can't be serious!" she said almost reflexively. She quickly added, "sir." She wanted to volunteer to be *part* of the team, not its captain!

"Oh, I see how it is," he teased her in mock disappointment, "you'll take my wife shopping, and then dive in front of a bullet for her, but you won't take on an extra assignment for *me*?"

"I'm sure people are getting tired of hearing me say this, sir," Claire said wearily, "but that was my job—the shopping *and* the diving. What *you're* asking isn't. I don't have any experience in managing a project like this. This could be *international* for all we know, right now. The last thing you want is for this to get screwed up because of my lack of qualifications."

"I've considered that, Agent Bradley," the President said. "But you'd hardly be alone. A good manager surrounds him or herself with the talent they need to get the job done. I sure as heck don't run this administration by myself. You'll have a pool of tens of thousands of individuals to draw from. I have every confidence that you'll succeed."

"Sir," she began, trying a different tack, "once the media finds out about my lack of experience, won't my appointment look like your campaign capitalizing on my fifteen minutes of fame?"

"You don't beat around the bush, do you, Agent Bradley?" the President said. "I'm beginning to see why Katherine has taken such a liking to you. You're very much like her. And you're absolutely right. The polls show you to be more popular than *me* at the moment. And that's an advantage I'd prefer not to throw away."

"They're taking polls about *me*?" Claire asked incredulously.

McClure laughed. "At this point in an election this close," he said, "someone is taking a poll about something, every hour of every day. Yes, they're taking polls about you, and your numbers are fantastic. What's not to like? You're young, attractive, athletic, courageous—and that press briefing upstairs showed you to be articulate and serious, but with a sense of humor, too. Hell, if it weren't so late in the election, I'd ask you to be my running mate!"

"No thank you, sir." Claire said with a laugh. "My courage has its limits!"

The humor served to relax everyone a little, but it was clear that the President wasn't dissuaded. "As your employer, I could, obviously, require you to take the position," he said, "but I don't operate like that. I'll leave the decision up to you, Agent Bradley, but I do believe that you can do this."

Claire felt like she did when she was a kid and her father would use the same guilt/logic to get her to do the "right" thing by leaving the choice up to her after making it abundantly clear what he thought the "right" thing was. But even the guilt-trip the President was laying on her right now could not make her cave. The success of this task force was far too important.

"How about a compromise?" Claire said after a few moments of thought. "What if I'm spokesperson for the ETF? I want to work the investigation, too, of course, but someone who has management experience should run it. Someone like Paul Levine."

"Oh, yes!" Diane Stevens interjected quickly. "I *like* the spokesperson angle, Mr. President! That could work perfectly!"

"What do you think, Mr. Gants?" the President said. "Is Levine the guy for the job? I know who he is from being in my wife's detail, but I don't know much about him."

"Absolutely, sir," Gants replied without a moment's hesitation. "Paul Levine is one of the most organized and disciplined people I have. He'd be the perfect candidate to coordinate a project like this. And he has great credentials. The media shouldn't have any questions at all about why he was chosen to head the team."

"All right then," the President said, "the ETF has a director and a spokesperson." Looking at his watch, he went on, "Now, I suggest ..."

"Um, sir." Claire interrupted. "I do have one condition on the spokesperson position. And I'm sure that Paul would have the same one, if he were here."

"And that would be?" the President said curiously. He was not accustomed to people putting conditions on assignments after he gave them, but Bradley's up-front demeanor intrigued, and even amused him.

"No lies and no politics," Claire replied flatly. "As spokesperson, I won't tell the media anything that's not true, and I won't tell them anything even if it *is* true, if it's obviously politically motivated. Otherwise the whole task force loses its credibility and its effectiveness."

"Fair enough," the President said with a smile. Turning to Diane, he added, "She even has integrity!" Back to Claire, he said, "You sure you won't reconsider that running mate position?"

"Would you really want a running mate with a no-politics platform?" she said, happy that the President had apparently not taken offense to her condition.

"Good point," he said. "We'll leave it spokesperson, then. Now, if that's all," he went on, getting back to his previous thought, "I'll leave the details up to you folks. Go and find yourselves a convenient room to start hammering out what you're going to do and how you're going to do it. Diane, I want you to set up a press conference for nine tomorrow morning so we can announce this."

As they were filing from the room, Gants said quietly to Claire, "Are you sure you know what you're getting into? No lies and no politics is an admirable goal, but we're talking about Washington DC here. I'm not sure you can hail a taxi in DC and keep those expectations. I would have thought that you'd want a transfer to Investigation so you could be right in the trenches."

In fact, Claire *wasn't* sure. When the President asked Diane to set up a press conference, it suddenly struck her that she was going to be talking not just to a room full of reporters, but to a national—even *international*—TV audience. She sure hoped her *voice* knew what it had gotten her into when it had held her back from asking Gants for that transfer.

Chapter 19

It was eight twenty-five Sunday morning when Dr. Whelk, head of the FBI lab in Quantico, placed his call to the President at the hospital in Boston.

Whelk was running late, having promised to call the President no later than eight-fifteen with whatever the lab had come up with overnight. McClure wasn't expecting much, but he wanted to show that the ball had been set in motion even before the announcement of the joint-agency task force.

With the same group in the office that had been there the night before, plus Paul Levine, the President put Dr. Whelk on the speakerphone.

"What have you got for us?" the President asked. "Anything I can use in my announcement this morning?"

"We have something pretty significant, sir," he said, "But I'm not sure you'll want to release this, just yet. It appears that the gun they found at the hospital was built as a special project for the CIA."

"The CIA!" half a dozen voices exclaimed at once.

"*Our* CIA?" the President asked in disbelief.

"Technically, no," Whelk answered, "not *your* CIA, Mr. President. If our information is correct, it was manufactured in the early eighties, apparently for President *Reagan's* CIA."

"Fill in the blanks, Dr. Whelk," the President said. It was an expression he used when he knew there were pieces of a story he wasn't being told right away. It was also an indication that he was losing patience with the speaker.

"Yes, sir," Whelk answered, recognizing the phrase and its implications. "We have a civilian consultant down here named Jack Hampton—he's kind of a special expert on making things out of metal. We've been using his services off and on for a couple of years. He can tell you if a part was made on a mill or a lathe, and what kind of tool did the cutting. We've used him with good results in several bomb-making cases.

"Pulling out all the stops, we called him in to look at the gun and all the parts of the aiming mechanism. We wanted to see if there was anything special about the parts that might point us toward where they were made. Whether they came from a sophisticated factory or could have been made in some nut's basement workshop, for instance.

"Well, he took one look at the gun this morning and he actually recognized it! Apparently, Hampton used to work for a company in Vermont called Dynametric, where he, himself, built this gun. He says he's pretty sure that the customer was the Reagan CIA."

"That would make that thing more than 25 years old!" Gants said skeptically. "Are you sure this guy knows what he's talking about? It looked pretty state-of-the-art to me."

"That's what I thought too," Whelk replied. "But Hampton sure knew a lot about it before he got within six feet of it. There's no question in my mind that he's seen it before. If he didn't *build* it like he said, then at the very least, he's been *around* it before."

"But in the eighties?" Gants pressed him. "Where the heck has it been since then?"

"He doesn't know," Whelk answered. "He worked on its development for several years, and then after they did the acceptance trials, it was crated up and he never saw it again after that. That was in 1984."

"You said he's 'pretty sure' the customer was the CIA," the President said. "Have you contacted anyone over at Langley to confirm any of this?"

"How about the people at Dynametric?" Claire added.

"I just got done talking to Hampton when I called you, sir," Whelk replied to the President, "so I haven't had a chance to call anyone over at

Langley yet. As for Dynametric, they closed their doors about six years ago, so I'd guess getting records and finding the right people to talk to may take some digging. But that's not the area we get into down here in the lab."

"Might I suggest that the task force contact the CIA and do the follow-up with Dynametric?" Claire said. "There's no time like the present to get started. I'd also like to talk to Mr. Hampton, if I could."

"I thought you didn't *want* to run the task force," McClure said, grinning.

"Sorry," she said, giving a glance at Levine. "I guess I just want to get going, especially with a hot lead sitting out there."

"I agree with Bradley, sir," Levine said. "The quicker we get started, the warmer the trail is. I'll set up an interview with Mr. Hampton and have the Service's research group check his background and start looking into Dynametric."

"I'll make a call over to Langley," Gants said. "I know just the person who'd know about this kind of thing."

"Well, I'm certainly not going to announce that the gun that was used to try to kill me was made for our own CIA—not without knowing its trail, anyway," the President said. "Do you have anything more benign that I can use in the meantime, Doctor?"

Claire offered, "Like how it could shoot two miles?"

"We had actually figured that out overnight by reconstructing the bullet," Whelk said, "but Jack confirmed our theory this morning. The bullet is self-propelled."

"I knew it!" Claire exclaimed. "I knew it had to be something like that!"

"The gun is a launching tube," Whelk went on. "It uses nearly-pure hydrogen peroxide and a silver catalyst to create a head of steam that accelerates the bullet up to just under the speed of sound—around 350 meters-per-second.

"The same fuel is carried inside the bullet—which is actually a small rocket—inside of a pressure bladder that's made from a piece of surgical tubing. As the peroxide exits the bullet's nozzle, it passes through a wire mesh made of pure silver, which causes the peroxide to vaporize into high-pressure steam. That propulsion keeps the bullet flying straight and true. Hydrogen peroxide, by the way, is the same fuel that they use in those one-man rocket packs."

"You said 350 meters per second," Levine said. "Why so slow? A typical sniper rifle has a muzzle velocity of 800 to 900 meters-per-second."

103

"According to Hampton," Whelk answered, "it was to keep the whole thing quiet. Same reason for using steam. He said it just made kind of a loud *whoosh!* when it fired, and then because the bullet stayed subsonic you never heard the crack of it breaking the sound barrier like you do with a regular rifle bullet."

"That's why no one heard the shot!" Claire said, more to herself than anyone else. That had been bothering her. "Was it some kind of self-guided bullet?" she asked.

Before Dr. Whelk could answer, the President said, "Please keep your answer brief, Doctor, we have a press conference in about eight minutes."

"Okay, here's the condensed version," Whelk said, speaking more rapidly than before. "No, the bullet wasn't guided, *per se*. But because it was self-propelled, and spun very rapidly, it would fly a much flatter and straighter path than a normal bullet. The *gun* was guided, however. It was aimed by a computer, using a telescope fitted with a camera, and some pretty sophisticated aiming software. It was even connected to an anemometer on the hospital roof to measure the wind speed. We're still digging into the software's capabilities and where it might have come from, but we don't believe it's home-grown."

"Thank you for the information, Doctor," the President said. "I'm sure there's much more you could tell us, but I'm afraid we're going to have to run with what we have for now. Keep up the good work down there, and give your staff a round of atta-boys for me. Good bye, for now."

"As official spokesperson for the investigation task force, Miss Bradley, you have about five minutes to put all that into announcement form," the President said. Then he added, "But no mention of the CIA connection."

Claire raised an eyebrow, silently questioning whether his directive didn't violate her "no lies, no politics" stipulation.

"*Alleged* CIA connection," the President clarified. "I'm not asking you to lie, Miss Bradley. At the moment, the CIA link is speculative. It would be irresponsible to bring up something like that without hard proof, wouldn't it?" With a grin he added, "That's what we have right-wing newspapers for."

"Agreed," Claire said, and with a grin of her own, added, "On both counts."

There was nothing humorous, however, about the thought that there might be some connection to people within the government. Her mind flashed back to all that she had read about the Kennedy assassination and the fact that, half a century later, some people still believed that he was killed from within his own administration. The idea that this investigation might leave such lingering doubts scared the hell out of her.

Chapter 20

A few minutes after Dr. Whelk's call, Claire was standing to the left, and slightly behind the President in front of a room full of reporters. She was wearing a dark blue business suit with a white blouse that Diane Stevens had come up with from God-knows-where.

As the President spoke, she stood with her hands clasped behind her back, watching him intently. Although she appeared to be paying close attention to everything he was saying, she was, in fact, thinking about what Dr. Whelk had told them.

The President's remarks were brief and non-political. He gave an update on Katherine's condition and received a round of applause when he announced that the doctors expected her to be well enough to be transferred to George Washington hospital, by Tuesday or Wednesday. He thanked everyone for their support, their prayers, their telegrams, and their e-mails.

He went on to explain that later in the morning he would be signing an executive order creating a special multi-agency task force to investigate and prosecute "... this act of terror that has been perpetrated on the American people."

"Playing a major part in the Executive Task Force," the President went on, "and taking up the position of spokesperson, will be a person who has become a personal hero of mine—Secret Service Special Agent Claire Bradley. I'm going to let her outline the structure and scope of the ETF for you, and then we'll take some questions."

As Claire stepped to the podium, it occurred to her that Levine, as head of the task force should be part of the question-and-answer team, too, but for some reason, that had never been discussed.

"Thank you, Mr. President," she said as he retreated to the wings, leaving her in full control of the briefing. "And thank you all for being here. As the President said, we have begun the process of setting up a multi-agency task force to investigate and then to aid in the prosecution of yesterday's attempted assassination.

"Using the Secret Service liaison division as a hub, a computer network is presently being created, which will link every federal law enforcement and investigative agency together in a manner that has never been done before. What we are creating is an even more closed-loop system than was established after 9-11, with enhancements born of the shortcomings of that experience.

"The plan is that every person in every agency who is working on this investigation will send their reports, their findings, even their *guesses* to a database within the liaison division at Secret Service headquarters in Washington. As the information comes in, it will be immediately categorized, indexed, and cross-referenced, and added to the searchable database. This will include all of the information produced by all of the agencies' researches and investigations, as well as any tips or inquiries from the field.

"A separate group within the liaison division will constantly monitor and cross-type the information coming into, and going out of the database, and will feed what it sees as pertinent information out to the various agencies, without them even requesting it. For instance, if a DEA agent gets a tip that there's a gunsmith in Huntsville that builds untraceable weapons for drug dealers, we're not going to wait for the FBI or the ATF to do a search for illegal gun manufactures. We're going to turn that information around *immediately*, and get it out to the Huntsville field office, as well as sending it to FBI and ATF headquarters.

"What we are doing here—creating this inter-agency, inter-department network—is not unheard of, but the scale on which we are doing it, and the level at which we will not only sort and store data, but proactively disseminate it, *is* without precedence. And we believe that the level of efficiency at which the various departments will be able to operate will also be unequaled."

In the wings, the President leaned close to Diane Stevens, and whispered, "She's good. Very confident."

Diane replied, "Yeah. And did you notice she hasn't looked down at her notes once? You may have met your match, Richard."

"As far as the operation of the ETF is concerned," Claire went on, "as the President mentioned, I will be the official spokesperson for the group, but the person who will actually be in charge of the structure and operation of the task force will be Secret Service Special Agent Paul Levine. Paul, could you come out here, please?"

Looking slightly disconcerted, Paul walked onto the stage and gave a polite nod to the press corps.

"Paul was not expecting to be out here this morning," Claire explained, "so I'm sure that he doesn't have anything prepared. As a consequence—and, I'm sure to his relief—I'm not going to ask him to speak to you right now." Turning to him, she said, "But I *will* want you by my side when the questions start, so don't go too far." He then stood there, a bit self-consciously, as she talked about his background, his years with the Service, and his qualifications to head up the ETF. She then thanked him, and with a small wave, he walked off stage to rejoin the President and the others.

With a smile, Diane said to the President, "That was *smooth*!"

"What was?" he asked.

She asked Paul, "Did you know that she was going to want you out there to answer questions ... before just now?"

"No," he said. "And I *so* love surprises!"

Diane chuckled and said to the President, "Without breaking stride in what she was saying out there, she managed to get a message to Paul to be available, and even gave him a little time to get prepared to answer questions." With another chuckle, she added, "I *like* this girl!"

On stage, Claire had deftly shifted subjects, telling the reporters that the police had, based on a citizen's tip, recovered Frances Dunham's abandoned car in a shopping center parking lot.

An item that Claire did not mention was that police had received unconfirmed reports that Dunham—who dressed like a man and preferred to be called "Frankie"—was gay, a so-called "butch" lesbian. Claire didn't bring it up, because she and Levine felt it was irrelevant at the moment, and being unconfirmed, might be seen as "profiling" and inflammatory by the gay community. One had to be so careful, these days!

She then gave a condensed version of Dr. Whelk's report on the gun, minus any mention of the CIA or Jack Hampton.

Five minutes later Claire motioned for Levine to share the podium with her. Most of the questions they fielded sought to probe further into what the FBI had learned about the gun and the computer from the hospital.

Claire was unable to answer any technical questions about the gun, stating truthfully that she didn't know any more about how it operated than she had already told them, and that she and they would have to await a more in-depth report from Quantico.

When a reporter asked if they knew who might have produced such an unusual weapon, Claire neatly sidestepped the question. "The FBI lab is still examining the gun," she said, "but so far they have not found any markings—a serial number, or manufacture's stamp, for instance—that would indicate its origin. Our best-guess, at this point, is that it's a one-of- a-kind device, however."

She told them that the FBI's computer-crimes division was analyzing the software in a clone of the computer's hard drive, while the original had been sent to the National Security Agency to see if there was any data on the drive that had been erased, but that might be recoverable.

Responding to a question about Dunham, Claire said, "We're turning over every stone we can find to try to locate her, but we also need the public's help. If anyone has even a tiny bit of information about this person, please call the tip line."

Later, as Claire sat making notes in the agents' lounge that had been set up across from the President's temporary Oval Office, Levine came in, and said, "You ready to go?"

"Sure. Where we going?"

"DC. One o'clock flight out of Logan. We should be in our respective offices by three-thirty," he replied.

"We have offices?"

"While you were blabbing to the press I made a couple calls and had some shuffling done at headquarters."

Claire looked at her watch. "Geez!" she said, "It's already eleven! That doesn't give us much time, unless you've arranged for a police escort to the airport, too."

"Better," Levine answered. "Marine One is going to give us a lift. Get your stuff together, and meet me on the helipad in twenty minutes."

"Twenty minutes," she repeated as she headed for the elevator.

Claire made a brief stop at the hospital's gift shop on the first floor, and then headed up to say good-bye to Katherine.

Claire was surprised to find Katherine looking almost miraculously better than she had the night before. Still heavily bandaged, with her right arm lying on a pillow across her belly, she was sitting up and had apparently had her hair done. Though she no longer had the oxygen tube in her nose, she was still connected to various monitors and had an IV connected to the back of her left hand. She wasn't wearing any makeup, but she was a woman who could get away with that in any setting, much less a hospital bed.

"Well, aren't you looking good!" Claire said, smiling broadly. "How are you feeling?"

"Not as good as I look," Katherine replied in a conspiratorial whisper, "but I'm trying to convince them I'm well enough to leave. So, have you tracked down the inept assassin who tried to kill Richard, and did this to me?"

Claire was constantly surprised by Katherine's ability to turn her attention to her husband's political life, no matter what she was going through. Clearly, it and he were the center of her world.

"Progress, but no arrests," Claire replied. "The Dunham woman keeps looking more interesting. She hasn't been back to her apartment since Saturday morning, and they found her car in a shopping center just outside of town. Security cameras show her entering and leaving the grocery store there, but she apparently didn't get in her own car to leave."

"So, you think she's skipped town with an accomplice or something?

"That's the went-willingly scenario. Another possibility is that she was the "inside" person on this thing, and the people she was working for needed to tie up loose ends, and we'll find her floating in the Merrimack River."

"You really think so?" asked Katherine.

"Trying to bump off a president is a pretty high-stakes game. Killing some simple-minded maintenance worker that you drew into the web with money or idealism, would be penny ante stuff."

" 'O, what a tangled web we weave ...'" Katherine mused.

"Kind of a big leap on the gun, though," Claire went on. "We still need to verify the information, but it looks like it was built in the early eighties for the CIA."

"The CIA!" Katherine exclaimed.

"That's pretty much everyone's reaction," Claire said. "Like I said, though, we still have to verify the information. Then if it's true, we need to find out where the thing's been for the last quarter century, and who had it last."

Claire glanced at the clock on the wall, and realized that she had to be heading for the helipad.

Reaching into the bag she was carrying, she took out a stuffed koala bear, about six inches tall, who was the representation of a character from a popular series of children's books. He wore a yellow baseball cap with an "M" on it, and held a sign that said "Get Well Soon."

"Do you know who this is?" Claire asked.

"Can't say that I do," Katherine replied as she held the soft toy against her cheek in an almost child-like manner. "But he's kind of cute."

Claire continued to be amazed by how different Katherine was, how completely unguarded she could be, when they were alone. "Read his name-tag on the bottom," she said.

"Martin!" Katherine read out loud with a laugh. "You're not going to let me forget that little flirtation, are you?"

"Nope! Never!" Claire said, smiling. "Well, I've got a plane to catch, so you take care of yourself."

"Thanks for coming, Claire," Katherine said. "You come and see me when I get back to DC, okay? I'll want all the latest poop on your endeavors to catch this Dunham woman and her incompetent friends."

"Promise!" Claire said holding up her right hand in an *I swear* gesture. With a smile and a wiggling-finger wave, she turned and headed for the helipad.

Inside Marine One, again, Claire couldn't help but think about Katherine and the last few days. How strange it was that she felt so close to this woman. There was something that connected them, something deep and enigmatic, and she hoped that no matter what happened, they would be able to remain friends.

Chapter 21

Sunday, October 19
Orlando, FL

After reading Claire's personnel file, and getting Henri's assurance that there had been no security lapse that he could detect, Frank was satisfied that Claire's "heroic action" was most likely based on what her supervisor had referred to in a performance evaluation as "...an apparent sixth-sense about impending danger." Frank knew exactly what her supervisor was talking about, because that same type of "premonition" had helped him on more than one occasion. He couldn't explain it, but he sure as hell believed in it.

Convinced that Bradley was not a threat, Frank had decided to delete her file from his computer, and move on with his "exit strategy," as planned. But as he watched the President's announcement regarding the creation of his "Executive Task Force", and Claire's appointment as its spokesperson, he changed his mind. He didn't know if it was one of those sixth-sense premonitions of danger, but something was telling him not to dismiss this Bradley woman so easily. Her continued involvement might require a change in plans. She might yet have to be dealt with.

Chapter 22

Sunday, October 19
Washington, DC

It was coming up on ten o'clock Sunday night, and Claire was sitting in her newly acquired office in the Secret Service headquarters on Murray Drive in Washington, DC. She had just finished reading Gants' on-scene report from Newburyport.

It had all been interesting, but she had been particularly struck by how many times one name, Officer David Perkins, had come up in the report.

It was Perkins who had first suggested to Gants how an "unconventional" weapon might be used to fire a round the two mile distance from the hospital to the stage. It was Perkins who had suggested looking in the facilities floor, even though it had already been checked by Secret Service agents. It was Perkins who discovered the gun's hiding place inside the air-conditioning duct—the duct that Perkins, himself, had installed several years earlier. It was Perkins who was the first to recognize the thermite bomb on top of the computer, and it was Perkins who correctly speculated that the access panels were booby trapped to set off the bomb.

How could Officer Perkins have known all those things? Could he really have deduced it all, or was he the world's luckiest guesser? Or was it a smoke screen? Could he have been involved in the plot to kill the President, and decided to avert suspicion by being the one to find the weapon? Not very smart, if that was the ploy.

Another thing she wanted to know was if he was the same Dave Perkins that she had gone to high school with.

She called down to the research group, which had gone on 24-7 duty per Paul Levine's orders, and requested any information they could find on Perkins, saying that she would drop by in the morning and pick up whatever they had by then.

Finally, deciding to call it a day, she pushed herself out of her chair, intending to head back to her apartment, shower, catch a few hours of sleep, and put on her own clothes before being back at seven in the morning.

She had just made sure that she had her car keys in her purse when it occurred to her that her Jeep was still out at Andrews Air Force Base where she and Katherine had caught the C-5 up to New Hampshire two days ago. Had it really been just two days? Well, technically it was almost three now, but it seemed like a month.

Claire stopped at the desk of Margaret Colby, the headquarters' administrative assistant, on the way out.

"Hi Margaret," Claire said, surprised but happy to see Margaret still at her desk. "Can you get somebody to give me a ride out to Andrews? My car's out there."

Margaret looked up at Claire over the top of the half-glasses she reluctantly used for reading. "You have your keys?" she asked.

"Of course," Claire answered. "I just don't have the Jeep to go with them."

"Give them to me," Margaret said, extending her hand. "Your Jeep will be here in the morning. I'll have somebody drive it in for you. You need your sleep." Then picking up her phone, she talked to somebody named Pete and said that she needed a car and driver to take Miss Bradley to her apartment."

"The car will be out front when you get down there," Margaret said. "Just tell him what time he should pick you up in the morning. Now, you go get some rest. That news guy, Mark Wallings, might think you're a super-hero, but those red eyes of yours say different."

"Thank you, Margaret," Claire said warmly. "But I think it was Tom Lawson who coined the super-hero label."

"Whoever," she said dismissively. "And you eat something for breakfast, too! And not some junk. You eat a good breakfast."

Claire thanked her again as she stepped into the elevator. Listening to Margaret, Claire was suddenly reminded that she hadn't called her mother in a while.

Chapter 23

Monday, October 20
Washington DC

At six-fifteen the next morning, Claire headed out the door of her apartment building, finishing the last bites of a Pop-Tart. She found a black Suburban with government license plates double-parked and waiting for her. Thirty-seven minutes later they pulled into the Secret Service headquarters' parking lot.

When Claire got to Levine's corner office, two other agents were just leaving. As she took a seat, he handed her a folder that had "Perkins; David (nmi)" printed across the top.

"I guess we both had the same idea," he said. "After reading Mr. Gants' report this morning, I called down to research and found you'd beaten me to the punch. They said they already had a report on David, no-middle-initial, Perkins waiting for you."

"Great minds think alike," Claire said as she flipped open the file. "How's he look?"

"Straight and narrow," Levine replied. "Born and raised in New-buryport. Born in the St. Jacques, as a matter of fact. No apparent run-ins with the law as a kid. After graduating from high school with mostly A's, he joined the Marines where he earned a Purple Heart and a citation for bravery in Iraq."

Claire had a hard time picturing the skinny Dave Perkins she went to school with as a Marine, much less winning medals.

"After an honorable discharge as a master sergeant," Levine went on, "he went back to Newburyport where he worked for his father in his heating and ventilation business. After a couple years of that he joined the Newburyport Police Department where he's been for almost three years. Excellent record with the department, if a little under average in handing out tickets. No civilian complaints at all. In short, nothing that would profile him to be involved in a conspiracy to kill a president."

"So he'd be the perfect conspirator," commented Claire.

"Exactly," agreed Levine. "I've asked research to go as deep as they can without making contact. Any unusual travel habits of late; any big purchases, cars, boats, a house; any ties with political or religious groups. I've asked them to get his tax records for the past five years, too."

Claire was studying the photographs of Perkins that were in the folder. One was a copy of his Marine ID photo, and the other was a copy of his police ID. There was no question that this was the kid that she went to school with.

"I know him," Claire said. "Well, I didn't know him so much as I just went to high school with him. The Dave Perkins I knew was skinny as a string bean. Five-foot-ten and a hundred and twenty pounds soaking wet. Looks like the Marines did him some good."

"What do you remember about him?"

"Nothing very specific," Claire replied. "He was one of those people who just sort of blended into the woodwork, you know? Ten minutes after you'd talked to him you couldn't remember that he'd been in the room. Frankly, his name never entered my mind since high school until I heard Mr. Gants mention him, Saturday. Even then, it didn't register that I'd gone to school with him. It wasn't until I was reading Gants' report that the name rang a bell. One of those invisible personalities, you know?"

"Again, that would make him perfect for something like this," Levine observed.

"I suppose so," Claire agreed conditionally, "but if you're Mr. Invisible and Mr. Beyond-suspicion, why throw yourself into the spotlight by finding the gun in some totally obscure place, and then make sure nobody gets hurt by pointing out the booby trap that's meant to destroy the evidence? Something's not clicking, there."

"Maybe he panicked when the shoot went wrong," Levine speculated. "Killing the President for some fanatical reason is one thing, but accidentally blowing away the First Lady would have been something else, entirely. Maybe his guilt got hold of him and he didn't have the guts to confess. Giving up the gun was the next best thing."

"Boy, that's awfully fast for guilt to kick in," Claire said. "But it could be, I guess. Anything's possible."

"You asked for the report first," Levine said, lobbing the ball into her court. "How do you see him being involved."

"I don't know that I do see him involved, necessarily," she admitted. "His name coming up that many times in one report just threw up a red flag. And then recognizing the name from high school, I guess I was more curious than suspicious. I do want to talk to him after we get the in-depth from research, though."

The intercom buzzed, and Margaret announced that Jack Hampton was there to see Levine.

It took Claire a second to process the name. Hampton was the FBI's consultant who claimed to have built the gun they found in the hospital.

While Levine went out to retrieve Hampton from the lobby, Claire made sure a conference room was available.

Hampton, a notably robust and energetic man for someone in his late seventies, was visibly surprised to see Claire, the hero that he'd seen on TV, waiting for him.

"I ... I didn't know that *you'd* be here, Miss Bradley," he said awkwardly. "I'm really sorry about what happened up in Newburyport, please believe me. I mean, I never guessed that something like this could happen ... you know, with something that I built. If I'd had any idea that that thing would be used to try to shoot the President someday, I swear on my grandchildren's heads that I never would have done it. I'd have just quit, I swear! God, I'm so sorry!"

Claire was a bit taken aback. She hadn't been sure what to expect from Hampton, but it certainly wasn't an apology.

"It's okay, Mr. Hampton. Nobody's blaming you. You're not a suspect. We'd just like to ask you what you know about the gun. Please, have a seat, Mr. Hampton. Would you like some coffee or anything?"

"No, thank you. And please call me Jack," he replied as he lowered himself into the chair. "I'll tell you anything I can if it will help catch whoever did this. You ask me anything you want to know. Anything!"

"Before we start," Levine said, "I need you to know that what we say in this room is being recorded. Is that okay with you?"

"Fine," Jack answered. "If that'll help."

"Just to be clear," Claire began, "you're reasonably sure that the gun that you saw in the FBI lab, the gun taken from the hospital in Newburyport is the same gun that you worked on back in the early eighties?

"Not reasonably sure, Miss Bradley," Jack said with a sigh, "I'm positive. That gun was invented at Dymo ... that's what we used to call Dynametric ... only one of them was ever built, and I made every part of it. It's just that simple."

"How can you be so sure, Jack?" Levine asked. "That was 20-odd years ago. Somebody could have built a second one in that time if they had the plans, couldn't they?"

"There's a breech block on the end of the gun where the projectile gets loaded—it's not an actual bullet, you know, it's some sort of a rocket. Anyway, when I was making that block, I put a hole in the wrong place when I was almost done with it. I forgot to add a hundred-thousandths for my edge-finder ... stupid rookie mistake."

Claire had no idea why *adding a hundred-thousandths for your edge-finder* was important, but she was sure that it didn't warrant interrupting him to find out.

"That block is a complex part to machine, and it's made out of Inconel—I probably had nearly forty hours in it by that time, and I wasn't about to scrap it and start over. We were on a deadline. So I plugged the hole with another piece of Inconel and polished it down so nobody could see I'd screwed up. And nobody ever did. But if you look real close—and know right where to look—you can make out where the plug is. Looks like a circular scratch 'bout the size of a pencil eraser. Well, that little scratch is on that gun. That's the gun that I built—no question about it."

Then he added quickly, "Not that I'm braggin' because I'm proud of it ... what they did with it, I mean. I'm just telling you everything I know about it, so maybe you can catch 'em, you know?"

"Of course, Jack," Claire said. "We understand. And we appreciate your being here. It's a big help, believe me."

"So did you ever see the gun in action?" Levine asked. "Or did you just make the parts?"

"You mean did I see it fired? Yeah, I was there when they did the final acceptance test. We did a demonstration shoot in December of '84, for a bunch of suits. We put four rounds in a three-inch group, within three-inches of the bull's-eye at four-thousand yards. That's two and a quarter miles!" he said, a bit of pride in that technical accomplishment seeping through.

"A bunch of suits?" Claire asked.

"CIA," Jack replied. "Dymo did a lot of development for the military—Army, Navy, Air Force. But there were certain projects that you just knew didn't have military application. We figured they were probably CIA projects—we called them 'suit jobs'. That's because if they were military, the people who came for reviews and demonstrations and stuff wore their uniforms. The folks who came in for the other projects always wore suits—usually dark suits. I guess now that I think of it, that was kind of a uniform, huh?"

"Did anyone ever hint at what this gun was going to be used for?" asked Claire.

"No," Jack replied. "Nobody ever talked about stuff like that. But the way the gun works, I figured it had to be to assassinate somebody. Why else build a single-shot gun that will shoot two miles, just about silently? I don't know who it might have been for, of course. Castro maybe? Probably not Gorbachev—that would have just opened a big can of worms. Maybe that guy in Iran—what was his name? Ayatollah Khomeini—I don't think Mr. Reagan cared too much for him."

"Do you remember the date, Jack?" Claire asked.

"Let's see," Jack replied. "Reagan took office in January of '81, and we started development in March. Course we couldn't put a round on target until June of '84, and didn't really have the thing perfected and ready for delivery until December that year."

"So the gun was delivered in late 1984?" Claire said as she took notes. "Do you know who took delivery? Where it went? Or did they take it with them after the demonstration?"

"It was never delivered to anyone, to my knowledge," Jack said. "The day after the demonstration, the shipping department crated up the gun, the spare parts, all the rocket bullets that were left, and even the pressure tank of peroxide. Everything was taken apart and packed into this one container that was purged and sealed—like they pack stuff that's going into storage for a long time, you know? Then it just sat in shipping for a couple of weeks." He laughed a little and added, "I remember sitting on the container—one of those fiberglass jobs—when I'd take my coffee break with Doug. Doug was in charge of shipping. Then one day Doug says that they told him to move the whole kit and caboodle into Dymo's storage bunker out back. That's the last I saw or heard of it." Then he added quietly, "Until Saturday."

"Could it have been delivered to someone later on?" Levine asked.

"I guess," Jack replied. "You'd have to ask Doug about that. He ran shipping right up until Dymo closed the doors."

"What's Doug's last name?" asked Claire.

"Polan. Doug Polan. Don't know where he is, these days," Jack answered. "But I suppose you folks can find him, though, huh?"

Levine swiveled his chair to face the computer in the corner and typed an e-mail to the research group downstairs. "We're sure going to try," he said, flagging the message "Top Priority."

"Do you know if Polan held any specific level of security clearance?" Levine asked Jack.

"Top secret. We all did. You couldn't get inside the gates without it."

Levine added that information and sent the e-mail. That would be plenty to get research on his trail.

"How much do you know about the gun?" Claire asked Jack. "Could you fire it if we asked you to?"

"Me? No!" he said. Then realizing that his answer sounded uncooperative, he added, "I mean ... I would if I could, but I don't know all the scientific stuff about the gun. I just made the parts. I know the thing looks pretty simple," he went on, "just a big long barrel with a breachblock at one end, and a hose connecting to it. But it didn't work the same as just a big rifle. Like I said, the bullet was actually a kind of miniature rocket. It used hydrogen peroxide for fuel. Like the stuff women use to bleach their hair, ya know? How they got hair bleach to be rocket fuel, I'll never know. That was the science part."

"Who did set it up to fire?" Claire asked, remembering that a computer had been connected to the gun, and imagining the complexity of a missile launch. "Did that take a whole team?"

"Not really," Jack said. "Oh, there were a lot of people around when we fired it, but only the two engineers who designed the gun really knew how to set it up and aim it and everything. They had their calculators and a whole list of formulas and stuff that they used. They were the ones who filled the little rocket-bullet with the peroxide—it came from this big pressure tank, like a welding tank, you know? Then they connected the tank to the gun and set different regulators and heaters, and I don't know what all else. Then they figured out the trajectory and all that, and aimed the gun using micrometers. After we had the gun set up on the firing range, I'll bet it took the two of them almost two hours before they were ready to fire the first round."

"Do you happen to recall the engineers' names," Claire asked trying to keep the excitement out of her voice.

She could see the light bulb come on for Jack as soon as she asked the question. If there were only two people who knew how to set-up, aim, and fire the gun, the investigators were going to be very interested in finding them.

"Whoa!" he said. "You think they might have had something to do with it?"

"I don't know," Claire said, "but we'll sure want to talk to them."

"Well, one of them was Walter Collins—he was the head engineer. And Roger McPherson was the other one. Come to think of it, McPherson—they called him Roddy—he was kind of an odd duck. Some of the guys thought he might have been queer, ya know? Course back then, you kept that hidden pretty well, if you wanted to work for the government."

"You don't happen to know where either of them went after Dymo, do you?" Claire asked as Levine was typing their names into a new e-mail to research.

"Sorry," Jack said. "I never really had much contact with them, except on that one project. No reason to keep in touch, or anything."

"Did this project have a name or number or something?' Claire asked. "I presume the folks at Dymo didn't just call it 'the big gun'."

"All the projects had official numbers," Jack said, "but I really can't recall what this one was. But nearly all the projects had unofficial names, too. Sort of nicknames that everybody used when they talked about them. We called the gun 'Johnny'."

"Johnny?" Claire asked.

Jack hesitated before answering, and Claire sensed that he was uncomfortable. "After a guy named Johnny Wadd. He made ... um ... well, he made sex movies. He was supposed to be ... you know, the *biggest* star there was."

"I see," Claire said, trying not to chuckle at Jack's quaint embarrassment. He was from a generation that didn't talk about such things with respectable young women. "Those were the days before political correctness, weren't they, Mr. Hampton? So, did the customers use these nicknames, too? Did the CIA folks call the gun 'Johnny", as well?"

"I think some of them might have," Jack said searching his memories from a very long time ago. "But I really didn't deal with them. And they didn't talk much at all when other people were around. Very secret bunch, they were."

The information about the gun and the engineers was a huge break, and Claire wanted to get working on it right away. "You have anything else for Jack, right now?" Claire asked Levine.

"Not at the moment," he replied. "But I hope we can contact you again, if anything else comes up, Mr. Hampton."

"We certainly appreciate you coming in, Jack," Claire added. "You've given us a great deal to work with here." She paused a moment then went on, "There is one more question I have to ask you, though." In officialeze, Claire said, "Jack Hampton, did you or anyone known to you take any part in the attempted assassination of the President of the United States on October 18th of this year? Please, don't take my question to be an accusation, Jack. It's something I'm required to ask you."

"The answer to your question is no," Jack said. "And I understand you asking. I've been through security checks before. No offense taken." He then abruptly stood up, ready to leave.

Claire and Paul looked at each other, both thinking, *Boy, when he's done talking, he's done talking!*

"I hate to seem rude," Jack said, "but could you point me toward a bathroom? I wouldn't wish this prostate on anyone. Well, maybe whoever used that gun. Then all you'd have to do is stake out all the men's rooms and he'd walk right to you," he added with a chuckle.

"Catch him with his pants down, as it were?" Claire said with a smile.

After Jack left, Claire and Levine remained in the conference room kicking around what he had just told them. "If McPherson's gay," Claire said, "and the Dunham woman is gay, do you think there could be some connection?"

"Some radical fundamentalist gay group that we've never heard of?" Levine replied. "One that's out to kill the President for his liberal stand in support of gay marriage?"

"Okay," Claire laughed, "When you put it that way ..."

"On the other hand," Levine went on, "if you were going to recruit coconspirators into something like this, you'd be likely to do it from among like-minded folks. If McPherson really is gay, he's not likely to seek help at a biker bar." He turned back to the computer, and said, "I'll pass your hypothesis on to research."

"Meanwhile," she said, "I'll call over to CIA in Langley, and see what they know about 'Johnny Wadd'."

Chapter 24

Monday, October 20
Washington, DC

C laire had just finished transcribing her notes from the Jack Hampton interview into her computer when Margaret buzzed her.

"There's an Officer David Perkins with the Newburyport Police on the line for you," she said. "Do you want to take it or should I put it through to voice mail? Or should I direct it to someone else?"

"Dave Perkins?" Claire repeated in surprise. *Why would Perkins be contacting me?* she asked herself. Had somebody in research made contact despite Paul's instructions?

"Put him through, please," Claire replied, unable to think of a reason *not* to talk to him, although she wished that she had that in-depth report in front of her.

"Special Agent Bradley," she answered the phone, "what can I do for you, Officer Perkins?"

"Have dinner with me," he answered.

"Excuse me?" she replied, caught completely off guard.

"Well, that's better than 'no', I guess," he said with a chuckle. "Which is what I expect you'd have said back in high school if I'd asked you out."

"You're calling to ask me to dinner?" Claire asked skeptically.

"Not entirely," Dave confessed, "but it sure seemed like a good ice-breaker. Of course I'm assuming you remember who I am, which is probably a really bad assumption, huh?"

"No, no," Claire said, "I remember you. It's just that … well, I guess I thought you'd want to talk about the investigation. You know, finding the gun, or what we've found out about it. Something along those lines."

"Well, I figured that you, the task force that is, would be contacting me eventually, but if I waited for somebody on your end to call, who knows who I'd be talking to. This way I not only get to talk to you, specifically, but I can finally ask you out after all these years."

"Why did you think we'd be contacting you?" Claire asked, avoiding the personal reference for the moment.

"I got to thinking about all that went on when I was with your SAC Gants up here the morning of the shooting," Dave said. "I correctly guessed where the shot had come from; I guessed the gun would be some kind of unconventional weapon; I found the thing inside a plenum chamber that I had personally built; I discovered that the gun was booby trapped; and I correctly guessed where the booby trap triggers would be. If I were in your shoes, I'd sure as hell want to talk to me!"

"Since you brought it up …" said Claire. She found it interesting that he had hit on all of the points that she had thought about.

"Really not that much to talk about," he said. "A few lucky guesses based on a professional knowledge of weapons and an intimate knowledge of the St. Jacques Hospital. I'm sure you know, by now, that I'm a former Marine sniper and that I helped to install the air handling system in the hospital."

"You used long-range unconventional weapons in the Corps?" Claire asked.

"No," he said, "My weapon was a Barrett 50-caliber. My best shot ever was just under a mile, and that was on the range. My knowledge of what's possible in the way of unconventional weapons comes from a much more sinister source; *Popular Science*."

"The magazine?"

"Yup. They had an article about six months ago on weapons of the future Army," Dave told her. "Everything from invisibility suits to long-range self-propelled ammunition and even smart-bullets that lock on a target and follow it. Of course, how much of that is real and how much is from some editor's imagination is anyone's guess, but I've pretty much stopped thinking that anything is impossible."

"So you were just in the right place, at the right time, having recently read the right article, after having worked with your father in the right floor of the right building," Claire said. "That about sum it up? Do you play the lottery, Office Perkins? You seem to be one lucky individual."

"Well put," he replied with a little laugh. "Actually, I do consider myself pretty fortunate, Agent Bradley, but that was just deductive reasoning based on a bit of specific knowledge. Please feel free to do whatever digging into my background that you'd like. Interview anyone who's ever known me, and even give me a polygraph if you'd like. I assure you that I had no involvement in Saturday's assassination attempt, and certainly had no prior or post knowledge of any such activities."

Claire was silent for a moment digesting what Dave was telling her. Then she shifted subjects and said, "Why did you think I'd say no if you asked me out in high school?"

"Are you kidding?" he laughed. "You were Claire Bradley—THE most desirable girl in Newburyport High, in my opinion, and I was 'Beanpole' Perkins. I figured I had as much chance of going on a date with you as I did beating you in a Judo match."

"You were in the Judo club?" She didn't remember that at all.

"No," he chuckled. "I used to go and watch your practices and matches, though."

"I see," Claire said. "You were afraid to ask me out, so you stalked me instead."

Dave laughed, hoping that Claire was just joking. "I guess that didn't come out right, did it? No, my cousin, Kendal LePage, was in the club and he was my ride home. Getting to see you kick the crap out of him was just a bonus three times a week."

She did remember Kendal. He had been good, but cocky, and she had enjoyed beating him since she was "just a girl" and he outweighed her by at least seventy-five pounds. But that was one of the beauties of Judo; you used your opponent's weight against him.

"Hey, I've got to go," Dave said suddenly. "I have a call. I'm still on duty here. What do you say? Dinner Wednesday night? I'm going to be down there in DC at a conference and visiting my uncle."

"I don't know if I'm going to have time for much socializing for a while, Officer Perkins," Claire said, feeling a little on the spot. "The investigation is going to pretty much consume my waking hours."

"Tell you what," he said hurriedly. "I'll call you when I get down there. If you can't have dinner, I'll understand, but if you consider it interviewing a potential lead, then you'll still be on duty, and you won't have to feel guilty that you're goofing off. Heck, you'll be working overtime! Think about it, okay? Gotta go!"

And with that the line went dead.

Claire was still shaking her head and smiling to herself when her thoughts of the transformed Beanpole Perkins were interrupted by the buzzing of her phone.

"Bradley," she answered.

Paul Levine got right to the point. "I have Bob Palmer from the NSA on hold over here. They've found something interesting on the computer from the hospital. You want me to patch you in from there, or come over here and do it on speaker?"

"I'm on my way," Claire said as she grabbed her notebook and hurried out the door. Her internal debate over whether she should take a little personal time to meet Perkins evaporated, and her mind was back on the investigation one-hundred percent.

Chapter 25

Monday, October 20
Washington, DC

Twenty seconds after Levine's call, Claire slid into his office, grabbing the door-frame to slow herself down from her full run.

"Okay, Bob," Levine said with an amused shake of his head at her entrance. "Agent Bradley just *bounded* into the office. Go ahead with what you were saying."

"Hello, Agent Bradley," Palmer said over the speaker. "As I was telling Agent Levine, we found some encrypted e-mails on the hard-drive from the computer that was hooked up to the gun, and we've managed to decrypt them. They ..."

"E-mails?" Claire interrupted. "The report we got from the site said that the computer was stand-alone, that it wasn't connected to the Internet."

"It wasn't," Palmer replied. "Not inside the hospital, anyway. These files were saved to the hard-drive earlier, when it was on-line, presumably at another location."

"What have you got?" Levine asked.

"Based on these e-mails, it looks like this hit came out of the Middle East."

"al-Qaeda?" Claire and Paul asked in unison.

"Hezbollah," he said.

"Are you sure?" Levine asked.

"From the language used, references to specific places, and the mentioning of one specific name, I'd say we can be ninety percent sure," Palmer answered.

"Can you give us the details?" Claire said with a little abruptness in her voice. She didn't like being handed conclusions without knowing the facts that supported them.

"Sure," Palmer said, ignoring or oblivious to Claire's tone. "Let's see if you concur with our analysis.

"We decrypted three e-mails and each makes direct reference to the gun itself. The first message said that the gun had been finished and had completed testing in Naameh. That's a small town in South Lebanon, under the protection of the Syrian Army. About the only thing located there is a well fortified subterranean military base used by the PFLP—that's the Popular Front for the Liberation of Palestine. But the PFLP is a major supporter of Hezbollah, specifically with regard to supplying weapons and paramilitary training. That e-mail is about eight months old."

"That's impossible," Claire told him. "The gun wasn't built in Lebanon. We just got finished interviewing a machinist who has first-hand knowledge of it being made in a factory in Vermont. In 1981!"

"I know," Palmer replied, "I saw the initial report from the FBI lab, yesterday. That's why I called you folks before posting this to the database. Something's wrong *somewhere*."

"What were the other e-mails?" Levine asked.

"The second e-mail is about six months old, and indicates the date, and on which ship, the gun left Lebanon. It went out through Beirut. This e-mail mentions the name al-Mughrabi. He's one of the highest level arms smugglers in the region, and is a major player in Hezbollah politics.

"The third e-mail told what shipment of 'machinery spare parts' the gun was hidden in, and when it had cleared customs in Miami. Which was about five months ago."

"Did it say who the consignee was?" Levine asked.

"No, but you folks can get that from customs, I'm sure," Palmer replied. "Once the crate cleared customs, it became domestic, and we can't look at it any more."

Claire had forgotten that it was illegal for the NSA, like the CIA, to investigate anything within the United States. A dumb restriction in her opinion, but that's the way Congress had set it up.

128

"Is there a possibility that this machinist could be part of the conspiracy?" Palmer asked. "That he's feeding you bogus information?"

"Anything's possible," Levine said, "but we don't think it's very likely. He's a Korean War veteran and a died-in-the-wool Yankee who's had a top-secret clearance for thirty-five years. Our people just finished a new background check on him, and he's as clean as they come. They're still going to do some personal interviews, but there's nothing to raise any suspicions at all. We also have people working on verifying his story by other means."

"Do we know where the gun has been these last two and a half decades?" Palmer asked. "If the CIA built it, how did Hezbollah end up with it?"

"We don't know, yet," Claire said, "but we're working on it. I'd hate to think that the thing became part of an arms-for-hostages deal or something."

"Like Agent Levine said, anything's possible," Palmer replied. "Who knows? Maybe there was some black-op that went wrong over there, and we lost the damned thing. Not everybody in the game is James Bond."

"Does the sender's address show up on the e-mails?" Claire asked, hoping for carelessness on the other team's part.

"Yes," Palmer told her, "but it's one of those freebee accounts, so I'm sure that whoever opened the account used a bogus name and address. We're still poking around, but getting official cooperation from European web-servers is pretty difficult. Of course, getting *unofficial* access to records is another matter. We have some sources we haven't tapped, yet."

"Great work, Bob," Levine said. "I'm glad you called before posting this. There's a chance of this leaking to the media once it's on the database, and I think the President and the Secretary of State will want a chance to review it before that could happen. Can you send the e-mails directly to me, along with your assessment? I'll see that the President gets them, and I'll get back to you with what he says. Or he may get with you directly. In the meantime, keep digging in your direction, and we'll do the same over here."

After they hung up, Claire looked at Levine, and said, "We obviously need to find out what happened to that gun after it went into storage at Dymo. I'm going to call over to Langley, and see how they're coming with their search for *Johnny*."

As Levine dialed his phone to call the President, Claire walked back to her office. Something was nagging at her about the e-mails, but she couldn't put her finger on it.

As she entered her office, deep in thought about the Hezbollah e-mails, the *bing-bong* sound from her computer announced that she had new e mail, herself

She opened it up to find the preliminary report from the research group regarding the Dynametric employees whose names Jack Hampton had given them.

Doug Polan, Jack's buddy in shipping, currently ran shipping and receiving for NCP Aviation Services at Pease Airport in New Hampshire. The report gave his home address and phone, as well as his work information and his cell phone number. Doug checked out clean so far, and the report noted that he had already been contacted, and had agreed to meet with Secret Service agents at the airport, on Tuesday morning. Claire found it interesting that he worked at the same airport where the President's plane had landed on Saturday, hours before the shooting.

As for Walter Collins, the head engineer on the project; he was dead. He had drowned in the summer of 1999, when the sailboat he was single-handedly operating had capsized in a sudden storm off the New Hampshire coast. His body washed up on the sand at the Hampton Beach resort area, two weeks later.

The research group was having a little tougher time with Roger McPherson. Claire found that interesting, too. They could find no record of him after March of 2000. No phone in his name, no current address, no updating of security clearance. He had not even filed an income-tax return since 1999.

The report also noted the possibility that McPherson had died, but so far, they could not locate a certificate of death nor an obituary for him, anywhere. It ended by saying that he was getting top priority.

Claire debated whether she would bring up his name as an investigative lead during the next press briefing. On the one hand, it was obvious that finding the sole remaining person who knew how to fire the gun was going to be critical to the investigation, but by announcing that they were looking for him, they might send him even further underground. If he had assumed a new identity somewhere along the way, it might be giving him a false sense of security that they could use to advantage.

Chapter 26

Monday, October 20
Washington, DC

Claire had left her office a little before nine-thirty Monday night, and after a shower, she had slipped into a pair of comfortable pajamas, and was now sitting on her coffee table waiting for the eleven o'clock news to start while towel-drying her hair. She mused, again, why she hadn't cut it short a long time ago.

When the news came on, the election, which was just two weeks away, was naturally the lead story. With the illuminated White House in the background, a young news woman began the broadcast as the words, "Live from outside the White House ..." traveled across the bottom of the screen, as if that added more credibility to whatever she was about to say.

"President McClure's lead over Senator Evans continues to grow," she said with an over-acted seriousness. "We'll look at those numbers and the reasons behind them tonight on *Election Watch*."

Following thirty seconds of throbbing theme music and an annoying sequence of rapidly changing images of the station's news team "in action", the channel's anchor, Kerry Andrews came on the screen.

At the mention of her name by an off-camera announcer, Kerry looked up from the papers on her desk. "Good evening, I'm Kerry Andrews," she said, "and this is what happened today ..."

Looking directly into the camera—the viewer's eyes—Kerry took on a grave look as she began the top story. "Making her first public statement since being nearly killed on Saturday by an assassin's bullet meant for her husband, the White House, earlier today, released this photograph, and a recording of the First Lady, made as she continues to recover in the intensive-care unit in Boston ..."

As Kerry spoke, an image of the First Lady came up on the monitor to her left. It showed Katherine propped up in her hospital bed, her right shoulder bandaged, and her right arm in a sling. Although her hair had clearly been combed, it still had the flattened look of having been slept on. She was smiling for the camera, but it seemed somehow forced, and despite the fact that she was giving a thumbs-up gesture, her eyes betrayed the pain she was obviously feeling.

Claire was shocked! Not only did this photo, that the White House officially released, look like something that would be on the cover of *The Enquirer*, it was nothing like the way Katherine had looked when Claire left her just yesterday. She looked awful!

As the recording of Katherine's voice began, her image enlarged to fill the screen. The audio tape started with the sound of Katherine taking a deep, but labored, breath, as if getting ready for some arduous task that she was really not up to. Then in a halting manner with frequent pauses, as if each word was an effort, she thanked everyone who had sent her cards, letters, and e-mails, wishing her a speedy recovery. After taking another labored breath, she went on to thank the people of Boston, in general, and the hospital, in particular, for taking such good care of her, and putting up with all of her disruptions. She concluded the short recording after a pause that included a throat-clearing, by saying that she had been told that it would be a long and painful recovery, but that with God's help, the love of her family, and the fantastic support of the American people, she knew that she would make it. "May God bless you all," she said finally, her voice just above a whisper.

Claire stared at the screen in disbelief. What had happened? Was she trying too hard to get herself released, and had now had a setback?

A minute later, Claire was on the phone talking to Bill Sweeny, the agent on duty at the hospital with Katherine that night. She asked him to see if the First Lady was awake, and half a minute later she was talking to Katherine.

"Hey, CB! I didn't expect to hear from you until I got back to DC. Or are you calling to tell me you caught the SOBs who put me here?"

"Ah ... no," Claire said, caught off guard by the exuberance in Katherine's voice. "I just saw you—well, heard you, actually, on TV. I was calling to see how you were. You didn't sound too good."

"Oooh … that," Katherine said as the pieces fell into place for her. "I'm sorry, sweetie. That wasn't meant for you. That was just a little … a little *dramatic license*."

"Then you're all right?" Claire said, infinitely relieved. "I thought you'd had a setback."

"No, no! I'm fine!" Katherine replied enthusiastically. "Well, as fine as can be expected under the circumstances. It's not like I'm ready to run a marathon, or anything." In a conspiratorial whisper she added, "I almost have my new doctors convinced to let me out of here tomorrow afternoon. Pretty cool, huh? Hey, you're still going to come see me when I get down there, right? Oh! Did you see Richard's numbers, Claire? There's no way Evans can touch us, now! No way!"

Claire wondered what the heck they were putting in Katherine's IV. She was blabbering as if she was drunk.

"Then why the dramatic license thing?" Claire asked.

"Votes, sweetie, votes," Katherine answered. "The polls show that the Poor-Katherine-McClure sympathy-factor is putting a minimum of eight percent of the undecideds into our pocket. One poll shows nearly *twenty* percent! Twenty percent, Claire! We've got to milk that for all it's worth!"

Relieved that Katherine was obviously feeling better than she had sounded or looked on the news, Claire was nonetheless miffed at having been, in effect, lied to through the TV. The whole country had. She wanted to say something about it, but she knew this wasn't the time or place, because she didn't feel that Katherine was really herself. So, as graciously as she could, she wished her friend a good night, and ended the call.

As she turned off her TV and headed for bed, Claire thought about how much she liked Katherine—the effects of her medication, notwithstanding—and how much she *disliked* politics under *any* circumstances.

Chapter 27

Monday, October 20
Washington, DC

In his hotel suite, Senator Evans had just finished listening to the First Lady's recorded statement while staring at her thumbs-up photograph.

"Well, that was frigging masterful!" he declared contemptuously.

"What was wrong with it?" Will Clark asked.

"Nothing," Evans replied. "I wasn't being sarcastic."

"What was so masterful then?"

"FDR once said that in politics nothing is accidental. If something happens, be assured it was planned that way," Evans said. "I'll lay you odds that Katherine McClure isn't in half as bad a shape as that piece makes her out to be. They are sucking everything they can out of this. Tie up their heart strings, and their votes are yours," he said wearily. "You can't fight emotions with issues, and he sure as hell knows it. You want to bet that this shows in McClure's numbers before noon tomorrow?"

"So what do we do about it?" Clark asked.

"If it didn't smack of copy-cat-ism, I'd have *my* wife shot," Evans said.

Clark was sure that Evans was joking, but he found it unnerving that the man wasn't even smiling. He knew that the reality of Evans' marriage was far darker than the façade that he and his wife managed to maintain in public. It made him wonder if the McClures' publicly-perfect marriage might not hide similar secrets.

"Have you talked with your friend lately?" Evans said, coming out of nowhere as he so often did. "Does he know what the call to Levine was about?"

From a combination of sources, Evans had learned that someone at the NSA had called Paul Levine at Secret Service headquarters. Then, ten minutes later, the President had taken a call from Levine. Five minutes after that, the Secretary of State, the Attorney General, and the Director of Homeland Security were hotfooting it to the oval office. But then, nothing of any great importance had shown up on the task force database. There was something going on, and Evans wanted to know what it was.

"I think he might know, but I'm having a hard time getting a lot out of him. He's a loyal party supporter, but a pretty straight arrow," Clark replied as he poured a cup of coffee from the carafe on the serving cart.

Evans slowly turned on the couch, and fixed Clark with a stare. Clark stopped pouring mid-cup.

"Motivate him," Evans said quietly, but firmly. "Give him more money. Find something you can hold over his head. I don't care. Just find out what that call was about!"

"I'm trying," Clark explained, "but this guy ..."

"I don't need excuses, Billy!" Evans cut him off. "I want to know what McClure was talking to Levine about, so I know what that meeting was all about. I am tired of fucking surprises!"

With that, Evans went into the master bedroom, and closed the door behind him.

Chapter 28

Tuesday, October 21
Washington, DC

For Claire, the morning had flown by. When she got back to her office after an early lunch, there were a number of phone and e-mail messages waiting for her. Most were from journalists seeking specific information, or requesting an interview.

Still marveling at the fact that she had "an assistant," Claire forwarded the bulk of them to the woman in her sixties who was an absolute whiz at handling correspondence.

One of the e-mails she did not forward was from the New Hampshire coroner's office. She had called them yesterday to ask for a copy of the coroner's report on the Walter Collins drowning. The message said that the file existed only in hard-copy, and that they would scan it and get it to her by the end of the day.

Another e-mail was from a Secret Service agent whose name Claire didn't recognize. Cynthia Caan had written to say that she had some information regarding Roger McPherson, and left her cell phone number.

With high expectations, Claire dialed the number. The phone was answered on the first ring.

"Hi, this is Claire Bradley; I'm calling in reply to your e-mail regarding Roger McPherson."

136

"Great timing," Cynthia replied. "I just got off the phone with a guy who may know where McPherson is."

"Fantastic! What have you got?"

"Well, I was just talking to his voicemail , actually," she said. "He's a commercial pilot, and in the air right now. I asked him to call me as soon as he gets my message."

"Where did you get this guy's name?" Claire asked. "What is it, by the way?"

"Jeff Stiller," she said. "We got it from a guy named Doug Polan. We interviewed him up in New Hampshire this morning. He used to run shipping and receiving at Dynametric. He gave us the date that the gun left Dynametric, and the name of the CIA guy who took it. *His* name was Charles Townsend."

"That's his real name?" asked Claire. "A CIA spook with the same name as the never-seen 'Charlie' from *Charlie's Angels*? That almost seems too cute to be true."

"I know what you mean, but we believe it's his real name. We've checked, and there *was* a Charles Townsend on the payroll at the CIA back then. The records show him being on station in Israel that whole year, however. They're trying to see if there's any record of him traveling back to the US around that date. They're also trying to come up with a current address for him. He retired in 2000."

"Nice work!" Claire said. "Let me know as soon as you know any more, okay?"

After exchanging good-byes, Claire noticed the time display on her phone; it was a quarter past twelve. She had a news briefing scheduled for two o'clock, and really wasn't sure what she was going to talk about. One thing she was sure of was that she was not going to release anything about McPherson, yet. She wanted to see where Agent Caan's lead went, first. Of course, that left very little that was new that she *could* talk about. This spokesperson thing, she thought, was beginning to lose its charm, pretty quickly. How did Diane Stevens do it for a living?

Back in her office after a briefing that lasted only fifteen minutes, she was just beginning to check her e-mail, again, when her phone buzzed, and Margaret announced that the First Lady was on the line.

"How are you?" Claire asked, after hellos. "When are you coming home?"

"That's just the reason I called you, sweetheart!" Katherine replied excitedly. "They're transferring me tomorrow morning!"

"That's great!" Claire replied, sharing Katherine's happiness.

"You're going to George Washington, I assume? I'll make sure I get over and see you tomorrow."

"Actually, Claire," Katherine replied, "I'd like you to meet me at Andrews. You can ride in the ambulance with me to the hospital. I think the wounded First Lady being escorted by the agent that saved her life will make a great photo op, don't you?"

That took Claire completely aback. Katherine wanted her to take time out from the investigation for publicity pictures? Had she forgotten what Claire was doing down here in Washington?

"Well ... I'm pretty busy here ..." Claire began to explain.

"Oh, nonsense!" Katherine scoffed. "The President is here with me, and he agrees that a few pictures with your boss isn't going to derail the investigation. Besides, you can use the ambulance ride to fill me in on how the investigation is going—like you promised."

It became clear to Claire that this wasn't just some casual request because Katherine wanted to see her. It was a calculated public-relations move, and refusal was not an option.

It seemed to Claire that this was pushing the limits of the no-politics-allowed policy they'd agreed upon, but she decided not to press the issue right then. Her father had always taught her to choose her battles carefully.

"You're right," Claire agreed, forcing cheeriness into her voice that wasn't quite there. "What time does your plane land? I'll be there."

For the next hour and a half, Claire went through the reports that had been posted to the task force database, as well as through her own notes, and put together an outline on her office whiteboard of what they had, so far.

She was standing there scanning the information to see if any pattern jumped out—any connections that she hadn't seen before, when her computer issued its musical *bing-bong* sound, announcing new e-mail. It was from the New Hampshire Office of State Chief Medical Examiner. The title indicated it was the autopsy report on Walter Collins that she'd requested.

Thirty seconds later, she was taking the eleven page attachment from the printer, and settling into her chair.

Eight of the pages were photographs. Three were taken on the beach where Collins' body washed ashore. Two more were taken of the naked body on the coroner's examination table, and one was of a set of lower dentures. The last was of a silver colored wristwatch.

The report stated that the body was "... in such a state of decomposition and disfigurement through natural actions as to make an identification by fingerprints or facial features impossible," and also noted that "... identification through dental records was complicated by the fact that all of the decedent's teeth had been removed during early adulthood. X-rays from that time, which would presumably show the upper and lower jaw bones, and, therefore, be useful for purposes of identification, could not be located."

The report went on to say that Mr. Collins' upper dentures had not been recovered with the body, but that the lower dentures were found in the decedent's mouth, and had been positively identified by the dental lab where they were made. Further confirmation of his identification was provided by a wristwatch which was attached to the left wrist of the body, which was positively identified by Mr. Collins' former wife, Helen Yates, as having been a gift from her approximately three years earlier.

Claire realized that, under normal circumstances, the evidence contained in the report would have been more than sufficient to establish the identity of the body. Now, she wasn't so sure.

If, for instance, Walter Collins had had a strong motive for wanting to disappear, all of the evidence noted in the report could very easily have been transferred to a "surrogate" body, which could then have been tossed into the sea in hopes that it would eventually be discovered.

At the time of Collins' disappearance, there had been no reason to suspect foul play, so the evidence was accepted, the case was closed, and what was left of the body was cremated with the consent of the next of kin.

Now, however, the circumstances were a little different. What if Collins had sold his technical expertise regarding the gun to someone? This would be a good way for Collins to make sure that the authorities would not be looking for *him* if and when the gun was used.

Another scenario was that whoever had purchased Collins' expertise, could have arranged his "accident" to tie up loose ends. In that case, the body really would have been that of Walter Collins, but the manner of death would have been homicide.

Then, of course, there was always the possibility that it was exactly what it looked like; Walter Collins' accidental death.

Claire picked up the report again, and flipped to the section on toxicology. "Examination of the blood for drugs of abuse and prescribed medications was negative," she read. "Trace amounts of alcohol were found, and were not considered a contributing factor."

She hadn't really expected that to be any help, but she wondered if they had kept the samples. If they had, and if she could locate some other cell sample known to be from Collins, then a DNA profile would settle her suspicions as to whether Collins had faked his own death. At the time of his drowning, DNA testing had been in its infancy, and would not have been used in such a clear cut, and low-profile case.

Claire placed a call to the Office of State Chief Medical Examiner in Concord, New Hampshire, and after several hand-offs, she found that there was, in fact, a frozen sample of the decedent's blood in storage. It had been retained because the cause of death had never been determined, even though the manner of death was listed as accidental. Claire asked what the procedure was to have the sample sent to the FBI labs in Quantico.

One down, one to go. But where could she get a sample of Collins' tissue, his blood, or a hair follicle from before his death? Perhaps if his former wife had a letter that he had sent at one time, they could get a sample of his saliva from the stamp or envelope.

All of the witnesses, examiners, and contributors whose testimony or opinions were cited in the report were listed at the end, which is where Claire found Helen Yates' phone number. Dialing it, she mentally crossed her fingers that it was still good. On the third ring a man answered.

"Hi, is Helen there, please?" Claire said cheerily.

She was pleased when the man didn't ask who was calling, but said simply, "Yeah, wait a minute." She heard the receiver clunk against something hard, and then heard the man's voice bellow, "Helen! Phone!"

As she waited for Helen, Claire could hear a TV blaring in the background. After thirty seconds or so, the receiver was picked up, and a woman who sounded like she'd been running, said, "Hello?"

Figuring that she would play the celebrity card only if she needed to, Claire decided not to introduce herself by name. "Hi, Mrs. Yates," she said. "I'm with the US Secret ..."

"Harold!" the woman shouted past the poorly covered mouthpiece. "Will you for Christ's sake turn that thing down! I'm on the phone!" Then back to Claire she said, "Sorry. He's about as deaf as a post and refuses to wear his hearing aids. Now, what were you saying?"

"I'm with the US Secret Service," Claire began, again. "I'm trying to put some pieces together regarding your former husband's death, and I wondered if you could help me."

"Walter?" Helen said in a hushed and somewhat agitated tone. "I thought all that was settled."

"Yes, well I'm just trying to nail down a couple of loose ends," Claire said. "I'm wondering if ..."

"I don't think I can help you," Helen cut her off, still whispering. "That's not a welcome subject in this house. I'm sorry, but I ..."

"No, wait! Please," Claire said before the woman could hang up. "This will just take a second. I just need to know if you might have an old letter from Walter—one that he mailed to you. It doesn't matter how old."

"Anything that that cheating son-of-a-bitch ever sent me or gave to me I burned, threw in the trash, or flushed down the toilet!" she told Claire. "Everything I could, that is. I got nothing left from that SOB but bad memories and a case of genital herpes that is, thank God, in remission, right now. And I sure as hell don't need this stress to get it going again! I can't help you, Miss. Good-bye!"

Before Claire could throw out her celebrity card, the line went dead. "Thanks for your help, Citizen Yates," Claire said sarcastically into the dead phone.

With her best hope a dead-end, she read through the report one more time, hoping that something else would jump out at her. It did not. Though they were rather unpleasant to look at, she also studied the beach and the coroner's-table photos of the body, more closely. Still, nothing triggered any ideas on how to verify Collins' identity.

She looked at the photo of the watch. Though it was a Seiko, and probably moderately expensive, she could see no way that it might be helpful to her, even if it still existed. Which was unlikely, because the report said that Collins' effects were released to his former wife, and she had just informed Claire that anything to do with Walter had been trashed.

The last photo was of the lower dentures. Though she was looking at a scanned copy of the original photo, she was still able to make out the sharpness of the edges of the teeth, which, she realized, meant that they must be fairly new. That was when a thought struck her.

Collins' dentures should have plenty of his tissue cells adhering to them. That should be true even if they had spent time in the mouth of some other dead person, because they would certainly not fit the imposter's gums the same as Collins', and with no saliva, Collins' cells wouldn't get washed away. But what about the salt water, she wondered. How thoroughly would that have washed them? Then she hit the same roadblock. The dentures probably didn't exist anymore. Who would save even a *loved-one's* dentures, much less those of someone they hated?

As she looked at the photo of the dentures, a new possibility occurred to her. She knew from her mother's experience that the first step in making dentures was to make a "before" casting by taking a flexible impression of the patient's mouth, after which a solid mold of the teeth was made by pouring plaster directly into the flexible impression. By simple transference, there would be millions of the patient's cells imbedded in the plaster like microscopic fossils! The question was could the mold from Walter Collins still be around? How long did dental labs keep those things?

Claire dialed the phone number for the dental lab that was listed on the report, all the time reminding herself that this, too, would likely lead to nothing.

This time she identified herself to the receptionist, and after receiving garrulous praise for saving the First Lady, she was finally put through to a lab technician.

The answer to Claire's hopeful question was disheartening, however. The technician said that castings were routinely disposed of after a year, because a person's mouth was constantly changing. After that, a new impression and new casting would have to be made for any new work.

The technician then asked, as Claire's name finally registered with her, "Are you the Claire Bradley that saved the First Lady's life?"

"Well, I think her doctors did that," Claire replied, having answered the question many times before. "I just tried to make sure they didn't have any *extra* work to do."

"Well, I think you're too modest," the technician said. "I've seen that video, and I think what you did was awesome!" Then a thought struck her. "Hey, does this thing about the castings have something to do with the shooting?" she asked, though she couldn't imagine what.

Claire didn't want to get into specifics of the case with an outsider, so she simply said, "It's background stuff, really. Just verifying some information."

"On who?" the technician asked excitedly.

Though Claire's training as an investigator told her not to mention Collins' name, her *voice* over-rode her training, and she told her. "Walter Collins. He passed away in 1999, and your lab helped to identify the body through his dentures."

"Snaggletooth?" the technician said. "What could he have to do with the shooting if he's dead?"

"Snaggletooth?" Claire repeated.

"Sorry. That's speaking ill of the dead, huh? He got that nickname around here because he had the crookedest set of teeth anyone's ever seen! Dr. Gary still shows that casting to colleagues. It's no wonder they pulled all his teeth. I'm surprised that he could chew anything tougher than oatmeal with a mess like that."

"Then you still have his casting!" Claire exclaimed, unable to believe her luck.

Ten minutes later, Claire had explained her request to Dr. Gary and had given him all the information necessary to overnight the casting to the FBI lab via courier.

She then placed a call to Dr. Whelk, and left a voicemail explaining what was coming his way and what she was looking for.

With a feeling of accomplishment, Claire swiveled around, put her feet up on her guest chair, and began reviewing her case outline on the whiteboard, again.

Almost immediately, the phone buzzed.

"There's a Cynthia Caan holding," Margaret said, "she says you're expecting her call."

"Yes, I am. Put her through, please," Claire replied optimistically, hoping her luck would continue on its roll.

"So, what are you doing tomorrow, around noon?" Cynthia asked after exchanging hellos.

Claire pictured herself riding in an ambulance with the First Lady, and replied, "I've got a meeting that I can't get out of. Why?"

"Jeff Stiller, that McPherson connection is supposed to be landing at Reagan around noon," Cynthia replied. "I thought you might like to be there to chat with him if you had the time."

"I'd love to," Claire answered, "But unless you can push it back to around 1:30, I don't think I can make it."

"He says he's scheduled to take off again at 1:20," Cynthia said. "Sorry. I know it's not much of a window."

"Hey, that's fine," Claire replied. "I appreciate the invitation. Just take good notes, and I'll call you after my meeting, okay?"

Looking back at her whiteboard, again, Claire's eyes gravitated to McPherson's name. She had a feeling that there was something very odd about the man, but she had an equally strong feeling that he was not a player in the conspiracy to kill the President. If her feeling was correct, unfortunately, that left her with a whole whiteboard of dead-ends.

Chapter 29

Wednesday, October 22
Washington, DC

Because of her appointment to meet Katherine's plane in the morning, Claire decided to work from home for an hour or so, and let the Service driver pick her up there.

Wearing pajamas, she made a cup of tea, toasted an English muffin, and then sat down at her computer to check her e-mail.

In her personal account she found several spam e-mails that went directly into the trash. In her office account there were a dozen or so e-mails, but they were all legitimate with varying degrees of importance. She skimmed through them, flagged a couple for personal follow-up, and then forwarded most of the others to her assistant for official replies.

One that she opened was from Dr. Whelk at the FBI labs, informing her that he had posted a report to the task force database regarding the dissection of the hard-drive from the gun's computer.

Logging into the database, she found the report, and began reading, only to be interrupted by her cell phone buzzing on the kitchen counter. It was Gants.

"You have your TV on?" he asked, knowing she was working from home.

Claire didn't like the sound of that. "No. Why?"

"Turn on CNN. Hurry."

As her set came on, she heard the news anchor say, "When we come back, we'll talk with CNN political analyst Todd Lathrop about this breaking story. The apparent Hezbollah connection to the attempt on the President's life."

Claire couldn't believe what she was hearing! "Where did that come from?" she asked Gants. "Did they name a source?"

"A high-level official within the Secret Service, speaking on condition of anonymity," Gants quoted what the newsman had said earlier.

"Bullshit!" Claire snapped in reply.

"Yeah, that was my reaction, too," Gants said, "but we better put a statement together that's a little more articulate than that."

"How the hell did CNN get it so quickly?"

"I think if you ask, 'who does this help?' the answer to who gave it to CNN is obvious. The President's been working his butt off to get all the players in the Middle East at the same table, almost since he took office. If one of the parties to his détente is trying to kill him, it doesn't say much for his foreign policy. It's just the kind of thing the Senator would love to get his teeth into."

"But where did Evans get it?"

"He's been in Washington longer than you've been alive, Claire. He probably doesn't even know all the sources he has, at this point. I've already talked to Director Witherspoon—we'll launch an investigation, but we're not going to pull much manpower to do it. For now, at least, we're just going to have to roll with this. We're also going to have to be a lot more careful with sensitive information. Apparently, the real-time database has its flaws."

"This wasn't posted," Claire said. "After Palmer at the NSA called us, Paul called the President, and he asked to keep it under wraps until he could talk with State and Homeland about it."

"Interesting," Gants said. "That sure limits the cast of characters, doesn't it? I'll bet that whoever passed the info on to Evans' people, however they got it, they don't know that it's not on the database. He or she probably thinks that about half a million people have access to it, so it'll be impossible to trace back to them."

"Mr. Gants, I have to get ready to meet Mrs. McClure out at Andrews," she said, "but thanks for calling me about this."

"No problem. It'll give you and Mrs. M. something to chat about on your ride in," he said with a teasing chuckle.

"Oh, yeah," Claire said, unenthusiastically, "talking about her husband getting beat up two weeks before the election should be a load of fun."

She went back to her computer and sent the FBI report to her printer. She'd read what they had found out about the shooter's hard-drive, on the ride out to Andrews.

Though she was beginning to feel positive about the progress that the task force was making, it irked her that someone, apparently *in* the task force, was willing to sabotage the investigation. And she wondered why. Did this person have an "Elect Evans" sticker on their car, or was it done for money. Either way, it was an unconscionable betrayal of trust, in Claire's view.

Chapter 30

Watching CNN in his office, Senator Evans picked up his coffee cup and raised it in a toast to his aide, Will Clark.

"Well done," Evans said. "Make sure your friend knows that this is appreciated—and that there's more appreciation where that came from if he can be of any *further* help."

"I'll do that, sir," Billy replied, "but I think he's going to want to keep a pretty low profile for a while. With all the access to the task force database, the first leak will be hard to find. But now that they know there's a hole, they'll be watching."

"That's fine," Evans agreed. "Just keep him motivated in case something pops up."

Billy laughed. "I think Crystal could keep the Pope motivated!"

"Ah, yes," Evans said. "I recall meeting Crystal. She does indeed have motivating qualities. Be sure that she knows she's appreciated, too.

*****

Peter Sewell sat naked in his bed propped against his pillows and

147

covered by a sheet. He was watching the CNN report on the Hezbollah e-mails, and he felt sick to his stomach. He had never even passed on office gossip before, much less anything that one would classify as a "leak". Now, suddenly, his words were on CNN! How could he have been so stupid?

As he watched a political analyst named Todd-something expressing his views on the impact of the Middle East connection on the upcoming election, Peter heard his shower stop. A minute later a stunning raven-haired woman came walking, naked, into his bedroom. One look at her answered his question about how he could have been so stupid the night before.

"Mornin' sugar," she cooed as she crawled onto the bed and positioned herself beside him. "Do you have time for a quickie before you have to go to work?" she whispered as she traced the outline of his ear with her tongue.

He pulled his head away from her tongue, and pushed her off of him. "Who did you tell?" he asked angrily, pointing at the TV. "What are you trying to do to me?"

He had met Crystal the night before in a club, and after a couple more glasses of wine than he normally drank, he found himself showing off to her with how he knew things about the "investigation of the century" that no one else did. And the tactic had worked for him. Knowledge is power, and power is the ultimate aphrodisiac. Crystal had come home with him and they had had the most amazing night of sex and shared-secrets.

Thinking back on it, he realized that although he had thought that he was seducing the lovely Crystal with his insider knowledge and male charm, she had actually set him up. *She* had taken the stool next to his, *she* had initiated the conversation about how interesting the assassination investigation was, and *she* had suggested that they go somewhere more private since she didn't want him to get into trouble if anyone overheard him talking about sensitive topics. Somehow, she must have known that he worked for the NSA, and she was digging for secrets to sell to the media. The whole thing was crystal clear, now ... so to speak.

Crystal looked at the TV and caught enough of what they were saying to make the connection. "Hey, don't worry, sugar. No one's going to know the source. What, do you think you're the only person who could possibly have known about those e-mails? Just relax and you'll be fine."

She moved back toward him, pulling the sheet away as she did. "I know just what you need to take your mind off it," she said, as she lowered her head.

He pushed her away again, and this time jumped out of bed. Crystal lay on her back, laughing, her enhanced breasts defying gravity. "Relax, sugar," she repeated. "What's done is done. You may as well enjoy your reward."

Peter couldn't believe this. What the hell had he gotten himself into?

When he heard that Todd guy say something about a special prosecutor possibly being assigned to the investigation of the leak, Peter suddenly felt nauseous and he ran for the bathroom.

Crystal lifted her head and watched his naked butt disappear around the corner. A few seconds later, she heard him retching into the toilet. She laughed and said derisively, under her breath, "Loser."

By the time Peter Sewell emerged from the shower, Crystal had gathered up all of her things, and was gone without a trace.

Chapter 31

Wednesday, October 22
Washington, DC

Claire was running late to meet the First Lady's plane, so she wasn't happy when the cell phone on her hip started to vibrate while she was strapping her .38 to her ankle. So that she could talk and get ready at the same time, she clipped her wireless receiver over her ear, and answered the call.

To Claire's surprise, it was the White House operator, putting through a call from the Oval Office. "Hello, Mr. President," Claire said as an anxiety knot formed in her stomach.

"Good morning, Agent Bradley. Can I assume that you've heard about the Hezbollah leak, by now?"

"Yes, sir, I have," she replied. "And I can assure you that the leak did not come from inside the Service, no matter what they said on CNN. Somebody is blowing smoke, sir."

"I just got off the phone with Paul Levine," the President replied, "and he gave me the same assurance. So you didn't talk to anyone about the e-mails, either?"

"No, sir," Claire answered emphatically. "I never even wrote the word 'Hezbollah' in my notebook. If Paul says he didn't tell anyone, either, then I can guarantee that the leak didn't come from inside the Service. No one else *knew*."

Claire looked out her front window and saw a black Suburban double-parked in front.

"Good," the President said. "I didn't think so, either, but I needed to hear it directly from you. The other reason that I called was to apologize for the way Katherine spoke to you on the phone yesterday. I think her medications are having a weird effect on her. She's—well, more aggressive than I've seen her before. I just wanted to give you a heads-up before you meet her this morning. If she seems more cantankerous than normal, understand that it's just the medication. It's nothing personal, okay?"

"No need to apologize sir, but I appreciate the warning. I'll just pretend that she's my mother, and not listen to anything she says."

The President laughed, and wished her good luck.

After pulling the FBI report from her printer, Claire sprinted down her front stairs, two at a time, and fifteen seconds later she was swinging up into the Suburban and apologizing for making the driver wait.

"No problem, ma'am," he replied with a smile while reaching up to flip a couple of switches on the overhead console. "It's been a while since I've gotten to play with the lights and siren, anyway." Through the generous application of both, the driver had Claire at Andrews Air Force Base well ahead of the First Lady's plane.

The driver parked on the apron next to the President's ambulance, and since they were about fifteen minutes ahead of schedule, Claire used the time to read the FBI report. She had intended to read it on the ride to Andrews, but weaving in and out of traffic with the siren whooping had proved a bit too distracting.

Claire was, at first, confused to read about the encrypted files on the hard-drive, and that they were not very hopeful that they would be able to break them. Then she remembered that she was reading an FBI document and that it was the NSA who had cracked the files on their duplicate hard drive.

Since the information about the Hezbollah e-mails had not been posted to the database—nor leaked until this morning—Dr. Whelk would not have known that the encryption had been broken by the NSA by time the he wrote the e-mail to Claire.

Along with finding the encrypted files, the FBI technicians had been able to reconstruct exactly how the "communication and fire-control module" of the computer functioned. The report went into great detail on what all sorts of abbreviations, such as AZM, ELV, VAC, and VAL stood for, and how they interacted. Claire skimmed through most of that.

A line-by-line analysis of the software that was used to aim the gun showed that it had been written around a commercially-available program that originally had nothing to do with weapons of any kind. The software had been designed to control security cameras.

According to the report, if photographs of the left, right, and front of a subject were fed into the program, it would combine them to create a three-dimensional model of that person, and store it in memory. Then, when connected to a motorized surveillance camera, the software would use the 3-D model to recognize that subject, and could even pick them out of a crowd. The program would then direct the camera to follow the person wherever they went, no matter which way they turned.

The software, which had been commercially developed for Las Vegas casinos, now had custom additions that turned the surveillance features into target-acquisition and gun-aiming functions.

The report then switched topics from software to hardware, describing the search for evidence in the nuts and bolts of the computer. The technicians had quickly determined that the system was not an off-the-shelf unit, but had been custom assembled from separate components such as its motherboard, power supply, memory sticks, and the various "driver boards" needed to control the gun-aiming motors.

The report said that the serial numbers of the components were all being traced to determine when and where they were sold, in the hope that records of the buyer or buyers would point somewhere meaningful. Claire doubted that that would lead anywhere, but every stone had to be turned.

The search for trace evidence, such as fingerprints or a hair that might have been left behind by whoever built the computer came up completely empty. Apparently the builder had worn gloves while working, and possibly even a hair net.

They had finally gotten a lucky break when they examined the wiring between the driver boards in the computer, and the motors on the gun. Each wire had an unusual pinch mark in its insulation at each end where it had been stripped to make a connection. Examining the items in Frances Dunham's tool belt, turned up a pair of semi-automatic wire strippers with a small burr in one of the gripping jaws which exactly matched the unique pinch marks. With solid evidence connecting Dunham's tool to the gun and computer, fingerprints, from the right, middle, and index fingers, were lifted from the grips of the wire strippers, and sent through the FBI's 200-million-fingerprint database. Unfortunately, no matches were found. They would have to find Dunham and match her prints to those on the wire strippers before they could solidly connect her to the gun.

Claire had just reached the end of the report when she noticed the driver looking out the window at the President's 747 approaching the runway. Several minutes later it was pulling up on the apron in front of them.

As a service truck was backing up to the side of the plane, Claire saw the cargo door in the fuselage open from inside. Two agents stood in the opening, watching as the box of the truck lifted straight up like an elevator. As the agents and attendants transferred the First Lady's gurney to the truck, the President's ambulance pulled alongside to take her in when she returned to ground level.

As Claire got out of the Suburban and walked over to the ambulance to greet Katherine, she found herself wishing that she had thought to pick up some flowers.

While the body of the truck was coming down with the First Lady, Claire was still trying to figure out how she wanted to greet Katherine. Officially? "Good morning, ma'am. Welcome back to Washington. How was your flight?" Or personally? "Katherine! It's so good to have you back! You look great!"

She needn't have wasted her time pondering the question.

When Katherine finally came into sight, Claire saw that she appeared to be unconscious. "Is she all right?" Claire asked with obvious concern, as the first two attendants jumped down and started to pull the gurney from the truck.

"Much better now," her doctor answered from inside the truck. "She was in a lot of discomfort from the ride between the hospital and Logan. Helicopters aren't known for their smoothness, you know—even Marine One. I had to give her a little boost on her pain meds to get her to relax." Hopping down from the truck he went on, "And I gave her another booster just before landing." Pointing to the truck, he explained, "I knew this would be uncomfortable for her, too."

"Um, she and I were supposed to talk on the way to the hospital," Claire said.

"Trust me," he replied, "even if she were awake, she wouldn't be much fun to talk to."

One of the attendants let out a *you-can-say-that-again* laugh.

"Well, she's supposed to have pictures taken when she gets to GW," Claire said looking at the unconscious First Lady, strapped to her gurney.

"She doesn't look too photogenic right now."

"Yes, I know about her photo-op," the doctor said, with obvious displeasure. "Don't worry. When we get to the hospital, I'm going to give her something that will bring her out of the medication very quickly. She'll be awake and smiling like that," he said snapping his fingers. "Then she'll end up with one of the worst headaches she's ever had. I tried to tell her to skip the cameras, and let it wear off by itself, but it's like talking to a stump!"

Claire laughed. "She can be a bit bull-headed," she agreed.

Again, the attendant laughed.

When, Katherine's gurney was finally strapped into the ambulance, and they were on the way to the hospital, Claire noticed that her driver in the black Suburban had pulled out in front of them, lights flashing and siren whooping. At least someone is having fun, she thought.

When they were in view of the hospital, the doctor stuck a needle into Katherine's IV connection, and slowly injected a clear liquid into her arm. Almost instantly, Katherine's eyes popped open, and she assumed a wide-eyed, where-the-hell-am-I look, like something out of a cartoon.

"What the hell did you just shoot her with?" Claire asked in surprise.

"Starbuck's double-espresso," the doctor deadpanned. "No cream, no foam." Then he leaned over, and putting his familiar face in front of Katherine's, he said soothingly, "Hello Katherine. It's Dr. Drewer. You're in an ambulance arriving at George Washington Hospital in Washington. Do you understand me?" He watched her eyes very closely to make sure she was able to focus on him.

Katherine simply stared dumbly for a moment then blinked a couple of times, and croaked, "Mouth is dry."

By the time the doors of the ambulance opened, Katherine was fully aware of what was going on, and in complete control of it.

She instructed one of the attendants to raise the back of the gurney to its most upright position so she would be sitting up when she was wheeled out. She told another one to fix her hair, and she told Claire to stay close beside her on the right side. Only then, would she allow them to open the ambulance doors.

When they swung opened, Claire saw a number of familiar faces. Secret Service agents formed a corridor from the ambulance about 20 feet to the hospital's Emergency Room doors.

Inside, a number of reporters, video cameramen, and photographers were waiting. Because of the restricted space, and because it was an active E/R area, the number of media people was limited, much to Katherine's disappointment.

Making the most of it, however, as she was wheeled through the doors, Katherine gave a thumbs-up gesture, and a seemingly pained smile. Like a ventriloquist, she whispered to Claire without moving her lips, "Smile."

Claire did *not* smile, however. She hated this photo op crap.

As it turned out, the video that made the news that night, and the photos that made the papers were even better for Claire's somber expression. She was seen as the young and attractive Secret Service agent, still deadly serious about protecting the First Lady. Another publicity coup for Katherine.

Chapter 32

Wednesday, October 22
Washington, DC

When Claire arrived back in her office after the photo session at the hospital, she had a voicemail from Dr. Whelk at the FBI labs. She returned it immediately, and luckily, got him right away.

"We received the Walter Collins blood sample and the dental casting this morning," he told her. "We were able to scrape enough cells off the casting so we'll be able to do a nuclear-DNA profile. That's going to give us some pretty robust results. I was afraid, at first, that we'd only be able to get a mitochondrial profile."

"That's great!" Claire said, knowing that a nuclear-DNA profile could lead to the identification of a specific individual, where a mitochondrial match could only establish family lineage, and only on the mother's side.

"Can you give me an approximation on when you'll have some results?" she asked hopefully.

"You understand, that there's not much we can speed up here," he said almost apologetically. "Working straight through, it's going to take the best part of twenty-four hours to run the polymerase-chain-reaction to amplify the short-tandem-repeats, and then get the samples into the gel and to electrophorese it."

The only part of that that Claire really heard was "... twenty-four hours ..."

"You're kidding?" she said. "Twenty-four hours?"

"I can't make the cells incubate any faster," Whelk replied a bit defensively.

"No, no!" Claire replied. "Twenty-four hours is great! Fantastic! I thought you were going to tell me a week or something."

"Well, to turn it that fast is pretty extraordinary," he said, "but then so is this case. Everybody down here is pulling out all the stops."

"Thank you!" she said. "And please pass my appreciation on to your team. This is a huge help!"

After checking her e-mails, and going through the usual sorting routine, Claire logged into the task force database and reviewed any new information that had been posted.

As with any investigation, the flood of information that marked the early stages was tapering off as the tough parts of the investigation took hold. Most of the updates were progress reports indicating little or no *new* progress.

As she was scanning the posts, a new report appeared, sent by Cynthia Caan.

Claire double-clicked it and began reading, happy to see that someone had made some headway today.

The report noted that Cynthia and her partner, Mark Liston, had interviewed Jeff Stiller, another former Dynametric employee, and had gotten the name of Roger McPherson's plastic surgeon. He remembered the name, Joseph Merrick, because it was the name of the person known as *The Elephant Man*, and he thought it was an odd name for a plastic surgeon. Unfortunately, Stiller did not know where McPherson, himself, might be. The report concluded by stating that, at the time of the posting, Cynthia was still trying to reach the doctor.

Plastic surgeon! Wow, McPherson really *did* want to drop out of sight, Claire thought. She looked at her whiteboard and saw the names Frances Dunham, Walter Collins, and Roger McPherson grouped at the top. Claire wasn't sure where Dunham fit in, but she could see an obvious connection between the two ex-Dymo coworkers who had both dropped out of sight around the same time. One by faking his own death, and the other by altering his appearance and changing his identity. Claire was feeling pretty good about things all of a sudden, but there was still a lot to do and a lot that could go wrong.

She dialed Cynthia's number, and got her on the second ring. "Hi, this is Claire Bradley. I was just reading the report you posted and I was wondering if you'd run the doctor/patient thing through legal yet?"

"Legal is in the process of getting a warrant as a back-up," Cynthia replied, "but they said that I could talk to him and explain the situation—that McPherson is the subject of a felony investigation—and see if he'll cooperate. According to the guy that I talked to down there, the doctor/patient confidentiality thing gets into some real grey areas if the doctor knows that their patient may be putting someone else or the public in danger."

Claire liked Cynthia's thoroughness. "So was your contact, Stiller, able to give you a description of what McPherson looks like now?"

"Yeah. *He* looks like a *she*. McPherson underwent gender reassignment," Cynthia said.

"McPherson had a *sex-change* operation?"

"Yup," replied Cynthia. "And according to Stiller—who is openly bisexual to the point that he was hitting on both me and my partner, Mark—a very complete one. He claims to have had sexual relations with him, or rather *her*, after the surgery, and in his words, 'Her indoor plumbing worked just like she came from the factory that way.'"

Claire chuckled at the phrasing, and then said "Could McPherson have become Frances Dunham?"

The question took Cynthia by surprise. Damn! Why hadn't she thought of that? "Good question," she replied. "Do you have access there to photos of the two of them?"

"Hang on a sec," Claire said as she put her telephone headset on to free up both of her hands. "Let me get them both on the screen at the same time."

"Boy, that would be a pretty good ruse, wouldn't it?" Cynthia said as she listened to Claire tapping at her keyboard. "A homosexual male transforms himself into a female, and then plays the part of a *butch* female pretending to be a man. My head hurts just thinking about it," she said with a laugh. "How could you remember who you were when you got up in the morning?"

Claire replied with a distracted "Mmm", but was concentrating more on her computer screen than on what Cynthia was saying. She had located the two images in the databank, and had just split the screen so that she could view them side by side. Resizing them, so they each filled their respective windows, she began shifting her eyes back and forth between the images, looking for similarities.

"Okay," she said to Cynthia, "I think that's a bust. McPherson's eyes are too close together. I don't think any plastic surgeon can move eye sockets. But how about this? What if they were lovers? The new Miss McPherson, and Dunham."

"Wow, there's another one to make your brain hurt," Cynthia said with a laugh. "Dunham, a gay female who would apparently rather be a man, hooks up with a female who actually used to *be* a man. And McPherson, who is so gay that he goes to the bother—and expense—of changing his sex, takes on a butch female as a love interest, rather than finding a *male* lover—which would seem to be the whole point of the sex-change thing in the first place. Boy, wouldn't Freud like to get his hands on that scenario?"

"Okay, if you're going to put it *that* way," Claire said with a chuckle, "it does sound like a stretch. But how about if McPherson is just using Dunham? All I'm saying is, let's not rule anything out."

"Hey, I agree," Cynthia replied. "Some writer once said that the difference between fiction and reality is that fiction has to be plausible. That's just *im*plausible enough to be true."

After brief good-byes, Claire grabbed her purse to head downstairs to the cafeteria. It was after one-thirty, and her stomach was growling.

She had just reached her doorway when the phone buzzed. She returned, and picked it up, hoping it was Cynthia, again. She was getting used to being surprised by good news.

"I have Officer Perkins for you," Margaret announced.

Claire had forgotten all about Perkins coming into town today, and his request to meet her for dinner. "Put him through," she said as she mentally rehearsed her sorry-I-have-to-work-tonight excuse for not meeting up with him.

"Hi," he began in a cheery tone, "I know I promised you dinner tonight, but something's come up with my uncle, and I'm going to have to beg your forgiveness for changing plans at the last minute."

Relieved that she didn't have to lie to him, Claire lied anyway. "Oh, that's too bad," she said. "I was looking forward to seeing you again after all these years."

"Same here," Dave replied. "So how about if I pick you up in front of your building, and we can grab some lunch, instead. I know you haven't eaten yet, and this way there's no 'date' pressure. Just a couple of old school chums in need of nourishment."

Claire couldn't believe she had walked right into that. "How do you know whether I've eaten or not?" she asked. "Are you stalking me, again?"

Dave laughed. "Nothing so sinister. I asked your secretary. So, how about it? My treat or we can go Dutch if it makes you feel better. I can be in front of your building in five minutes."

"Okay," she said, in a resigned tone. "But something fast. I've got a lot of work to do. I was just going to grab a salad and eat at my desk."

On her way down in the elevator, a grin crept across her face. Surprisingly, she found herself liking this guy. He was witty, charming, and articulate, and he was persistent without being creepy. And he was damned cute, too! He'd changed a *lot* since high school!

Standing on the sidewalk, Claire was surprised when a black Lexus limousine pulled to a sudden stop, double-parking right in front of her. The back door opened, and a man hopped out. It was Dave Perkins. "Hi, Claire!" he called to her. "Come on, before we get a ticket. The traffic cops are murder in this town."

More than a little surprised, Claire climbed into the back of the car, followed by Dave. As the door closed, the driver was pulling out into the traffic.

"If this is how you do lunch," Claire said, "I'm sorry I'm going to miss dinner. A limo really wasn't necessary, you know. There are six or eight lunch places within walking distance."

"This is my uncle's," Dave said. "He insists I use it whenever I'm in town. I have to admit, it's a darned sight better than trying to *drive* in this city."

"Who's your uncle?" Claire asked, wondering if he might be in Congress. "Is this coming out of my tax dollars?"

"No," Dave answered. "Uncle Ron's never been elected to anything, that I'm aware of. He's just a shrewd investor with a knack for being in the right place at the right time."

A mile or so down the road, the driver pulled into a burger place, and threaded the car into the drive-through lane.

"When I said 'fast', I didn't mean that we had to eat in the car," Claire laughed.

Patting the leather seat, Dave said, "I guarantee this is more comfortable than the hard plastic inside." Lowering the window to speak into the order box, he asked Claire, "What'll you have? Price is not an object."

Dave ordered for the two of them and then asked the driver, "What'll you have, Sam?"

Claire was surprised when the driver answered. Her short hair and sunglasses, and the fact that she had never turned around had kept Claire from noticing that Sam—probably Samantha—was a woman. An attractive woman. Claire mentally kicked herself for missing it. She was trained to spot things like that!

After stopping at a small park overlooking a duck pond, Sam took her food into the front seat, and then discreetly raised the glass partition separating herself from the passenger compartment.

"So," Dave said, unwrapping his grilled chicken, "I told you if you'd have dinner with me, you could use the time to interrogate me. So ask away."

Claire recalled him saying that, but she hadn't been thinking along those lines. She was rather enjoying the almost silly spontaneity of this whole thing. Dining on drive-through sandwiches in the back seat of a chauffer-driven limo. The only thing missing was drinking *Dom Perignon* from Flintstones glasses.

"Okay," she said after swallowing her first bite of veggie wrap, "business before pleasure. I've read Gants' on-site report and the FBI's lab report on the booby trap that was meant to melt the computer in the hospital. What I want to know is how did you know that's what it was? I mean, from the photos I saw, it looks like a coffee can full of dirt. How did you know it wasn't a can for cigarette butts?"

"A butt can probably wouldn't have had wires running out of it," he said, "and it probably *would* have had butts in it. Plus, from the Marines, I'm familiar with thermite. I know how to make it, I know what it looks like, and I know what it can do."

"Which is?"

"You set a can like that on the hood of a truck, and light it off, and it'll make a molten ball so hot it will literally melt its way right through the engine block and end up on the ground. It would have fried that computer a hundred times over."

"Why the overkill, do you think?"

"Fry the computer and set the hospital on fire at the same time, and it makes the whole mess even harder to sort out. If the hospital went up in flames, who knows how long it would have been before they found what little would have been left of the gun."

"Why leave the stuff out in the open like it was," Claire asked around a mouthful of sandwich. "It was just sitting there saying, 'defuse me'."

"I like the way your mind works," he said with a grin. "I was having the same problem, myself. And why wire the device to the two access doors in the plenum chamber, but not to the trap door that I accidentally discovered—the one that opened to let the gun fire?"

"Exactly!" Claire said, excited to have found someone who was thinking the same way that she was.

Dave went on, "And why leave the cover off the can so the bomb squad could just vacuum out all the thermite without having to risk cutting wires? You'd think that whoever set up the booby trap, *intended* for it to be found and defused."

"It was either a very sloppy job," Claire said, "or a very clever one." Then something that she had read in the FBI lab report struck her, and she added, "And I'm going to put my money on *clever*. The detonator that was buried in the bottom of the thermite was defective!" she told him. "They analyzed it at the FBI lab and they found that one of the wires had what they called a 'cold-solder joint'. It had broken away from its contact, so the device would never have gone off even if they hadn't defused it. The report implied that the defect was accidental—poor workmanship—but now, I'm not so sure."

"So what does the shooter gain by letting us find the gun and computer intact?" Dave mused.

"For one thing, he doesn't burn down a hospital with a couple hundred people in it. Maybe he got an attack of conscience," Claire suggested. "Assassinating the President to make some political point is one thing, but wholesale slaughter is something else. Especially if it's just to cover your tracks—the President was supposed to be dead already by the time the thermite would have gone off."

"Then why set up the booby trap at all?" Dave said. "Or, if it was already set up when his conscience kicked in, why not just unplug it?"

"Maybe whoever set it up was following specific orders from higher up," Claire speculated. "And from what the FBI has found, the set-up person appears to be the Dunham woman. Maybe she couldn't just ignore the orders, but her conscience wouldn't let her carry them out, either. So she sabotaged the booby trap, making it look like a technical snafu, to save the hospital without her employer or her cohorts suspecting her."

"I think you're on to something!" Dave said. "And maybe that's why you can't find her. Maybe they *did* suspect her, and she paid the price for her disloyalty.

"On the other hand," he went on, "maybe the point was to make sure that you got the computer intact so that you would find those e-mails, but without making it look too easy. Maybe the Hezbollah connection is a red herring."

"Interesting that you should say that," Claire said, amazed by how much she and Dave thought alike. "I'd been thinking the exact same

162

thing. But if that was the case, then why encrypt the e-mails? Why take the chance that they wouldn't be broken? I mean, the FBI couldn't do it. It was only the fact that the NSA got involved that allowed us to read them, and it was only a liberal application of anti-terrorist laws that allowed them to *get* involved. Until they decoded the e-mails, the crime had been completely domestic, so technically, they shouldn't have been part of this, yet."

"The e-mails were encrypted?" Dave asked. "I hadn't heard that. And they cracked them in two days? Wow, that's extraordinary!"

"Why would you think that's extraordinary?" Claire asked. "That's what the NSA does."

"I know," Dave said, "but this past spring I finished a computer forensics course at the State Police Academy up in Massachusetts, and one of the things they told us was that if we came across an encrypted file, we should probably forget about it and move on to the next piece of possible evidence. The instructor said that even a $20 encryption program can scramble files so completely that they're virtually unbreakable. He even mentioned the NSA, and that even they couldn't unscramble most encryption codes used by other governments—it's effectively impossible."

"Really?" Claire said. "I didn't know that. The guy that we talked to about it at the NSA didn't mention that it was anything unusual to crack the code so quickly. So what does that mean to the e-mails? I'd say it tends to support the red herring theory."

"Maybe, maybe not," Dave said. "Maybe the NSA folks just got lucky."

"You mean lucky as in being able to disarm the booby trap before it could fry the computer and the e-mails?" Claire said. "And lucky as in there being an 'accidental' fault in the booby trap triggering device that would make doubly sure that we got to see the e-mails? And then lucky as in being able to crack an impossible encryption in two days? When I see too many lucky breaks, I begin to think somebody's stacking the deck."

"So now you *do* think the e-mails were planted to throw off the investigation."

"A minute ago—before you told me about encryption—I'd have said, no. But now I'm not so sure. But I'm definitely going to have a chat with somebody over at NSA when I get back."

"Speaking of which ..." Dave said, "I should be getting you back before you turn into a pumpkin."

"You're probably right," Claire said, looking at her watch, amazed to see that so much time had passed. "But, hey, I appreciate the lunch, and the ride, not to mention kicking around ideas with you. This was a lot more pleasure than business. Thanks."

Pressing the intercom button, Dave said, "Sam, we have to get Miss Bradley back to work. She has a crime to solve."

"I'm really sorry that you can't get away for dinner tonight," Claire said. "I think I'd have enjoyed that very much. Next time you get to town, be sure to give me a call."

"Do you really mean that? Or are you just saying it to make me feel good?"

"I really mean it," she assured him.

"Well, I understand if you've already made other plans," Dave said a bit sheepishly, "but the offer actually still stands."

"What about your uncle?" Claire asked him.

"The truth is that I never had a commitment with my uncle tonight. He's not even in town—he's in Belize. I just told you that to let you off the hook. It occurred to me that I kind of ambushed you into the dinner date, and I didn't feel right about it. I'm sorry. Not a very good first impression, huh?"

"Actually, I think it's kind of sweet," Claire said, "and amusing. Sweet that you'd *let me off the hook*, as you say, even though you'd waited years to get a date with me. And amusing, because when Margaret said that you were on the phone earlier, *I* was ready to break the date with *you*."

"Which leaves us exactly where?" Dave asked.

"I guess it leaves us going out to dinner tonight," Claire said as Sam pulled up in front of the Secret Service building. "But with the caveat that if anything comes up between now and then, I'll have to beg off."

"Understood," Dave said as Claire opened her door. "Where would you like to go?" he asked.

"Surprise me," she said. "Girls like that kind of thing." Handing him her card with her e-mail address, she said, "What time?"

"How about eight? Assuming I can get a reservation somewhere, of course."

"I guess we'll see how creative you are, won't we?" she said. "See you at eight."

Chapter 33

Wednesday, October 22
Newburyport, MA

Eldred Beazley, a fastidious little man in a bow tie, walked, unannounced, into the chief administrator's office at the St. Jacques Hospital, holding a six-page printout. Beazley was the hospital's accounts-payable supervisor, and he was not happy.

One of Beazley's pet peeves—and there were many—was employees using hospital phones to make personal long-distance calls—a practice that Beazley regarded as just as much stealing as walking out the door with bed linen or a case of aspirin.

Not everyone agreed with Beazley's vehemence on the matter, but the policy was well explained in the employee's manual and Beazley even made sure that Human Resources specifically covered that point with new hires.

"Are *they* stupid, or do they think *we're* stupid," Beazley said holding up September's telephone bill.

"Come in Eldred," Miranda Randal said in a weary tone, having been through this numerous times before. "Have a seat. I take it they've been abusing the phone system again." she said, setting aside the report she had been reading.

"Do they not understand that a record of every single long-distance call ends up on this bill?" Beazley said as he took a seat. "And that our phone system keeps a log of calls made from every extension? Why do they keep doing it when they know they're not going to get away with it? I just don't understand these people," he said, pushing the bill in front of Miranda.

At one time, a couple of years ago, this had been a big problem. Personal Long-Distance Calls, or PLDCs, as Easley called them, had topped $2,000 one month, and the hospital had cracked down, issuing a reminder of the policy and stern warnings about phone-privilege misuse.

"How much?" Miranda asked, glancing at the bill and the numerous times that the same number was marked with yellow highlighter.

"It's not how much," Beazley replied, "it's how many, Mrs. Randal—and all by the same person." In fact the PLDC's only amounted to $87.24; an amount that was a drop in the bucket compared with the total phone bill.

"Look at these calls," he said, pointing with his precisely sharpened No. 2 pencil. "Every one is to the same number—twice, sometimes three times in one day—and *every* day! I've dialed the number several times myself, to find out who's receiving the calls, but there's never an answer."

"Who is *making* the calls?" Miranda asked, flipping pages in the bill, but not really knowing where to look. "Whose pass-code was used?"

"Every one was made by Bryce Donnelly, downstairs in maintenance," Easley told her. "I confronted him about it, but he swore he didn't make them, even though I have the evidence right here. I mean, how stupid does he ..."

"Maintenance? When was the last call made?" Miranda interrupted him.

He flipped to the last page of the printout from the hospital's phone system, and circled the date with his pencil.

She looked up at him and said, "That's the day before the shooting."

"Yes, I know that," Beazley replied. "I don't see what ..."

"Dunham," she said. "All the calls were made from maintenance, and they stopped on the last day that she was seen here." Searching her desk for James Gants card, she added, "I could be leaping to the wrong conclusion here, but I think the Secret Service will want to hear what you've found, Eldred."

166

Chapter 34

Wednesday, October 22
Washington, DC

Claire was still smiling when she got back to her office from her lunch with Dave. She hadn't felt this good about meeting a guy in a long time. But she quickly shifted gears and was back to work.

Dropping into her chair, she pulled up the database and quickly scanned it for new entries. There were several recent postings from the tip lines, but nothing earth shattering. She then pulled up an inter-agency phone directory, and found the number for the NSA headquarters in Fort Meade, Maryland.

After explaining to several different operators and receptionists who she was and who she was looking for, she was finally connected with a young man named Kevin Mathews, a decryption specialist, or what the NSA referred to as a "code warrior." He was the specialist who had broken the e-mail encryption code.

"I'm curious about how you decoded the Hezbollah e-mails so quickly," Claire said. "I don't need to get into anything top-secret, but I've been told that encrypted files are extremely difficult, sometimes impossible, to break. Did you just get lucky on this one?"

"How much do you know about how encryption works, Agent Bradley?" he asked.

"Not a lot, I guess. I know that when you type in your password, it comes up as asterisks on the screen. Beyond that, it's all magic," she replied good-naturedly, with only a little exaggeration.

"I like an honest answer," Kevin said with a chuckle. "Okay, here's a condensed version of encryption 101. First of all, encrypting isn't the same as protecting your work with a password. A normal password only prevents a file from being opened by a program that would normally be able to run that type of file—in this case, a text document. Once the password is cracked or if you find another way in—say by dissecting the hard drive—then the whole file is there for the taking, just sitting there on the disk. For us, cracking most peoples' passwords is almost too easy. We won't even use the Cray's for it. Heck, I've cracked forgotten passwords for friends on their home computers in a few minutes with software I wrote myself."

Claire had been afraid when she placed the call to the NSA that she would end up talking to some Ph.D. who would talk so far over her head that she wouldn't even know if he *had* answered her question, much less what it meant. She was surprised and relieved to be speaking with someone who spoke the same English that she did.

"Without going into all the technicalities of how it does it," he went on, "when you encrypt a message, a unique 'key' is created—sort of a password, but much more complicated. Using that key is the only way that the message can be decrypted and made readable again—*ever*."

"Sort of like feeding it through a cross-cut paper shredder?" Claire said.

"Nope," Kevin said. "With enough time, a shredded document can be put back together. We do that all the time. When a document is encrypted, everything in the document is changed through a mathematical algorithm or formula, and every time even the same document is encrypted, the formula is different. Without having that *exact* formula—the 'key'—the document is just computer gibberish. Its not even words, anymore."

"You mentioned using the *Crays*," Claire said. "You're talking about the Cray super-computers, I assume. Is that how you figured out the formula—the 'key'—so quickly?"

"Yes and no," Kevin replied. "The Crays couldn't have done it alone—not under normal circumstances. If you were using a good encryption program—which you can download off the Internet for about twenty-bucks—take a guess at how many possible encryption keys could be generated."

"A couple trillion?" Claire replied, taking a wild guess.

"Way low," Kevin said, knowing that she would be. "Encryption keys use fifty-six bits, and because computers are binary in nature—that is, they know only two things; zeros and ones—that means that the total possible combinations there could be is two to the fifty-sixth power, or just over 72-*quadrillion*! That's 72-million billion!"

"Wow!" Claire replied, though not fully able to comprehend a number that size. "That's a lot of combinations, but isn't that what your super-computers are for? Crunching really big numbers really fast?"

"That's what they do, all right," Kevin answered, sure that she wasn't grasping just how big the number was. "So, let's say that we can crunch numbers at a rate of one-hundred-thousand per second. I'm not allowed to tell you what the Crays actually *can* do, so we'll just use that as an example, okay? Well, to try all 72-quadrillion possible combinations at one-hundred-thousand tries per second, it would take about eleven-*thousand* years!"

"Holy cow!" Claire exclaimed. "But that would be under normal circumstances, right? You implied there was something *abnormal* about this."

"It was something we found on the hard-drive that really shouldn't have been there," Kevin said. "We found the source-code for the encryption program on the same drive as the encrypted files. That's *very* unusual."

"I don't understand," said Claire. "Wouldn't it have to be there if you were going to encrypt and decrypt with the computer?"

"You'd need an encryption/decryption *program*," Kevin explained, "but that wouldn't normally include the source-code for how the key is generated—and it's different for every program. The source-code is usually kept on a secure server somewhere, not in a system out in the field. If you leave it on a field system, things like *this* can happen," he said with a chuckle. "So, by being able to decompile and then analyze the source-code I was able to get a pretty good feel for how this particular program formulated the algorithm that then generated the key. With that, I was able to knock that 72-quadrillion down to maybe 100 or 150 million. And that's a real manageable number in the world of super-computers!"

"If it's not classified," she asked, "how long did you have to number-crunch once you analyzed the source-code, and got the possible combinations down to 150 million or so?"

"About eight minutes," he answered. "When you have a realistic number and you happen to have a Cray super-computer handy, the rest goes pretty quickly."

"And a skilled analyst," she added, giving him a pat on the back. "I won't pretend to understand everything you've just told me, Kevin, but one thing I *don't* understand, is why the source-code would have been left on the computer if it wasn't necessary to be there?"

"From what I understand," Kevin answered, "the computer was booby trapped to get fried after the President was shot, so I'd guess that the guy was just being lazy. He probably figured there was no need to take care of the housecleaning."

Claire's mind was racing. Everything Kevin was saying was fitting into the theory that she and Dave had come up with over lunch. That somebody had *wanted* them to read those e-mails.

"Kevin, you've been a tremendous help," she said. "This all makes a lot more sense to me now. Thanks a lot."

After hanging up, Claire changed some things around on her white-board. She didn't erase the Hezbollah connection, but she moved it down in priority, pretty sure now, that it was a decoy.

From what they had gathered so far, she still felt that finding McPherson was going to be critical to tracing the path of the gun from the Reagan-era CIA to the St. Jacques Hospital. She would like to talk to Dunham, too, but she had a bad feeling about that. Claire didn't think that they were going to find her—not alive, anyway. Half an hour later, she got a call that proved her feeling to be correct—sort of.

An agent from the Secret Service field office in Toledo called and told her that using the information that Dunham had given human-resources when she got the job at the hospital, they had traced her back to the small town in Ohio where she had been born—and still lived. The real Frances Dunham, who had obviously had her identity stolen, turned out to be a frail black woman who had been surviving on the street as a prostitute for ten years, and had never been outside of Ohio in her life. Frances Dunham, at least in name, was a dead end, if not actually dead. Finding the woman who had been using her identity, without some kind of tip, would be nearly impossible.

Chapter 35

Wednesday, October 22
Washington, DC

Claire kept herself so busy for the rest of the afternoon that she had completely forgotten about her dinner date with Dave until his e-mail popped up in her computer, just before six.

Once again, her work ethic nagged at her, and she was tempted to beg-off. But there were pieces of the puzzle that she didn't have, and wouldn't have until tomorrow at the earliest. And they were critical pieces, such as a determination from the FBI on whether the body from the beach was really Walter Collins, more information on the where-abouts of Roger McPherson, and the long shot of locating Frances Dunham. She decided to go. After all, she would never be further from the investigation than she was from her cell phone.

Dave's e-mail read, "I hope your afternoon has gone well and that you'll still be able to join me for dinner. I understand, of course, if you have to cancel in favor of the investigation, but if you are able to make it, I think I've found just the right place. Elegant, but not stuffy. If we're still on, I'll pick you up at seven-thirty. Remember to send me your address."

By seven-fifteen, Claire was wearing the only piece of evening attire that she owned—a dress that she hadn't worn since her cousin's wedding more than a year ago—and she felt wonderful! For one reason, the dress still fit! For another, she had a better reason to be wearing it than someone else's wedding.

As she checked herself in the mirror for the tenth time in half an hour, she realized that she was nervous. A few days ago, she had thrown herself between the First Lady and some unseen sniper, and hadn't thought twice about it. Now, a date with an old schoolmate had her stomach twisted in a knot. She had to laugh at the irony of that.

At precisely seven-thirty, her doorbell rang. Opening the door with as much composure as she could fake, she actually took a step back when she saw Dave standing there. *Oh my God!* she said to herself, *It just keeps getting better!*

Dave was wearing a white tuxedo, that looked like it had been molded for his body, and in his hand he held a single red rose.

"You look … *fantastic!*" he said. He was a little disappointed that he couldn't think of a stronger adjective to describe how beautiful she looked.

The knee-length black dress flowed over the curves of Claire's body like a satin glaze that had been poured over her. It had spaghetti straps that crisscrossed her bare back almost to the base of her spine, and a neckline that revealed just enough cleavage to be elegant. Around her neck she wore a delicate ruby and diamond necklace, and on her wrist she wore a matching bracelet. The jewelry had been a gift from her grandmother when she had graduated high school, and she always felt special when she wore them. They were certainly working their charm, now.

She had styled her hair with just a few more waves and flips than her every-day casual toss, and had spent more time with her makeup tonight than she normally did in a whole week. And the look in Dave's eyes made it all worthwhile.

Draping her wrap over her bare shoulders, he took her key, locked the door for her, and dropped the key into her evening bag. Not that Claire dated a lot, but no date had *ever* done that for her before! She was liking Dave more and more all the time!

As Sam pulled the limo out into the traffic, Dave reached forward and removed a half-filled champaign flute from a chilled holder, and handed it to her.

"To renewed acquaintances," he said, raising his own glass.

Smiling, she clinked her glass to his, and said, "Here, here."

Claire wanted to know a lot more about Dave—and not in a professional sense—but she wanted that to be conversation over dinner. So instead, as she admired the monogrammed champaign glass, she said, "Tell me about your uncle."

"His name is Ron Egan, but he's not really my uncle," Dave began. "Ron's got to be seventy or so, and he's just been such a close friend of the family, forever, that I grew up calling him Uncle Ron.

"He and my Dad served in Korea together. He was married once— before I was even born, but now he's a confirmed bachelor."

"Sworn off women, has he?" Claire asked.

"Hardly," Dave said with a chuckle. "He's just sworn off marriage. He's always advised me, 'Never get married. If you want loving and companionship, date good looking women and raise dogs.'" Immediately, Dave wished he hadn't said that.

"Interesting philosophy," Claire said coolly and with a look that women reserve for men who have begun to dig their own graves.

"That's *his* philosophy, not mine," Dave said defensively, not quite sure if Claire was kidding or was really offended. "I didn't say I subscribed to it."

"Then you don't care to date good looking women?" Claire asked, turning the screw just a bit.

This time he caught the lilt of humor in her voice, and he knew she was pulling his chain. "Can I just take the Fifth on this?" he said.

"Getting drunk won't help your cause," Claire quipped. "So, do you own a dog, Officer Perkins?"

He laughed at her quick-wittedness regarding the "Fifth", and confessed, "Yes, I own a dog, but that doesn't mean ..."

"The prosecution rests!" she interrupted in a mock huff.

"You win!" he said with a laugh. "I admit it. It's a stupid, chauvinistic attitude, and it's offensive to all women and most dogs. I apologize on behalf of my uncle and I promise to have a talk with him."

"You're no fun," Claire said with a pretend pout, "you give in too easy." In fact, he *was* fun. He was easy to talk with and could take a joke. She was beginning to see that he had a personality that matched his looks.

A short while later, Sam pulled into the driveway in front of a high-rise condo building. The driveway split and a sign indicated that residents should go to the left and guests to the right. Sam went to the left.

"There's a restaurant here?" Claire asked, not seeing a sign.

"Actually," Dave answered, "this is my uncle's place. He owns the building and lives in the penthouse suite. I know how hard you're working on the investigation, and guessed that you'd want to be home early. So I asked Uncle Ron's chef to put something together for us. I hope that's okay."

"Hmm," Claire mused. "Getting me all dressed up, bringing me a perfect red rose, plying me with alcohol, and then bringing me back to you're uncle's bachelor pad in a limo. Now what should a young single girl from a small town read into *that*?"

"If it makes you feel safer," Dave said, "I can have Sam come up to chaperone."

With an impish grin, Claire said, "What makes you think *I'm* the one who needs to feel unsafe?"

In the elevator, Dave pushed a pass-card into a slot below the rows of buttons, and the elevator whisked them silently upward.

When the doors opened again, Claire was surprised to find that the elevator had taken them directly into a lavish penthouse apartment. As she stepped out into the living room, all she could muster was "Wow!" Even in the low light, Claire could see that the room was elegantly—and expensively—decorated, but it was arranged in a manner that did not try to compete with the spectacular view of the city lights in the distance.

"I'm told that there are few restaurants in the city that can match this view," Dave said.

"I believe it," Claire said as she moved toward the wall of glass that faced the city. "Is that a hot tub?" she asked, noticing steam rising from what looked like an arrangement of boulders on the balcony. "Wow, wouldn't that be nice at the end of a long day? Kick back in the bubbles, sip some wine, and watch the city lights. I have to admit that your uncle sure knows how to live—in spite of his Neanderthal philosophies."

When Dave slid the patio door open so they could step out onto the veranda, Claire was expecting to be struck by the cold, but it was just a little less warm than indoors. Looking up, she saw a series of glass tubes glowing a dull orange in the ceiling that covered the patio.

"UV heaters?" she asked. "My mother used to tell me all the time to close the doors because we weren't heating the outdoors. I guess your uncle *does*."

"That's new since my last visit," Dave said with a grin. "His latest girlfriend must not be a big fan of the cold."

Dipping her hand into the steaming water, Claire found that it was just the temperature that she liked her baths. For a brief, but very enjoyable moment, Claire pictured the two of them sitting in the steaming water, looking out at the glimmering city below. She quickly reminded herself, though, that this was a first date with someone who was not even an old friend—a man who had just shown up on her doorstep, so to speak.

Dave led Claire to the kitchen, and poured them each a glass of wine. As she sipped, he took the center-cut tenderloin from the broiler, and deftly sliced it in two. Placing the halves on separate plates, he drizzled them with Chateaubriand sauce, and then added several stalks of asparagus from the vegetable steamer.

The dining room table sat next to a picture window with an unobstructed view of the city sparkling in the night. In the distance, Claire could see the blinking light atop the Washington Monument.

As Dave refilled her wine glass, Claire said, "Three times I've had the opportunity to decline this dinner invitation, and three times, I almost did. I'm glad I listened to the voice, and accepted."

Dave looked at her in mild surprise.

"What?" Claire said, hoping that her confession hadn't offended him somehow. "It's not personal. It's just that I ..."

"You *listened to the voice*?" Dave interrupted her.

Claire felt a bit embarrassed. "That probably seems a little flaky, huh?"

"Not at all! I can't believe you used that phrase. '*Listen to the voice*' became my mantra when I was in the Marines. I firmly believe that my *voice* kept me alive more than a few times. Most of the guys in my outfit became believers, too."

As they swapped *voice* stories, Claire couldn't help but wonder if *voices* did more than just warn of danger. If they might have matchmaking abilities, for instance.

Claire was about half way through her melt-in-the-mouth Chateaubriand when her cell phone started ringing inside her purse on the table in the foyer.

Her first instinct was to ignore it and let it whoever it was leave a message. Then, setting down her knife and fork, she said, "The *voice* says to answer it."

"I can't argue with that," Dave said with a smile. "I'll get the coffee while you take your call."

"Claire Bradley," she answered, not recognizing the number.

"Agent Bradley, this is Bob Palmer with the NSA—we spoke yesterday regarding those encrypted e-mails."

"Yes, Bob. I remember." Claire wondered if this was about her talking to Kevin Mathews about the decoding process earlier in the day. Turf wars and chains-of-command were a part of the Washington bureaucracy that Claire detested.

"I hate to bother you at this time of night," he said, "but Agent Levine didn't answer, and you were the next person on my list."

Suddenly, Claire knew that this had nothing to do with her talking to Kevin, and her pulse quickened.

"That's okay, Bob. What's up?"

"Again, I hate to interrupt your evening, Agent Bradley, but I think we have a pretty major development. Is there any way that you can drive out here to Fort Meade tonight?"

"I take it you don't want to talk about it over the phone?" she said.

"Absolutely not," he replied without hesitation.

"Okay," she said. "But it's going to take me a while to get there. I'm on the wrong side of the city, right now."

"We'll be here," he said, and hung up before Claire could ask who "we" was.

With seriously conflicting emotions, Claire walked back into the dining room, where Dave had just finished pouring two cups of coffee. "I truly hate to do this, Dave, but I have to go. Something's come up in the investigation."

"I understand completely," he said. "Like you said this afternoon, business before pleasure. Can I get Sam to drop you somewhere? You need to go back to the office?"

"Actually, I need to go out to Fort Meade, so I better drive myself. But if you could have her drop me back at my apartment ..."

Dave was already on the phone, calling Sam.

Twenty minutes later Dave climbed the stairs to Claire's door with her, unlocked it and pushed it opened. She stepped inside and as he handed her the key, she took his hand and drew him inside, as well.

He put his arms around her waist, and she looked up into his face. "I had a wonderful time, Dave," she said, smiling. "Thank you, so much. I'm sorry it had to end early, but I really ..."

"Hey, I'm a cop, too," he interrupted, "I know the drill."

He leaned down, and as she closed her eyes, he placed the gentlest of kisses against her lips.

In spite of the lightness of his kiss—or perhaps because of it—electricity streaked through Claire's body in every imaginable direction, but with *very* definite focal points. She was suddenly aware of erogenous zones that she had only read about in Cosmo.

He broke the kiss and took in the beauty of her smiling face. "Thank you, Claire," he said. "This evening was worth every day that I've waited since high school. Is it okay if I call you again?"

"You'd better!" she said with a grin, "or my *voice* will be having a talk with your *voice*!"

Closing the door behind him, Claire leaned against it and wondered where the night might have gone if she hadn't gotten that call from Bob Palmer.

Chapter 36

Thirty minutes after trading her little black dress for her usual dark slacks, white blouse, and navy windbreaker, and driving north for almost an hour, Claire arrived at the entrance to Fort Meade in Maryland. Another ten minutes, and she was in Bob Palmer's outer office.

Waiting there were two men that Claire did not recognize. "Bob Palmer?" she asked, looking back and forth between them.

"No, ma'am," the larger of the two said. "I'm Kevin Mathews. We spoke earlier today. And this is Craig Landry. He's the data recovery tech that's been working on the hard-drive. Craig is the one who found that source-code we were talking about."

"Nice work," Claire said, "both of you."

Kevin showed Claire into Palmer's office, and he came around his desk to shake her hand. "Thank you for coming, Agent Bradley. I'm sure you'd rather be home in bed at this hour."

She let the irony of his statement pass, having shifted gears back to investigation-mode during the drive. "I'm sure you wouldn't have asked me to come up if it wasn't important," she said.

"I assume that you've read Mr. Landry's report on the contents of the hard-drive from the Newburyport computer," Palmer said, motioning everyone to a small round conference table.

"Yes," she said, having seen it posted earlier in the afternoon. "And I have a couple of thoughts on it. The report talks about a self-executing program that deleted some, but not all of the files. I think that its being there proves that the Hezbollah messages are a ruse—a smokescreen."

"That's pretty much the same conclusion we'd come to, as well," Palmer said. "If the computer was meant to be melted down, why go to the bother of deleting files at all? And if deleting files was a back-up in case the fire-bomb didn't go off for some reason—as it didn't—then why not just clean the entire drives? Why be selective?"

"Exactly!" Claire said, pleased that she wasn't going to have to debate her conclusions. "So, is there a way to reconstruct those deleted files," she asked, "to try to figure out what they *didn't* want us to know while they were spoon-feeding us horse-poop about Hezbollah?" Then, suddenly, it all clicked. "Oh," she said hopefully, "tell me that's why you called me out here! Please!"

"Well, it's one of those good news, bad news things," Palmer said. "We—Craig that is—*was* able to reconstruct a partially deleted file. Unfortunately, only one."

As Palmer reached for a folder on his desk, Craig explained that the file he had reconstructed was a picture file—a type referred to as a "J-peg". He went on to tell her that when a J-peg picture file was reconstructed, but with some of its information either missing or filled with null-data from being overwritten, the result was like abstract art.

The top of the image—15 or 20%—might be perfectly normal, and then the center of the image might shift to the side, with the left side of the image looking like it was wrapping around and coming back into view on the right side. Below that, the image might be aligned properly, but have its colors altered.

The good news, Craig explained, was that you could generally make out what the original image had been, despite the distortions.

Palmer handed Claire the folder and she flipped it open. Though the image was indeed rearranged into the abstract format that Craig had described, there was no doubt that she was looking at a photo of Katherine McClure.

"Jesus!" she said looking up at Palmer, "Does this mean that the First Lady was the real target all along?"

"Taken with some other things that the self-executing program did and didn't do," Palmer answered, "we're pretty sure, now, that she was. We also believe that the image of the President that was found running on the aiming program when the computer was discovered, was as much of a smokescreen as the Hezbollah messages."

"What other things did the self-executing program do and not do?" Claire asked excitedly.

"Well, one of the significant things that it *didn't* do," Craig said, "was to delete any of the J-pegs of the President from the disk. I think we were supposed to find those."

"And the main thing that it *did* to support this theory," Palmer added, "was to send a file named 'Pres.ddd'—which is the 3-D image of the President—to the aiming software. The kicker is that according to the computer's event log, it did that *after* the shot had already been fired. We don't know for sure what 3-D image was in the aiming software before it was overwritten by Pres.ddd, but that it was an image of the First Lady doesn't seem like too much of a stretch to me."

"There's something else to support the theory," Claire said. "I had the FBI lab calculate the time-of-flight for the rocket bullet that the gun fired, and at its subsonic speed, it took over ten-seconds to get from the gun to the First Lady. When I first heard that the shot had come from two-miles away, the time-of-flight thing began to bother me. How can a sniper hope to hit a walking target when it's going to take ten-seconds for his bullet to get there after he squeezes the trigger? The fact that Mrs. McClure was sitting in a chair, right out in the open, makes much more sense. I think you've hit it right on the head; Katherine McClure was the target all along."

Saying that out loud triggered something, and she quickly reached for her cell phone.

"Aaron," she said, when Powell answered, "this is Claire. Where are you?"

"I'm in the hospital lobby, checking IDs with Harrison," he said, picking up on the urgency in her voice. "What's up?"

"Aaron, I'm up at the NSA," she said as she stepped away to Palmer's outer office, "and we just figured out that Katherine was the real target all along. You need to jump her security up to level three, right away."

"Jesus!" he replied. "Do you know who? —or why?"

"Nope," she answered. "Neither one. Aaron, I've had a nagging thought in my head that she might have been the real target almost from when she got shot, but I just couldn't think of a reason why someone would conspire to kill *her*. I mean, if some nut runs up and takes a shot at her because they don't like her stand on environmental issues, or feminism, or something, that's one thing. But this is a well thought out, well financed conspiracy to assassinate her. What the hell for? Nobody could hate her that much. It has to be for a reason! But who gains by her being dead?"

Claire realized that she was running on, but this had been bottled up for a while now.

"I'm getting into the elevator, right now," Powell said. "If I lose you, I'll call you back, but you know, the thought of her being the real target crossed my mind, too. And I wouldn't rule out that hate thing too quickly. Hate can be a damned powerful motivator, whether the reason is real or imagined. People strap dynamite to their bodies and blow themselves up on buses with little more reason than hate."

"Yeah, I've thought about that," Claire said, "Could it be just a universal I-hate-America thing? Some misguided attempt to throw the country into turmoil? Screw up the election?"

"Hey, that's another angle," he replied. "What if they figured the trauma of his wife's death would make McClure drop out? Maybe out of fear for his daughter's life."

"No way," Claire replied having already thought of and dismissed that notion. "If they know anything about Richard McClure, they'd know better than that. He'd dedicate everything he did in his next four years to her memory, and he would be relentless in getting what he wanted. Killing her would have exactly the opposite effect from keeping him out of office. First, he'd be a shoo-in to win because of the sympathy vote, and then he'd be the most fiercely dedicated president, probably in history. No. Killing her puts McClure *back* in the White House. It doesn't keep him out."

There was simultaneous silence on both ends of the phone as the significance of that last statement sunk in.

"Holy crap!" Claire said softly. "Could that be it? Someone who actually wants McClure *in* the White House, is willing to kill his wife to make sure it happens?" Then second-guessing herself she said, "I don't know, though. It sounds too much like a plot from *Mission: Impossible.* You'd have to put an awful lot of faith in how the American public would react."

"Well, if that *is* the reason somebody tried to kill her," Powell said, "their faith in the American public was well placed. The President's numbers took off right after the shooting, and haven't come down since. It's an interesting hypothesis."

"I wonder what McPherson's political affiliations are," she said almost to herself.

"Hey, I gotta go, Claire," Powell said, "I'm at the ICU, and I've got some calls to make—agents to wake up."

Next, Claire speed-dialed Paul Levine, but he was apparently on his phone, and the call went right into voicemail. She decided to try him again later, and called Gants, who answered on the first ring. In the background she could hear the whoop of police sirens.

"What's going on?" she asked.

"We're on our way to a house in Seabrook, New Hampshire that Dunham was apparently calling on a regular basis from the hospital," Gants answered. "It's a rental—rented to a guy named Lawrence Douglas. We don't know what the connection is yet, but it has to be more than casual. I'm thinking coconspirator."

"When did all this happen?" Claire said. "I didn't see anything about a New Hampshire house on the database."

"This morning. Right after I talked with you and Powell," Gants answered. "I got a call from the hospital administrator at the St. Jacques, and then went right to work on a search warrant, before flying up here. I've been working it, so I haven't had time to get it posted, yet."

"That's great!" Claire said. "We're finally finding the cracks in the wall. And here's another big one. I'm up at the NSA in Maryland right now, and they just pulled enough pieces off the computer disk to make a pretty strong case that Katherine was the intended target all along."

"Did you tell them at the hospital?" he said immediately. "They need to get her security detail upgraded!" Then more to himself than to her, he said, "Damn it! I should have stayed in DC!"

"Don't worry, sir. I called Powell right away, and he's jumping the detail up to level three," she replied. "I haven't called the President, yet, but I'm sure he'll will want to know, right away. Do you want me to call him, or do you want to do that?"

"I'll do it," Gants told her. "What did Levine say?"

"He doesn't know yet," she replied. "I think he was on his phone when I tried to call him. I'll try him again, right after this."

"Anything on *why* she was the target?"

"Nothing on the computer, if that's what you mean. Plain old anti-American hate leaps to mind, but it's possible that somebody wanted to manipulate the election, too."

"You mean trying to get the President to drop out?" Gants replied. "Why not just shoot *him* then?"

"I'm thinking maybe it was to get him *elected*," Claire said, and briefly outlined her hypothesis, presenting what skimpy support she had for it.

"Well, I certainly wouldn't rule it out at this point," Gants said thoughtfully. "I wouldn't rule *anything* out after what you just told me about Katherine being the target. Look into it, but let's not put too many eggs in the basket, okay? It seems like a stretch." There was a little pause and he said, "Okay, I'll let you go, now. Good work, Claire—and good luck."

"Good luck to you too, sir," she replied. "And don't worry about Mrs. McClure, sir. She's in good hands."

When she called Levine back, she explained what they had found up at the NSA, and that she had already contacted Powell and Gants.

"I'm thinking we should have a press briefing on this, ASAP," Claire said. "Like tonight. This needs to get posted and sent out to all the agencies, but as we've seen, once it hits the database, the media may not be far behind. I'd prefer that they get it directly from the horse's mouth, this time, rather than taking the chance of looking like the other end of the horse, like we did with the Hezbollah leak."

When she hung up with Paul, Claire called the media office at the Secret Service. After mentally calculating the time to get back into the city and putting some notes together, she had the media office announce that they would have a special briefing at eleven-fifteen. Just in time to catch the end of the nightly news.

Returning to Palmer's office, she waited a moment for him to end the call he was on, and then explained that she had decided to have a special news briefing to announce the NSA's discovery, and that she had to get back to DC right away.

"I'll walk you out," Palmer said as Claire picked up her purse.

They walked from his office through the corridor and into the lobby in silence. Claire was sure there was something that he wanted to say, but he seemed to be having second thoughts.

At the front door he stepped outside with her and said, "I don't know if you'll want to add this to what you're going to talk about in your briefing later on, but I just got off the phone with the FBI, and it seems that my office assistant, a young man named Peter Sewell, just admitted to being the one who leaked the Hezbollah e-mail information to CNN. Well, not to CNN directly, but to somebody who then passed it on to them. The Bureau's been talking with him all day." Palmer looked Claire in the eyes with a downtrodden expression, and said, "Pretty embarrassing, huh? Sure makes *my* security instincts look good."

She thought for a moment before answering, "I don't think I'll use that tonight. Once I tell them that the Hezbollah messages were a red-herring, knowing who leaked the information becomes anti-climactic. You and your team did a great job flushing out the information about Mrs. McClure—that'll be plenty for the eleven o'clock news."

Claire sat in creeping bumper-to-bumper traffic as four lanes of traffic merged into one to squeeze past a roll-over accident on the beltway. She hadn't calculated this into her travel plan to get back to the office, and she wondered if she was going to make her 11:15 schedule. The only saving grace was that the slow going allowed her to think and to make some notes into her voice recorder about what she wanted to say.

The lights of the fire trucks and the police cars were finally in sight when Claire's cell phone rang. The display showed that the caller's ID was blocked, so she answered with a simple, "Hello."

"Agent Bradley?" a man's voice asked.

"Yes. What can I do for you, Mr. … ?"

"You can stop pretending you're something you're not," the caller said.

"Excuse me?"

"You're no hero, Agent Bradley. All you did is what you're paid to do, and you didn't do *that* very well. The American people have to be the stupidest group on the face of the earth to put *you* on a pedestal."

The blunt insult caught Claire off guard, but she recovered immediately. "May I ask who's calling?" she said.

"No, you may not. You may listen to what I have to say, because it might save your life."

The man didn't sound angry, but he sure sounded serious.

"If you know what's good for you, you'll stop trying to find Frankie Dunham. She's the real hero in all this; she's trying to save the country from that nincompoop, while you're grandstanding on television like you're some kind of Sherlock Holmes. Well, trust me; you don't know what you're talking about. You don't know anything."

"For what it's worth, sir, I think you're right," Claire said, forcing herself to stay composed, and non-confrontational. She had no way of knowing if this guy was just a nut who thought that Richard McClure was unfit to be president, so was empathizing with Dunham, or if he really did know Dunham—or who she really was—and something about the plot. "I don't consider myself a hero, either. I was just doing my job, the best I could. I wish I could have done it better. And I agree that we don't know much of what's going on. I'd be happy to

184

have you explain it to me, if you would. Why did Frankie Dunham want to kill the President? And where did she get that curious gun?" She was hoping the caller would correct her about the attempt being on the President. It would lend a great deal of credence to whatever he said.

There was a long pause on the other end. Apparently, the man wasn't expecting to have Claire agree with him or talk to him like they were sitting in a bar, chatting over a beer. Finally, he said, "You wouldn't understand if I explained, so I'll just tell you again, to lay off of Frankie if you know what's good for you. You don't know who you're dealing with here." With that, the line went dead.

Claire sat there for a moment pondering how seriously to take the call. There was no substance, to speak of, but it didn't feel like a crank call, either. And she wondered where he had gotten her cell phone number. As she was finally passing the accident, she made a call to the IT department at the Secret Service headquarters, through which all of the Service cell phones had their calls routed. "Hi. This is Claire Bradley," and she rattled off her security code. "I just took a call from a man who wouldn't leave his name, and his caller ID was blocked. Can you run a trace on it for me?"

"You want to hold, or do you want me to e-mail it to you?"

"How long will it take?"

"About thirty seconds."

"I think I can hold."

Twenty seconds later, the young-sounding tech recited the phone number to her.

"I don't recognize the number or even the area code," Claire said. "Can you pull up a name?"

"The 603 area code is for New Hampshire. The number is a land-line listed to a Lawrence M. Douglas. You want a street address?"

Claire's heart skipped a beat and she nearly dropped her phone. "Yes. And thanks a lot!"

She immediately called Gants, who was already inside Douglas' house. "Crap! You must have just missed him!" she said when Gants told her that the house was empty. She told him about the call, and that IT said it had come from the phone line in that house.

"We've been here for fifteen minutes Claire. If you just got off the phone with this guy, he didn't make the call from here." Gants covered his phone, but Claire could still hear him ask loudly, "Any of you guys see a phone in the house?" She could hear someone talking to Gants, but she couldn't make out the words. When he came back on the line, Gants said, "Mystery solved. One of the techs here just pointed out that the computer in the den is hooked up to both an Internet cable and a regular telephone line. He's checking, but your friend probably called into the computer over the Internet—which he could do from anywhere—resent the call, and made it look like it originated here. Obviously, he doesn't care that we found this place. He had to have known he'd be handing us the address when he called you."

"Damn!" Claire said. "I was hoping he was technology-challenged enough to think that blocking his caller ID made the call untraceable. That just gives us another loose end. Damn it!"

"As soon as the sun comes up, we'll see if we can get a description of Douglas from the neighbors," Gants said. "In the meantime, why don't you call Research, and see what they have on him, so far?"

Claire dialed the number for the Research Department, but she didn't hold out much hope. If he gave it up that easily, she had to believe that Douglas' ID was stolen, just like Dunham's had been.

It was eleven o'clock when Claire squealed into the parking lot at the Secret Service headquarters.

She dashed directly to the media room, where, waiting in the wings, she caught her breath, took her voice-recorder from her purse, and pressed "play."

"Five minutes, Miss Bradley," a tech wearing headphones said to her. "Will you be ready? I can push it out a few, if you need it."

"No, no. I'll be fine," she said optimistically.

Many of the voice-notes she'd made during her drive back were disjointed fragments of sentences simply meant to jog her memory, so she began scribbling in her notebook the complete sentences she would need in a few minutes' time.

At eleven-fifteen on the dot, Claire began her briefing. "I have three announcements regarding the investigation, which we believe are important enough to warrant the unusually late scheduling of this briefing," she told the assembled press corps. "Some of this is, literally, breaking news, so I'm not going to be able to give you a lot of background on it. I also won't be able to take questions after the statements. Rather, we have people working on a press package right now, and as soon as that's available we'll get it out to you.

"The first piece of information," she went on, "regards Frances

Dunham. We now know that that is not the real name of the person-of-interest from the St. Jacques Hospital. The identity was stolen from a woman living in Ohio, whom we have cleared of any involvement. This makes the search for the woman from the hospital much more difficult, but I am confident that with the public's help we can locate her." In fact, Claire felt no such confidence.

"The second item concerns the encrypted messages which were recovered from the computer that was attached to the gun discovered in the hospital. These are the so-called 'Hezbollah-connection' messages that were leaked to CNN and reported on this morning. Further analysis of the computer's hard-drive by the NSA, has lead us to the conclusion that those messages were *planted* on the computer with the intent to mislead this investigation.

"The third announcement is based, in part, on that same excellent analysis work done by the NSA up at Fort Meade and supported by ballistics simulations performed by the FBI lab in Quantico. With 99% certainty, we have determined that First Lady, Katherine McClure—and *not* the President—was the intended target of this assassination plot. Accordingly, steps have been taken to increase her security beyond the high level already in place."

With that Claire closed her notebook and said, "I know that you all have a hundred questions about this, and so do we. Unfortunately, there's nothing more I can give you right now. As I said, when we get more information on these topics we'll pass it along as quickly as practical. Thank you, and good night."

A barrage of questions followed Claire off the stage. "Is the First Daughter in danger?" "What motive have you determined for wanting to kill the First Lady?" "How can you be so sure that Hezbollah is not involved?" "What did the President say when he was told?" "Was the timing of this Hezbollah-statement dictated by Senator Evans' statement earlier this evening? —isn't that using the task force for politics?"

Paul Levine was standing just off stage, and Claire had to ask him what the last question, about an Evans statement, was all about.

"Oh, Evans released a typical slam at the President's foreign policies," he told her, "with a specific dig at his Middle East diplomacy. The interesting part is that Evans said he was going to set up a special commission to investigate the connection that you just stated didn't exist. The reporters probably don't believe that it was coincidence that the messages being a hoax was announced *after* Evans' statement, and *before* McClure's rebuttal. Some reporters see ulterior-motives in everything.

Don't worry about it. Diane Stevens can take it from here, that's what she gets paid to do."

It was nearly midnight when Claire finally pulled out of the parking lot and headed for home. Not wanting to be caught out of the loop again, as she had by not having heard Evans' earlier statement, she switched on her radio in time to catch the news at the top of the hour.

She heard the tail end of the announcement she had made less than an hour before, followed by the anchorperson paraphrasing her statements and analyzing the timing of the news conference and its political significance. Then there was the issue of her not taking questions. Blah, blah, blah.

Claire tuned the commentator's voice out as she thought about Katherine. She wondered if *she* had any idea who might wish her harm. The jingle for a beer commercial started playing, and Claire reached over and turned off the radio. She considered driving over to the hospital, to personally check on Katherine's security, but she had complete confidence in Powell, and besides, the First Lady was really not her assignment, any more. She would also have liked to just talk with Katherine, but if she wasn't asleep at this time of night, she should be. She made a mental note to call her, first thing in the morning.

*****

In Orlando, Frank was just pulling into his motel parking lot. Although it was highly unlikely that Bradley and her task force would be able to trace the call he had made to her an hour ago back to its true origin in Florida, in anything short of a week, Frank wasn't still alive because he depended on the unlikely not happening. If it was even remotely possible, he took precautions. In this case, the precaution had been to drive an hour east to Cocoa Beach to make the call as Larry Douglas. If they got lucky in tracing the call, they might be in the right state, but would be looking in the wrong city. And Frank had already disposed of the cell phone he'd used, so even if they opened a real-time trace on it, it would do them no good. If he decided to contact Bradley again; if he thought she needed more prodding, it would probably be through her personal e-mail, just to keep her off balance.

He sat in his rental car listening to the end of the headline news. So, now they knew that the President wasn't the real target, and that the Hezbollah e-mails were meant to be found. They were making good progress with the investigation. But there was nothing to indicate that he should change his exit plan.

Chapter 37

Thursday, October 23
Washington, DC

Thursday morning dawned cold and rainy, and Claire was glad that she had no appointments outside the office all day—at least not yet anyway. As bad as the traffic was in the city, it got twice as bad when it rained. If the rain turned to snow ... well, that was something that people in DC preferred not to think about.

On her drive in, she listened to the news again, and was surprised to hear a statement from the President. It wasn't even seven o'clock, yet. He and Diane must have been up into the wee hours to have it ready for release for the morning commute news.

"The President, this morning, released a strongly-worded statement," the news anchor said, "aimed squarely at yesterday's criticism by Senator Evans of his foreign policy. In his statement, President McClure took the Senator to task for what he referred to as 'jumping to conclusions.'" They then played the relevant excerpt from the President's recorded announcement.

"Perhaps the most important thing that whoever is sitting in the White House must be able to do," McClure said, "is to refrain from jumping to conclusions. When you command the most powerful military force that the world has ever known, you had better be sure of your facts before acting or even speaking. I would like to thank the dedicated folks up at the NSA as well as the FBI and every member of the task force who had a hand in defusing this disturbing piece of disinformation in such a timely manner.

"And while the news about Katherine shocked me and sickens me, I also want to thank the same folks for exposing last Saturday's assassination attempt as an attempt not on my life, but on the life of a selflessly dedicated wife and mother, and a tireless ambassador and icon of all that is great about this country. I can only hope that they will be as swift and successful in apprehending the perpetrators of this outrageous act, and in determining a motive, which to me, right now, is completely unfathomable.'"

From her office, Claire called the First Lady, and was happy to hear that she was feeling well and getting better, although she was as baffled as everyone that she was the real target, all along. After hanging up, Claire went through her e-mail and message-checking routines, and then checked the database for new postings.

Later, after her routine tasks were completed, she went to her whiteboard, and erased the bottom half, where she had made notes about the computer and the thermite bomb. She felt that those issues were pretty well put to bed, and she needed the room.

In the newly cleared space, she wrote:

TARGET: KATHERINE McCLURE
MOTIVE:
        PERSONAL GAIN
        REVENGE
        POLITICAL GAIN
        HATE
        FANATIC

She was just considering what to write beside each of the headings, when Aaron Powell walked into her office.

"This is a surprise," she said looking at her watch. "What are you doing here?"

"I'm working the six p.m. to six a.m. detail at the hospital," he said as he scanned Claire's whiteboard. "So, I thought I'd pop by and see how things are progressing in mission control. Whatcha got here?" he asked.

"Highlights of the case," she answered. "I'm waiting for something to jump out at me that I'm overlooking. But help me fill some blanks about motive, will you? If we can figure out *why* somebody wanted Mrs. M. dead, it might point to who they are. Throw out some ideas with me."

After ten minutes of no-holds-barred brainstorming, where nothing was too far fetched to write down, they had added a number of possible motives—however outlandish they might be—to each category.

PERSONAL GAIN; Insurance: Notoriety
REVENGE: Fired employee: Other woman: Jilted lover: Jealousy: Bad business deal
POLITICAL GAIN: Sway election: Screw-up President mentally: Disrupt election
HATE: Terrorists: Anti-Semitics
FANATIC: Religious: Anti-Feminism: Pro-Life

Powell and Claire began going back through the list assessing each point and eliminating the highly-unlikely motives. Rather than erase them, however, Claire simply drew a line through them, just in case they wanted to resurrect a discarded motive if new information surfaced.

The sole beneficiary of Katherine's million-dollar life insurance policy was a trust set up for her daughter Melissa. There was a second policy for $50,000 but it was to be used specifically for her funeral expenses with any excess going to a charity that Katherine had named. Claire drew a line through *Insurance*, and tapped the board next to *Notoriety*.

"Since no one's jumped up to claim responsibility," Claire said, drawing a line through the word, "that's probably not a factor."

Next she pointed to *Fired employee*.

"*That* could be an interesting list," Powell said.

"I'll get Research going on a list of all past employees right after we're done here," Claire said.

With very little discussion, Claire was able to draw a line through *Other woman, Jilted lover*, and *Jealousy*. If either Richard or Katherine had been having an affair during the past four years, their respective security details would have to, at least, *suspect* it. They would, unquestionably, be discreet about it, as they had with Jack Kennedy and Bill Clinton, but it would be known among the agents.

Claire and Powell knew that the McClures had various business investments, all of which were being handled by a trust during Richard's time in office, but they knew little about them. Was it possible that there had been a dealing so horrific that it could drive someone to want to kill Katherine. That was another assignment she'd give to Research.

They had just started to talk about Claire's pet motive—swaying the election—when her desk phone buzzed. Margaret announced that Mr. Gants was on the line.

On speaker, Gants filled Claire and Powell in on the status of the investigation at the Seabrook house, and Larry Douglas.

"Research has traced Douglas to an address in Boston, and we have agents on the way there, right now. Based on how easily we were able to locate him, though, I'm putting my money on another stolen identity. We have a trace going on the call that came into the computer and went back out to you, Claire, but that's going to take a little time. And if this guy is good with computers, and it appears he is, he could have routed it through a bunch of hijacked systems anywhere in the world. We may never know where the call originated."

"I hope there's going to be a *but-the-good-news-is* coming up here, pretty quickly," Claire said.

"Actually, there is," Gants said. "It appears that the place in Seabrook was used as a workshop for putting together the computer we took out of the hospital, and the gun, too. The FBI lab has already taken a look at the hard drive from the Seabrook computer, and they say it's a virtual clone of the hospital drive. We also recovered some tools that would fit with having assembled the motorized system that aimed the gun. And get this; one of the local cops who came out here with us noticed that a big limb had recently been cut off an elm in the back yard. Then he noticed that other trees behind the house—that weren't even on the property—had been trimmed, too. Well, it turns out that if you stand in the back bedroom and look out of the east-facing window, there had been about a dozen trees trimmed all in a line that gave a clear view to an old barn ... two miles away."

"The distance from the hospital to the stage!" Claire said.

"Yup," Gants confirmed. "And when we went out there, we found some imbedded fragments of what looks to be ceramic in the side of the barn. The FBI is checking to see if it's consistent with what was taken out of Mrs. McClure, but I'm betting that was how they sighted in the whole aiming system. And because the gun is nearly silent, they could do it in the middle of a residential neighborhood, and nobody would know."

"Do you recall what the local cop's name was, by any chance?" Claire said.

"He was a New Hampshire State Trooper, named Jackson. Why?"

"Oh, just a random thought. If you told me it was Dave Perkins, I was going to have to rearrange my whiteboard, again." *And my ability to read people*, she added to herself.

Gants laughed. "Yeah, that would be a bit hard to chalk up to coincidence."

"Anything else from the house? Prints or trace-evidence?" Powell asked.

"The place was surprisingly clean as far as trace evidence goes," Gants replied. "Obviously, it had been wiped down before they left. They dusted the silverware, the tools they left, even what they left in the refrigerator. All clean. Then they got lucky ... in the bathroom. On the underside of the toilet seat, they lifted a good partial of what is probably the right index finger. Apparently, they wiped the top of the seat, but forgot the bottom. Depending on whether it was left when the seat was being lowered or lifted it could be either Dunham's or Douglas'."

"If Douglas was any kind of gentleman," Claire commented, a bit tongue-in-cheek, "he'd have lowered the seat when he was done, so the lady wouldn't have to touch it."

"Whatever," Powell said, rolling his eyes. "Anything else?" he asked Gants.

"We're hoping so," he replied, "but it's a long shot. One of the items they left behind was a paper shredder. It's one of those cross-cut jobs that chews the paper into about a million one-inch strips a quarter-inch wide. It's a pretty cheap model, and it looks like that's worked in our favor. The guys in the mobile lab were able to pull out a half-dozen of those strips that were jammed up inside the cutters. They didn't fall through into the basket like they're supposed to, so even though Dunham and Douglas had emptied the basket, they left a few shreds behind. The lab guys explained to me that cross-cut shredders are designed to cut the strips with the long direction up and down, so when you feed in a sheet of paper the long way, the strips will show one or two letters from several sentences that were one-above-the-other on a page. That way, individual strips don't make any sense; don't show complete words.

"But, guess what happens if you fold a piece of paper in half across its middle, and then feed it in the long way? The paper is sideways, now, so the little strips are in the same direction as the words! And rather than getting meaningless one-above-the-other letter sets on the scraps, you get strings of letters or whole words. Well, a few of the scraps they pulled out were cut that way. One had the letters 'ew sched' on it. "We're guessing that was 'new schedule' before it was chopped up. Another read 'ent in f.' We're not sure what that might mean, yet."

"Payment in full?" Claire guessed, being very good at word games.

"That's a possibility," Gants acknowledged. "But it could also be 'went in first,' 'dent in fender,' 'sent in funds,' or a couple dozen other things. The third scrap has a number on it: 97057991. The lab tech said it looked like there was something printed directly before and after the number—not blank spaces—so this is probably just a piece of a longer number."

"Could it be a phone number?" asked Powell.

"It could be," Gants answered. "But it could also be part of a bank account number, a serial number from something, or it could even be part of an encryption code. The NSA is going to try it on those unbroken messages. It could also be a piece of a simple numerically-coded message, or about a hundred other things. We'll just have to see what, if anything, we can flush out of it."

"Well, I'll let you get back to work," Gants said. "I just thought you'd want to hear this in case you want to use any of it in your briefing, today. I'll get it into the database as soon as I get to the office."

After Powell left, Claire went to her whiteboard, and wrote the shredder number up near the top. She puzzled over it for a while, then gave up trying to guess its significance, if there was any. The Research group was far better equipped to figure that out than she was.

Shortly after she got back from lunch, Claire got a call from Cynthia Caan. Although she had a court order as back-up, Roger McPherson's plastic surgeon had cooperated fully as soon as Caan explained why they were looking for his patient. The doctor had given agents from the local Miami field office a current address for McPherson, who was now going by the name Kelli Morrison, and living in California. He had also supplied an "after" photograph of the transformed McPherson.

"McPherson makes a good looking woman," Claire had to admit after she had pulled the photo up on her computer.

Cynthia agreed and added, "It doesn't look like she's involved at all from what we've come up with so far. She's working as a waitress in Santa Monica, California, lives in Culver City, hasn't traveled much since getting there a year ago, and has no record of unusual long distance calls from her house phone or her cell. None at all to the east coast."

"Have you talked with her yet?" Claire asked.

"Yeah, first thing this morning, her time," Cynthia replied. "The LA field office went to her house, and she agreed to a teleconference interview with us back here.

"She says she had forgotten all about the gun until she saw it on TV. She told us that she had just put that whole life out of her mind—like it was somebody else. I asked her about Charles Townsend, and showed her his CIA photo over the video link. She said she remembered him, and that her boss at Dynametric had told her to bring him up to speed on how the gun had operated. She claims that that was the only contact she ever had with him."

"You believe her?" Claire asked.

"No reason not to, so far," Cynthia replied. "My gut says she's being straight with us, and the polygraph guys have gone over the audio and video, and they don't see any deception flags. I hate to say it, but I think McPherson is a dead end."

"How about her boss? The one that told her to educate Townsend," Claire asked.

"Name's Travis Westbrook," Cynthia told her. "We've talked with him before. Nothing jumped out then, and his account of delivering the gun is pretty much the same as McPherson's. We'll talk to him again, but I doubt that he's involved."

"Well, thanks for calling and letting me know, Cynthia," Claire said, the disappointment obvious in her voice.

"Don't worry," Cynthia said. "We're just getting started. This will come together. You'll see."

When she hung up, Claire went over to the board and changed Roger McPherson's line to read, "a.k.a. Kelli Morrison: transgender female (cooperative lead)."

Scanning the board a couple of times while backing toward her chair, her eyes lingered on Walter Collins' name. She decided to give Dr. Whelk a call. Maybe the results were in from the DNA tests.

As she reached for the phone, it buzzed, and Margaret announced Dr. Whelk.

"I was just reaching for the phone to call you," Claire said after a warm hello.

"You must be psychic," he said. "The results of the DNA tests were just handed to me, and I have good news for you. They're a perfect match. The blood sample and the casting definitely came from the same individual."

"You're certain?" she asked, the disappointment obvious in her voice, yet again.

"Positive," he replied. "I thought you'd be happy."

"I was working on a faked-death angle, and this pretty much kills it," she explained. "I don't suppose you've run the profile through CODIS by any chance?"

CODIS stood for Combined DNA Index System, and was the central database created by the FBI for law enforcement use to store DNA profiles much the same way that they collected and stored fingerprints.

"I have," he said, "but it came up empty. When did you say this guy died? '99? Unless he had been a sex offender, or a pretty high-profile felon, his DNA wouldn't be there."

"Apparently, he was just an engineer who liked to sail, and got unlucky," Claire told him.

After thanking the doctor for pulling out all the stops for her wild goose chase, she hung up, went to the whiteboard, and erased Collins' name. Apparently, this just wasn't her day for theories, she thought. Suddenly, all the promising leads were fizzling.

Chapter 38

Thursday, October 23
Washington, DC

As Claire turned to look at her whiteboard again, the cell phone on her hip vibrated and she flipped it open. Noticing that the caller's number was blocked, she answered expectantly, "Hello. May I help you?" She was hoping that it was "Larry Douglas", again. Even though they had determined that that was a stolen identity, continued contact with him, whoever he was, could only be a good thing. Instead, she was surprised by a voice that she recognized.

"Hello, Angel," the caller said in a very good imitation of John Forsythe, the actor who provided the voice of "Charlie" on *Charlie's Angels*. "How is the investigation going? I hear that you've been looking for me."

"May I ask who's calling?" Claire asked suspiciously, though the voice, the angel reference, and "I hear that you've been looking for me" all clicked together. It had to be Charles Townsend!

"Call me Charlie" he replied still in the Forsythe voice. Then in his own voice—with a slight British accent—he said, "Charles Townsend at your service, Agent Bradley. How may I be of assistance?"

"Hello, Mr. Townsend," she said, still wary. "Yes, we do have some questions we'd like to ask you. Thank you for getting in touch. Without trying to sound ungrateful that you called, do you mind if I ask why you called *me*? I understand that your former contacts at the CIA have been trying to get in touch with you, and having little luck. They said that you'd dropped off the radar after your retirement. I expected something a lot more clandestine that a call to my cell phone."

"One of the keys to successful espionage/counterespionage is to never do what the other bloke expects you to do. Unless, of course, you *want* him to know what you're up to, in which case, he probably won't believe whatever he finds out, anyway. Ours is an odd business. But in answer to your question, the long and short of it is, I called you because I like you, Agent Bradley," he said. "I have a keen sense of people, and I've been watching you on the telly. From your debut as a superhero with that dive across the stage to protect the First Lady, through all of your media briefings. And I like what I see. You're gutsy, you're intelligent and you have integrity. There's substance to you, and that deserves to be protected—and rewarded.

"My reluctance to jump into the fray, straight away, is because I've tried to make a clean and complete break from that past life. In that business you are either in or you are out—there is no middle ground. And although, as you are obviously aware, I know some things about the gun in question, I was quite on the fence about sticking my head up and getting involved—at least in any *official* way. So I figured I'd contact you personally, give you what I can, and hope that you'll allow me to maintain a low profile."

"I'm flattered, Mr. Townsend," Claire replied, though the feeling was also a little spooky. It had somehow escaped her until just then that millions of people were seeing her every day and making personal judgments about her, feeling that they knew her. For Claire Bradley—whose circle of close friends was more like a triangle than a circle—that thought was a little unnerving.

"By *low profile*," Claire said, "I assume that you want this to be off the record then?"

"If you're asking if I'll testify to any of this," he said, "well, let's just see where it all leads, and we'll work that out when the time comes. It's not like you're going to just take my word for any of this, anyway. I fully expect you to verify everything I tell you through other sources. Frankly, I'd be sorely disappointed if you didn't. For all you know, I could be Frances Dunham disguising my voice and feeding you a load of crap."

"The thought had crossed my mind," Claire said bluntly, always particularly suspicious of getting help before it was asked for. "You do seem to be good with voices. How *do* I know you are who you say you are?"

"Ask me a question that only the real Townsend would know the answer to," he suggested. "I can give you my Agency ID number or fax you my driver's license, but I don't think that would convince you."

"Rattle off the number anyway," she said, trying to think of a better question.

Without hesitation he recited the number, and then added his mother's maiden name, and the name of his dog when he was a kid.

Claire had no idea if the names, or even his ID number, were correct or not. She had seen his data sheet, but she hadn't memorized it. And she certainly doubted that his mother's or his dog's names would be on it anyway. Then a thought struck her, and she quickly pulled up the report that Cynthia Caan had posted.

"When you picked up the gun at Dynametric back in '88," she said, "what make of station wagon were you and your partner driving?"

Townsend laughed. "That's cute, Angel" he said. "I wasn't working with a partner; the year was 1989; and I was driving a U-Haul rental truck. You don't actually have my agency file handy there, do you?"

"Nope," Claire replied honestly. "Was your dog's name really Beelzebub?"

"He was the biggest, friendliest Saint Bernard I've ever seen, but he had these spots on his belly, that if you looked at them just right they looked like a 6-6-6 marking. We were going to call him Satan, but he just looked more like a Beelzebub. We ended up calling him Bubba most of the time, anyway."

"Cute story," Claire said, still on her guard. "I'll have to check it out. So let's say you are the real Charles Townsend; how do I know you're not part of the conspiracy, and just calling to send us down the wrong path?"

"The simple answer is, you don't," he replied. "But even if you did trust me, you'd still verify everything I'm telling you, right? And I'm not going to tell you who-done-it, because I don't know. I'm just giving you what I believe is a good lead. It's up to you and your task force to turn it into evidence."

"Fair enough," she said. "So how should we do this? Do you mind if I ask you specific questions?"

"Ask away, Angel. I'll give you whatever I can."

"Okay. First of all, why are you only coming forward now? You of all people should know how important your information is to this investigation."

"As I've told you," he answered, "I've been trying to stay completely out of the game, so I planned to just watch from the sidelines, and see how the investigation went. It looked like you were doing pretty well until that Hezbollah stuff hit the papers. That's when I started thinking seriously about calling. Up until then, I figured you must already know everything that I know about the gun, so you really didn't need me. I figured you'd have access to all the CIA records about that operation. But apparently not, huh?"

"What operation is that?" she asked, her excitement about getting to the heart of the matter tempered by her instinctive skepticism.

"What I'm going to tell you is classified," he said, "but I'm sure that since you're allowed to stand next to the President with an automatic weapon under your coat, you have a high enough security rating to be hearing it. Besides, it's pretty old news. Nonetheless, if it ever comes down to it, I'll deny that you heard this from me. As I said, you need to verify this through other sources.

"You're young, but I assume that you remember, or at least read about the PanAm 747 that blew up over Lockerbie, Scotland in 1988," he began. "You probably studied it at the academy. Bloody good investigation. Well, right away, before the fires were put out, we—the CIA that is—got information from some usually-good sources in Iran that the Ayatollah and his towel-head buddies were behind it."

"Wait a minute," Claire said, her inconsistency-antennae on high-alert. "Didn't they convict some Libyan terrorists of that?"

"Yes, well, we didn't find out about *that* connection until much later," he replied with a hint of contrition in his voice. "Basically, we were hoodwinked by a group of Iranian revolutionaries who used the Lockerbie attack to get the CIA to support an overthrow plot that they were hatching. Like I said about this being an odd business.

"Anyway, Bush-the-elder had just been elected, and with him being former Director of the CIA and all, and given the fact that the Ayatollah had, as you Yanks say, been pissing in Reagan's corn flakes for the past eight years ... well, it didn't take much convincing by the Iranians to get us to lend a helping hand. In a meeting at Langley, on *how* to help, I suggested getting 'Johnny' out of mothballs at Dymo, and getting it to the revolutionaries—which I did."

Claire picked up on Townsend calling the gun, "Johnny". Not too many people would know that nickname, and she began to trust him a little more.

"As it turned out, their plot got discovered and about a dozen guys were executed," he continued. "They were beheaded for their blasphemy.

Fortunately, the gun had only made it into the country the day before, and the only guy who knew where it was stashed escaped the fate of his comrades. Wisely, he went so far underground after that, that I completely lost track of him—and by extension, the gun."

"So you lost the gun somewhere in Iran in 1989?" Claire summarized.

"Long-story-short, yes," he agreed.

"Did it ever surface again?" Claire asked. "Before last Saturday, I mean?"

"There was a captain in the Israeli Defense Force Intelligence Group that did some document-faking for me to help me smuggle the gun into Iran," Townsend said. "A couple of years later he told me that he had heard rumors that the Palestinians had come up with this rocket-firing super-rifle and that they were going to use it to assassinate Prime Minister Shamir. This was right after the Gulf War—the first one—and the Palestinians were pissed off that Sadam hadn't been able to suck Israel into the war and crush them like he said he would do.

"If the rumors were true, my Israeli friend suspected that it might be the same gun he'd helped me with, and he contacted me to get some particulars on it—what it looked like, how quickly it could be set up, its range, stuff like that—so they could be on the lookout for it. To my knowledge, neither the gun nor the plot to kill Shamir ever materialized."

"So, as far as you know," Claire paraphrased, "the Palestinians have had the gun and been sitting on it since 1991."

"Yes. Assuming, of course, that my IDF friend's information was correct back then," Townsend said. "That was a long time ago, of course, and things change pretty quickly over there. But there's a piece of evidence that you've generated on your own that corroborates that conclusion."

It took a second for Claire to get what he was talking about, but then it clicked. "The Hezbollah e-mails!" she exclaimed.

"Precisely. I think that was probably the turning point for me," Townsend said. "When I heard you categorically state that those e-mails were bogus, I decided you needed my help. Like I said, I like you—I don't want to see you crash and burn."

"I appreciate that, Mr. Townsend, I really do. I just wish you'd have called me a day earlier."

He laughed. "Hey, up until last night, it looked like you were doing pretty well on your own."

"So, who is this Israeli captain?" Claire asked. "Can you arrange for me to talk with him?"

"No," Townsend replied bluntly. "First off, that would be getting back into the game, which I won't do. Secondly, I know he'd never agree to talk to you. You're just going to have to take the information at face value and consider the source to be dead."

"Is he?"

"As far as you're concerned."

"Okay," Claire pressed, "how about if you leave me out of it? Just talk to him yourself. See if he knows anything else about the gun or where it might have gone?"

"Which part of '*I'm out of the game*' are you having trouble comprehending, Angel?"

"Oh, come on, Mr. Townsend," she said, not willing to let go of something so promising. "You spent twenty-odd years with your life on the line for your country, and now, all of a sudden, you don't care any more? I can't believe that one discreet call is going to plunge you back into the espionage business like you're some kind of recovering spy-aholic."

There was a moment's pause before he answered. "I'll think about it," he said, "but don't hold your breath. If he knew where the gun was at one time, and it slipped through his fingers to turn up later being fired at the President—or First Lady—of the United States, he's probably not going to want that getting around."

"I guess you've got a point," Claire agreed reluctantly. "But ask anyway, would you please? Maybe he'll feel like he's redeeming himself if he helps us out."

"With the things this guy has done in his career—the things we've *all* done," Townsend said, seriously, "redemption will have a much higher price than that. But that's not your concern, Angel. So, do you have any other questions for me?"

"One," Claire said. "Do you remember the name Roger McPherson?"

"Yeah," Townsend answered. "He's the engineer back at Dymo that showed me how the gun worked. Queer as a nine bob note."

"That's the rumor," she said, choosing to protect McPherson's new identity. "Was that your only contact with him?"

"That was it," he assured her. "If you're thinking that he had anything to do with getting the gun back somehow, and using it to shoot Katherine McClure, forget it. From the conversation we had, I could see he was about as violent as Gandhi. He was quite a paradox for an engineer who invented weapons."

"Well, if not McPherson then who? Any ideas? I understand that only he and one other now-deceased engineer knew how to set up the gun. Plus *you*, of course," she added with special emphasis.

"Of course," he repeated dryly, enjoying the verbal sparring with Claire. "Plus whoever in Dynametric wrote the operator's manual, plus whoever edited the manual, plus anyone who may have read the manual that was with the gun when it was delivered to Iran."

"Touché," Claire conceded. "But that doesn't narrow the field very much."

"Hey, it puts you in the right hemisphere, doesn't it? Have you gotten any input from your CIA people over there?"

"Nothing that I'm aware of," Claire admitted. "But I've been pretty focused on the domestic side of all this up until now. If they've been working on this, I haven't seen any reports yet."

"Oh, they've been working on it," Townsend said with a chuckle, "you can count on that. They're probably just playing it close to the vest and not putting out any status reports until they're sure of what they're hearing. We're always pretty skittish about burning sources on dead ends, and after that Hezbollah e-mail leak they wouldn't take any chances by posting information to your databank unless they have a pretty sure thing.

"You might want to see if you can talk directly with the station chief over there in Israel—face to face if possible. She might be a little more open talking to an individual than posting reports for God-knows-who to see. Her name is Avi Geller. She's as sharp and as tough as they come. She grew up in the Golan Heights. She did some undercover stuff over there, back when I was active, that would have scared the crap out of *me*."

"Thanks for the name," Claire said, jotting it down. "How about a motive. Any thoughts on *why* anyone from your hemisphere might want to kill Katherine McClure?"

"Just to fuck with the U. S. of A. springs to mind," he said bluntly. "They don't need any more motive than that. I hear they're thinking about amending the Koran to include that as a direct ticket to heaven-number-seven."

"You don't think it might be something specific?" she pressed.

"Specific like what?" he asked, taking more time to talk with Claire than he had originally intended. "I assume that you have a theory."

"I'm wondering if whoever did this might have been trying to affect the outcome of the election," she said. "Would that make sense with any of the groups you know of over there?"

"It's possible," he said after a few moments of thought, "but I seriously doubt it would have been the *prime* objective. They like their cause-and-effects to be much more direct."

"Then why shoot the First Lady? Why not the President?" Claire said, finding her conversation with this oddly-charming stranger to be surprisingly stimulating. "That would certainly have screwed with the U. S. of A. a whole lot more."

"Maybe, maybe not," he said. "I think there might be a couple of reasons that *she* was the target and not him.

"First of all, some folks in the Hezbollah might secretly agree with McClure's mid-east policies. He's been trying to negotiate a fair and livable peace in contrast to Evans' hands-off, let-them-kill-each-other posture. They would want McClure to be President. So killing him, while it might have a bigger disruption-impact, would certainly be counterproductive. His wife could have been a compromise among extremists.

"You have to remember that in an act of terrorism you want to have the greatest impact on the largest number of people. If not physically, then mentally. She could have been the target because she is actually more popular—more *admired*—than her husband is.

"One more possibility is that the First Lady is an easier target. She doesn't go wandering all over the stage the way he does. When she's speaking she stands at the microphones, and if not, she's almost always sitting on the stage behind him—a nice still target either way. And from what I know about the gun, and what you've released about a computer aiming it, that would be important. Then there's the possibility that it was a shooter's choice. Maybe the President was the *prime* target, but if they couldn't get off a clear shot at him, they'd settle for the First Lady."

Claire hadn't thought of that possibility. Could the aiming software handle multiple targets? Since it was a customized version of surveillance-camera software originally used in casinos to pick out *personas non grata*, it must be able to handle multiple targets! She scribbled a note to call the FBI lab and the NSA as soon as she and Townsend were finished, and have them explore the possibility.

"If you don't have any other questions, Angel, I really need to be getting on," he said. "I'm afraid that I don't have any more to offer, but if I come up with anything, even an interesting theory, I'll give you a call, okay?"

"Please think about contacting your Israeli friend, Mr. Townsend,"

Claire reminded him. "That would be most helpful."

"I'll think about it, Angel," he said in his Forsythe voice, "I'll think about it."

After hanging up, Claire turned to her computer and made a request through the databank for Townsend's CIA file. A one-word message popped up. "RESTRICTED" it read. She wasn't surprised. She'd have to go out in person to the CIA headquarters to view his file. Maybe she could initiate procedures to contact Avi Geller at the same time.

*****

After hanging up, Townsend turned to his computer and typed a short e-mail in French.

Henri,

I have sown the seeds per your request. We must now wait to see if they bear fruit.

CT

Chapter 39

Friday, October 24
Langley, VA

Typical of DC weather, Friday dawned as meteorologically opposite to Thursday as day was to night. The sky was a brilliant blue, virtually cloudless, and the weather-girl on the radio promised a high in the low 70's. Not bad for the end of October.

At a little after nine a.m., Claire was pulling up to the front gate of the CIA headquarters complex in Langley, Virginia. She handed the guard her Secret Service ID, and waited as he checked her name against a registration book.

In the lobby of the New Headquarters Building, Claire was met by a young woman who verified Claire's identity by scanning her thumbprint. She then had her photo taken, and sixty seconds later, she was wearing a temporary visitor's badge around her neck, along with her Secret Service ID, and she was being escorted to a reading room. The room had half a dozen low-walled cubicles where authorized individuals could read "eyes-only" files. A big sign on the wall warned, "You ARE being videotaped!"

The young woman led Claire to one of the desks, and said that she would return in a moment with Townsend's file.

Thirty minutes later Claire had finished reading it. The details he had given her over the phone were correct, though there was no mention of why his dog had been named Beelzebub.

She had an idea that not every assignment he had taken on during his twenty-year career with the Agency was in this folder, but she was particularly disappointed to not find any reference to the gun, to the Iranian plot to kill the Ayatollah, or to any Israeli operatives.

Claire signaled her escort, who had been standing by the door the whole time, and she came over and picked up the folder. Claire waited in the cubicle while the escort returned the folder to the adjacent room. Through the glass wall, Claire watched as the woman placed the folder on a tray where the bar code on the face of the folder was scanned, and a moment later the exact weight of the folder was displayed on a readout, and a green light came on. As they walked back to the lobby, her escort explained that every "eyes-only" file was weighed to an accuracy of $1/100^{th}$ of a gram when it left the vault room, and when it was returned. Since a typical sheet of paper weighed around 4 ½ grams, it was a very accurate way to check that nothing had been taken from or slipped into the folder.

In the lobby, Claire was asked to wait for another person who would talk to her about her request to contact Avigail Geller. Fifteen minutes passed before a tall man with a rapidly receding hairline approached and extended his hand.

"Sorry to keep you waiting," he said, "I'm Leo Bond." As they shook hands he took a folded dollar bill from his left jacket pocket and added, "A buck if you can come up with a joke about my name that I haven't heard yet."

"Claire Bradley," she replied with a smile. "I can imagine that working for the CIA and being named Bond, that you *have* heard them all."

"You're not even going to try?" he said, clearly disappointed.

She wasn't going to, but then a thought struck her. She dug in her purse for a penny, while taking the dollar bill that Bond was holding. She held the penny against the dollar, and held them both up next to her face. "Who am I?" she asked.

He laughed and nodded his head. "Very clever, *Miss Moneypenny*," he said in a James Bond imitation. Then in his own voice he went on, "Looks like you made yourself a buck, Agent Bradley. You're a branch thinker—and quick, too. That's good. I see why the President gave you this assignment. When you're done with the investigation, come talk to me about a *real* job. So what's this about wanting to meet Avi? How did her name come up?"

Deciding that being straight with Bond was probably going to be the best approach, she said, "Charles Townsend," and watched for his reaction.

He cocked his head a bit in a you-don't-say gesture. "Charlie, huh? And, what did ol' Charlie have to say?"

"He contacted me yesterday and offered his insight. He seemed to think the assassination plot might have originated in the Middle East. He thought Ms. Geller might be a helpful person to talk to."

"He thought that, huh?" Bond said. "What made him think the plot came out of the Middle East?"

"Sort of a gut reaction, I guess," Claire replied, mentally debating whether to mention what Charlie had told her about the gun and the CIA's involvement in the plot to kill Khomeini.

"Nothing more solid than his gut?" Bond mused.

She couldn't figure out whether he was probing to find out what else Townsend had told her, or if he already knew and was trying to see if he could get it out of *her*; testing her ability to keep secrets.

The way the CIA network functioned, there was a pretty good chance that Townsend had been in contact with a few insiders all along, despite his adamant out-of-the-game assertion. Since the CIA presumably knew he wasn't a threat, they'd have no reason to hand him over to the task force. The CIA had always been fiercely independent—and distrustful—of the other intelligence branches and *they* all felt the same. The creation, in 2002, of the Department of Homeland Security and the folding of all of those agencies under the same roof did nothing to ease the tension. Many said that it made it worse.

"You understand that I hold a Top Secret security clearance don't you, Mr. Bond?" Claire said, deciding on an approach to take. "Well, because of that, Mr. Townsend was able to confide in me that he had direct knowledge of the Dynametric gun being in Iran in 1989 and *indirect* knowledge of its being in Palestinian hands in 1991. That, together with his knowledge of the region is what convinced him, I believe."

"That was smooth, Agent Bradley," Bond said, clearly amused. "You covered your source's butt over disclosing classified information to you by claiming that you're authorized to have such information. Only, he knows better, even if you don't.

"If such an operation had taken place—and I'm not saying that it did—it would not even show up in the normal files, and he'd never discuss it with you based solely on your Top Secret clearance—those are a dime-a-dozen in this city. He must have some other reason to trust that you'd keep what he told you confidential. I doubt that he's ever met you, Agent Bradley, so I wonder what could make him trust you so?"

"The fact that I'm a super-hero?" Claire quipped, setting her arms akimbo.

Bond laughed. "Knowing Charlie, it would be more likely that it's because he finds you attractive. But how about that he thought you were in trouble with those Hezbollah e-mails?"

Claire just stared at Bond for a moment. "What *don't* you already know?" she asked, half in awe of his information, and half peeved that she was being tested.

"We don't know who bankrolled your Frances Dunham for one thing," he admitted. "But we're working on it."

"And were you going to share?" she asked with more of an edge in her voice that she had intended.

"Come on," he said. "I want you to meet someone."

As they walked down a series of corridors and through automatic doors that Bond opened with a swipe of his thumb over a fingerprint scanner, he explained, "The world of spooks is a little different than what you're probably used to, Agent Bradley. Don't get me wrong—I'm not minimizing what you do. It's just that here in DC, only about half the population is armed and dangerous, whereas over there—the Middle East—it's more like ninety-eight percent, and it includes kids. And everyone thinks everyone else is a spy for either the Mossad or the CIA. So those who really *are* spies have their lives on the line, quite literally.

"Remember, the justice system to them is two people who say you're a spy and a bullet in the back of the head. If you're guilty you got what you deserved. If not, then you get a free pass to heaven as a martyr.

"It's not that we don't like sharing our information, Agent Bradley, we're just particular about who we share it with while our SOG's are still out there gathering *more* information."

"You have a Special Operations Group working this?" Claire said, the edge back in her voice. "And you didn't think that was worth mentioning?"

"Believe it or not," Bond told her, "I had it in my planner to call you and Mr. Levine and arrange a private meeting the morning that the Hezbollah messages leaked on CNN. After that little slip, however, I decided to postpone that meeting—indefinitely. Then Avi called me to make double sure that nobody outside knew about the SOG she was running. If I had already talked to you and told you what we were doing over there, she'd have pulled the operation for fear of further leaks, and I couldn't have blamed her."

"So what made you—or Ms. Geller—set up the special operation in the first place?" Claire asked. "Was it just because you knew the gun had been over there? Or was there more?"

Bond stopped in front of an open doorway, and held out his hand, indicating that Claire should go inside. In a plain office, at a plain metal desk, sat a plain woman, looking through a folder of papers.

"Claire Bradley, I'd like you to meet Avigail Geller," Bond said, then excused himself and pulled the door closed on his way out.

Avi Geller was the definition of the word average. Standing five-foot-four and weighing about 120 pounds, both her figure and her face lacked any particular focal point. Unless Claire had known that she came from the Golan Heights, she could just as easily have come from Cairo, New Delhi, Naples, or Cleveland. She was the perfect spy—she could be virtually invisible anywhere she went.

"I'm pleased to meet you," Claire said. "I thought I'd have to wade through a truckload of paperwork just to talk with you on the phone. What an interesting coincidence that you're here on the day I dropped by to check on an 'eyes-only' file."

Avi regarded her for a long moment before replying. "I doubt that you believe in coincidences any more than I do, Agent Bradley. If I thought you were that naive we wouldn't be talking right now. Please forgive my abruptness, but I need to ask you a question and how you answer it will determine how long this conversation lasts."

Although Claire was taken aback by Avi's directness, she did not find it abrasive. She could easily tell that it was not a display of ego, but was born of a need to cut through the crap and get to the facts. Claire was taking an instant liking to Avi. "Shoot," she replied.

"After Townsend told you about the Middle East connection to the gun, I know that you didn't post a report," Avi said, "and for that I'm glad. But I need to know who you *discussed* the information with after Charlie's call."

"No one," Claire answered.

"Not even your supervisor, Mr. Gants? Why?" Avi asked.

"I wasn't completely sure about Townsend," Claire explained. "After all, I had no way to know if he was who he said he was. I guess I was just being cynical, but I didn't want to say anything to anyone until I had a better base of evidence than a phone call out of the blue from somebody imitating John Forsythe."

"And after reading his file, are you convinced he was telling the truth?" Avi asked.

"I think I'm convinced that he was who he said he was," Claire answered, "but that's no proof that was telling the truth about anything else. No offense, but you folks are in the lying business. It's what you do."

Avi chuckled. "It's an odd game," she said. "Each side lies as much as they can in the hope of prying a grain of truth from the other side, and then distrusts it when they get it."

Avi took the folder that she had been looking at, and turned it around on the desk. "What I'm going to show you and tell you has to stay in this room," she said. "You can't post this information to your database, because if any of this should leak out it would jeopardize several operations that we're running and could put a number of very valuable informants in grave danger. Do I have your word?"

"Why bother to give me information that I can't use?" Claire asked, beginning to see how the CIA got its reputation for being difficult to work with.

"You can use it," Avi replied, "you just can't post it without developing it through your own sources. It can't become known that this came from me, or even from the CIA. But knowing where to look should make independent development a lot easier. So, do we have a deal?"

"Deal," Claire said, understanding that Avi would be concerned about the security of the task force database, in light of the Hezbollah e-mail leak.

Opening the folder, Avi revealed a photograph of a number of men around a battered military truck. From the background, the looks of the men, and her previous conversation with Townsend, Claire guessed that the picture had been taken somewhere in the Middle East—not that that narrowed the scope very much.

"Do you recognize anyone in that photo?" Avi asked.

Claire looked at each of the men closely before admitting that she did not. Avi handed her a magnifying glass. She studied each man once again, but with the same result.

"The man near the front fender," Avi said. "Try to visualize him without the beard and mustache."

Suddenly she saw it. "My God! He looks like Frances Dunham! Is he a brother? Where was this taken? When?"

"It was taken in Ramallah—in Palestine—about ten months ago. And we don't know for sure, but we suspect that the person with the beard *is* the person you know as Frances Dunham. We don't even know for sure if it's a man or a woman since, if you look closely, you can see that the beard appears to be fake. But it would be pretty unusual for these people to allow a woman to be part of a raiding party, much less to let her dress up like a man, since that's against their religion. Either it really is a man or it's a very important woman—one with an invaluable talent, perhaps. My personal guess is that your Dunham is actually a man."

The next picture was a blow-up of Dunham's hospital ID photo. Looking back and forth between the two photos, Claire finally said, "I don't know. The nose isn't right. Dunham has a wider nose—larger nostrils."

"I agree," Avi said. "But that can be faked almost as easily as the beard. Look at the left ear. Ears are as distinctive as fingerprints, and difficult to change with makeup in a way that looks natural."

"I see it," Claire replied. "What else do you have on him?"

"Not an awful lot, I'm afraid. Not for sure anyway. Do you know the name Ilich Ramirez Sanchez?" Avi asked.

"Sanchez ... Sanchez ..." Claire repeated slowly, rolling the name around in her mind. Then it clicked. "That's Carlos the Jackal, isn't it? You're not saying Dunham is the Jackal are you? He's in prison in France, isn't he?"

"Yes," Avi confirmed. "He's still in a Paris prison. And no, I don't think Dunham and Sanchez are one and the same. I do believe they know each other, however. Dunham—for want of a real name—has wisely chosen not to take on a moniker, like *The Jackal*, and has also done his best to keep his exploits out of the media, again unlike his world infamous mentor.

"Mentor?" Claire said. "You think Dunham studied under Carlos the Jackal?"

"We don't have any hard evidence," Avi replied, "but it's what we've heard from more than one source. Then, working on his own, we have reports of Dunham being involved in the planning and/or the execution of the bombing of the Air Force housing complex near Dhahran, Saudi Arabia, in '96, and also the truck bomb that went off in Sri Lanka's capital later that year. Then a Tel Aviv café bombing in '97.

"From there he seems to have gotten more sophisticated—and choosey. We think he got out of the blow-everything-to-hell business, and took up political assassination. Do you remember when the Hamas bomb-maker Mohiyedine Sharif was killed in March of '98?" Claire shook her head. Avi explained, "He was blown up in a car bomb that he was allegedly going to drive into Israel and leave on a street somewhere. Well, it went off before he even got out of the garage. The interesting thing is that the coroner's report from the Palestinian security force said that he had been shot three times several hours before the explosion dismembered him.

"Hamas naturally blamed Israel, and Israel, of course, denied that they had anything to do with it. Shortly thereafter, we began to hear reports from both sides of the fence that it was your Dunham character that did that job—probably on a Mossad secret payroll so there'd be no link back to Israel."

"That's getting out of the bomb business?" Claire observed dryly.

"The bomb blast was apparently a cover, but even if it wasn't, the explosion had only a single body count," Avi replied. "Besides, it was probably hard for him to quit cold-turkey, especially with a car full of explosives just sitting there.

"Anyway, after that, he seems to have left the Middle East for a while. My contacts aren't quite as good down there, but he appears to have taken a few jobs down in South America, helping drug lords kill each other, and what-not. At least one of those executions is rumored to have been contracted by the Columbian government, itself.

"There have been two killings in Canada attributed to him, although without much in the way of hard evidence, and another two murders— equally uncertain—in Great Britain."

"That's your idea of not an awful lot?" Claire said.

"It's a lot of quantity," Avi replied, "but the quality is lacking. There's no hard evidence that these were all the same guy; it's all hearsay, although hearsay from usually reliable sources."

"If this photo is almost a year old," Claire said, "what made you suddenly connect it to our picture of Dunham? I can't imagine anybody was so familiar with the details of this picture, that they recognized this as Dunham."

"No, you're right. We've been watching this group for some time now," Avi said, pointing to the photo. "The special-op I'm running finally got a guy inside that group. They're a terrorist cell and we're trying to get a handle on the rest of their network. But that's my concern, not yours. Anyway, it seems this Dunham person has popped in and out a couple of times, but my guy says it's just been during strategy meetings or strike-planning sessions. It's as if he's a consultant. In fact, the Israeli Intelligence Group has codenamed him: The Teacher."

"I'm still not seeing a connection between the photos," Claire said. "What made you suspect that this consultant to a terrorist cell in Palestine might be the person who shot the First Lady? That seems like quite a leap."

"It would be," Avi agreed. "Frankly, a connection between the two would never have crossed my mind. But here's what happened.

"We had heard a couple of rumors that Hamas had some high-tech super-gun that came out of Russia after the collapse, and that it might be available for somebody to use for a really high-level, high-profile assassination.

"All the checking we did turned up dead ends, though. Now bear in mind that the rumor had this gun coming out of Russia, so there was no reason to be looking here in the US for confirmation. We figured it was just another one of those urban legends that are always going around over there ... until Charlie called me."

"So, he's not out of the game like he claimed," Claire said, surprised and angered. "And the CIA really *does* know where he is! I knew it! Jesus! We're all supposed to be on the same team here!"

"Don't be angry, Claire," Avi said. "Charlie's whereabouts isn't a CIA secret, it's a Charlie secret. The brass doesn't even know that he's been in touch with me and very honestly, I have no idea where he is. *He* contacted *me*—just like he did you. Do *you* know where he is, just because he called you?"

"Good point," Claire agreed in an apologetic tone. "Okay, so now you know that this super-gun really does exist and that it really did get used for a high-profile assassination—or at least an attempt. How did you link the gun to this cell you've been watching?"

"You helped us do that," Avi replied with a grin. "Or at least your task force did. Remember that number that your people pulled out of the shredder up in New Hampshire? Well, when Leo saw it posted in your daily reports, he called me right away.

"Do you remember the number?" Avi asked. "97057991. 970 is the international telephone country-code for Palestine," she said. "579 is the city-code for Ramallah. And 91 is the first two digits of a cell phone number belonging to this man." She pointed to the man at the far right in the photo, and told her, "His name is Yacoub Hamoudi. He's the leader of the cell."

Claire couldn't believe that the CIA had this much information and hadn't said a thing until *she* contacted *them*. Trying to keep the annoyance out of her voice, Claire said, "Have you checked his phone record for international calls? Specifically to or from New Hampshire or the Newburyport area?"

"We have checked," Avi replied. "There were three calls made from the US to that number in the past nine months—we're assuming by Dunham, but that's really just a hopeful guess.

"The first call was from Washington DC, nine months ago. The second was from Amesbury—right next door to Newburyport—on Friday, the day before the shooting. The last one was from a town named Valdosta in Georgia, two days ago. The first and last calls were made from throw-away cell phones. The one from Amesbury was made from a cell phone that was later reported stolen."

"Two days ago from Georgia!" Claire said, her anger apparent. "When did you find this out?"

"Yesterday," Avi answered.

"Yesterday! And you didn't think that was worth sharing? Jesus! We could have had people on that town like a blanket and caught him before he slipped out."

"No, you couldn't. All you'd have done is tipped your hand that you were on his trail, and given him reason to be more careful in the future. Remember, this was a throw-away phone. Service was activated on the morning of the call—probably using a stolen identity—one call was made from it, and there's been zero activity since. That's a pretty common maneuver when you don't have access to any secure phone lines. Even if you'd been watching Hamoudi's phone activity day and night, by the time you saw the call come in, figured out where it was coming from, and then triangulated the cell phone area, Dunham would have tossed the thing in a dumpster, and been out of town. You're not going to catch this guy by knowing what he *did*, you're going to have to know what he's *going* to do, and be there waiting for him."

Claire looked down at the photo and took a couple of deep breaths to relax herself again. Avi was right and Claire knew it. It was all just so damned frustrating!

"So, what now?" Claire asked.

"Now, we wait. From what my guy in the cell has heard," Avi said, pointing to a house in the background of the photo, "he believes that The Teacher is going to be there again within the next week—two at the outside. So there'll *be* an opportunity to be there waiting for him if it doesn't get screwed up. Obviously, you're going to have to keep a lid on that number a lot tighter than you did on the Hezbollah messages. If Dunham finds out that you have that number, he won't go within a thousand kilometers of that house."

"Just so you know," Claire said, getting a little tired of the references to the Hezbollah-messages leak, "that information did not leak from the task force. We've discovered that it came from another agency all together, and have the guy in custody."

"Doesn't matter," Avi said flatly. "A leak is a leak. It means that your system has holes in it. If he gets wind that you have that number or that we're watching that house, Dunham will go so far underground that you may never sniff his trail again. It will also undo literally years of undercover work on our part, regarding the Hamoudi cell, not to mention putting my informant's life in jeopardy."

As Avi slid the photos back into the folder, she asked, "Do you think you can keep this buttoned up long enough to set a trap for this Dunham of yours?"

"Yes," Claire said, conveying more confidence than she actually felt. "One way or another, we're going to have to."

Chapter 40

Friday, October 24
Washington, DC

As soon as she got back to her office, Claire called down to the Research Group to see if they had made the phone number connection yet. As innocently as she could, she asked, "Have you made any progress with that number that came out of the shredder, yet?"

"Funny you should call," the tech said. "It looks like it might be a phone number in Palestine."

"Palestine?" Claire said with convincing surprise. "Interesting. Has that been posted yet?"

"Marcy is just finishing up the report to post to the database now," the tech said. "Mathematically, there's a hundred possible phone numbers that that number could be when you add the last two digits, and we have names and residential or business addresses for about half of them. The rest may either be unpublished, unassigned, or belong to cell phones that aren't in any directory. Once this gets posted, maybe the CIA or NSA will be able to do what they do best, and ferret out the rest of the list."

"Good work," Claire said. "But when Marcy gets the report finished, don't post it, okay? Just hang onto it until I get back to you. Understood?"

"Understood," the tech replied. "Is this getting a security bump?"

"For now, yes," Claire told him. "How many people know what

218

you just told me?"

"Down here, three, maybe four," he replied.

"Okay, make sure that number doesn't grow," she said, "and tell the other's who *do* know that anything to do with that number is sealed until further notice. If anyone inquires about it, refer them to me."

Claire called over to Levine's office and found out that Gants happened to be there, as well. She met them there, and behind a closed door she recapped her conversation with Townsend, her trip to Langley, and her conversation with Avi.

She also informed them that Research had made the Palestine phone-number connection on their own, but that she had them holding the information, for now. They all agreed that it made sense for the all-information-gets-posted edict to be suspended on this.

For the next twenty minutes they discussed the possibilities of leaks, how to contain them, and the ramifications if they couldn't be contained.

They didn't know if any of the other agencies were currently looking into the Seabrook number, but they decided that they should remove it from the database anyway. It seemed the best way to keep the loop as small as possible. If anyone noticed that the number had suddenly dropped off the radar, they would deal with that when the time came.

In the end, they had to admit that there was no bullet proof containment method now that the number had been posted to the database. The only course was to move forward as quickly and as discretely as possible.

For the remainder of the afternoon, Claire felt charged up. There was still a lot to do, and a million things that could go wrong, but for the first time, she saw an actual path to success. With the cooperation of the CIA and probably the Israelis, they had a very good chance of catching Dunham ... or whatever his name turned out to be.

The big question for Claire still remained motive. Why would Hamas, Hezbollah, the Palestinians, or whomever, want Katherine McClure dead? Claire still favored the sway-the-election theory, but she knew that there was little to support it. Even getting hold of Dunham might not provide the answer. If he was the professional that Avi Geller implied he was, then he wouldn't be likely to expose his clients, even to cut some kind of deal for himself.

The prospect of not having all the blanks filled in when this was over, did not sit well with Claire, but if she could at least bring the people responsible for shooting Katherine to justice, then she thought that she could live with it.

Chapter 41

Friday, October 24
Washington, DC

Claire was just getting ready to leave for home when her cell phone vibrated. She didn't recognize the number, but at least it wasn't blocked, this time. She answered generically, "Hello, can I help you?"

"You can have dinner with me, again ... all of it this time." It was Dave, and just hearing his voice made her smile.

"Maybe we should start with dessert next time," she replied, "in case we get interrupted again."

"I like the way you think," he said, "but I'm probably reading more into '*dessert*' than you really mean, huh?"

Claire laughed. "Down boy," she said. "I was speaking literally, not metaphorically ... as in crème brulee."

"I'll make a note," he said. "Unfortunately, it's going to have to wait a while. I have a plane back to Boston in a few hours."

"You need a ride to the airport?" Claire asked, hopefully.

"If you're sure you can get away, that'd be great," he said. "This is Sam's afternoon off, so I'd be stuck with public transportation."

Thirty minutes later, in front of his uncle's condo building, Dave tossed his suit bag into the rear seat, and swung up into Claire's Jeep. As she pulled out into the traffic, Dave asked, "So, you go off-roading in this?"

"Not if I can help it!" she said with a laugh. "That's why I bought it—to stay *on* the road. We get half an inch of snow and this city needs disaster relief! I think the city owns two plows and one sanding truck, and has to get Congress to act to put gas in them."

When they got to Reagan National, Dave offered to pay for parking so Claire could come inside and wait with him. Since neither of them had had dinner, they each got a beer and bratwurst at one of the many overpriced eateries along the airport concourse.

"This doesn't count as taking me out to dinner again, by the way," Claire joked. "They don't have crème brulee."

Dave smiled at her joke, but she could see that there was something on his mind. Whether it was her *voice*, her women's intuition, or just having been through this before, she was pretty sure she knew what was coming, and a knot began to form in her stomach. It was the "I had a nice time, but …" speech.

To her relief, both her *voice* and her intuition were wrong.

"This is kind of fast, I know," Dave said, "I mean, we haven't even had one complete date, yet, but, if *you're* interested, I'd really like to see you again. It's obvious to me now, that I was right to have that crush on you back in high school. I guess I just hadn't learned to listen to my voice at that point, or I would have acted on it then. Well, I don't want to make that same mistake, twice."

"Have you ever been in a long-distance relationship?" Claire asked, recalling dating a guy in Phoenix while she went to school 125 miles away, in Flagstaff. "It's not easy, Dave. I tried it once before with pretty poor results." With a serious expression, she went on, "With you in Newburyport and me in DC, I haven't the slightest idea how we could make a relationship work."

He took that to mean that she wasn't interested, and just looked down into his beer.

Then breaking into a smile, she added, "But the problem-solver in me is a sucker for a challenge and it says that this would be a *great* puzzle to tackle!"

Chapter 42

Saturday, October 25
Washington, DC

When Claire arrived at the office Saturday morning, Margaret told her that Mr. Levine wanted to see her as soon as she was settled. She also mentioned that Agent Powell was with Levine.

A few minutes later, her notebook in hand, Claire walked into Levine's office.

"Morning, Chief," she said cheerily, "you wanted to see me?" Dropping into the chair next to her fellow agent, she said, "Hey, Powell. How's it going?"

She saw him give Levine a wink, and then he said, "So, was that a new style of interrogation you were using on Dave Perkins at Reagan, last night? I was at the airport, too, dropping off my mother-in-law, and saw you trying to suck the truth right out of his mouth! How'd that work out? Did you get him to confess?"

Claire couldn't help but flush, as she said defensively, "Can't a girl have a private life around here?"

"Private?" Powell laughed. "You were making out like a teenager in the middle of Reagan National Airport! You want private, get a room!"

"What can I say?" she said, quickly regrouping and going on the offense. Looking at Powell, she said, "A girl has needs. He's a nice looking guy with a great personality, and butt you could crack walnuts on. Not bars that are set all that high around *here*."

Turning to Levine, she said, "Was there anything else? Or did you just want to see me to bust my chops about my personal life?"

"Easy, killer," Levine said with a smile, knowing that Claire was putting on the wounded act. *"I'm* not busting your chops, and you'd think there was something wrong with Powell if he *didn't*. Besides, I'd call it a draw with that crack about the height of the bars—that was a good come-back."

Despite the teasing, Claire felt very comfortable with these two men. She felt that she could, literally, trust either one of them with her life.

"But yes," Levine went on, "there was real business I wanted to see you about. It's about that number from the Seabrook house. Research has managed to match it to a bank account number from one of those don't-ask-don't-tell banks in the Cayman Islands. The State Department is trying to get some cooperation, but right now it's about fifty-fifty whether they'll help us."

Claire was puzzled. Why was he telling her this as if it were breaking news? This was the cover story *she* had come up with the day before. Then it clicked. This must be for Powell's benefit. She didn't know why, but she'd play along.

"I guess that's good, but not great, huh?" she said. "It would have been better if it was an address, or a social-security number, or a phone number or something, but I guess this could pay off if we can get some cooperation. I assume Research is still hunting, in case this is a dead end."

"They are," Levine said. "Well, that was all the fresh news as of this morning. I just thought you'd want to start your day off on a little bit of an up-note."

As she got up to leave, Powell said, "And just for the record, I could crack walnuts with my butt when I was that age, too."

"Who are you kidding?" Claire laughed. "You were never that age."

Twenty minutes later, after Powell had gone, Levine walked into Claire's office and took a seat.

"So, what was that all about feeding Powell the bank-number story?" she asked, "You think he's a security risk?"

"No, of course not. But he's not on the need-to-know list, either. I just wanted to test the story on someone to see if he picked up on it as being a ruse. Apparently, he didn't, so let's hope nobody else does, either. At least not anybody we can't bring into the fold, if necessary."

The two spent the next half-hour discussing what Claire should include in her eleven-thirty press briefing, and at the appointed time, Claire was standing behind the podium in the Service's media room.

She explained to the press corps that she had very little new information to share, except on the subject of the person known as Frances Dunham. "Based on close examination of photographs of Dunham and interviews with people who knew her while she was in the Newburyport area," she said, "we have revised our look-out bulletin to include the possibility that Frances Dunham may be a male posing as a female."

Claire went on, "I realize that that doesn't shrink the search group very much—in fact, it actually expands it. But this new information is important because we're now going to be searching other databases and sources that we might not otherwise have been focusing on."

Fifteen minutes later, after a relatively benign question and answer session, Claire was on her way back to her office. She was just stepping through the door when her cell phone buzzed.

"Hi, there," she answered brightly, recognizing Dave's number. "Did you see me on TV?"

"Yeah," he said. "You were sexy."

"Sexy?' she said, taking mock offense. "That was supposed to be my authoritative look."

"Well, yeah—that's what I meant," he replied, pretending to get out of hot water that he knew he wasn't really in. "Sexy in an authoritative way."

"Oh," she said. "You're into that, are you? The whole mistress/slave thing?"

"Hey," he said as if it were perfectly obvious, "why do you think I joined the police? We get to carry handcuffs all the time. But that's not ... Uh oh. I've got a call coming in. I gotta go. I'll call you tonight, okay?"

Without even a chance to say good-bye, he was gone. Flipping her phone shut and sticking it back on her belt, it occurred to Claire that a relationship with Dave would have to endure a lot more than just long distance. They were both in law enforcement, which meant being on call virtually twenty-four hours a day. And her job was even worse, involving almost constant travel.

She thought about her words at the airport, the day before. *A great problem to tackle*, she had said, happily. Now, she was wondering if it was *too* great of a problem.

Chapter 43

Saturday, October 25
Tel Aviv, Israel

Shortly after Avi Geller's El Al jumbo-jet touched down at Ben Gurion Airport in Lod Israel she was riding in the front seat of a Mercury sedan being driven by a man in a crisp Israeli Army uniform.

Chronologically, the man was in his early sixty's, but he could have easily passed for a man at least ten years younger. Moshe Yousif was a colonel in the IDF—the Israeli Defense Force—assigned to the Intelligence Group. He was well built and handsome, and had been not only a close friend, but even a surrogate father to Avi for years.

Moshe had helped Avi and her family after her father had been killed in a suicide bombing of an army outpost on the West Bank, and had even sponsored her commission into the Intelligence arm of the Israeli Army when she came of age. He had also been the one to encourage her to take the offer when she was later recruited to work for the CIA.

Moshe had greeted Avi with a warm hug, but it had not taken long for their how-was-your-flight, how-is-your-wife conversation to turn to business.

As they drove northwest toward Tel Aviv, some twelve miles away, he said, "Things are nearly ready in Ramallah I'm told. All we need now is for The Teacher to show up. How did it go with the Bradley woman?"

"Useful," Avi told him, "She's cooperating as we thought she would. I'm told that the government's researchers figured out that the number from the shredder was a telephone number, but Bradley managed to keep it out of their leaky database. I think the lid will hold long enough. I'll have to remember to thank Charlie, next time we speak."

"It doesn't have to hold much longer," Moshe said. "All the chickens are nearly home to roost."

"I don't care about all the chickens," Avi said. "I just want Hamshari."

"And I want Hamoudi and his brothers," Moshe replied, "The Americans can have The Teacher—just so long as he's out of *my* hair."

Avi raised an eyebrow. "That's a change," she said. "I thought you wanted him, too."

"I just want him out of business," Moshe replied. "Whether he dies hanging from an Israeli gallows or rots in an American prison cell makes little difference to me. Just so long as he is no longer able to teach Palestinian worms like Hamshari and the Hamoudis."

Ashraf Hamshari had been on Avi Geller's personal most-wanted list for several years—ever since he had sent her a videotape of one of her Army Intelligence operatives getting his brains blown out after being discovered as a spy within Hamshari's bomb-making cell.

Her reaction to that video was two-fold. First, she threw up. And then she made a solemn vow to God that she would exact revenge on Hamshari.

Yacoub Hamoudi and his brothers Muhammad and Sa'id had been tried *in absentia* by an Israeli court of masterminding two Tel Aviv bus bombings. They were convicted of recruiting and training the suicide bombers, and supplying them with their explosives.

Each brother had been sentenced to forty-six consecutive life sentences. That was the number of men, women, and children who died in the two explosions. One of those forty-six victims, a twelve year old girl named Galilee, was Moshe Yousif's only granddaughter.

The operation about which Moshe and Avi were talking—the capture of their respective most-wanted's—had come together almost by accident. Working deep undercover for nearly two years, one of Avi's SOG agents had finally managed to get inside the Hamshari cell. A week later, he had reported to her that the Hamoudi brothers and their followers were joining forces with Hamshari.

A plan was quickly formulated to send in an Israeli commando strike-team and raid the cell's house in Ramallah. That team was to be led by Moshe Yousif.

On the evening before the raid, Avi's agent sent an urgent message that the person they knew as The Teacher was going to be at the house in a week's time. The raid was postponed so that they could pull in yet another big fish with one cast of their net—the only cast they would get.

Unfortunately, the meeting with The Teacher did not take place in the Ramallah house, but in the back of a moving truck—a last-minute suggestion made by The Teacher who seemed to be able to smell traps.

Avi's agent had not been able to get word to the strike force, and when the advance guard scouted the house and found it empty except for a couple of women, the mission was called off. Avi's man later reported that The Teacher had left immediately after the truck meeting, but that the Hamoudi's talked about his return in the near future.

One week later, Katherine McClure had been shot in Newburyport Massachusetts. Neither Avi nor Moshe, nor anyone else, had had any reason to connect the incident in Newburyport with the terrorist cell in Ramallah until the discovery of the number jammed into the paper shredder in New Hampshire.

That was where Leo Bond entered the picture. Along with his long-standing habits of watching the news on CNN and scanning the New York Times, checking the latest postings to the Executive Task Force's database had recently become part of Leo's morning ritual.

On the morning that the "shredder number" was posted, he had called Avi immediately, having instantly seen the country code and the city code possibility in the number, and he told Avi to check it out.

To Leo's credit he *had* intended to post to the databank his suspicion that the number was a Palestinian phone number, but when Avi had discovered that the number had a good probability of belonging to Hamshari, she had asked Leo to keep the information under wraps while she checked further.

Digging out the photo that she would later show Claire, and comparing the men in the picture to the "wanted" photo of Frances Dunham, Avi had concluded, to her own satisfaction, at least, that Frances Dunham and The Teacher were one and the same. She shared her discovery with Moshe, and between them, they had hatched the plan that they were now discussing.

They had decided that, rather than compromise Avi's agent inside the cell or expose any other of their own intelligence sources, they would let the Americans "discover" (with a little help through Claire) the terrorist cell that was responsible for attempting to kill their First Lady, and to let the Americans request the raid that Avi and Moshe had been planning for weeks.

In Avi's short absence to the United States, Moshe had learned of the Hamoudi's and Hamshari's return to Ramallah, and he had put his strike force on alert. He wanted The Teacher, but he wanted the Hamoudi brothers far more. They would not slip through his fingers again, even if it meant missing the American's big fish.

He was confident, however, that that was not going to happen. Like most men in his profession, Moshe had developed a large number of contacts over the years, and one of those contacts, was Henri Marchaund. Henri claimed to have direct knowledge of The Teacher's movements, which he told Moshe were in the direction of Ramallah. The only question was exactly when he would arrive.

Some of Moshe's contacts were Israeli patriots, loyal to their homeland to a fault. Others were petty criminals who would sell their grandmothers to stay out of jail, while still others were simply paid snitches. Henri Marchaund, however, was none of those.

*****

Henri Marchaund pronounced his first name "on-REE", and it was by that single name that the majority of people who dealt with him throughout the vast, corrupt, often deadly world of the black market knew him.

Henri was a third-generation international-criminal and blackmarketeer. A provider of goods and services. In fact, that is exactly how his calling card read:

Henri Marchaund
Provider of Goods and Services

Inheriting a nefarious association of contacts and connections from his father that ranged from street criminals to government officials, Henri built upon that base to create a staggering world-wide network of both criminal and legitimate business holdings that provided him with an equally staggering income. In fact, the only reason that Henri continued to do what he did was because he enjoyed it.

When Forbes magazine published its annual list of the richest men in the world the only reason that Henri was not in the top five was that Forbes seemed disinclined to include criminals in their database.

Even that was a technicality that should not have been a problem, however, as Henri had no criminal record—anywhere. During his entire life of crime he had never been arrested once and had only been investigated by the authorities a couple of times, during his youth. Considering his history, that fact was as staggering as was the breadth of his empire and his wealth.

There were few criminal activities that one could name with which Henri had not had some acquaintance. From pickpocketing, to loan sharking; from weapons sales, to drug smuggling; from pornography to prostitution; from selling information, to spreading mis-information; from breaking bones, to murder. Henri's card should have included the line, "*No Job Too Big Or Too Small*".

For prices that varied with the importance of the victim and with the client's ability to pay, Henri had arranged to have many men killed over the years and even a few women. But he had only ever killed one himself.

When Henri was seventeen, he had come home to the Paris flat where his mother and he lived, to hear a man's yelling coming from the kitchen. It seems that this man had gotten wise to a con that Henri's mother was pulling, and he was demanding his money back.

At first she had feigned innocence, but she had finally relented, and had given him all of his "investment" back in five and ten Franc notes.

Unfortunately for her—and even more so for him—the man knew something about counterfeiting, and spotted the fake notes mixed with the few real ones right away.

Henri came around the corner just in time to see the man's huge fist crash against his mother's jaw, sending the petite woman into a crumbled heap at the foot of the stove.

It was the last thing the man ever did—aside from crying, "No, no," as Henri beat him to death with a marble rolling pin.

Now, in his early eighty's, Henri conducted most of his business from a picturesque old villa located on the coast of Cartagena Spain, overlooking the Mediterranean. Although his criminal network was now larger than it had ever been, he rarely found it necessary to leave his compound to conduct business, anymore, thanks to the Internet. Henri might be getting old, but he remained assiduously *au courant* in all things technical, as well as world events. Although Moshe Yousif, with the tacit approval of his government, had been a customer of Henri's for years, it was Henri's well-known technical curiosity that brought he and Yousif together in their current dealings.

Yousif had, for some years, been in possession of a very unique weapon he had seized during a raid on a Palestinian training camp in the desert. He and his top officers that day decided to keep the strange gun a secret, and buried it in Yousif's back yard against the time when a worthy target would make its unique capabilities valuable. That target, the Colonel finally decided, would be the terrorist they had come to call The Teacher. But Yousif wouldn't shoot him with the gun. Instead, because locating The Teacher, for even a conventional hit, had proven impossible, Yousif decided to barter the fascinating gun to Henri in return for setting up The Teacher. That Henri had, in turn, used the gun as part of that setup, Yousif saw as an interesting irony.

Seated by a wall of glass that looked out over the deep blue of the Mediterranean, Henri reread the e-mail that he had just received from the man he knew as *François*, whom the Israeli's knew as The Teacher.

Henri,

I am on my way now to see the good doctor. I will be arriving for the reunion as planned. I look forward to seeing you, again, old friend.

F

Henri typed an e-mail in response to François' confirmation of their plans, set its security level to "high", and sent it to Colonel Yousif. He then replied to François, stating that he would have a car sent to his hotel to bring him to the get-together.

Leaning back in his chair, he smiled to himself, immensely pleased with how well things were coming together.

*****

Approaching a checkpoint just outside of Tel Aviv, Moshe Yousif's cell phone chirped its signal that he had received a new e-mail. In the slow moving traffic, he typed in his password and read the brief message.

Pressing a button to delete the e-mail from the phone, Moshe said to Avi, "That was about The Teacher. My contact confirmed that he'll be there on Wednesday."

"Finally!" she said. "I'll have to call Bradley and make sure things are moving quickly over there. That's not much time for the Americans to get their bureaucratic asses in gear."

Chapter 44

Saturday, October 25
Washington, DC

S aturday afternoon, Margaret put a call through to Claire from the First Lady. Katherine wanted to know why Claire hadn't been by the hospital to visit since her arrival. It was obvious from her tone and her choice of words, that Katherine was trying to make her feel guilty for not having visited, but thanks to her mother, Claire had, long ago, developed antibodies to guilt-tripping.

Claire *had* intended to stop by, but it had just never worked into the schedule. Katherine's personal request had been just the catalyst she needed to *make* time, however, and she had told her that she'd be there in a couple of hours. Katherine asked her to make it one.

As Claire stepped off the elevator on Katherine's floor, she was met not only by Powell, but by Dan Burger, whom she hadn't seen since Newburyport.

"Hey! It's the superhero!" Burger teased. "Can I have your autograph?"

"I'll send you an autographed box of Wheaties," she replied. He looked at her quizzically, and she said, "It's a long story; I'll tell you later."

They exchanged a few pleasantries and a quick hug, and then Claire asked, "So what's going on? Has she got a publicity shoot going on in there, or something?"

"Actually, it's more like a coming out party," Burger replied. "Her first news conference since being shot. They've got a room set up for her downstairs."

It suddenly became clear why Katherine had wanted her there in one hour, and not two. Claire was not happy with being manipulated like this. *That* was a condition for which she had *never* developed antibodies.

Inside Katherine's room, a male nurse, the President, Katherine's mother, and Melissa were helping Katherine from her bed into a wheelchair. It appeared to Claire that there were probably three too many people helping, and that the nurse could have done it faster and simpler, alone.

Finally settled into the chair, Katherine closed her eyes for a few moments and bit her lower lip, fighting down the pain from having her arm jostled by her well-meaning family members.

When Katherine opened her eyes, she drew in a deep breath and looked around the room. A big smile spread across her face when she saw Claire.

"You made it!" she said brightly.

Claire made her way across the room, and gave Katherine as good a hug as could be expected under the circumstances.

"Will you do the honors of pushing?" Katherine said to Claire, indicating the handles of the wheelchair.

Claire noted the look of disappointment flash across Melissa's face. She gave Melissa a wink, and then said to Katherine, "How about if your daughter does the pushing, and I walk alongside, so we can chat?"

"How about if you do what I asked?" Katherine snapped.

The room went quiet and Claire gave Melissa a surprised look, while Melissa just shrugged and backed away from the chair.

"I'm sorry, Claire, Liss ... everybody," Katherine said. "That's the pain talking. It just makes me ... *snippy* ... for want of a description that doesn't start with a *B* and rhyme with *witch*."

"Why don't we just call this off?" the President suggested, sympathetically. "If you're not ready, we don't need to have the press conference right now. I'll have Diane go down and tell them ..."

"No!" Katherine cut him off. "We *do* need this!"

Claire correctly guessed that "We do need this," meant that, in Katherine's mind, her husband's campaign needed this.

Then, in an apologetic tone, Katherine said, "Really, Richard—I'll be fine."

Turning her head to find Melissa, she said, "Liss, how about if you push me to the elevator, and Miss Bradley takes over when we get downstairs?"

"Sure, Mom," Melissa answered, her dislike of being *appeased* not very well masked.

As Claire wheeled Katherine out into the hospital's media room, the members of the press and guests rose, and began applauding.

Katherine smiled at the cameras and waved with her good left arm as Claire rolled the chair to center stage behind a table arrayed with microphones. As she bent to set the wheel locks on the chair, Katherine said quietly, "Claire, I'd like you stay here with me."

"That's okay, ma'am," Claire said as if Katherine's order had been a polite suggestion. "You've got your family here—I'd just be in the way."

With that she turned and walked to the side of the room before turning around to look at Katherine. Katherine's eyes defined the expression, "If looks could kill ..."

Claire knew, of course, why Katherine wanted her on the stage with her, and it wasn't because she wanted the support of a friend. It was because she wanted Claire's high-profile, vote-getting face in her damned photos!

Claire also knew that short of shouting out a direct order for her to get her ass back beside the wheelchair, there was little that Katherine could do right then, so she watched as the First Lady turned to the microphones, and with a wide smile thanked everyone for coming; everyone for the cards, letters, and e-mails; everyone for their prayers—and so on, and so on.

Twenty-five minutes later, after her speech and a session of questions and answers, the President rolled Katherine back off the stage to another standing ovation. As she rolled past Claire, Katherine looked up and said flatly, "I'd like a word with you."

Upstairs, Claire was more than a tiny bit nervous as she waited outside of Katherine's room, while the nurse and Helen helped get Katherine situated in her bed once again. It had occurred to Claire, after hearing the tone with which Katherine had said *I'd like a word with you,* that there may have been some substance to those *Dragon Lady* stories, after all.

"She'll see you, now," the nurse said as she, Helen, and Melissa left the room.

When Claire went in and let the door close quietly behind her, she found Katherine freshly tucked into her bed, the back angled up to a sitting position, and two pillows fluffed behind her head. Her eyes were closed, but Claire knew that she couldn't be sleeping.

Her breathing was slow and regular, but very deliberate. With each exhale, she pursed her lips and gently blew out the air. Claire assumed this was some kind of pain-management method, but wasn't sure if the technique might also include meditation, so she was reluctant to interrupt. Finally, she said softly, "Excuse me, ma'am. You wanted to see me?"

Katherine opened her eyes and looked in her direction, but did not lift her head. "Yes, I wanted to see you. And I hope you know why," she said.

"To ask for my resignation?" Claire replied, believing that that was a distinct possibility.

Katherine laughed, and then quickly recoiled from a jolt of pain. Recovering, she said, "What the hell would I want that for?"

"Insubordination, ma'am?" Claire answered, still not convinced she was off the hook.

"You mean ignoring my order and walking away from me downstairs? That wasn't insubordination," Katherine said with a small grin. "That was a willful young woman exercising her right to disagree with a cantankerous old woman."

"I wouldn't refer to you as 'old', ma'am," Claire said, playing straight man to the obvious setup.

"But you have no problem with *cantankerous*," Katherine said pretending to take offense.

"You've been known to have your moments, ma'am," Claire said, glad that she was still on kidding terms with Katherine.

"Come sit down," Katherine said, patting the bed, "I want to talk before my meds kick in and I turn into a babbling fool."

Claire sat on the edge of the bed and for the first time saw in Katherine's face just how much pain her friend must be enduring.

"Are you okay?" Claire asked with genuine concern. "Do you want me to call the nurse?"

"I will be," she replied, looking at Claire through half-open eyes. "The meds will kick in in a couple of minutes and I'll be fine. Of course, ten minutes after *that*, I'll be comatose."

"I hope that's just a figure of speech," Claire said.

"It is," Katherine said. "Though sometimes I wish it *was* a coma—the pain gets to be so much sometimes."

"Really? I'd have thought that after a week your chest and shoulder would be feeling at least a little better," Claire said with a concerned frown. "Are there complications?"

"It's not the wound," Katherine said. "It's my head. I've been having these killer headaches."

"Migraines?" Claire asked, recalling the agony that her father had endured with them.

"I almost wish they were," she said, "they'd know what to give me for *that*. No, they're still trying to figure out what's causing them while they give me different drugs to see if anything will help. I'm a regular lab rat.

"But that's not what I want to talk to you about. I've only got a few minutes, so forgive me if I rush a little bit. First of all, about the 'insubordination' as you called it. I understand that you don't like publicity-shot photo ops and I can't say that I really blame you. But I don't think that you understand why they're important to me."

Claire began to explain her feelings on the subject, but Katherine held up her hand.

"The most important thing in my world right now is to see that my husband gets re-elected. And not just because it's nice living in that mansion over on Pennsylvania Avenue. It's because this country needs the leadership—the continuity—that only Richard can deliver.

"Claire, I apologize for using you to get votes, but believe me, you're not the only person that I've used. Not that that makes it okay, I just thought you might want to know that I haven't singled you out for exploitation."

"The President is way ahead in the polls right now," Claire said, puzzled. "And he has been for over a week. Every pundit that I've heard has said that there's almost no way that Evans can make up that much ground. He'd have to ..."

"The key word in your sentence is 'almost'," Katherine interrupted her. "Ask Thomas Dewey about that. You remember that photo of Truman holding up a newspaper that read, 'Dewey Wins!' right after Truman was declared the winner in the 1952 election? I agree, we don't need any more votes than we have right now, but we can't afford to lose any either. And a lot can happen between now and Election Day.

"Which brings me to the second thing," Katherine said, visibly more relaxed as her meds took hold. "How is the investigation going? I mean *really*. Not the fluff you feed the media. Are you going to *solve* it by Election Day or what?"

Claire was a little surprised by the almost accusatory tone of Katherine's question.

"It's going pretty well, actually," Claire said. "We've recently developed a couple of very promising leads. I wasn't aware that we were working to a deadline, though," she added defensively. "I thought our mandate was to find the truth."

"You're right! You're right!" Katherine said, her speech a tiny bit slurred, as if she was becoming intoxicated. "I didn't mean to imply that you were dragging your feet or anything. It's just—you know—if you could solve it by then—well, I mean, that would go a long way toward—you know ..."

Claire smiled at how relaxed Katherine was becoming—and how quickly. It was like watching a block of ice morph into Jell-O.

"I'll see what we can do, ma'am," she said patronizingly, guessing that Katherine probably would not remember much of the conversation anyway. "If there's nothing else ma'am, you should probably get some sleep now."

With sleepy eyes and as serious an expression as she could muster through her medication, Katherine said, "Just one more thing. Did you and that police stud from Newburyport hit the sheets, yet?"

"What!?" Claire said with a surprised laugh. "Who told you that I ...?" She didn't bother to finish the sentence as she remembered Powell teasing her, and knowing his penchant for telling what he thought were humorous stories to anyone within earshot. Katherine must have overheard him telling another agent about the airport encounter.

"A little birdie told me," Katherine said in a child-like voice. "The way I heard it, you and Dave were smooching at the airport, and groping each other like a couple of horny teenagers."

Claire couldn't help but smile at Katherine's sudden drug-induced silliness, and actually laughed out loud when she began to sing, with a goofy, drunken expression, "Claire and Davy sittin' in a tree, K-I-S-S-I ... N ... G ..." Then she was asleep.

Claire was smiling, but her eyes filled with tears. She stood and gently kissed her friend on the forehead. "Please, get well, Katherine," she whispered, "Please, get well."

Chapter 45

Saturday, October 25
St. Petersburg, FL

One week prior, as the First Lady was on her way to Mass General, Frances Dunham had been wiggling out of the elaborately padded bodysuit that gave her a set of droopy boobs and a wide butt. For the final time, she went through the metamorphosis of changing back into a man. The man that the Israelis had dubbed The Teacher; that Henri knew as François, and who answered to Frank. Wearing no disguise, but carrying yet another false identification; that of one Thomas Beard, he had then been able to travel freely, unconcerned about being recognized as Dunham.

But the *persona* of Thomas Beard would have an even shorter life expectancy than had Frances Dunham. Frank knew that he had enemies who would recognize him in his natural state, and he couldn't very well live the rest of his life wearing bulky disguises.

At a gated residence on Sunset Drive in St. Petersburg, Florida, Frank pulled alongside the call box and pressed the button.

"Thomas Beard to see Dr. Polyakov. I'm expected," Frank said looking straight at the box, knowing there was a camera inside.

Almost immediately, the big gates swung silently open and Frank was instructed by a voice from the box, to drive to the south side of the house where someone would meet him.

At the side of the huge Georgian-style house a man in a white servant's jacket was waiting for him. "Dr. Polyakov is expecting you, Mr. Beard," the man said in a thick Russian accent. "Right through there, please."

Frank stopped just inside the door, letting his eyes adjust to the rather dim artificial light of the room. As he stood there, taking stock of his surroundings, a door at the other end of the room opened, and the light from the brightly-lit adjoining room silhouetted a broad figure in the doorway.

"Come, come," a deep female voice commanded impatiently. "You have left us little time to accomplish much." Her Russian accent was only a degree or two less thick than that of the man outside. Frank entered the room behind the woman and found himself in a starkly-white doctor's office.

"It's a pleasure to see you again, Doctor," Frank said, shaking her beefy hand. "Business must be flourishing. This is a remarkable house."

"As long as I have loyal customers like you, who keep coming back, I will never go hungry, no?" she said with a smile, as she unwrapped a blood pressure cuff.

"This will be the last time, I'm afraid," he replied, unbuttoning his shirt. "I'm going to retire."

"Da! Is a good time to do that!" she replied. "You have become a bit too famous, no?"

"I'm afraid so, but it was unavoidable," he said. "That's why this time needs to be a little more radical than what you've done for me before. Ears and all, this time."

Taking his chin in her hand and turning his head back and forth, she studied his face closely. She turned it far to the right, looking closely at his hairline, and made a "Tsk, tsk," sound as she said, "You can't even see the scars. What a shame to have to cut into such magnificent work, yet again."

"Last time!" Frank said raising his right hand. "I swear. After two days here, you'll never see me again."

"Is not good to travel so soon after you are having such surgery, you know. You should stay with us for a week, at least. Two days is hardly enough time for a *nose-job* to heal. Is much too fast for this operation. Why do you wait so long to come see me?"

"Couldn't be helped," he replied. "I have a very small window of opportunity coming up, so I'm just going to have to take my chances. You can give me some antibiotics to ward off infection, can't you?"

"Have you at least followed my instructions?" she said with a sigh of exasperation. "Nothing to eat since midnight and nothing but water since noon?"

"I have," he said. "I remember the routine."

"All right," she said motioning to the hallway that led to her operating room. "We should not be wasting any more time, no?"

"No," Frank agreed, and followed her down the hall.

Chapter 46

Saturday, October 25
Washington, DC

Claire made it home to her apartment a little after six pm. While eating a supper that consisted of a can of ravioli, a slice of buttered bread, and a glass of Gewurztraminer wine, she had an enjoyable conversation on the phone with Dave. Telling him about Powell's having seen them at the airport, and about his teasing, Dave said that he was really sorry to have caused that. When Claire told him about her conversation with the First Lady, and *her* teasing, Dave couldn't find the words to apologize enough.

Claire just laughed it off, but she found it sweet that Dave was so concerned about her embarrassment.

After they said their good-byes, Claire got undressed, and while she was naked and going to get a pair of pajamas, her cell phone began ringing in the kitchen. Thinking—*hoping*—that it might be Dave again, and feeling a bit uninhibited from the wine, on a whim, she went to pick up the phone *au natural*. She was feeling uncharacteristically sexy and playful, and was thinking about making him guess what she was wearing.

When she saw in the display that the calling number was both restricted and secure, every bit of playfulness vanished instantly.

"Claire Bradley," she answered with a touch of apprehension.

"Hi, Claire, this is Avi Geller. I hope I haven't called at a bad time, but this is important. Is this line secure?"

Claire assured her that it was, as all traces of fuzziness from the wine immediately disappeared.

"Good. Listen, I just received word that The Teacher—a.k.a, Dunham—is going to meet with the people in the Ramallah house on Wednesday and Thursday, and then leave on Friday," Avi said. "I think this is that golden opportunity to be ahead of him for once, so I want to raid the house while he's there, and take him and the whole cell at one time. Obviously, though, I can't do that myself, and I can't go storming through Palestine with a CIA SWAT team. There are sovereignty issues, you know? I need the *Israelis* to lead the raid, Claire, but I'm afraid if I request this through the normal channels, the red-tape between the US and Israeli governments will take us into next week some time, and by then he'll be gone again. We'll never get another opportunity like this one."

"I agree," Claire said, her mind racing. "But is there any proof that the cell is part of the plot with Dunham? I mean, if there isn't, then an operation to nab Dunham by himself while he's *en route* to the house, might be easier to pull off. It'd be a lot less dangerous and probably faster to get organized."

"There *is* proof," Avi assured her. "My mole has seen hard evidence inside the house that the cell is connected to the plot. That's another reason to move quickly; to avoid leaks. The first thing they'd probably do if they found out that they were compromised is destroy that evidence."

"What kind of hard evidence?" Claire asked excitedly, wondering if it was anything that would point toward a motive.

Avi explained that a couple months earlier, her mole inside the cell had overheard Yacoub Hamoudi talking with The Teacher as they climbed into the back of a truck, and that they were talking about the wife of the American President. Hamoudi had said that if she were *his* wife, he would do Allah's will by putting her in her place with his boot.

"That's not exactly *hard evidence*," Claire said, wanting to believe, but wary of unsupportable leaps.

"I agree," Avi said. "But it was overhearing that comment, together with having heard about the assassin's gun on the news that tipped my guy off that something he saw just yesterday connected the two things.

"This afternoon I retrieved a note in one of our dead-drops from my mole inside the cell. He said that yesterday he saw Hamoudi flipping through a book, and he happened to see a drawing that looked just like the photos in the news of the gun that you folks found after the shooting of the First Lady. He asked Hamoudi what it was, and he told him, 'It is for doing Allah's will.'

"Not exactly a confession, but my mole managed to see enough of the book to form the impression that it was an *instruction manual* for the gun. Considering that he's not aware that I'm working with you on this *or* that we suspect that the man he knows as The Teacher is the actual assassin, it was pretty remarkable that he put all this together and got a message off to me. I mean, this has nothing to do with the operation that I'm running with him. He took a big risk to get me this information just so I could pass it on to someone else. But then, he's one of the best guys I have over here."

Claire's pulse quickened as she thought about there finally being some hard evidence—*physical* evidence—to work with. "Let me make some calls on this end," she said. "I'm sure we can cut through the tape, Avi."

"I don't know what you have in mind for getting past the bureaucracy," Avi said, "but don't tell anyone that you don't absolutely have to about this. And for God's sake, don't put it on your database!"

"I didn't plan to," Claire said, just a little peeved at Avi's condescending tone. "I have channels that might surprise even you," she told her, thinking that she might go directly to the top and call the President.

After ending the call, and while she was thinking about how to present her case to the President, Claire went and pulled on a long pajama top. Talking to Avi while naked had been awkward, but talking to the President with no clothes on would be ... well, like something out of one of her weird dreams.

Claire flipped open her cell phone and punched in the password to get to her list of restricted numbers. She held the button to scroll down the list to "President," but on the way she watched her entry for "Gants; Cell" roll by, and she immediately changed her plan.

"Hi, Chief," she said to Gants when he answered on the third ring. "Sorry to bother you at night, but something's come up. Can you talk, or would you rather call me back?"

"I'm fine," he said. "What is it?"

"I just got a call from Avi Geller," Claire explained. "She says that there's some hard evidence at the house in Ramallah that the cell she's been watching is part of the plot to kill the First Lady, or at least may have supplied the gun to Dunham for that purpose. And she says that Dunham is going to show up at the house on Wednesday. She suggested pulling some strings to see if we can get the Israelis to mount a raid on the house while he's there. Secure strings that won't have any chance of leaks."

There was a longish pause before Gants replied, "Who else knows this?"

"I don't know about Avi's end, but you're the only person *I've* called," Claire answered.

There was another pause while Gants thought about the situation. "Okay," he said finally. "Plan on being at the White House in an hour and a half. I need to make a few calls to make sure some others are available to join us. If the meeting can't happen or if the time needs to shift, I'll call you."

*****

When he hung up Gants immediately called Katherine's room at the hospital. Gants was still at his office in the White House, and he knew that the President had gone over to visit his wife and had not yet returned. Melissa answered the phone and quickly passed it on to her father.

"Can you talk?" Gants asked.

Through a covered mouthpiece he heard the President say, "Will you run down and get me a soda from the machine, Sweetheart?" He caught only part of Melissa's response, but it included, "... just tell me to leave, why don't you ..."

To Gants the President said, "Go ahead. What's happening?"

Gants gave the President a recap of what Claire had told him about Avi's evidence and her request for help in arranging a raid. He ended with his suggestion about meeting at the White House to discuss details. The President agreed on the meeting and the time, and then clicked off.

Next, Gants called Paul Levine, and after that conversation, he called Leo Bond.

An hour and a half later, the four were going through the security procedures at the West Wing entrance to the White House, and Gants was leading them upstairs.

In the Oval Office, the President was just hanging up the phone when the group was ushered in. First into the room, Claire had heard the President ending his call with, "... I love you, too, Kat."

"Agent Bradley; gentlemen," he greeted them. "Please have a seat. I assume that you're all aware of the nature of this meeting, but since you suggested it, Mr. Gants, why don't you recap what you have in mind to be sure that we're all on the same page."

"Well, sir," Gants began, "I'd like to start by apologizing to all of your absent Cabinet Secretaries. I specifically asked you not to invite them, because I think it would only complicate the matter and drag out what I think is a pretty simple and obvious decision.

"Mr. President, I'd like to suggest that you call your counterpart in Israel and formally request that a joint strike force be formed immediately, between the CIA's Special Operations Group in the area and Israeli Army Intelligence. The purpose of the strike force would be to raid the house in Ramallah and capture the terrorist cell there along with the person we're calling Frances Dunham, whom they know as The Teacher."

The CIA, being an Executive Agency under the President, was under his direct authority, so it was not only legal, but was often *prudent* for the President to make a unilateral decision of this kind. Congress did not need to be notified.

The President looked up at the small bank of clocks that was arrayed across the wall opposite him, and noted that the time in Jerusalem was just approaching four-thirty in the morning.

"I think a joint-agency raid is a good idea, and I'm pretty sure that the Prime Minister will agree," the President said, "but I think I'll wait couple of hours before I call him to discuss it. In the meantime, Mr. Gants, what do you think of having Agent Bradley join our CIA people over there, and take part in the capture of Dunham? Or at least be there when he's taken by the Israelis, and escort him back to US soil."

"What!?" Gants said incredulously.

"Hear me out," the President said. "I think it makes sense for someone from the task force to be present. It shows continuity and demonstrates the task force's part in all of this. And I believe you've told me on more than one occasion, Mr. Gants, that you'll put your female agents up against anyone else's males any day of the week. I'm quite sure that Agent Bradley can handle the assignment. It's not like we're sending her in there alone."

"Of course she can handle it," Gants agreed, "but it's an unnecessary risk, sir."

"I have to agree," said Bond. "I think it would add a needless burden to the strike-force to have to take along an observer." He turned to Claire, and added, "No offense."

"None taken," she replied, and then turning to the President, she said, "Permission to speak freely, sir?" He nodded, and she said bluntly, "This was your wife's idea wasn't it, sir?"

He looked at her for a long moment during which her lock on his eyes never flinched.

"As a matter of fact, it was, Agent Bradley," he said. "But it's an idea that I happen to agree with." His tone was firm, but not angry. "Forgive me for being a politician, but I want to win this election. You may not realize ..."

"You want to send Bradley to Palestine as a *publicity stunt*!?" Gants interrupted him, too shocked to even add, "sir." "Are you insane? For want of a few votes, you'd ...

"You're overreacting, Mr. Gants," the President interrupted him, his voice calm, but the authoritative edge, unmistakable. "And you're also testing the limits of my tolerance," he added, reminding Gants who he was talking to. "I'm not asking Agent Bradley to parachute into enemy-held territory and single-handedly bring back Satan, and this is *not* just for votes.

"If we get Dunham back here, and then don't get a conviction we're all going to look pretty stupid. I want someone to be there when Dunham is taken into custody to make sure his civil rights aren't violated, and to make sure that any evidence that's found is going to be admissible when it gets back here. I believe Bradley has training in both those areas."

"As well as a high recognition-factor when CNN starts broadcasting," Gants added dryly. "With all due respect, sir, the risk is ..."

"I don't see the risk as being that high," the President interrupted again. "She wouldn't be going into *combat*. She'd be there as a civilian observer. A *well trained* civilian observer."

"Begging your pardon sir," Levine weighed in, "but people get killed over there riding the bus to school in the morning. Just being American and being there is a risk."

"And we have people," Bond pointed out, "who are already in-country who can handle securing any evidence and getting Dunham back here. I have to agree with the others; even if the risk is low, it's still unnecessary."

The President drew in a long breath and rubbed his temples. Looking at Claire, he said in a resigned tone, "They *are* right, of course. There is a risk. I won't order you to go over there. I won't even *ask* you to go. It's certainly not in the mission-statement of the Secret Service, so I'm just going to leave it on the table. The decision will be up to you, Agent

Bradley. Strictly voluntary, no hard feelings, either way. I'll be calling the Prime Minister in two-hour's time, so please have an answer for me before then."

"You can have my answer now, sir," Claire said. "I'd be honored to be part of the strike force that captures Dunham, Mr. President." Although she wouldn't admit it to anyone, a large part of the inducement to say yes was Larry Douglas' call, warning her to lay off Frances Dunham.

Gants gave Claire a look that went beyond cold and into cryogenic, and it came close to literally making her shiver.

"If there's nothing else, sir ..." Gants said to the President, "Apparently, I have travel orders to cut. Permission to return to my office, sir?"

The President got to his feet, indicating that the meeting was over, and the others rose immediately.

"Thank you all for your input," he said. Extended his hand to Claire, he added, "And thank *you*, Agent Bradley—again."

"Will you call me as soon as you know if they'll have me, sir?" she said. "I'll have some arrangements to make. Call me any time, sir. As soon as you know."

Outside the Oval Office, Claire expected Gants to light into her for volunteering when he was so obviously against the idea, but instead, he simply walked off in the direction of his office without so much as a goodbye. It occurred to Claire that she had never seen him so angry.

Was it because she had, in effect, disobeyed him? Was it because he was genuinely worried about her safety? Or was it because he had stood up to the President on her behalf, in front of subordinates and a peer, and she had not even supported his stance?

Gants was a good and close friend and a fantastic mentor, and she didn't want to lose him in either of those roles. As much as she wanted to talk to him about the reasons behind her decision, however, she knew that this was not the time.

Chapter 47

Claire stood in the Tel Aviv bus station, closely watching the people getting on and off the buses.

It was a warm day, and she noticed a man with a dark complexion wearing an unseasonably heavy jacket. The man looked nervously about before getting on one of the buses after a group of teenagers in school uniforms.

Claire hurried to the bus, and before the man could take a seat, she feigned bumping into him from behind. There was something hard and cylindrical under his jacket. A dynamite-vest!

Standing behind the man, she took a step back and reached for her gun. She would put one round into his head at the base of the skull. An instant kill, giving him no time to react.

But her gun wasn't there! Where the hell was it? The airport! She had left her gun at the airport! Jesus!

Just then, the man turned toward her and opened his jacket revealing a dozen or more sticks of dynamite strapped to his body. He reached up and took hold of a grip with a switch in the top of it.

With no time to reach for her ankle gun, Claire lunged at him just as his thumb mashed down on the detonator.

Instead of a thunderous roar, however, the vest just made an electronic ringing sound. As Claire stared at it uncomprehendingly, the man released his thumb and the ringing stopped. Then he pressed it down and the ringing began again.

It wasn't until the start of the third ring, that Claire came out of her dream enough to fumble her bedside phone to her ear, and in a groggy voice, answer, "Bradley ..."

"Apparently, I woke you up, Agent Bradley," the President said, "but you did say to call any time."

"That's okay, sir," she said, recognizing his voice. "The phone pulled me out of a dream that I think would have ended poorly."

"Well, I'm glad I could be of service," he said, "but I'm actually calling to let you know that the Prime Minister agreed to my request for a joint strike force *and* to my request that you accompany the strike force when they go to Ramallah.

"I talked with Mr. Gants, again, and although he's still not happy, he is on board. He suggested that in order to keep this tightly under wraps, you should make your travel arrangements yourself, rather than through the Secret Service. You'll be reimbursed when you return, of course."

"Thank you, sir. I'll get on that right away," she said with a trace of sleep still in her throat.

"Why don't you finish your night's sleep, first?" he suggested.

"Thank you, sir. If you insist."

"I do. And Mrs. McClure said to make sure that you come visit her before you leave."

Sleep never really took hold, again, however, and forty minutes later her alarm clock put an end to the futile attempt.

After she had showered, Claire called Avi. Claire found herself a bit annoyed that Avi already knew about the go-ahead for the joint-force raid, and that Claire would be coming over to join the team. It bothered her that information seemed to pass much faster on that side of the fence.

"Do you foresee any problems with my being part of the strike force?" Claire asked her.

"Well, it's not like you're going to be in the first wave blowing down the front door," she replied. "*I* don't see any problem, but Colonel Yousif is another matter."

"Colonel Yousif?" Claire inquired.

"Colonel Moshe Yousif," Avi replied. "He'll be leading the strike force, and quite frankly, he was not happy to learn about your participation in the operation. In fact, he's still fighting it."

"Will he succeed?" Claire asked, suddenly concerned that some unknown player could pull the rug out from under her. "Does he have that power? Can he just veto my involvement?"

"Colonel Yousif commands a great deal of respect from those above him," Avi said, "and they *will* listen to him. But ultimately, he'll carry out the orders that they give him. And considering that this request started with the President of the United States and was passed on through Israel's Prime Minister, it seems unlikely that a colonel in the army will have much chance of overturning it."

Claire's reaction was one of simultaneous relief and anxiety. She wanted to go, of course, but she didn't relish being in a combat group where she wasn't wanted in the first place.

"How do you think I'll be involved in the whole thing?" Claire asked.

"The Colonel and his team will be leading the operation, so they'll do all the planning," Avi replied. "Even as CIA station chief, I won't get briefed until Monday sometime. I guess you'll just have to wait until you get here to find out. So when are you leaving?"

"I was going to ask you about that," Claire replied. "What airline do you suggest? Can I get somebody to meet me at the airport? Should I make hotel reservations or will I be staying on base somewhere?"

"Fly El Al," Avi told her, "but you'll have to catch the shuttle to New York—they don't fly out of Washington. There's a flight that leaves around midnight. You should be able to make that. I'll pick you up at Ben Gurion Airport, and you can stay with me. And pack light," she added. "Most anything you need—which won't be much—we can get for you over here. And don't even *think* about bringing a gun! Not even in your checked luggage. You have no idea what a hassle that would be, Secret Service ID, or not. Besides, you won't need it."

Chapter 48

Sunday, October 26
Washington, DC

Just after five, Sunday evening, Claire was hefting her one suitcase into the back of her Jeep, and tossing the backpack she would use as a carry-on onto the passenger seat. A half-hour later she was pulling into the parking lot of George Washington Hospital.

When she entered Katherine's room, Katherine was sitting up, typing with one hand on the keyboard of a laptop computer that sat on the roll-away dining table.

"Hi!" Katherine said cheerfully when she saw Claire. "I'm glad you had the time to stop by. Just let me send this, and I'll be right with you."

After a few more clicks and a little electronic sound that indicated success, Katherine closed the top on the computer and pushed the table back out of her way.

She patted the bed beside her, and Claire came over and sat down. Claire hadn't noticed it the last time she was here, but this time she saw the little koala bear that she had given Katherine back in Boston. She was touched that she had brought it with her and even had it beside her on her night stand.

Katherine noticed Claire looking at the stuffed animal and said, "Your little friend is quite a reminder for me. That was a remarkable day." She picked it up with a chuckle, she began singing, "Katherine and Martin sittin' in a tree ... I still laugh every time I think about that."

A thought—or was it a memory—seemed to occur to her. She looked at Claire quizzically, and asked, "Was I singing that yesterday when you were here?"

"Like a drunken sailor," Claire confirmed with a laugh. "Only you changed the words to, 'Claire and Davy sittin' in a tree ...'"

"Gotta love the medications!" Katherine laughed.

"Speaking of which," Claire asked, "how are your headaches?"

"They come and go—coming more often than I'd like, but going faster than they used to. My neurologist seems to be getting closer with the drugs he's giving me, anyway. At least this stuff doesn't make me quite so snippy—or so drunk that I start singing. Speaking of which, how is your Mr. Perkins? What's he think about you shipping out to the Middle East?"

"I haven't talked to him since I found out," Claire replied. "I'm just going to tell him I'll be out of town on business—I won't tell him where I'm going."

"Afraid of a leak?" Katherine asked.

"I don't see Dave as a security risk, but obviously, the fewer people who know, the better," Claire told her. "I also don't want him to worry while I'm gone."

Katherine studied the younger woman's face for a moment, and then said, "Why *did* you volunteer to go, Claire? Richard said that Mr. Gants was quite vocally against it, and even the others saw it as an unnecessary risk."

"I want Dunham," Claire said without hesitation. "I want the son-of-a-bitch who put you here—pardon my French."

"I'd like to see him caught too," Katherine said, "but it's not so important that you should risk your life, you know."

"I thought it was your idea in the first place," Claire said, wondering if the meds were having an effect on Katherine's memory.

"It was," Katherine admitted. "I'm ashamed to say that all I could see was votes when Richard told me about the raid that Mr. Gants had suggested. Wrapping up the investigation and bringing in the shooter right before Election Day ... You couldn't write a better script! How could we lose? And then I thought of you, our national hero. Who better to be seen escorting America's most-wanted back to the United States to face justice? Well, that would just be icing on the cake!"

"And now you don't see it as such a good idea?" Claire asked, wondering what had caused the flip-flop.

"It's unnecessary," Katherine replied, "*dangerously* unnecessary. Claire, I couldn't live with myself if anything happened to you over there, knowing you were there because of my greed for votes. Votes, as you pointed out, that we don't really need."

"Frankly, ma'am, I wouldn't be going if I believed it was just about the election," Claire said. "I honestly believe that that's a done deal." She paused for a moment before she went on. "The reason that I volunteered is a lot more personal, I'm afraid." Again, she stopped and thought. Not about *what* she was saying, but whether she wanted to *say* it—to speak it out loud. She had only recently admitted it to *herself*.

"What I said about wanting to bring Dunham in is true," she finally went on. "But it's not just to see justice done—it's also to feed my ego."

Claire watched Katherine for a reaction, and got a single raised eyebrow—a silent request to go on.

As if unburdening her soul, Claire explained, "I've never been a person with dreams of being famous, Katherine. I've always been able to satisfy myself with simply striving to be the best at whatever it was that I was doing.

"But then all this happened, and suddenly I find myself a celebrity. Strangers say hi to me by name and ask for my autograph. I've been asked to speak at a graduation that won't take place for another six months. I've been on national—actually *worldwide* TV, and I've been on the cover of *Newsweek* and *Time*. And I've had two publishers contact me about my memoirs. And you know what I discovered from all that?"

Katherine smiled knowingly, and answered her question. "It's addictive as hell, isn't it?"

Claire let out a little laugh. "So my shallowness is that obvious," she said. She wasn't sure whether she was more relieved that Katherine understood, or embarrassed at being so transparent.

"You're not shallow, Claire. Just human," Katherine consoled her. "Who doesn't want to be loved? Admired? Respected? The trick is to let those things happen *because* of who you are, and not to let them *define* who you are.

"You have the occasional drink and you're not an alcoholic," Katherine went on. "You've had sex without becoming a nymphomaniac, haven't you? Fame isn't much different. You just have to decide what you want out of it and keep it under control. Hey," she joked, "you've taken the first step—you've admitted you have a problem."

Claire laughed. "So I need to join a chapter of Egomaniacs Anonymous?"

"That's a little oxymoronic, isn't it?" Katherine said with a laugh that ended abruptly with a grimace of pain.

"Are you okay?" Claire asked, suddenly very serious. "Do you need to take something? Should I get the nurse?"

With closed eyes and staying very still, Katherine said quietly, "I'm fine. I just need to be still for a minute. Damned headaches come on like a sledgehammer!"

After taking a few deep breaths, and blowing out like Claire had seen her doing the day before, Katherine said, "So tell me, Miss Celebrity; if you're so all-fired addicted to the spotlight, why wouldn't you stand in it with me, yesterday?"

"Because I *hate* being manipulated even more than I *like* the spotlight," Claire said bluntly.

"And yet," Katherine said, "knowing, full well, that I *manipulated* your inclusion in the Palestine raid, you volunteered, anyway. You know what that tells me? It tells me that you don't want to *share* the spotlight. I think that maybe you have *celebrityitis* even worse than you thought."

"So, what's the cure, Doctor?" Claire asked with a grin.

"There is none," Katherine told her. "Your only hope is to go into politics as soon as you get back."

Claire laughed, and Katherine gave a little chuckle that she immediately regretted, and she quickly took refuge in stillness and silence.

For a minute or so, Claire watched her friend without saying a word, to make sure that she was all right. She was relieved to see that the controlled breathing seemed to be helping her to relax.

"I should really be going," she whispered, finally. "I've got to get out to Dulles. Are you sure I can't do anything before I go? Pour you some water, pull the drapes—anything?"

"Just make me a promise," Katherine said, opening her eyes slowly as if even that sudden movement might cause her head to explode—again. "Be careful over there. No heroics. Dead people are famous too, but it's really only fun if you're alive." She punctuated her comment with the slightest of chuckles, but immediately recoiled from a jolt of pain. "Damn!" she said in a whisper.

Claire had to blink away tears as she looked down at her friend. She bent down to give her at least a symbolic, if not a physical, hug, touching Katherine's cheek lightly with her own. "Please get well," she whispered.

As she left, she looked back at Katherine to see that her eyes were closed and she was lying perfectly still. Her only movement was from the fingers of her left hand, wiggling a slow good-bye.

In those few steps to the door, Claire's emotion turned from deep empathy for her friend, to boiling rage against the person who had done this to her, and with the image of Frances Dunham in her mind, she said to herself, *I can't <u>wait</u> to meet you, you son of a bitch!*

*****

Two hours later, Claire was lifting off from Dulles Airport, and after the small commuter plane landed at JFK in New York, Claire had another three hours before boarding her El Al flight for Israel. During her layover Dave called her, and while they didn't discuss anything important, Claire felt good just to be talking with him. It had been a very long time since she had felt this way about a guy.

In the course of conversation, she had told him that she would be away on business for a day or two, and he had asked no questions. She was grateful for that, but she also wondered about it. She told herself that it was just the fact that he, too, was a cop, and that he knew that there were certain things that she couldn't talk about. But what if her initial reaction to seeing his name in Gants' report had been correct. What if he was, somehow, involved in all this, and he already knew where she was going, and why? She certainly didn't know him well enough to say that that was impossible, and she never had seen that in-depth profile that Research was supposed to put together.

She was beginning to mentally berate herself for not being able to accept when good things happened without the need to scrutinize them to death, when Dave got a call from his dispatch officer.

"Hey, I have to go," he said. "You be careful over there, okay? You're already a hero—you don't need to prove it again."

"Over where?" she replied, trying to keep the surprise out of her voice.

"Israel. Or wherever you might be going from there," he said.

"How ..." she began, and then caught herself. "What makes you think I'm going to Israel?"

He laughed and said, "Because, *Mata Hari*, somebody in the background there has been paging '*El Al passenger Yuri Golden*' for the last five minutes."

Not bothering to deny it, she just said, "That's classified, okay?"

"Of course," he said. "You just be careful, all right?"

"You, too," she said.

After they hung up, she heard, for the first time, the page for Yuri Golden. Some spy *she'd* make!

Chapter 49

At nearly the same time that Claire was reaching cruising altitude, Henri Marchaund was reading an e-mail on his computer in Cartagena, Spain. It read:

> This is to inform you that Agent Bradley with the US Secret Service will be in attendance when the Ramallah raid takes place. Please make a careful review of the plans based on this new information. It is highly desirable that no harm come to her, though of course, the success of the project is still paramount.

Henri gave a little laugh as he clicked the "Delete" button. Agent Bradley, he thought, had developed quite a fan club, somehow. This was the fourth e-mail he had received alerting him to the fact that Claire would be part of, or at least peripherally involved in the raid, with all of them expressing concern for her safety.

Given the line of work that Henri was in, it was not surprising that many of his clients happened to know one another. People who buy and sell guns on the black market tended to know others in the same trade, just as used car salesmen or lawyers would know others in *their* professions.

What *was* surprising was that very few of Henri's clients, even those who knew each other well, realized that they all had Henri in common.

Part of the reason was that Henri was very particular about those clients with whom he dealt directly. He preferred that the vast majority of his dealings be carried out through a well-run criminal bureaucracy, bigger and more organized than some third-world governments.

By being selective in his personal clients he was able to maintain a discreet separation between most of them, thus avoiding the problem of his name popping up in dinner conversation. Adding to the secrecy-by-separation was the *two-way-street factor*. If one wished for their activities to remain a secret from the police, or their government, employer, spouse, partner, or whomever, it was best to keep one's acquaintance with Henri Marchaund a secret, as well.

A perfect example of the two-way-street factor, even without benefit of secrecy-by-separation, was Avi Geller and Moshe Yousif. The two, who could hardy be closer, were both utilizing Henri's services to apprehend their respective most-wanted targets, and yet neither suspected that the other even knew that Henri Marchaund existed.

The same held true for Leland, the man who had contracted the "Weaver" project, as well as for Charlie Townsend, François, and even The Teacher himself, to name but a few.

So it was that Henri Marchaund had become an orchestra leader of sorts, directing the needs and services of numerous clients to create a symphony of deceit that impressed even Henri himself.

Though each of the members of this bizarre symphony was playing an intricately woven piece of the whole, few of them knew that any of the others even existed, much less were part of the same grand ensemble. And although each was paying Henri handsomely for what they, personally, needed from the opus, Henri would have done this for free just to watch how it all played out. He had not had such fun in years!

Chapter 50

Monday, October 27
Negev Desert, Israel

It was shortly after four o'clock, Monday afternoon in Tel Aviv when Claire's plane touched down at Ben Gurion Airport. For Claire, it was ten in the morning, and although the flight hadn't exactly been restful—having been crammed into a coach seat for more than ten hours—she felt good and was wide awake when Avi met her at immigration.

Once in the privacy of Avi's car, Claire asked with hardly a breath in between, "So have you had your briefing yet? Is the raid still on for Wednesday? I'm still going, aren't I?"

"We had a strategy meeting this morning," Avi said as she headed the car south from the airport. "The operation will take place early Thursday morning, and yes, you're still part of the plan." Avi looked at Claire, and said in a very serious tone, "Just make sure you do what you're told, okay? Colonel Yousif still isn't exactly keen on the idea, and if you give him much of an excuse, he'll scratch you from the operation instantly, and you won't have anyone to appeal to.

"Any suggestions on what I should do?" Claire asked, thankful to have an ally in this foreign land and foreign situation.

"Yeah," Avi said, feeling that she was repeating herself, "Exactly what you're told. No more and *certainly* nothing less. Don't ask why; just do it. I may be CIA station chief over here, but Colonel Yousif is in charge of the operation. If you piss him off, I won't be able to help you.

"For now, though," Avi said, "you should get some sleep. It's going to be a long night. We've got about 150 kilometers to go, so you've got an hour and a half to nap."

Claire had been able to sleep on the plane and felt fairly fresh, all things considered. But it was obvious that Avi wasn't interested in talking about specifics of the operation, so Claire laid her head back and closed her eyes just to appease her host.

An hour and twenty minutes later, mouth dry from hanging open, Claire was shaken from her sound sleep as the car left the smoothness of the asphalt for a washboard dirt road.

After about ten kilometers of constant bumping, the car finally stopped at what appeared to be a small village nestled between three small mountains in the Negev Desert.

The village was, in fact, a military installation used for training in urban combat. For the next two days it would be under the exclusive command of Colonel Moshe Yousif for practice exercises for the Ramallah raid scheduled for the predawn hours of Thursday morning.

Inside the largest of the buildings at the east end of the compound, Avi and Claire were escorted through a door in a wall that divided the building into offices and an auditorium.

The auditorium was austere, with rows of folding chairs that faced a podium and projection screen at one end. A number of men, all of them wearing desert camouflage fatigues, were standing or sitting in small groups, talking quietly.

They all turned when the door opened and Avi and Claire walked in, and even before they were instructed to do so, they began taking seats.

Avi led Claire up the front of the room to meet the man standing at the podium. "Colonel Yousif, this is Claire Bradley with the US Secret Service. Claire; Colonel Yousif."

Claire extended her hand, and said, "It's a pleasure to meet you, Colonel. Thanks for allowing me to be part of your group."

"You are not part of any group, Agent Bradley. You are an observer," he said brusquely, without even looking at her. "Please take a seat at the back and listen closely. Don't ask questions—just listen. Is that clear?"

Claire was completely taken aback. She had at least expected civility! She had even thought that she might be introduced to the rest of the group, rather than being dismissed like some unwanted stepchild. He hadn't even bothered to shake her hand!

"Yes sir," she answered after a dumbstruck moment. "Perfectly clear."

When Claire didn't move right away, he looked at her and said sarcastically, "And yet you're still here."

Without another word Claire turned and started down the center aisle between the seats. She felt the color come up in her cheeks, sure that every man there was looking at her and laughing at having seen her put in her place.

The quick glances that she took, however, indicated otherwise. She saw no one looking at her at all ... amused or otherwise. Instead they were all looking ahead at Colonel Yousif.

It wasn't until Claire reached the back row and turned to take her seat that she realized that Avi was not with her. Rather, she was standing by the podium, next to the Colonel.

As Claire sat, the lights went down, and an image came up on the screen, displayed by a computer-projector in the ceiling. The image showed the faces of six men.

Five of them were dark complected, with distinct Middle Eastern features, and Claire guessed that these were the members of the terrorist cell that Avi was going after.

Claire recognized the sixth photograph, immediately. It was a blow-up from the photo that Avi had shown her back in Langley. It was the man that Avi suspected was Frances Dunham—the man she referred to as The Teacher.

"These are the subjects," the Colonel began in a voice that didn't require a PA system. "You have copies in your folders. Memorize their eyes, noses, and ears. They may or may not have beards when we go in, so make sure you can recognize them either way."

As the Colonel continued to talk, Claire was surprised to see that Avi was working the computer, changing the images on the screen. Apparently, there was a stronger CIA/Israeli connection to the operation than Claire had gathered from Avi's comments.

Avi clicked on one of the photos of the Middle Eastern men, and it zoomed to fill the screen.

"This man is known as Samer al-Abassi," Yousif told them. "His real name is unimportant, but remember his face, because he is one of us. He knows we are coming and he will naturally cooperate, but he will act like one of them and try to resist you. Whoever makes contact with him, take him down and make it look good, but don't hurt him unnecessarily. He is a very valuable asset to Captain Geller's group, so don't expose him, and certainly don't kill him."

Captain Geller? Avi was a *captain*? In what? The Israeli army? Why the hell hadn't she mentioned *that*? Suddenly, Claire wasn't sure there was *anyone* she could trust anymore.

Next, Dunham's face filled the screen. "This is the man that we've come to know as The Teacher," the Colonel said. "The Americans believe that he might also be the man responsible for shooting the wife of their president. They also believe that all of these individuals may be part of that same assassination plot. That is the reason that Special Agent Bradley, back there, will be with us for the next couple of days."

Claire expected a least one or two heads to turn in her direction, but none did. Every man in the room kept his undivided attention on the Colonel.

"We will want to take all of these men alive if possible," Yousif went on, "but for diplomatic reasons, this man, The Teacher, is especially important. If you have to shoot him, do not—repeat—*do not* shoot to kill."

As Avi clicked their photos onto the screen, the Colonel introduced the brothers Yacoub, Muhammad, and Sa'id Hamoudi, and then Ashraf Hamshari. Then he added that there may also be two women in the house, who should be subdued, as well.

The next image was an aerial shot of a group of small, detached buildings. "This is south east Ramallah," the Colonel said. Then using a telescoping pointer he indicated a house near the middle of the screen. "and this is our objective. As you can see, it's set apart from the other houses around it and that's going to work to our advantage.

"At 0300 Thursday morning, we will deploy from the helicopter due east about six kilometers, and double-time to the rally point here." While pointing he went on, "Red Team will circle to the north through here, while Green Team goes south between these buildings. You'll join up here, and then work inwards, securing the area. You'll hold at this line, and each team will send two men forward to take observation positions. Zoom." The command was to Avi, but Claire noticed that the image enlarged even before he spoke. Obviously, this was not the first time that the Israeli Colonel and the CIA Station Chief had worked together.

For the next thirty minutes the Colonel went over, in minute detail, what each member of the raiding party was going do, covering everything from the direction from which they would approach the house, to where they would wait, to what the go and no-go signals would be. *Nothing* was assumed.

At one point, a hand went up, and Yousif pointed at the man.

"If we encounter any civilians, sir?"

"Neutralize and detain," the Colonel answered firmly. "Use only what force is necessary, but do not allow the operation to be compromised."

The briefing lasted another twenty minutes with Yousif going over contingencies in case things did not go as planned. Finally he said, "Okay, let's get some rest. We start our run-throughs at 2100 hours. Be back here at 2030."

The run-throughs, would be full dress rehearsals of the entire operation. They would include the six kilometer double-time march through the desert from where the helicopter would drop the teams, and would end with a simulated attack on one of the buildings in the compound.

There would be at least two run-throughs, but the Colonel would have the teams repeat the exercise as many times as necessary until they had every element of the operation down like clockwork.

As the projector went off, and the lights came up, the men stood and headed for the two exits. Before Claire could make it to the front of the room to talk to the Colonel, he, too, had left the room.

Avi was still there when Claire reached the podium. "I don't think your Colonel likes me too much," Claire said, trying to sound like it didn't annoy the crap out of her.

"Don't take it personally," Avi replied. "It's not that you're a woman, or American, or that you're anything else. It's what you're *not*. You're *not* one of us."

"You mean Jewish?" Claire asked, surprised.

"No. One of the strike force," Avi said.

"You're a member of the *strike force*?" Claire said in astonishment. "I was going to ask you about your rank of Captain, but I thought it would have been in an army reserve or something. Isn't it some kind of conflict to be in a foreign military and work for the CIA?"

"Yes," Avi answered, "And I did resign my commission when the CIA recruited me. But the Colonel and I go way back, and he got me temporarily reinstated for this action, since it is a joint-government operation.

"Like I said, don't take the Colonel's actions toward you personally. Think about this if it was reversed and he wanted to come along and take part in your guarding of the President on a tour of Jerusalem. You and your team have trained together for years, right? You know all the moves, the signals, the contingencies, it's all second nature. He might be equally well trained, but he'd never be part of the same loop. Just having him there would give you one more thing to be concerned about. You'd never be completely sure that he'd do what one of your own people would do in a given situation. That's what I mean about not taking it personally. The Colonel's son-in-law would feel no more welcome here than he's making you feel—and he's a major in the Israeli Air Force."

Claire saw Avi's point, but she didn't necessarily agree with it. "How can I prove myself?" Claire asked.

"In a day? I can't imagine," Avi replied as she pulled a memory stick from the computer under the podium. "My advice to you is to roll with whatever he throws at you. Don't challenge him—don't even question him. Like I told you before, if you give him an opening, he'll scratch you from this operation in a heartbeat, and you'll end up waiting right here for us to come back."

Claire hated to be cowed, but at the same time, she realized that this wasn't about her—it was about the investigation and bringing Dunham back with enough evidence to convict him. And if she had to kiss some arrogant butt to get him, then so be it. Pucker up, she told herself.

Avi led Claire across the compound to another cement-block building. Though the heat was not oppressive outside, the air conditioning still felt luxurious as they entered a medium-sized one-room building. The room was austere, to say the least, having bunk beds lining both walls, and three shower stalls and two toilets at the far end.

"In honor of your visit we women have our own barracks tonight," Avi told her. "Normally, there's no segregation around here. We all eat, sleep, and work as one. Makes for a real close-knit team."

"I'll bet!" Claire replied, not sure that she would be completely comfortable with that arrangement.

"Pick a bunk and try to get some sleep," Avi said as she unlaced her own boots and kicked them off. "I'll wake you when it's time to go."

With that, Avi flopped back on one of the lower bunks, punched her pillow to fluff it up, and was asleep in thirty seconds.

Claire, however, was too keyed up to be overtaken by sleep. If the excitement of being this close to Dunham hadn't been enough to keep her awake, then the questions streaming through her mind surely would have.

What was Dunham's part in all this, she wondered. Was he simply a hired assassin with no personal motive for wanting Katherine dead? And what *was* the motive, whether it was Dunham's or the cell's? Glancing at the sleeping Avi Geller, she wondered about her, too. Her sudden involvement in the case, at exactly the right moment and following Charlie Townsend's unexpected call, had, at first, seemed almost too convenient. Claire had pushed the feeling aside at the time, happy that any progress, at all, was being made, but now, seeing her closeness with Colonel Yousif, she wondered if Avi's being at Langley on the same day that *she* was there, was a lot more than coincidental. Coincidental like Dave Perkins showing up *at exactly the right moment* and nudging her toward the belief that the Hezbollah e-mails were a ruse, so that Charlie would have a plausible reason to contact her, and lead her toward Avi.

As Claire lay there staring up at the ceiling, she tried to tell herself that things couldn't possibly be that tangled, that the web of deceit she was imagining was just in her mind. She tried, but she wasn't succeeding.

Chapter 51

Monday, October 27
Negev Desert, Israel

Claire woke with a start at 2015 when Avi gripped her shoulder, and said, "Let's go. Get your shoes on and use the can. I'm on my way, now. Don't be late."

Five minutes later Claire was entering the briefing room through one door, as Colonel Yousif entered through another.

"Good evening, Colonel," she said, intercepting him as he approached the podium. "I was wondering if I'd be able to get some boots for tonight." Lifting one sneakered foot from the floor, she pointed out, "These weren't exactly designed for a run through the desert."

He looked at her with an expression somewhere between amusement and annoyance at her boldness in assuming that she was going with the teams on the run-through. "But they'll be fine for standing in the compound out of the way," he said bluntly.

"Are you afraid I can't keep up with your men, Colonel?" Claire replied. She saw Avi, who was standing to one side, roll her eyes.

He began to snap a reply, but checked himself before a second syllable came out. He stared at Claire for a brief, but intense moment, and then, in a tone that made Claire think that maybe she didn't want to win this argument, he said simply, "Fine."

The Colonel turned to Avi, and said, "Geller, have Levy get her some boots and a DCU—and a helmet." He looked back at Claire, and said mockingly, "Anything else?"

"Just a place to change, sir," she replied, trying to sound much more confident than she actually was.

"I don't really care where you change, Agent Bradley," he said in a tone that was half impatience and half challenge. "But if any person misses one word of this briefing they're scratched. And since this briefing is going to start in exactly six minutes, and you don't actually have your new clothes yet, it would seem your options are limited." Glancing down at the list of names in his folder, he added, "Dismissed."

As Claire walked over to the door through which Avi had left, she glanced at the men standing nearby, and seated in the first row. If any had overheard the conversation—and she couldn't imagine how they had not—none were reacting to it. No snickers, no condescending glances, no elbowing of one's buddy. Claire was surprised but impressed, as she imagined the reaction from guys like Powell.

"Sergeant Levy will have your stuff in a few minutes," Avi said coolly when she returned a minute later. "You know Bradley, if you're just going to ignore my advice you should probably stop asking for it in the first place."

Before Claire could reply, Avi walked off toward the podium.

How to win friends and influence people ... Claire said to herself.

It was 2029 when Sergeant Levy opened the door while balancing a stack of clothes that was collectively known as a Desert Camouflage Uniform, or DCU, on one hand. Claire had hoped to be done changing before the briefing began, but since that was now out of the question, she took the stack of clothes to the back of the room and pulled a chair from the back row. Just as she sat down to take her sneakers off Colonel Yousif began the briefing.

"Assignments," he began on the dot of 2030, with no introduction or fanfare. "Red Team: Myer, you're team leader. You'll take Cohen, Eli, Friedman, Ruben ..."

As the Colonel announced the names, Claire couldn't help but wonder at his motive for forcing her to change her clothes here in the briefing room. Certainly she didn't need to hear the roll call, since she didn't know who any of these men were, anyway. Was he just trying to grind her down one more notch—trying to get her to break? *Well, fat chance, Colonel!* she thought as she began unbuttoning her shirt.

Claire had worn a comfortable bra for the long trip from Washington to Tel Aviv, but it was not much good for jogging. To her surprise she found an army version of a sports-bra in the stack of clothes, along with a pair of army-green biker-shorts type underpants.

Claire considered turning her back to the room when she removed her bra and donned its GI counterpart, but would the Colonel somehow construe that as missing part of the briefing? Use it as an excuse to scratch her? Besides, if he was trying to prove that he could get under her skin by embarrassing her, he didn't know who he was dealing with!

Keeping her eyes locked on the Colonel—who was looking at the men he was addressing—she watched for any reaction as she stood up slipped out of her shirt, then reached behind and unclasped her bra. In one fluid movement she pulled off the bra, leaving herself naked from the waist up.

She had expected at least a momentary look, during which she planned to give the Colonel a "Fuck you!" smile.

He didn't react at all, however, though she knew damned well that he could see her, at least in his peripheral vision! He just kept reciting names and assignments, without the slightest pause or glance in her direction.

She had planned on putting on the GI bra then the camouflage shirt, and letting the shirt cover her when she changed underwear. But now, feeling that she was engaged in a battle of wills with the Colonel, she decided to up the ante.

Again, her eyes fixed defiantly on the Colonel, she unzipped her slacks, pushed them over her hips, and pulled them off one leg, and then the other.

Still no reaction.

Taking a deep breath, Claire went for all the marbles. Hooking her thumbs into the waist of her panties, she pushed them down, stepped out of them, and stood there naked except for her socks.

Nothing! Not a glance! She wasn't sure whether to feel triumphant that she'd met his challenge without flinching, or deflated that she was standing naked in a room full of men, and none of them cared. She suddenly felt like she was in one of her own weird dreams!

Then, she happened to notice Avi, who was standing on the other side of the podium and looking directly at her, wearing an unmistakable "What the hell are you doing!?" look.

Claire quickly looked away, embarrassed. Not so much for her nakedness, as for having so obviously lost her challenge to the Colonel.

She grabbed the underpants from the pile and put them on followed by the bra. In less than a minute she was dressed the same way as everyone else in the room, and was lacing up her boots.

"One more thing," the Colonel was saying as Claire snugged up the last boot. "Special Agent Bradley will be coming with us on the first run-through. Myer, put her right behind you when you leave the chopper. As she falls back in the line, each man report when you've passed her. When the last man passes her, just mark her GPS coordinates, and keep moving."

Then he looked at Claire for the first time, and said, "When that happens Agent Bradley, sit down, drink your water, and wait for us to come back for you. Do not leave that spot after your GPS has been marked. I will not spend the night looking all over the desert for you. Is that clear?"

"Yes, sir," Claire called out in a clear voice. To herself she added, *Wandering off won't be a problem, Colonel Asshole, because the only way you're going to mark my GPS is if I drop dead! You won the first round, but you will not beat me again!*

The Colonel looked at his watch and said, "Okay. At the helo pad at 2100. Dismissed."

Claire picked up her helmet and headed for the front of the room. Once again, the Colonel was gone before she got there, but Avi was still at the podium. Claire decided not to even try to explain what she had been doing back there. Instead she simply asked, "So, which one is Myer?"

"That's me, ma'am," a man said from behind her.

With no need to reply, Avi just turned and left the room. Claire watched her walk away, suddenly feeling very much on her own.

"This way, ma'am," Myer said as he started toward the door.

As she fell in beside him, Claire took note of the emblem embroidered into his collar and extended her hand saying, "Claire Bradley. Pleasure to meet you, Captain Myer."

"Likewise, ma'am," he said, shaking her hand. "That was quite a thing you did when your First Lady got shot, ma'am. You're quite a celebrity, even over here."

"Really?" she said genuinely surprised. "You wouldn't know it by anyone's reaction around this camp."

"Don't mind that, ma'am," he said as they stepped outside. "Out here we're focused a hundred and ten percent on whatever operation we're training for. When we get back to Tel Aviv these guys will all be buying you drinks and fighting to get to dance with you."

Claire smiled for the first time since she'd gotten there. "Thanks

Captain," she said. "That's good to hear."

Just then, the Colonel approached and fell into step on the other side of Claire. "Excuse us a moment, Captain," he said.

"Yes, sir," Myer said and made an immediate left turn.

Yousif stopped walking, and Claire turned to face him, heart pounding, trying to be ready for whatever was coming.

"That was quite a show you put on for me in the briefing room," he said. "You must think you're pretty sexy. Well, when this is done, I'd be happy to fuck your brains out, if that's what you're looking for—but until this operation is over, you keep your tits in your shirt, and you pants on.

"Between now and then, if you pull another stunt like that around here, I'll have your skinny ass on a plane headed back to Washington before you can get your clothes back on! Are we clear, Bradley?"

She blinked once, swallowed, and said, "Yes, sir— Sorry, sir."

"Apology accepted," he said as he turned and walked toward the helicopter pad. As he passed Captain Myer, he gestured with his thumb and said, "She's all yours."

Claire just stood there feeling monumentally stupid. *So much for showing him who he was dealing with*, she thought to herself.

In the distance she could hear the *whoomp, whoomp, whoomp* of a big helicopter as Myer called out, "Let's go, ma'am."

They approached a truck that was parked next to the helicopter pad from which equipment was being handed out to the soldiers. About twenty feet from the truck, Myer said, "Wait here. I'll bring you your gear."

She watched as the men strapped on their gear and helped each other get it properly adjusted. Finally, Captain Myer returned and handed her a web belt with a canteen hanging from one side, a pistol holster hanging from the other, and three pouches across the back.

"I didn't think I'd be carrying a side-arm," she said as she wrapped the belt around her waist.

"No, ma'am," Meyer said with a grin. "It's a flare gun. Despite what the Colonel said, it would be a little embarrassing if we had to explain to your President that we had misplaced America's latest hero on night maneuvers."

Claire felt that she was in very good hands as Meyer helped her on with her gear, and explained it to her as he went.

"This pouch contains two extra flares," he told her. "This is your GPS—which you shouldn't need—and over here, is your SAR radio.

That's search-and-rescue, so don't turn it on unless you're lost."

He then helped her to adjust the fit of her helmet, and hooked up its built-in radio headset. "This is a scatter-frequency radio," he told her. "It's almost impossible to eavesdrop on, but it's only good for about a kilometer—a half mile or so. That's why you have the SAR radio. That's good for ten kilometers."

With helmet and army belt, Claire felt a little like a kid playing soldier, compared to the way the Captain was outfitted. His body virtually bristled with weapons and high-tech gear. Claire had psyched herself up for the upcoming three-and-a-half mile jog through the desert, but she was sure glad that she wasn't going to be carrying all of the strike force's equipment!

When the big helicopter touched down and the whine of the engines subsided somewhat, Colonel Yousif called out, "Load up!"

In the reverse order of how they would exit the chopper, the twenty-three men and two women entered it. Avi went in eighth as the leader of White Team. Claire was third to the last to get on board, followed by Myer, and then Colonel Yousif.

As the helicopter crew-chief threw a switch that raised the rear loading ramp, Colonel Yousif plugged his headset into the chopper's intercom wiring, and told the pilots to take off whenever they were ready.

Flying at the leisurely pace of 150 kilometers per hour, it didn't take long to cover six kilometers to the LZ—the landing zone. The door was open almost as soon as the wheels touched the ground, and Claire jumped out right behind Colonel Yousif and Captain Myer.

Running about fifty yards from the chopper to get away from its noise and rotor wash, they crouched down to await the rest of the three teams. Once they were together they all did a quick radio check and those wearing helmet-cameras, like the Colonel, Avi, and Captain Myer also did the same for their video link.

On Colonel Yousif's signal, the group began to move out in single-file. For Claire, the pace was a fairly easy trot, but since they were not following any kind of path, it was much more challenging than jogging around The Mall back in DC.

In the low-light conditions, every fourth man wore his night-vision goggles, with the three men behind him expected to keep up well enough to follow virtually in his footsteps. If there was anything requiring extra caution, the man with the goggles would call it out over the headsets.

For the first mile or so, Claire felt pretty good about how she was keeping up. She was still in control of her breathing, and she had no real aches to speak of. She didn't care for how her helmet bobbled on her head, however, so as she trotted behind Captain Myer she readjusted the chin strap.

Taking her eyes off Myer's feet for just a second was all it took for her to kick a well-rooted rock and lose her balance. She nearly caught herself, but in the end gravity won out, and she went down.

She tucked her arms in, rolled, and came back up onto her feet almost like she meant to perform the little tumbling trick. The soldier behind her who had caught up to her just as she regained her feet, said quietly, "Nice recovery. You okay?"

Giving him a thumbs-up, she quickened her pace to catch up with Myer, although a pain in the side of her right calf told her that she'd probably cut herself on something. As long as she hadn't severed an artery, though, she wasn't stopping for it.

When they had returned to within a half mile of the compound, Colonel Yousif stopped the groups and studied the buildings representing those in Ramallah, through his night-vision binoculars.

She couldn't speak for the others, but Claire certainly welcomed the break. Her lungs were beginning to ache a bit, and her heart was pounding. But she had stayed right on Myer's heels the whole way and she felt damned good about it! Her calf, however, *didn't* feel so good.

Not wanting anyone else to see, she stole a quick look as she squatted, waiting for Colonel Yousif to give the order to move out once again.

With her pants tucked into her boot she couldn't actually see the cut but she was pretty sure there had been blood running from it into her boot. She just couldn't tell how much, nor did she have long to think about it.

"Okay!" came the Colonel's voice over the radio, giving her a start, "Red Team to the north; Green Team to the south; White Team straight away behind Geller. Go!"

The last half mile seemed worse to Claire than the other three combined. But with her objective in sight, she would be damned if she'd quit now!

Right behind Captain Myer, Claire came around the outer-most buildings in the compound, and on Myer's signal, the team stopped and held position. Then as one, they ran up to the next building where they stopped again and surveyed the area. With a hand gesture from Myer, the next man in line ran past them to the next building, stopping with his weapon at the ready. Leapfrogging like this two more times, Claire found herself standing behind Myer, at the corner of the building next door to their objective.

As each of the scout teams called in their all-clears, Claire noticed, with some surprise, how much the target house resembled the photos of the house in Ramallah that had been shown in the briefing. Even the security bars on the windows had been duplicated exactly. The Colonel, Claire could see, took his run-throughs very seriously.

Finally, the Colonel ordered the White Team to advance, and Claire watched as a dozen soldiers, including Avi, converged on the target building, taking up positions next to each of the doors and windows. Two of the men quickly placed explosive charges on the bars covering the front window, and reported, "Charges set."

"Grenades ready," the Colonel commanded over the radio, and counted down, "Three—two—one—GO!"

Claire heard the crash of glass, followed by loud *"whumps!"* which were accompanied by bright flashes. Those were flash-bang grenades, designed to stun and disorient the people in the building without inflicting serious injury.

Immediately following the flash-bang explosions, the charges on the window bars went off with surprisingly little noise or flash.

Those explosions were followed by more *whumps!* and flashes, after which Claire watched two of the soldiers crash through what was left of the front window. Right on their heels was the rest of White Team.

From inside the house came more *whumps!*, which were followed by the unmistakable sound of shotguns going off. With each shotgun blast, Claire heard "One down," in her ear piece.

Had Claire not been in on the briefing earlier, she might have thought that the strike team was practicing to kill everyone they encountered. Instead, she knew that they were going to be using "non-lethal" rubber bullets to subdue their targets.

In the excitement of the mock raid, Claire hadn't noticed before, but she now realized that the helicopter was approaching.

As the succession of shotgun blasts and "One down," announcements continued, the chopper settled to the street in front of the building, its rotors continuing to spin at flying speed, with only their pitch keeping the bird on the ground.

"Red and Green Teams cover evac," the Colonel commanded, and immediately, two soldiers from the White Team came out of the front door, running to the waiting chopper, taking up defensive positions next to opening loading ramp. Right behind them were two more soldiers, half dragging, half carrying a life-size, 200-pound dummy "prisoner" between them. When all eight dummies were aboard the copter, the Colonel called out, "White Team and Red Team, load up. Green Team, secure the area."

"Let's go!" Myer said to Claire, and the two sprinted for the helicopter.

Claire's sprint included a limp that she tried her best to hide. Her calf had become stiff while she was standing for just that short time, and now it hurt like hell to run on it.

With gritted teeth she made it to the side door of the chopper, but then misplaced her first step up, and banged her calf against the edge of the door. She let out a reflexive, "Fuck!!" as the pain exploded up her leg.

Rolling onto her back to get into the helicopter, she quickly scrambled to her position on the floor, so that the three men behind her, together with Avi and the Colonel could get on board.

The door was still closing as the big helicopter lifted off the ground and pitched forward to gain airspeed. "Green Team, fall back to evac-two," the Colonel said over his headset. "Yousif out."

After its emergency ascent, the run-through was complete for the helicopter crew, and the pilots took the bird in a lazy turn around the compound before approaching the landing pad where they had started. Claire was sitting there, eyes closed, trying to will the pain from her leg, when Captain Myer said, "Are you okay? Did you twist your ankle getting aboard?"

She looked up, and saw Colonel Yousif looking down at her, too.

"No, Captain," she replied. "The ankle's fine. I got a little cut during the hike, and I bumped it getting in, is all. No big deal."

"Get her to the infirmary when we land," the Colonel said to Myer. "Then get over to the briefing room. We'll wait for you."

"Colonel, I'm fine. Really," Claire protested, getting to her feet as the chopper touched down. "I don't want to be scratched from the operation for a little cut on the leg."

He looked at her with an almost amused look, and said, "You can't be scratched from an operation you were never going on, Bradley. You've had your adventure, now drop it." With that he hopped from the helicopter and headed toward the briefing room.

Claire stubbornly refused Myer's offer of help hopping down from the chopper, and quickly regretted it. Although she landed with most of her weight on her good left leg, the jolt sent such a stab of pain through her right, that it nearly caused both of them to buckle.

274

As she limped toward the infirmary, Myer at her side, she wasn't sure whether she was more pissed off at the Colonel at that point, or herself.

"I hope you're okay, ma'am," the Captain said as he left her in the care of the med-tech. "You did real well out there." With a wink, he added, "For a shikseh." He then headed back to the briefing room, at a run.

"What's a shikseh?" Claire asked the med-tech.

"Non-Jewish girl," he replied as he unlaced her boot. "High praise from these guys."

Twenty minutes, three shots of lidocaine, and six stitches later—three of which were intramuscular—the tech was putting a sterile bandage over the surprisingly deep wound. "You'll need to keep pressure off of that for a while," he told her. "Wait here and I'll get you some crutches."

As he left the room, Claire heard the engines of the helicopter winding up, and she realized they were getting ready for the second run-through.

She hopped down off the table, and found that although her leg still hurt, the lidocaine had reduced the pain to a dull throb. Through sheer force of will, Claire walked hurriedly across the compound with barely a trace of a limp.

"I'm okay to go again, Colonel," she said finding Yousif standing next to the helicopter talking to Myer. "It was just a deep scratch, really. I'm fine."

"Well, you're *not* going," he said dismissively with hardly a glance at her.

"Why won't you keep your end of the deal, Colonel Yousif?" Claire said, having expected an argument. "Despite your prediction, I kept up every step of the way. I think I've earned this, Colonel!"

"Why are you so fucking dumb, Bradley?" the Colonel snapped. "I am not taking America's celebrity *du Jour* on an operation into unfriendly territory where she could very easily get killed. How hard is that for you to comprehend? The people we're going after—not even counting your Dunham—are psychopathic killers. They've blown up women and children on buses, and then bragged about it, for God sake!"

Somehow, she hadn't expected an explanation from the Colonel, just an argument, and she found herself a bit off guard.

"And they would *love* to brag that they had shot your First Lady, and then when the USA—the Great Satan—foolishly sent a woman to apprehend them, they killed her, too. Just drop it, Bradley. You're not going on the operation, so there's no point in you cluttering up any more run-throughs. End of discussion."

As he turned to walk away, Claire threw out her trump card. "With all due respect, sir, my President and your Prime Minister have ..."

"Fuck your President and my Prime Minister!" the Colonel growled through clinched teeth as he spun back toward her. "You are really beginning to piss me off, now! I have made it clear to everyone above me, *including* the Prime Minister, that I do not want you on this mission. It is a stupid fucking idea to have civilian observers on a military operation of *any* kind, much less one as unpredictable as this.

"Unfortunately for me, I couldn't convince my superiors of that, so, because I am able to follow orders—unlike *some* people—I'm stuck with you.

"As field commander, however, what I do with you is entirely up to me. You may consider me an asshole, but I am trying to accommodate a whole raft of people who want to stick their noses into my job, and still accomplish my objective without getting anyone killed.

"To that end, and in deference to my Prime Minister, and not to you, my current plan calls for you to be sitting in our tactical-communications van and keeping your mouth shut while the operation takes place tomorrow night. That part of the plan is very flexible, however, so if I have any more shit out of you between now and then, I'll classify you as a security risk, and have you thrown the hell out of Israel. Am I getting through, Bradley?"

Though her heart was slamming in her chest, she managed to control her voice and reply, "Yes, sir. I guess I misunderstood my role in all this, sir."

"That's the difference between you and us, Bradley," he said. "You feel the need to *understand* an order before you agree to follow it. If the men defending this country acted that way, our neighbors would have pushed us into the sea decades ago." With that, he turned to Captain Myer, and said, "We ready to go?"

Without another word or glance at Claire, the Colonel strode off toward the helicopter.

As the chopper lifted off, Claire limped back to the infirmary, her leg beginning to throb more as the lidocaine wore off.

As she dropped heavily into a chair, the med-tech said, "If you don't follow the instructions, you void the warranty, you know. Don't come limping back in here expecting me to fix your stitches after you've been running around without crutches."

"Sorry," Claire said, "I thought I was going somewhere. I'll be happy to take those crutches, now. Also, some pain killers, if it's not too much trouble. And anything you might have for a badly bruised ego," she added.

Chapter 52

Tuesday, October 28
Miami, FL

Shortly after noon on Tuesday, a medical transport van was pulling up in front of concourse-G at Miami International Airport. As the wheelchair ramp was lowered a porter ran up and took the passenger's flight information from the driver. Even though the platform barely bumped the pavement at the end of its travel, the man in the wheelchair let out a pitiful moan of pain. His right arm was in a wrist-to-shoulder cast, and his right leg was encased in plaster from his toes to his knee. A bandage wrapped around his head covered both ears, and was topped by a yarmulke bobby-pinned in place. He had two black eyes, his lips were swollen, and more gauze covered his nose and chin.

As the porter released the locks on the chair and pulled it off the ramp, he said in a happy-go-lucky tone, "My, my, Mr. Levitz, what happened to you?"

When the wheels bumped the pavement, "Mr. Levitz"—a.k.a. François DeCarlo, the man who had been Frances Dunham a week and a half ago—cried out in make-believe pain. Through barely moving jaws he whined in a thick Jewish accent, "What happened? You want to know what happened? My *meshugga* son-in-law tried to kill me, that's what happened!"

Without even acknowledging the remark, the porter said, "Well, don't you worry there, Mr. Levitz; we'll take good care of you," and he pushed him up the anti-slip ripples of the disability ramp, eliciting more moans, groans, and whines with each bump.

The porter wheeled Frank to the front of the El Al check-in line and handed the attendant Mr. Levitz' ticket and passport. A second porter heaved Mr. Levitz' suitcases onto the luggage scale in the counter, and received an accented rebuke for his effort. "Whoa, Mr. Gorilla! You're training for some new Olympic event here? The suitcase throw?"

Experienced in dealing with cantankerous customers the three people attending to the man just smiled at one another, and *Mr. Gorilla* said, "You have a good flight, Mr. Levitz," and patted him on the shoulder.

"OY!" he moaned, "My *shmuck* son-in-law is paying all of you, isn't he? It wasn't good enough he tried to kill me in his car, now he's sending assassins after me!"

When the porter reached security, Mr. Levitz agreed to be helped from the wheelchair and assisted through the metal detector—moaning and whining all the way, using more Yiddish expletives than any of the people on duty had ever heard. As he rambled on about his murderous son-in-law and how they were surely all conspiring to make sure he never came back to the United States, they all just smiled behind his back. Some passengers could be real pains in the butt, but Mr. Levitz was more a source of amusement.

Being a source of amusement was fine with Frank; the whole point in the overbearing-accident-victim charade was that he not be a source of *suspicion*. And as far as he could tell not a single person thought to compare his bandaged and bruised face to the look-out photos of Frances Dunham that hung next to their x-ray monitors. Thank God for incompetent people, he thought.

It was a little after nine Wednesday morning when "Mr. Levitz's" plane touched down in Tel Aviv. As soon as he was in his hotel room, he removed Dr. Polyakov's bandages from his face and head. He then retrieved a pair of gift-wrapped pruning shears from his checked luggage, and cut the casts from his arm and leg.

He looked at himself in the mirror and marveled at how the doctor had altered his appearance. Once the swelling and bruising went away, it would be even better. In a few week's time, very few people would be able to pick out the features that gave away that Levitz, Dunham, Douglas, and Beard were all one and the same. Recognizing him as the person known as The Teacher, would be even harder. This was the fourth and most radical plastic surgery of his career, but even before this round of cutting, neither Interpol, nor even the Mossad knew what he really looked like any more.

He plugged his laptop computer into the hotel's network, connected to the Internet, and sent a short e-mail to Henri.

H-

I have arrived, finally. All went as expected before I left. Are the plans for the reunion still on track?

F-

Ten minutes later, after a quick sponge bath—Dr. Polyakov having warned him about getting his stitches wet—Frank checked his computer, and saw that he had received a reply to his message.

F-

So glad to hear that everything went well. Now that you're here, the reunion can go on as we had planned. Can't wait to see you again!

H-

Thirty minutes later, his recent surgery hidden by a long wig, false beard and mustache, and large dark glasses, Frank stepped out of the hotel dressed as an Hasidic Rabbi. He crossed the street and climbed into the back of an off-duty taxi that Henri had arranged to have waiting. As the driver pulled out into the traffic, Frank thought about how good it was going to be, in two days time, to be on a plane bound for Australia and to have this whole life behind him. But first, he had one last meeting to attend. A meeting that his old friend, Henri, had arranged.

Chapter 53

Tuesday, October 28
Negev Desert, Israel

Back in the barracks that she and Avi were sharing, Claire put her leg up as the med-tech had suggested, and lay there listening to the muffled explosions, gun shots, and *whoomp*, *whoomp*, *whoomp* of the helicopter, as the teams performed two more run-throughs at the other side of the compound.

Because of Claire's six-hour jet-lag, when Avi made it back to the barracks at six in the morning, it was midnight to Claire. So, for quite different reasons, both women were able to fall asleep, easily.

It was a little after noon on Tuesday when Claire awoke. Avi was still asleep, so as quietly as she could she took a shower, and put on a clean DCU, which she found on the bunk next to hers.

As she was lacing up her boots, she heard Avi stir. Using one crutch, Claire made her way over to Avi's side of the room. She sat on the bunk next to Avi's, and said, "I'd like to apologize for being such an ass during the Colonel's briefing yesterday."

"Being or showing?" Avi replied wryly.

"Yeah ..." Claire said. "You're probably wondering what the hell I was doing back there, huh?"

"Not really," Avi replied. "You were trying to show the Colonel that he couldn't intimidate you, right? That you were tougher than anything he could throw at you."

Claire was a little surprised and embarrassed that she had been so transparent. "I guess it was a stupid reaction, but he just had me so pissed off ..."

"I don't think you know *how* stupid, Claire. Not to mention unprofessional," Avi told her. "You may have seen that as a gutsy move, trying to one-up the Colonel, but if the rest of the men in that room had turned and seen you, almost all of the respect they have for you would have gone right out the window. I don't think you know how big of a risk you were taking. Not only that, it was a waste of time. The Colonel wasn't trying to intimidate you in the first place."

"You don't think so?" Claire said. "Having me change my clothes in a room full of strange men isn't supposed to be intimidating?"

"It might have *been* intimidating to you," Avi said, "but if you'll recall, Colonel Yousif never told you that you had to change your clothes there. He told you that if you missed a word of the briefing, that you'd be automatically scratched. He didn't just make up that rule on *your* account. That's standard procedure in any of his briefings, and it applies to all of us. Colonel Yousif doesn't play games, Claire. He'll tell you exactly what he thinks whether you're a buck-private or the Prime Minister, and he sure as hell doesn't sugarcoat what he has to say."

"Yeah, I got a taste of that last night," Claire said.

"The Colonel may appear to be an asshole to you, but he has never lost a man on a combat mission, so that makes him more like a God to us."

While she wouldn't compare the two men in any other way, she immediately thought of Gants, and that same type of respect that she had for him.

Later, after a quick lunch in the mess hall, Claire made her way to the small building that was Colonel Yousif's office and quarters. She knocked on the door and heard him call out, "Come."

Inside, the one-room building was very military—sparse, but functional. The Colonel was sitting at a metal desk typing at a computer keyboard. He glanced up at her, said, "Sit", and finished typing his e-mail. He hit the "Send" key, and then closed the program.

He leaned back in his chair and looked at Claire, noticing the crutch she had leaned against the wall. She saw his eyes go to the crutch, so she was surprised when he didn't comment about it. Instead, he simply said, "Yes?"

"Sorry to interrupt you, Colonel," she said. "But I have a question about the operation. In your briefing, sir, you didn't mention anything about collecting evidence from the house after it was secured. Is that the reason that Green Team is being left behind?"

He looked at her for a long moment before answering. "Green Team is being *left behind*—as you put it—because the maximum load for the helicopter is twenty-eight men, plus crew, and we're going in with twenty-four. We have to take an additional eight people out, so that puts us four men over-limit. It's safer to leave the whole team, than just half of it. They'll be picked up about half a mile west by the tac-com van in which you'll be sitting ... and keeping quiet.

"As for evidence," he went on, "I'm aware of an operator's manual, supposedly for the gun that shot your First Lady. Green Team will look for it before they pull back."

Trying to avoid any hint of challenge in her voice, Claire said, "Sir, do you think there might be any way that I could get into the house—after it's secured, that is—and collect the evidence myself?"

His face took on an expression that virtually shouted, *"Didn't we go over this, already!?"*

"Sir, I'm not questioning how you've planned the operation," she said before he could say anything. "It's a chain-of-evidence issue. If the prosecutors want to use whatever comes out of that house to convict those men of attempting to kill Katherine McClure, there'll need to be an unbroken link between where the evidence was collected, and the court-room, otherwise the defense lawyers will get it thrown out.

"If your men collect the evidence they'd have to be available to tes-tify—probably numerous times—when the trial begins. That's fine. That'll work from a legal standpoint. But if I can collect the evidence myself, then *I'm* the beginning of the chain, and the whole matter is out of your hair."

Again, he simply looked at her for a long few moments before saying anything. Was he contemplating her reasoning? Deciding whether she was trying to bullshit him? Or was he, Avi's assurances to the contrary, thinking of a way to screw with her?

"Okay," he said finally. "But it will depend on how the operation goes. If the area remains secure, I'll have the van come all the way in to the house to evacuate Green Team, and I'll have them give you five min-utes inside the house. If I think there's any risk at all, we'll stay with the current plan. The courts will just have to deal with it."

"Thank you, sir," she said, getting to her feet, and slipping the crutch under her arm. As she reached for the door knob, she paused and said, "Um, sir? There is one more thing."

He let out an exasperated sigh, and looked up at her.

"I'd just like to apologize again, for my actions in the briefing room yesterday, sir. That was an uncalled-for reaction to a reasonable request." She went on with equal parts humility and nervousness, "I was hoping that maybe that whole thing could stay ... you know, just between us ... sir."

Turning back to his computer, he replied, "I take it by your request, that you were unaware that all briefings are videotaped for possible use in training." Without looking up at her, he concluded the conversation with, "Dismissed, Agent Bradley."

Claire was sure that her heart stopped! Was he joking? He wasn't *smiling*! Oh, shit!

Before she could think of what to say, he added without looking up, "That means leave, Bradley. Now."

Without another word she hobbled outside and pulled the door closed behind her. She looked up and said quietly, "Oh God, let him be joking!" as visions of her *indiscretion* flashed before her eyes, circling the world on the Internet.

Chapter 54

Thursday, October 30
Ramallah, Palestine

On the dot of 2200 hours, Wednesday night, Claire's interminable waiting was finally coming to an end. Colonel Yousif began his last briefing before the start of the operation by saying that Avi had earlier received a message from her man inside the cell.

"al-Abassi has confirmed that the three Hamoudi brothers are there, that Hamshari is there, and that The Teacher is on his way and would be there before midnight. al-Abassi told her that there has been no discussion about any possible trouble, meaning that we still have the element of surprise. That's the good news.

"The bad news is that the cloud cover that we had hoped would be blocking the moon tonight is breaking up, so we're going to have sporadic periods of relative brightness."

During the briefing, as discreetly as she could, Claire looked around for a video camera. She didn't see any, but she knew enough about modern surveillance equipment to know that not seeing it didn't mean it wasn't there. Damn!

Twenty minutes later, the Colonel had finished going over specific things that he had noted during the three run-throughs on Monday night, and the final one on Tuesday. When he finished he said, "Now, go get a few hours sleep. We're on the helipad at 0230. Dismissed."

Claire didn't expect to be able to get much sleep between her jet-lagged body-clock and the anticipation of the operation, so she was surprised when Avi was shaking her awake at 0200.

Thirty minutes later, the teams started filing into the helicopter, with Claire and two team members that she hadn't seen before, getting in just ahead of the Colonel. She soon learned that they were the audio/video technicians that would be in the tactical-communications van with her. Although her leg was not fully healed, the day's rest on Wednesday had it feeling pretty good, so she decided to forego the crutch because she felt that it would be in the way in the helicopter, in the van, and certainly during her search through the house, if that came to pass. If it meant getting the evidence to convict these bastards, then she could put up with a little pain.

The helicopter took off, climbed to 1000 feet, and started its long-way-around course to the outskirts of Ramallah.

During the flight, Claire kept running the mission through her mind, especially the part where she would, hopefully, enter the house and have five minutes to look for evidence.

Claire had asked, but Avi had not been able to provide any more information about the manual, or where in the house al-Abassi had seen it, except to mention that he said that it was handwritten, and not printed. That didn't help her much, but at least Claire knew that she wasn't looking for a bound, military-looking document. It was probably a notebook or a binder, she thought.

Sitting on the deck of the chopper, absently rubbing her leg, Claire was mentally replaying the training animation that the Colonel had presented during the first briefing. Part of it had shown the Ramallah house with its roof removed, to show the team members the layout of the building. That was the part she had in her mind's eye, now. The animation had accurately shown the rooms and even the closets in the house, but the details that Claire would need to be concerned with, such as dressers, bookcases, shelves, desks, and such, had been just generic pieces furniture to make the illustration of the house appeared lived-in. The Colonel had pointed out to his men, that the animators had no way of knowing what furniture might be in the house or how it might be arranged. Aside from room layouts, then, the animation was of little help to Claire in planning her search.

So, instead, she tried to think of what she might do with such a document if she had it in her possession. Now that the gun was gone, the manual probably held far less importance than it once had, so it was probably not under lock and key. Of course, the other side of that coin occurred to her, as well, and she didn't like that thought. No longer having access to the gun, the manual was worthless to those in the house, so it might be discarded at any time.

Claire's thoughts of the search were interrupted as the chopper banked steeply, slowed, and then touched down. Immediately, the big rear cargo door lowered to the ground, and Claire jumped up to quickly follow the Colonel and the two techs down the ramp.

As the rest of the teams came out of the helicopter, Claire watched as the Colonel, using hand signals rather than trying to shout above the noise of the still running helicopter, indicated to one of the techs that he should take Claire and head for the van. She then saw him lean in close to the tech's ear to tell him something, while at the same time nodding and putting a hand to his ear. Then, shaking his head side to side in a "no" indication, he changed his hand gesture to a flat horizontal motion that would normally indicate "cut" or "stop".

What was that all about? she wondered as she trotted, with just a trace of a limp, toward the van that she hadn't even seen until the tech took her by the arm and pulled her toward it.

The van, expertly camouflaged to blend into the desert terrain, had been driven there, cross country, by the two strike force troops who now stood guarding it. The vehicle was a modified HUMV, or Hummer, with an eight-foot tall, eight-foot wide, and ten-foot long enclosed "room" on the back. On the roof of the room was a porcupine array of different size and shape antennae.

The two guards remained outside the vehicle under the netting, while the two techs and Claire climbed inside to join the other tech who had ridden out with the vehicle so that he could check all of the equipment before the arrival of the strike force.

As the newly arriving techs briefed the on-site tech on what was discussed during the Colonel's last briefing, Claire stood and looked about the van.

The forward wall was virtually covered with video monitors. Starting at the ceiling, there was a bank of four rows of six screens each, with each one having about a nine-inch display. Below that was another row of four monitors, each having about a nineteen-inch screen. In front of that row was a desk-like shelf that held two computer keyboards and a number of switches and pushbuttons.

The adjacent wall was lined, floor to ceiling, with electronic gear, much of which Claire couldn't identify precisely. From her training at the academy, and her experience in the Service's communications van, however, she recognized enough of the equipment to make the educated guess that much of it was jamming and tracking equipment, specially suited to strike force type operations.

One of the techs directed Claire to a folding jump seat at the back of the van, while he and the others took the operators' seats and donned headsets with microphone booms. Immediately, they began speaking to the team members, who were doing their radio checks. At the same time, Claire watched images appear on the monitors as those with helmet-cameras turned them on and requested video checks.

Claire recognized about half of the pictures on the screens from their green color and uniform brightness of living and inanimate objects as light-amplified, or starlight night vision images. The others, made obvious by the "glow" of the team members in the images, were being taken with infrared or IR cameras designed to pick up the "heat signature" of humans, even in total darkness.

At the bottom right corner of each picture was a letter and a number indicating which team member was broadcasting the image. Claire saw that the Colonel's starlight image was marked W1, presumably, for White-One, indicating that he had taken over the role of team leader from Avi. Claire scanned the monitors and found Avi's image, also a starlight, marked W8. Had she been *demoted* for some reason? Or had she just been a stand-in leader so that the Colonel could assess the training exercises?

She then found the image from Captain Myer's camera with an R1 in the corner. He wore an IR unit. She noticed that all of White Team had helmet cameras, but only a few in each of the other teams had them. She correctly guessed that that was because it was White Team that would actually be entering the house, and the techs in the van would be monitoring every step as a second set of eyes for the team members.

After watching for a minute or so, Claire tapped one of the techs on the shoulder, and when he pulled his headphones from one ear, she asked, "Will I be able to hear?"

"Sorry. I forgot," he said, reaching under the desk panel and pulling another set of headphones from a drawer. Before handing it to Claire, however, he unplugged the microphone from the connector on the ear cuff and slid it off the end of the boom. He then set a selector to the right wireless frequency, and handed the headset to Claire.

As she took it and put it over her head, she understood the Colonel's gestures back at the helicopter. *"She can listen, but don't let her talk,"* he had apparently told the tech.

Judging the Colonel on an objective, purely professional basis, Claire had to admit that she respected the man, or at least his abilities and accomplishments. On a personal level, though, she couldn't recall anyone that she *disliked* more!

Finally, the checks complete, Claire heard the Colonel give the "Move out" order, and all of the images on the screens began to bob as the teams started their trek toward the house. At the head of the column, the image from the Colonel's camera was displayed on one of the big monitors on the bottom row. After a while, the image began to break up and flick on and off. One of the techs touched his mike button and said, "Com to White-One; That's about the limit of your video range, Colonel. Let's set up a repeater there somewhere."

"Roger, Com," came the Colonel's voice. Then he said, "White-One to Red-four; did you copy that?"

"Roger, White-One. Repeater is active—now," came the reply.

As the word "now" came over the radio, the Colonel's camera image returned to its earlier clarity.

The repeater, was a small portable amplifier used to receive the video signals from the relatively low-powered transmitters that the troops wore, boost their strength, and resend them to the next repeater or to the van if it was within range. This process was repeated three more times before the teams reached the hilltop that looked down into the small group of buildings, a little less than a kilometer ahead of them.

One by one, all of the images became more or less steady as each of the troops wearing a camera made it to the rallying point and took a prone position while the Colonel and each of the team leaders scanned the area ahead with their binoculars.

After a minute or so, Claire heard the Colonel's voice say, "White-One to Red-One and Green-One; do you have a go?"

The reply came back immediately. "Red-One here; affirmative, we're clear to go." Then the same reply was repeated by Green-One.

"Okay," the Colonel's voice answered. "Red Team to the north; Green Team to the south; White Team straightaway behind me. Let's go."

As Claire watched the images of the teams' advance, her pulse rate began to quicken. She found herself watching Myer's image mostly, combining it with her memory of her run-through into almost being there.

When the teams reached their first outer-circle checkpoints, within sight of the house, they called in their "all clears" and waited for the

Colonel's order to move up.

Though her eyes were trained on one of the upper, smaller monitors, watching Myer's picture, her attention was immediately drawn when a bright spot flared in the center of the Colonel's image on the larger monitor in the bottom row.

"Hold positions!" the Colonel's voice commanded with an obvious tone of urgency. "I have a subject near the back door. He just lit a cigarette. Com; do you copy the image?"

"Com to White-One; affirmative. Let me try to enhance. Hold as still as you can for a capture on my count. Three—two—one," and he touched a button on the console. Immediately a still shot of the man appeared on the screen next to the Colonel's video image.

"Com to White-One; good capture; stand by."

Using his keyboard, the tech then zoomed the image until the man's face filled the screen. As it grew in size, the detail of the green image with its odd shadows became more and more grainy, making it all but impossible to determine which of the subjects the man might be.

"Com to White-One; no positive ID on the subject," the tech said. As he was speaking, however, a break in the clouds allowed the moon to light up the area, and the video image of the subject smoking the cigarette was instantly improved by a factor of five or ten times.

"White-One," the tech said quickly, "hold for another capture on one."

Before he could start his countdown, however, the Colonel replied, "Negative! I think he's seen me!" Looking closely at the video monitor, they saw that the man appeared to be looking directly into the Colonel's camera. The tech hit the capture button anyway, but the image that came up on his monitor, while brighter, was blurry because of the Colonel's movement.

Quickly, the tech zoomed in and tried to manipulate the image with some editing tools, but still, neither Claire nor the techs could recognize him.

"Com to White-One," the tech radioed to the Colonel, "negative ID. Repeat; negative ID. This appears to be a new subject."

As the tech spoke, they watched the center monitor and saw the man toss his cigarette on the ground and start walking directly toward the Colonel's position. The clouds had once again hidden the moon, but they could see that the man continued to stare intently at where he must have seen the Colonel's movement a moment ago. As he walked, they watched him reach into a jacket pocket and withdraw what appeared to be a handgun. With the graininess of the low-light image they couldn't tell for sure, but the tech keyed his mike and said, "Subject appears to have a weapon!"

"Roger that and confirm," the Colonel replied, indicating that he, too, had seen the gun. "White-One to White-Three," the Colonel commanded, "Take him—kill shot."

White-Three, who was positioned about thirty feet to the Colonel's right, fired a single shot from his silenced Mauser 86SR sniper rifle.

Claire heard a soft pop in her headphones, and then watched as the man took his next step and crumbled to the ground, laying there motionless in a distorted heap.

Although the shot through the rifle's silencer was quiet, it was not actually *silent*, and everyone remained frozen for several tense moments, watching the house, and listening to see if anyone might have heard it as it interrupted the stillness of the night.

Finally, Claire heard the Colonel say in his typical monotone, "White-One; all clear. Positions, report." Claire found herself almost shaking from the adrenaline in her veins, so she was amazed that the Colonel's voice sounded as flat as it had in the briefing room. She hoped to God that she would never get that used to people dying in front of her.

One by one the other team members reported that they, too, had all-clear conditions, and the Colonel said, "White-One to all teams; resume advance."

From that point on, as Claire and the techs watched the monitors and listened to the communication, the operation went almost exactly as planned and rehearsed.

Claire's heart was racing as she watched the jerky video images of the soldiers running through the house. First, a pair of monitors would go white and she'd hear a loud "*blam!*" as a flash-bang went off. Then, two images of the same room would appear, one from a slightly higher angle than the other as the first soldier knelt in the doorway training his Uzi into the room, and the second, from a standing position, aimed his shotgun with its non-lethal ammunition at whoever was in the room.

Claire would then hear the "*boom!*" of the shotgun and see the subject recoil or fall down, depending on what he was doing when he was hit.

Once each man had been incapacitated from the shotgun blast, Claire watched as a hood was pulled over his head to keep him disoriented, and his hands were bound behind his back using plastic zip-tie handcuffs.

With each capture, the call of "One down" was repeated until Claire had counted seven men and women in custody. And although the video images were jumpy, Claire had been able to recognize each of the terrorist as they were taken down. The one face that she didn't see was Dunham's, and a very bad feeling crept into her stomach.

"White-One to Evac-One," Claire heard the Colonel call to the helicopter. "On the ground in three minutes." Then to his team he commanded, "White Team, prepare your prisoners for evacuation." Finally, to Myer, he radioed, "Red-One, take two men and get the body from the back yard. He goes with us."

"Com to White-One," Claire heard one of the techs in front of her say, "from the video feed we can confirm that you have the three Hamoudis, Hamshari, and al-Abassi, along with the two women. It looks like you're missing The Teacher."

"Roger, Com," the Colonel replied in a tone that hinted to Claire that he had already figured that out, but wasn't particularly concerned. "White-Eight did you copy?" he asked Avi.

"Roger, White-One," Avi replied. "I just asked al-Abassi why The Teacher wasn't here, and he told me that he is. He said we wouldn't know it was him because a doctor changed his face. He must be our midnight smoker in the back yard."

"Roger, White-Eight," Yousif said a flat tone. "White-One to Com; all subjects accounted for; one deceased. Preparing to evacuate with all subjects. Com, commence your evacuation of Green Team. Over."

As the tech began his reply, Claire's anger and frustration exploded, and she shouted at the Colonel, "You killed him! Why the fuck did you have to kill him, for Christ's sake!?"

Hearing her rant over the tech's open mike, Claire heard the Colonel tell him in an icy tone, "Put Agent Bradley on for a moment."

"It's for you," the tech said, handing Claire his headset with its voice-actuated microphone.

Seething, she pulled the headphones on and shouted into the mike, "Why the hell did you..."

"Shut up, Bradley!" the Colonel cut her off. "Shut up or I'll have them *duct tape* your mouth shut!" With a seething silence on her end, he went on, "Not that I owe you an explanation, but just to keep you from bouncing off the ceiling and getting on my men's nerves, the reason I called for a kill shot is because wounded men can still shoot and raise alarms, and the lives of my men come first, followed by the success of the operation. Only after that do I start thinking about the welfare of the people who would like to see me and my men dead."

"What the hell happened to the non-lethal rounds?" Claire shot back.

"Number one, he was too far away," the Colonel began in a condescending tone as if Claire was ten years old. "Number two, the noise from the shotgun would have woken up the whole fucking neighborhood, and number three, he sure as hell wasn't going to be using NLR's when he started firing at us in another few seconds."

"I still don't ..." Claire began

"We're done talking, Bradley," he cut her off. "But you still have a job to do down here, so I suggest you get focused on collecting your chain-of-evidence. Now give the mike back to Linden."

Twenty minutes later, after a bumpy cross-country trek, the com-van pulled to a stop between two houses where it could more easily be defended by Green Team than out in the street. Everyone within two blocks of the house was awake after the assault and the big helicopter landing and taking off, but very few had ventured outside to investigate. Such was life in this area of the Middle East.

As one of the techs opened the van door, he said to Claire, "Five minutes, and we're out of here." She climbed out of the van and ran toward the house, her adrenaline masking most of the pain from her leg. Once inside, Claire was like a contestant on a beat-the-clock shopping-spree game-show, pulling books from shelves, flipping pages, and tossing them as fast as she could. She quickly exhausted all of the obvious places, and then started into the closets, pushing clothes aside, emptying shelves, and even looking for false panels.

Finally, in the closet in the back bedroom, she found a four-drawer file cabinet turned so that the drawers faced the side wall.

Yes! she said to herself as she struggled to pull it out where she could open it. She took hold of the handle of the top drawer, but suddenly, her *voice* told her to look in the bottom drawer first. There, she hit pay dirt! She pulled out several school-type spiral-bound notebooks filled with handwritten characters that she recognized as Arabic, a language that she was, unfortunately, not able to read.

Flipping quickly through the first book, she found an electrical schematic of what looked to be a timing device. For a bomb perhaps? She flipped through more of the books, finding similar sketches and even a couple pictures of automobiles that had been clipped from magazines.

At last, in the notebook at the bottom of the stack, she found it! A hand-drawn sketch of the assembled Dynametric gun!

"YES!" she said out loud, this time.

Setting the stack of books on top of the file cabinet, she grabbed the handle of the top drawer and pulled. But instead of the drawer opening, she felt herself being slammed from behind by someone's full body weight, while a pair of strong arms wrapped around her and yanked her fingers from the drawer pull.

A harsh voice began to say something, but was cut off when Claire instinctively threw her helmeted head up and back as hard as she could, cracking the man in the mouth. The man yelped, and followed it with a string of oaths as Claire brought her boot up hard, raking her heel up his shin and cracking his kneecap. Still in his bear-hug grip, she put both feet against the file cabinet, and shoved with all of her might, sending the two of them backwards into the wall. She slammed her head into his face once again, and wedged her arms up between his, finally breaking his grip. She spun out of his arms, planting one foot on the floor, and swinging the other up in a line for his crotch. Suddenly, she saw that she was fighting one of Yousif's men! The realization caused her to hesitate her kick for just a split second, and he was able to deflect it by turning his leg, and taking the blow in the thigh, while at the same time grabbing her boot. He pulled her foot up to shoulder height, and shoved, knocking her off balance and onto her back. To his surprise, though, she carried the motion of his push through into a smooth back-roll, and came up on her feet, ready to attack again. Instead of springing at him, however, she held her position as she found herself staring into the muzzle of a Sig Sauer 9mm pistol.

"Just stop! Okay? Stop!" the man shouted as blood ran from his split lip. "Damn!" he said, spitting on the floor. "I should have let you just open the fool thing!"

"You're too late." she said, stalling for time, while setting her balance for a kick at the gun. "I already opened it. I *have* the notebooks."

Through experienced eyes, the man easily read Claire's body language, and said as he lowered his gun, "I'll save you the trouble of that kick, Agent Bradley. Just stop fighting, okay? I'm sorry I startled you—real sorry," he added licking his bleeding lip, "but cabinets like that are a favorite place for booby traps."

"Apparently you're wrong," she said, still on her guard. "Like I said, I already opened it."

"Either I'm wrong, or you're very lucky, but I wouldn't recommend opening any more drawers to find out which. If I were you, I'd be satisfied with whatever I found already, and get out while I'm still in one piece. Which, by the way, is what I'm going to do."

Though she was ready to kill the man a moment ago, her *voice* told her that she should be trusting him on this. She grabbed the notebooks, and as she headed for the door, right on his heels, she said, "So what do you do with the cabinet? Do you blow it up, just to be sure?"

A few minutes later, as Green Team was getting into the van, Claire's "attacker" handed her the ends of three ropes that had been strung into the house through a smashed out window and tied to the drawer pulls of the file cabinet still inside where they left it. "Let's see if I was justified in attacking you," he said.

Claire pulled hard on the first rope, and she could hear the drawer slam open, but there was no blast. She pulled on the second one, with the same result. As she yanked on the final rope, she readied herself to hear an explosion, but there was nothing more than the drawer opening again. "I guess our skirmish was for naught," Claire said. "But I appreciate ..."

He held up a finger to stop her, and said, "... three ... two ... one." An explosion shook the house and made Claire jump. A hollow feeling hit her stomach as she realized that if it hadn't been for the man who stood there smiling at her—with a split lip—that that explosion would probably have killed her.

Taking the rope from her, and looking at the knot in the end, he said, "Top drawer. That's the one most people would open first. What made you open the bottom one?"

"A little voice told me," she answered, and mentally said a thank you to it.

Chapter 55

Thursday, October 30
Negev Desert, Israel

The com-van drove south until it reached Atarot Airport in Jerusalem. There it drove to the far end of a runway that was currently under reconstruction. Thirty minutes after they arrived, the Super Frelon helicopter that had been used in the raid flew in low over the nearby buildings and picked up Claire and Green Team.

As the chopper was lifting off, the two troops who had driven the com-van to Ramallah were pulling out and heading toward Tel Aviv.

With only the nine passengers in the helicopter, Claire got to sit in one of the web jump-seats that lined the walls, rather than on the floor as she had when the chopper was loaded to its maximum.

As they flew south, returning to the base from which the operation had started, Claire thought about the man that had been shot behind the house in Ramallah.

She didn't want to believe that it was really Dunham. Not that she was sorry that he was dead. It was just that his death left a lot of loose ends dangling.

Looking at her backpack, she thought about the notebooks inside, and hoped that they might shed some light on why the people they *had* captured had wanted to kill Katherine McClure.

Claire had been looking forward to asking that question of Dunham himself, but she saw that opportunity as all but extinguished now. Desperately, she still held onto a faint hope that it wasn't really him that they had zipped into the body bag.

The only way they would know for sure would be to take fingerprints from the deceased's hands and compare them to those that the FBI had lifted from Dunham's wire strippers and from the toilet seat in Douglas' house.

When the chopper touched down in the compound for the final time of the operation, Claire slung the backpack over her shoulder, and headed for the Colonel's office. Inside, she found Avi, as well, which didn't really surprise her, but it did bother her. She wondered what Avi had meant when she said that she and Yousif went way back.

"Imagine my surprise," the Colonel said, "to have you paying me a visit as soon as your boots hit the compound."

Ignoring the remark, she said, "I'm sorry to interrupt, Colonel, but I need to have access to that body. Could you tell me where it's being kept?"

He looked at her more than a little surprised that she wasn't ranting and raving about the fact that it *was* a body, rather than a *prisoner*. "Why?" he asked finally.

"To identify it," she replied in a tone that indicated that she thought the answer was obvious.

"We have a doctor coming in later today to do that," Yousif said dismissively. "He's going to see if he can determine what the surgeon had changed and hopefully reconstruct what this man might have looked like before the surgery. Unless you're a plastic surgeon yourself Agent Bradley, I'm not sure what your looking at the body will accomplish."

"I don't want to look at it, Colonel," she said, trying to keep the sarcastic tone out of her voice. "I want to take fingerprints from it."

"Fingerprints?" Avi said in surprise. "You have fingerprints of The Teacher? Where did those come from?"

"We have *Dunham's* fingerprints from tools that she used and left behind at the hospital," Claire replied. "One of those tools has been directly linked to the computer and gun."

"You're sure they're from Dunham?" Avi asked, knowing that The Teacher's fingerprints had been a Holy Grail of the authorities for a long time.

"As sure as we can be without having taken them ourselves," Claire said. "Whether they are also your Teacher's, is another matter."

"Do you have the prints with you?" the Colonel asked.

"I have a copy, yes," Claire answered. "I wanted to be able to verify his identity before I left Israel with him."

"That's great!" Avi said. Then looking at the Colonel she said, "Do we have a fingerprinting kit here?"

"I'm sure there's one over in detention," he replied, reaching for his phone.

Five minutes later, two soldiers were lifting the body bag off the floor in the walk-in cooler in the infirmary. They placed it on the table, and the med-tech who had stitched Claire's leg pulled back the zipper. Claire's heart leapt as she realized that it was not Dunham! But then it sank as quickly, as she remembered that Avi's man had said that he had had plastic surgery. In the bright light of the infirmary, it was easy to make out the cuts and stitches that were invisible to the night-vision cameras. Even the ears had been altered. Still, there was a *chance* that this wasn't Dunham.

Ten minutes later, Claire sat at a desk, looking through a magnifying glass at a pattern of loops, ridge-endings, bifurcations, and a whirl in the right middle fingerprint taken from the body.

With a sense of profound loss, Claire said quietly, "I've got a match—seven good points." She didn't want to believe that she had come this far, and had gotten this close to Dunham, only to hit a dead end—literally. She then checked the index fingerprint that had been lifted from the toilet seat, and got another match.

"Congratulations, Agent Bradley!" the Colonel said, patting her shoulder in what seemed to Claire to be a condescending gesture. "You have what you came for—you have your man!"

"I have a *body*," Claire replied, tersely. "I wanted to be able to talk to him."

"If you thought you were going to get anything out of him," the Colonel said, "like a confession, then you're more naive than I thought you were. Did you think you were going to intimidate him into confessing," he asked, "or were you going to use your feminine charm?" he finished sarcastically.

With amazing self-control, Claire fought down the urge to tell the Colonel to go fuck himself. But she knew that that was exactly the reaction he wanted, so instead she asked calmly, "Is there anyone here who can translate the notebooks, Colonel? Avi, perhaps?"

"I'm afraid not," he replied.

Claire was sure that she picked up a hint of disappointment in his voice that she hadn't reacted to his goading, and it caused a tiny grin to crease her lips.

"That's something that will be done when the team from Intelligence gets down here. Although you currently have the notebooks in your possession to preserve a chain of evidence, they technically belong to the state of Israel. You might want to prepare yourself for the possibility that you'll be relieved of them, Agent Bradley."

Again, Claire sensed that the Colonel was trying to push her buttons.

"That's fine," she said, hoping to disappoint him, again. "I'm sure that our respective State and Judicial Departments will be able to work something out."

Picking up the prints she had taken from the body, and adding them to her backpack, she stood up, and said, "I'll be in the barracks, Colonel. Would you please have somebody let me know when the folks from Intelligence get here?" Then, letting her own tone of sarcasm filter into her voice, she added, "Thank you, Colonel Yousif. You've been a tremendous help."

Chapter 56

Thursday, October 30
Negev Desert, Israel

Although it was just after three in the morning in Washington, it was nine in Israel, and Claire placed a call to Paul Levine using her secure satellite phone. He had told her to call any time, day or night, if she had *any* news.

The grogginess with which he answered the phone left his voice immediately as he realized who was calling. "What's up?" he asked.

"It looks like Dunham is dead," Claire said, getting right to the point. "He was killed during the raid, and I've ID'd the body from both of the wire stripper and toilet seat fingerprints. He had plastic surgery within the last week or so, so the strike team didn't recognize him. When he became an apparent threat to the operation, one of the team's snipers took him out. I don't agree with having to take a kill shot, but I think an investigation—if they have one—will show the shooting was at least supportable, if not exactly unavoidable."

"Jesus!" Paul said. "That's a twist I didn't see coming. I'd have put my money on his not being there at all. You're sure of the print match?"

"Yeah," she said, her disappointment obvious. "I'll be bringing the prints I took from the body back with me so our people and the FBI folks can confirm my ID, but I got seven good points on one print, and eleven on the other. That puts him at both the hospital, and at the house in Seabrook. I'm positive it's him. I was kind of wishing that the toilet seat print wouldn't match, though. I was hoping it belonged to Douglas. That leaves us with nothing to connect him to the house, if we happen to find him.

"What about Dunham's body?" Levine asked. "Will they turn that over to you?"

"I don't know," she replied. "I haven't asked yet. But I don't think there's anyone here who could make that call, anyway. I was thinking that maybe you could contact somebody in State and get the ball rolling from higher up. There's also the extradition of the rest of the gang to have State and Justice start on."

"I'll give them a few hours to wake up," Paul replied. "They'll be more pleasant that way. How many are in the cell?"

"At least four men," Claire answered. "There are two women as well, but the folks here seem to think they're peripheral. It would probably be pretty hard to build a case against them."

"You have a good case against the others though?" Paul asked.

"I'm not sure yet," Claire answered. "I collected a half-dozen handwritten notebooks after the raid, but they're all in Arabic, so I don't know if there's anything in them to tie the others to Dunham. But one of the books is—I'm guessing—an Arabic translation of the manual to the Dynametric gun. There's even a hand sketch of it in the book, which is apparently the page that Avi Geller's mole had told her about. That at least ties Dunham to the house, if not the cell."

"Unless it has both Dunham's and some cell member's prints on it, it might not be much good for building a conspiracy case," Paul pointed out.

"I know," Claire replied. "My ace is Geller's mole. A guy they call Samer al-Abassi. He should be able to tie Dunham and somebody in the cell together with dates that we can hopefully corroborate."

"Wow," Paul said. "That's not a lot to hang your hat on. Maybe it's just as well that Dunham is dead—at least he can't be sprung for lack of evidence."

"My thoughts, exactly," Claire said with a hint of defeat in her voice. "As much as I wanted him alive, I'm beginning to see it the same way. I'd really be pissed if we had him, and had to let him go!"

"Man, wouldn't that be a kick in the teeth?" Paul agreed. "Okay, I'll get together with Gants first thing after the sun comes up, and we'll figure out how to proceed from this end. When will you get the notebooks translated? Or will you just bring them back, and have it done here?"

"They're pretty territorial about their stuff, I'm quite sure I won't be carrying the originals back with me. There's a team coming down from IDF Intelligence within a couple of hours, but I have no idea what their itinerary is going to be. I'll call you as soon as I have anything worthwhile."

After signing off with Paul, Claire pulled her laptop from her luggage and began working on a draft of her report. She did it mostly to kill time while waiting for the Intelligence people to arrive. It wasn't necessary for her to write things down while they were fresh in her mind—she wasn't likely to forget the past few days very easily.

Chapter 57

Thursday, October 30
Negev Desert, Israel

It was nearing seven at night before the IDF Intelligence team had wrapped up their investigation for the day. There would be plenty more to do, but in Claire's opinion, they had made a very good start. She liked the way the wheels turned over here. Back in the States, it would be a month before agreement was reached on who should even *do* the investigating, and then someone would be taking *that* decision to the Supreme Court.

The Intelligence team had looked into the shooting of the person known as The Teacher, and identified by Claire as Dunham, but they had not reached a finding on whether the shooting was justified, or not. They had only collected evidence and interviewed those involved.

They had then translated the notebooks that Claire had found, allowing her to sit in on the process, and had then allowed her to watch, via closed circuit TV, while the terrorists captured in the raid were interviewed.

It had been a very long day for Claire, but oddly, she didn't feel tired. While the IDF Intelligence agents retired to their temporary offices to begin their reports, Claire went back to her barracks and called Paul Levine. It was just about noon, his time.

"Well, it looks like we finally have a motive," she told him after salutations. "And we were all wrong with our guesses. Apparently, Katherine had a religious death sentence issued against her, and the leader of the cell, Yacoub Hamoudi, saw fulfilling it as his ticket to Heaven. So he paid The Teacher, a.k.a. Dunham, to kill her. Apparently," Claire commented wryly, "you can also get your ticket to Heaven punched if you only *arrange* the killing of an infidel. You don't have to actually do it yourself."

"A death sentence?" Levine repeated. "What the hell for?"

"Blasphemy," Claire replied. "Like Salman Rushdie back in the late eighties, early nineties. Remember the Ayatollah Khomeini declaring that Rushdie had committed blasphemy against Islam in writing the book *The Satanic Verses?*"

"How in the world did Katherine McClure blaspheme Islam?"

"One of the notebooks that I recovered went into pretty venomous detail about that," Claire replied. "You may not remember, but back during her husband's first campaign, Mrs. McClure did an interview for a woman's magazine that caused quite a flap.

"In the interview, she was talking about the turmoil in the Middle East, and she knew that she would be talking directly to a nearly exclusively female audience, so, in a less than shining moment, the future First Lady told the interviewer that it seemed to her that if women held positions of power over there, or if some of the men would listen to their wives rather than militant clerics, that there would be little or no violence, and a workable peace plan would have emerged years ago. I think she was being a little tongue-in-cheek, but it didn't come out in print that way. In the line that made the cover of the magazine—and a few hundred newspapers—she said that if women were in power over there, there would also be shopping malls all over the West Bank, rather than terrorist training camps, missile batteries, and bunkers. That may not be an exact quote," Claire said, "but that's the gist of it."

"I remember it vaguely," Levine said. "I thought it was something of a tempest in a teapot. Obviously, it didn't cost McClure the election."

Claire replied, "It drew some flap from pro-Israeli groups who took offense to being lumped together with the Palestinians, and who pointed out that women *did* hold many powerful positions in the Israeli government—Golda Meyer having been Prime Minister. They also blasted her, saying that it takes a lot more to run a government than building shopping malls.

"It was the only serious gaff that I can recall Katherine making during the whole campaign, but McClure's opponent never missed an opportunity to bring it up, as if Richard had made the comment himself."

"For that, someone issued a death warrant?" Levine asked incredulously.

"Well, technically, I guess the answer would be, no, but it was *interpreted* that way," Claire answered.

"Explain," said Levine.

"The comment apparently pissed off whoever was keeping this particular notebook. Presumably, Yacoub Hamoudi. He had torn the page from the magazine and glued it into the book. There were some extremely derogatory remarks about Mrs. McClure written—actually more like *engraved*—in the margins of the page, in Arabic. Whoever wrote the commentary was *really* angry when he did it!

"One comment said, in effect, that this kind of stupidity is why the woman should always walk behind the man, and should never talk. Another referred to Mrs. McClure as the daughter of camels, and another suggested that her family tree was infested with monkeys. Pretty vile insults over here, I'm told."

"I'm with you so far. He's not a big fan of Mrs. M."

"Well, according to Avi's mole in the cell, Hamoudi went to some Islamic mufti—that's like a religious lawyer—and asked if Mrs. M's remarks were blasphemous. Apparently, since her commentary questioned the subservient role of women that the Qu'ran teaches, the mufti said that they were. So on Hamoudi's request, the mufti issued a formal fatwa."

"The death sentence," Levine concluded.

"No," answered Claire. "What the folks from Intelligence told me was that a fatwa shouldn't be confused with a death sentence. That's what the media made it seem like when Khomeini issued a fatwa against Rushdie, but a fatwa is just a ruling on a point of Islamic law—an interpretation of the Qu'ran by a religious official. They can, but they rarely include specific death sentences, they told me.

"Unfortunately, radicals sometimes read that fate into the mufti's opinion on their own. It would be like you asking your priest or minister for his opinion on whether something your neighbor did was a sin, and then when he said it was, you deciding on your own, that the punishment for that sin should be death.

"The good news is that it's customary for fatwas to be issued in writing and recorded in official books. The Intelligence folks over here are going to try to dig something up on it."

"So," Levine queried, "if Hamoudi hired this Teacher guy to carry out the death sentence, why didn't he come forward and take credit? You'd think he'd want his compatriots to know what a hero he is."

"Apparently, he was going to. They translated what sounds like the draft of a press release in the same notebook as the magazine article. It was pretty strongly worded, and mentioned her by name. The guess is that it wasn't published because the execution failed. Not something a guy like Hamoudi would brag about."

"Do you know how much Dunham was paid?"

"No, but he only got half of it anyway, apparently. The mole said that he overheard The Teacher and Hamoudi arguing over the second half of the payment about an hour before the raid. An hour before The Teacher—Dunham—was killed."

"You know," Levine said thoughtfully, "as interesting as all that is, it's purely hearsay and supposition. I think we should be glad that Dunham was killed. I can't imagine prosecuting him with no more than that."

"I know," Claire said wearily. "There are some other things in the notebooks that point toward conspiracy, but they're not exactly nails in the coffin. There was a page of dates and places, for instance, where the President was speaking, and whether or not the First Lady was scheduled to be with him. But that's still not much to go to court with. Especially if you can't directly connect Dunham to the notebook."

"So when are you coming back?" Levine asked.

"I'm scheduled to fly out of Tel Aviv Saturday. Avi's going to drive me back into town tomorrow, and show me a few of the sights."

"You need a ride from the airport," Levine asked.

"No, my Jeep's in off-site parking. I'll be fine, but thanks," Claire said, "So, how are things on that end? How is Mrs. M? They ready to spring her from the hospital yet?"

"More like throw her out," Paul replied. "The closer it gets to Election Day, the more cantankerous she becomes. She's made it absolutely clear—to us and to her doctors—that on Election Day she will be by her husband's side, and it won't be because *he's* in *her* hospital room."

Claire laughed. "That sounds about right for her. Count me in on her detail, okay?"

"You sure? Gants figures you're due for some R&R after your trip," Levine said. "Especially since it looks like the investigation is sliding into the conclusion-and-report phase."

"I hope so," Claire said unenthusiastically.

"That was pretty unconvincing," Levine said. "What's up?"

"Oh, I'm just not sure that we're going to be able to build much of a case with what we have," she replied.

"You ID'd Dunham yourself. How much more sure do you want to be?" Levine asked.

"It's not Dunham that's bothering me," she told him. "It's the connection to the Hamoudis and the motive behind the shooting. There's nothing I can put my finger on, but the *voice* says something's wrong."

"Ah," Levine said. "The *voice*."

"Hey, don't dis the voice!" Claire replied kiddingly. "Its batting average has been pretty damned good these past couple weeks. It even kept me from eating a hand grenade last night."

"Well, kudos to the *voice*, then," Levine said. "I can't wait to hear all your stories when you get back. Sounds like quite an adventure. In the meantime, I'll let Gants know that you have concerns about making a case."

"No," Claire replied, "let's not do that just yet. I'd rather see if anyone else comes up with similar feelings on their own, okay? Have you, by the way? Anything in all this disturb you at all?"

"Well, all I have so far are your verbal reports," Levine replied, "so I don't have all the little details that I'm sure you have. But so far, I guess the only thing that strikes me is how quickly all the pieces fell into place once they started falling. Not that that makes the pieces bad necessarily—it's just an observation, I guess. Speaking of details; will you be bringing back transcripts or videos of the interrogations, so the rest of us can get the full effect?"

"That 'observation' is *your* voice talking to you, Paul," Claire chided him. "You should learn to listen to it. But no, I probably won't be bringing much back with me besides my own notebook. Nobody here appears to have the authority to turn over copies of anything. Justice or State is going to have to get that done. I hope they're already working on it."

"I'm sure they are," Levine replied. "Gants wouldn't let them drop the ball on something like that."

After hanging up from Levine, Claire laid back on her bunk, going over all the pieces in her mind, and trying to get the nagging element to surface. Slowly, she began to see that it was al-Abassi, Avi's mole. Maybe it was that he was such a good actor, or perhaps the feeling came from the fact that he was, effectively, a traitor to the people he was living with. Whatever it was, though, there was definitely *something* about him that she didn't trust.

Chapter 58

Thursday, October 30
Negev Desert, Israel

Claire had slept for only an hour, or so, when she woke up and real-ized that someone had turned the light off. She looked at her watch. It was nine at night, but she didn't feel tired. Looking over, she could make out Avi's shape in her bunk, sound asleep.

As quietly as she could, Claire walked to the end of the room, and took a shower, which, considering the accommodations, felt luxurious. She dressed in her civies for a change, and was sitting at her between-the-bunks desk, reading over the entries in her notebook when she heard Avi's voice from across the room.

"You missed the doctor," she said.

Claire turned to face her, and said, "Doctor?"

"The plastic surgeon," Avi replied, getting up and walking over to Claire's bunk. "He took a look at the body while you were out."

"Why didn't you wake me?" Claire asked, obviously annoyed.

"You didn't miss anything," Avi said with a wave of dismissal. "His conclusion was pretty inconclusive. He said he'd have to do an autopsy on the face—actually open it up to confirm where he thinks bone grafts are, and where there was bone shaving. But he said that based on our photo of The Teacher from a year ago and your hospital ID photo of

Dunham, that this could be the same person. He emphasized *could be*, and said that it would probably never get much more positive than that. It looks like if it weren't for your fingerprints, we'd have little more than a John Doe in the cooler. Even al-Abassi, couldn't have made a positive ID if he hadn't heard the guy speak."

"Speaking of al-Abassi," Claire said, "is he going to be able to testify at our inquiry—in the States?"

Before Avi answered, the door to the barracks opened, and Colonel Yousif walked in. Avi started to get to her feet, and without really thinking, just following Avi's lead, Claire did the same. She immediately felt stupid for it. The Colonel wasn't *her* commanding officer.

"Sit!" the Colonel said brusquely as he crossed the distance to Claire's bunk in four long strides.

"General Lindenthal with the IDF has a helicopter on its way to pick you up," he said to Claire. "Be ready in five minutes." Then to Avi, he said, "See that she has everything she came with, and as soon as she's gone, come to my office." With that, he turned for the door.

"Colonel," Claire asked as he walked away, "will I be getting copies of the evidence before the helicopter gets here?"

"Not from me," he replied in a smug tone without turning to face her. "Good-bye, Agent Bradley," he said as he left the building.

As the door banged closed, Claire said, "Is he always that charming?"

"Only if he likes you," Avi replied. "Otherwise he can be a real prick."

Claire just laughed and began to pack her duffle bag, but it occurred to her that that was the first derogatory thing that Avi had said about the Colonel, and *it* was in jest. She made a mental note to see what else she could find out about Avi and the Colonel when she got back.

Ten minutes later Claire was seat-belted into one of the passenger seats of a Bell-430 commercial helicopter.

Earlier that morning, she had been crammed into a spot on the bare metal floor of a sixties vintage military helicopter, and that's what she had expected would be sent for her now. Instead, she found herself in a flying limousine, with leather seats, thick carpeting, and upholstered sound-deadening walls. It reminded her of Marine One, just a lot smaller.

As the chopper climbed and made a banking turn around the compound to pick up a northerly heading, the copilot called back to her,

"Welcome aboard, Agent Bradley. We'll be at Jerusalem airport in about twenty minutes."

"Jerusalem?" Claire repeated. "Not Tel Aviv?"

"No, ma'am," he said. "Foreign military aircraft don't use Tel Aviv."

"Foreign military?" she said in surprise. "I have a flight booked on El Al out of Tel Aviv, on Saturday."

The young man shrugged his shoulders and replied, "We were told to collect you and your gear from Colonel Yousif, and to deliver you to the mil-trans terminal at Jerusalem."

"Why the change in plans?" Claire asked him.

"I don't know about any changes, ma'am. These are the only plans I'm aware of."

Claire realized that prodding for any more information would just be a waste of time, so she sat in silence watching the moon-lit countryside whiz below for the rest of the trip.

After a short downwind approach, the helicopter touched down lightly in front of a row of hangars that bordered a long runway used almost exclusively by military aircraft.

About fifty yards directly in front of where the helicopter stopped was a US Air Force C-32A—the military version of Boeing's 757-200.

Almost immediately, an American Air Force captain and an airman trotted over to the helicopter, stooping slightly under the still-spinning main rotor. As the airman retrieved Claire's duffle from the baggage compartment, the captain opened the passenger door. He exchanged courtesy salutes with the pilot and copilot, and then offered his hand to Claire to help her out.

"This way, ma'am," he said close to her ear and pointing toward the steps of the C-32.

"Why the change in schedule, Captain?" Claire asked as soon as they were away from the noise of the chopper. "I wasn't supposed to be leaving until Saturday. I assume I *am* leaving Israel, right?"

Claire had thought about the change in plans all the way from the desert compound, and had arrived at the conclusion that Colonel Yousif had to be behind it.

"I'm not aware of any changes, ma'am," the captain said with the same expression that the helicopter's copilot had had. "Our orders are to pick you up and bring you back to DC. Non-stop to Andrews, ma'am."

"Why the rush?" Claire asked. And then a troubling thought occurred to her. "Has something happened to the First Lady?"

"No, ma'am," the captain replied, "not that I'm aware of."

310

"Then what's up?" she tried again as they climbed the steps into the C-32.

"Sorry, ma'am," he replied. "Beyond informing you of our destination, I'm afraid I can't help you."

"Because of orders?" she asked.

"Because I don't know," he replied as he reached out to pull the aircraft's door closed. "If you'll take a seat and buckle in, we'll be under way in a few minutes."

As the crew guided the big plane out to the runway, Claire once again tried to figure out why Yousif was in such a hurry to get rid of her. Perhaps he didn't like having people around who wouldn't jump to his every command, and who asked questions that he'd prefer not to answer. She was sure that it went far beyond just being a *real prick*.

Chapter 59

Ten hours and thirty-seven minutes later, during which time Claire enjoyed a ham sandwich, three diet sodas, two cups of coffee, a microwaved egg and sausage breakfast, and about three hours of sleep, the plane touched down at Andrews Air Force Base.

As the plane taxied to its parking location, the captain came back and said, "Welcome back to the US, ma'am. If you want to reset your watch, it's 2:06 Friday afternoon."

As the stairs were being wheeled up to the side of the plane, Claire looked out and saw, to her relief, a black Secret Service Suburban sitting on the apron. She had wondered how she was supposed to get home from here.

After the airman put her duffle into the back, Claire slid into the passenger seat, and before she had her seatbelt buckled, the driver had the vehicle moving.

Claire looked at her watch, and tried to decide whether she should call Dave when she got home. He'd still be on duty, but he'd want to know she was back safe and sound. Almost absently, she said to the driver, whom she didn't know, "You have my address, I take it?"

"Um, no ma'am," he replied, obviously a bit confused. "I was told to bring you directly to the White House—no stops."

"The White House?" Claire asked, far more confused than the driver. "Whose orders?"

"Mr. Gants, I believe, ma'am," the driver replied. As he exited the base, he flipped on the flashing lights, and accelerated to about eighty miles an hour as quickly as the big vehicle would do it.

"And we're in a hurry?" Claire said. "What's going on? What the heck happened while I was gone?"

"I was told to pick you up and deliver you as quickly as possible, ma'am," the driver told her while weaving through traffic, blipping the siren as required. "They didn't tell me why."

Claire was getting pretty tired of no one having—or sharing—any information. "Is Gants going to be at the White House?" she asked. No sooner had she finished the question when she held up her hand, and said, "No, wait. Don't tell me—you don't know."

He looked at her curiously, and said, "Sorry, ma'am, I don't."

Claire rode in silence for the rest of the trip, trying to guess what was going on. She was beginning to wonder if Colonel Yousif really *was* responsible for her sudden departure. He could most likely get her evacuated from Israel, but he couldn't have her sent to the White House.

They arrived at the West Wing entrance to the White House, where she was hurried through security, and escorted to the Oval Office. Already in the room were the President, the Secretary of State, the Attorney General, Paul Levine, Mr. Gants, and a man whom Claire had never met.

As she was shown into the room, the President rose and came around from behind his desk. The other men got to their feet as well.

"Welcome back, Agent Bradley," the President said, extending his hand. "Good job! We're all proud of what you accomplished over there. How's the leg feeling?"

"Um, fine, sir," she said as she shook his hand, a little surprised that he knew about her injury.

The others offered their congratulations as well, as the President went back to his seat behind his desk. Following the President's lead, the others sat, but Claire remained standing more or less in the middle of them.

"Thank you, sir," she said. "Thank all of you. But I'm not sure congratulations are really in order. In my eyes the operation wasn't much of a success. Our prime suspect is dead, and the evidence to connect the Hamoudi cell to the assassination plot is flimsy at best. We're going to have a heck of a time even getting these guys extradited, much less convicted."

As all of the men looked silently toward the President, Claire felt the proverbial rug being pulled from under her. She looked at the President, irritated, once again, that she was out of some apparent loop, and said in tone more demanding than she had intended, "What?" quickly adding, "sir."

"Your concerns are well founded, Agent Bradley," the President replied. "That's why we've decided that we're not going to pursue the extradition of the others."

Claire squinted at the President as if she couldn't see him very well all of a sudden, and said, "What!? You're not going to pursue extradition? What the heck does that mean? Why? —sir!"

"Have a seat, Agent Bradley, and I'll explain," the President said.

Shaking her head in disbelief, she sank into the seat next to Levine.

Introducing the unknown man, the President said, "This is Retired General Yuri Lindenthal of Israel's General Security Services. You've been working with his people for the past few days."

The General got to his feet once again, and extended his hand toward Claire. "It is a pleasure to meet you, Agent Bradley. I have received very favorable reports about you."

Claire stood, shook his hand, and replied, "Thank you, General. It's a pleasure to meet you, too." She wanted to ask who had sent him a favorable report ... certainly not Colonel Yousif!

When she sat back down, she simply looked at the President, waiting for him—almost challenging him to continue.

"As you astutely observed, Agent Bradley," the President went on, "any possible case against the Hamoudi terrorist cell is going to be weak at best." Gesturing to the others in the room, he said, "We have discussed that point, at length, and we have concluded that it will be in the best interest of the United States, and Israel, if we leave the Hamoudis and Hamshari in the hands of the Israelis, and issue a final report on the assassination attempt, without the expense—and more importantly—the *risk* of a public trial of the Hamoudi cell."

Claire gave him a you've-got-to-be-kidding-me look.

"We believe we're all better served by leaving them right where they are," the President continued, "As long as they're in prison—whether an Israeli prison or a US one—the prime objective is met: their threat is removed from society.

"But as a backup, the US and Israeli Justice departments will work out the details of an open-ended extradition agreement that will take effect immediately, if any of the cell members are ever to be released from Israeli custody."

"Which will never, *ever* happen," Lindenthal interjected. "You have my personal word on that."

After what she'd been through over the past few days, Claire was primed and ready to debate this decision. But she stopped even before she began, as she realized who she would be debating. She was in the company of the President of the United States, the Secretary of State, the US Attorney General, and the head of security for the state of Israel. She didn't need her *voice* to tell her that a young special agent for the Secret Service was not going to change a decision that these men had made.

Moreover, while she didn't like this course of action, she could see the logic in it—at least from the President's point of view. But it didn't explain her being whisked from the compound in Israel direct to the Oval Office. There had to be more going on.

"I see your point, sir," Claire said. "... even if I don't completely agree. But I don't think I was brought here just to be told that you're not going to extradite Dunham's co-conspirators. Nor do I think that General Lindenthal came here just to shake my hand. But I do think that my being here at the same time that he is, is no coincidence. Am I right, sir?"

"Very perceptive, Agent Bradley," the President replied. "Yes. That the two of you are here this afternoon is not mere chance. General Lindenthal has made a special request on behalf of his government, that, in the interest of preserving their asset, the operative known as Samer al-Abassi, that we not use any of his pre-operation information or his post-operation interview statements in our final report. They've sealed the videos of his interview, but as a witness to that interview, and inasmuch as you'll be contributing a great deal to the final report, your cooperation will, of course, be critical to that end."

Claire didn't even *try* to hide the tone of challenge in her voice as she replied, "al-Abassi's testimony is the only thing we have that ties Dunham to Hamoudi, and Hamoudi to the fatwa. How can we hope to write a report that doesn't directly connect Dunham to the motive?"

"If I may, Mr. President?" Lindenthal said.

"Please do," McClure replied.

"The deep-cover placement—as I believe you call it," Lindenthal began, "of our operative, al-Abassi, represents a substantial investment in both time and money, not to mention his own personal risk. Beyond that, his position within the Hamoudi cell is virtually priceless from an intelligence standpoint."

Was this, Claire wondered, where her bad feeling about al-Abassi had come from? That he was going to be removed from the equation?

"Now, you may think," Lindenthal went on, "that since the Hamoudi cell has been *busted*, as you Americans say, that al-Abassi's value as a mole has been busted as well. Not so. In fact, we believe that the situation may strengthen his ability to move within the ultra-militant terrorist cells.

"When the cell members go to trial, the most that al-Abassi will be charged with is accessory-after-the-fact since none of the acts with which they will be charged occurred after he joined the cell.

"With a good lawyer and a sympathetic judge, he could conceivably be set free, but we will probably allow him to be convicted, and sentenced to perhaps six months in a prison. This will enhance his credibility among other Palestinian militants, and will allow him to make contacts inside prison that would otherwise be literally impossible."

Allow him to be convicted! The Israelis certainly played by a different set of rules, Claire thought. Rules that she wasn't too comfortable with.

"Regardless of this intelligence opportunity, however," Lindenthal went on, "I want you to know, that if al-Abassi's testimony would mean the difference between a conviction and an acquittal of your Frances Dunham, believe me, I would not be making this request of your government. But whereas Dunham is dead—identified by you, personally—then compromising such a valuable asset can have no advantage."

"How about the advantage of telling the truth?" Claire snapped, her adrenaline getting ahead of her judgment. Immediately, regretting the comment, she said, "I'm sorry General. I didn't mean to imply ..."

Lindenthal cut her off with a wave, saying, "No apology necessary, Agent Bradley. I understand your dedication—indeed your *passion*—for your cause. I too am passionate about my cause—the security of my homeland. And I, too, am a great believer—and defender—of the truth. But separating private truths from public truths is sometimes necessary in the name of one's cause."

"With all due respect, General," Claire replied, "any time you put qualifiers on absolutes—like the truth—they cease to be absolutes."

"I disagree, Agent Bradley," Lindenthal countered. "Not only *is* there a difference between private and public truths, their *must* be a difference for society to function.

"When a friend or coworker asks you how your date was last night, do you tell them if you had sexual relations and which positions were most enjoyable for you? I think not. Those are your private truths. But holding those things back doesn't make whatever else you tell them *untrue*, does it?"

316

"It's an interesting analogy, General," Claire replied, "but the details of my sex life and the unimpeachability of our final report are on slightly different planes.

"Without al-Abassi's testimony, a connection between Dunham and Hamoudi is circumstantial at best, and without that connection, Dunham has no motive. What kind of a report is that going to be?"

"I agree, Agent Bradley," the Attorney General chimed in. "The evidence for a connection to Hamoudi and, thereby, to a motive will be purely circumstantial. Although, from what I've heard about these notebooks, it sounds like they can be quite damning. And even though convictions have been won with only circumstantial evidence, I agree that we would be very lucky to get a conviction with the notebook evidence alone. We might not even get an indictment. Fortunately, however, that's not a complication we have to worry about.

"As far as assembling a credible report, though, I think that the evidence we have—even without Mr. al-Abassi's statements—will be more than enough when presented in the proper format. In fact, from an unimpeachability standpoint, Mr. al-Abassi's statements actually add very little. As I understand it, his testimony would amount to relating overheard pieces of conversations, and witnessing Mr. Hamoudi write something in a journal which he, al-Abassi, never actually read. I wouldn't want to go to court with that."

Seeing that she was obviously outnumbered—probably even alone—Claire said to the President, "Well, you've apparently had time to discuss all this and have obviously reached a consensus. So what exactly is the plan, sir?"

"With Election Day three days away," the President began, "we're not going to have time to put together and edit a full-blown final report before then. Instead, we're going to issue a preliminary report stating the major facts as we perceive them, and follow that in a couple of months with the more detailed final report."

Claire wondered whose idea that was. Did it come from the political advisors in the room, or from his campaign people? Then she recalled her conversation with Katherine, just before she left, and she thought she knew.

"You really think Senator Evans is going to let you get away with that, sir?" Claire asked. "He'll be all over that as a political stunt. And he won't be wrong, will he sir?"

"I disagree with your term 'political stunt', Miss Bradley," the President replied, "but I do agree that that is how my esteemed opponent will categorize it.

"But since the report will contain nothing but the facts as we know them at this point in time, he really won't have much to sink his teeth into. The American public has been given information as it has developed all through this investigation, has it not? Why should it be any different now, just because it's close to Election Day? Evans would be on me just as bad—maybe worse—if I withheld information that might be *unfavorable*."

It was obvious to Claire that the President and his team had hashed this plan out pretty well, and would most likely have an answer to any argument that she could come up with. So rather than waste any more time beating that dead horse, she decided to get into the report they had in mind. And she was quite sure that they had that pretty well thought out, as well.

"This preliminary report that I'm going to help write," she said, "how much of it has already been written?"

"None of it," the President replied. "I asked Mr. Levine to put together an outline of the investigation to date, but the text hasn't been started yet. And we don't have much time." Turning to look at him, the President said, "Agent Levine?"

Levine handed Claire two sheets of paper on which the highlights of the investigation were written in outline form. Claire scanned down the entries, and noticed that a good deal of it looked exactly like the whiteboard in her office.

"Well, I see I've made a good start," she said coolly. She didn't like the fact that everyone—including Levine—was out in front of her on this. She had that distressing feeling of being manipulated, again.

"Hey, no sense in reinventing the wheel," Levine said with a grin.

Toward the end of the outline Levine had added the information that Claire had given him from Israel, including the highlights of al-Abassi's interview. Those entries now had lines drawn through them. Near the very end was the topic heading "Motive", and under it was written, "Religious fatwa issued by unknown Islamic mufti because of an allegedly blasphemous statement made four years ago."

"I'm a little concerned here, Mr. President," Claire said. "It's about the motive. If we announce that the reason that the First Lady was shot was because of this obscure and unconfirmed religious ruling, we're going to be inviting every fundamentalist Muslim nut to take up the cause and come after her to try to score points with their Almighty.

"Not that we can't protect her, but why open that can of worms if we

318

don't have to? I think before we announce this, we should try to get someone—perhaps General Lindenthal can help here—to number one, see if this fatwa was really ever issued, and two, if it is for real, to see if we can't get it quietly reviewed by somebody higher-up the Islamic religious ladder, and maybe have it overturned.

Seeing that the President was actually listening to her for a change, she decided to go further. "You could offer an official, highly publicized apology from the First Lady if they promise to reverse the fatwa, or throw it out, or whatever they call it," she suggested. "You could play it up as a good-will fence-mending thing to get the peace-ball rolling in the Middle East.

"And while I have no doubt that you can get some political advantage out of it, *my* main objective is to protect the First Lady from any further attempts on her life. These people never give up. Just look at Salman Rushdie! It might delay the release of the report, but I think your wife's life is worth that."

She had expected an immediate agreement with her point from somebody, but when no one spoke, and the President just looked at her, a knot quickly formed in her stomach. "What?" she asked him.

The President didn't answer immediately, but Claire watched his eyes, and saw a change come into them that made the knot in her stomach turn into a leaden ball. "What?" she demanded, not giving a damn about protocol. "It's Katherine, isn't it? What about her? What!"

"Katherine is dying, Claire," the President finally said in a resigned tone. "Her doctors have given her a week—two at the outside."

Claire stared at the President in disbelief. "How ... What ... What *happened*?" she finally managed.

"Katherine has a degenerative neurological disorder," the President said in what sounded like a long, sad sigh. "There's nothing they can do for her but try to make her comfortable. I hate to drop this on you like this Claire—and we can talk more about it later—but obviously it has a direct bearing on what we're discussing here."

Claire said nothing in reply—she was completely stunned.

An awkward silence followed the President's remark. No one wanted to be the first to turn the subject back to business.

Finally, however, the Attorney General said, "I'm sorry that you had to hear about this this way Agent Bradley, and I understand your point of view—I would probably even agree with it if—well, under different circumstances.

"But in light of the fact that this fatwa isn't going to have any ...

well, any *significance*, in a couple of weeks, I don't believe that we should even consider negotiating with the extremists who issued this death warrant in the first place. I think the fatwa-motive should be the focal point of the report, and that it should be issued as soon as possible. If that should alienate a handful of lunatic Muslims, well just file that under 'W' for 'Who the hell cares?' I think the world needs to know who's behind all this!"

Normally, Claire would have jumped all over the AG's suggestion, pointing out that, as yet, the fatwa in question was just that, *in question*. *Her* suggestion had at least included an *investigation* before making a public statement about it.

But the sudden news that Katherine was dying had sapped nearly every bit of the resolve that had kept her going these past two weeks, and she just sat there numb, only hearing the Attorney General's comments on some subconscious level.

Paul Levine, however, was not similarly stunned into quiescence, having heard the news about Katherine in a private briefing with the President earlier in the day. So Levine voiced those very concerns about a premature release of unsubstantiated information.

For the next ten minutes, the pros and cons of the different approaches were debated. Should they release an official report before Election Day that announced Dunham's death, but that left the motive "under investigation by joint US and Israeli investigators"? Should they wait and release an official report that included both news of Dunham's death and the fatwa-motive, assuming it was confirmed? Or, should they release an official report before Election Day announcing Dunham's death and *leak* the unconfirmed report of the fatwa and watch for reactions?

They finally agreed on the report/leak combo as giving them the best bang for the buck. It allowed them to announce, officially, that the alleged shooter was deceased and that there was hard evidence—fingerprints—tying him to the gun. This would allow the task force—and by extension, the President—to chalk up a major success on the eve of the election.

Since the report would be labeled "preliminary", some details could logically be withheld and the blanks filled in later, after further analysis. The motive would fall under the heading, "under investigation."

The leak, or more correctly, the "... information from a member of the task force, speaking on condition of anonymity ..." would indicate that a connection between the deceased shooter and a Palestinian terrorist cell was being investigated, and that the motive might have been an Islamic fatwa issued some time in the past four years.

This would allow al-Abassi to remain safely in the shadows, while at the same time testing the waters for a Muslim reaction and possibly even flushing out whether the fatwa was for real.

"Should we include something about a possible election-swaying motive?" Levine suggested. "That adds a second possibility to the purely religious-fanatic angle, in case the fatwa doesn't come off as true."

"No!" the President said firmly, surprising everyone. "I've talked this over with Mrs. McClure," he said, "and she is adamantly against using her dying as a means to win sympathy votes. She feels—and I agree—that such a victory would be tainted at the very least. That's why her illness will not be made public until *after* the election.

"An election-swaying theory falls into the same category, only worse. It would mean that someone actually set out to influence the election by trying to kill her—and succeeded in doing so! I, personally, don't believe that hypothesis, and I will not let it demean what Katherine has gone through these last weeks."

Lost in her own thoughts, Claire had not uttered a word while the discussion went on around her. She suddenly didn't care one bit about the investigation, about Dunham, about the election, about the President—about *anything*.

Gants, who was sitting across from her, had been watching her, and when she offered no opinions on what would normally have been hot-button issues for her, he recognized that she was in the classic first stage of dealing with the sudden death of someone close—shock and numbness.

But that surprised him a little, because he didn't realize that Claire and Katherine had become that close. And of course, Katherine wasn't actually dead, yet. Perhaps the stress of the Israeli operation, and possibly even a little jet-lag sleep-deprivation were factors in her reaction.

At hearing the President using Katherine's name, Claire suddenly came to, as if awakened from a hypnotic trance. She stood up, and announced to no one in particular, "I have to go see her."

Gants was on his feet at the same time that she was, and he turned to the President and said, "Excuse us, Mr. President. I'll be right back."

Once they were in the corridor, Claire eyes filled with tears and she snapped, "The world sucks, Mr. Gants! It sucks! How can this happen after all she's already been through? It's not fair! And don't give me any 'who said life was fair' crap! It's time it was unfair to someone else!

She's gone through enough, Goddamn it!"

Gants was surprised at her sudden change, but he saw it as the second phase—rage. He had just never seen anyone move through phases that quickly before!

Getting the attention of a young male intern, Gants asked him to go down to security with Claire, and to see that she got a ride over to George Washington Hospital. Gants then returned to the Oval Office.

The ride to the hospital, though only a few minutes, reminded Claire of the two-hour bus ride she had made from school in Flagstaff to her home in Phoenix, when they had called and told her that her father was dying. That was the longest trip she had ever taken, and this was coming in a close second.

Chapter 60

Friday, October 31
Washington, DC

When Claire got to Katherine's room, she found Melissa and Helen sitting in chairs on opposite sides of her bed. Katherine appeared to be sleeping.

Claire was almost afraid to walk into the room, but Melissa noticed her and silently motioned her in.

As she approached the bed, Helen stood to greet her, and as they embraced, she could see that she had been crying.

Claire's anger at the unfairness of all of this had pushed her crying reflex into the background, but seeing the look in Helen's eyes stimulated it once again, and tears were rolling down her cheeks as Melissa came around the bed to give Claire a hug.

As Claire was taking deep breaths, trying to regain her composure, Katherine's voice came from beside her. "Well, I take it from your expression that you've heard the news."

"I just came from the White House," Claire said wiping the tears away with her palms. "How are you feeling? Is there anything I can do?"

"Not unless you got your degree in neurobiology while you were gone," Katherine replied in a voice much stronger than Claire expected. "I'm actually feeling better now than when you left. No more headaches, at least. They've finally admitted the inevitable—with my persuasion—and stopped giving me those damned drugs."

"The drugs were giving you the headaches?" Claire said, confused. "I thought the drugs were to ease the pain."

"It seems that the drug's only function was to prolong my life," Katherine said dryly. "It was a *side-effect* of the drug that gave me the headaches. The wonders of modern medicine, huh? Here's a drug to make you live longer, and the longer you take it, the more you'll wish you were dead."

Claire was a little surprised by Katherine's flippant manner regarding her own death.

Katherine read Claire's expression and said, "I'm sorry Claire, you haven't had as long to get used to this as I have."

"What do you mean?" Claire asked. "How long have you had this—whatever it is? How long have you known that ..." Claire found herself unable to finish the question.

"That I'm going to die?" Katherine finished it for her. "It'll be a year November 12th, that I've known. And they hit it pretty damned close. They said I had about a year to live when they told me, and here we are. How long have I had it? This neurodegenerative-whatever? Apparently all my life. It's a genetic thing."

Claire's eyes blinked, and she began to turn toward Melissa. "No," Katherine said, anticipating the question. "Melissa's been tested—she doesn't have it. Apparently she got that particular gene from her Dad. Right, Liss?"

"Right, Mom." Melissa sniffed.

"But you seem better now than when I left," Claire said, turning back to Katherine, still confused. "The President said that you—that ..."

"That I have a week, maybe two? That's right. And you only think I'm better because I'm off that damned medication and don't feel like my head will explode any second.

"Apparently this insidious little disease—which I'm told they may re-name Katherine McClure Disease, after I'm gone—great, huh? Anyway, it appears to eat away at the neural connections that control the muscles. So, while my mind is just fine, the support structure is going to hell.

"You should have been here yesterday, when I thought I felt well enough to get out of bed. What a mess that was. Right, Mom?"

"Honey, you should really be resting," Helen replied in classic mother fashion.

"Resting for what?" Katherine replied. "I'm going to have plenty of time to rest in a week or so."

Melissa erupted in renewed tears, and Helen snapped, "Stop that! Stop talking like that!"

Katherine closed her eyes, and said, "I'm sorry—I really am. I'm pretending to be tough here, and all I'm doing is making this harder on you. I'm sorry, Liss baby, I really am. Come here and give me a hug."

After Melissa regained her composure, Katherine asked, "Liss and Mom? Would you mind if I talked with Claire for a few minutes alone?"

As they were leaving the room, Katherine patted the bed, and reading the expression in Claire's face, she said, "Go ahead, you've got a thousand questions—ask away."

Claire did have a thousand questions, but she didn't know where to start. Finally, she said, "Are you in pain?"

"Surprisingly, no," Katherine replied. "I feel weak—like my legs weigh a hundred pounds—but there's no pain to speak of. You'd think that something eating your brain would be painful as hell, wouldn't you? But apparently the brain itself has no nerve-endings—it can't feel pain. Did you know that? I didn't. Pretty strange, huh?"

Claire recognized the pattern of nervous chatter. "Are you scared?" she asked.

"Shitless!" Katherine replied without a second's thought. "They've told me how I'm going to die, and I'm not looking forward to it. Woody Allen said, 'I'm not afraid of dying, I just don't want to be there when it happens.' That's pretty much how I feel right now.

"They said my organs will begin to give out, but the one that will do me in—because it uses the most muscles—will be my lungs. I'm going to suffocate."

The frankness—the almost coolness with which Katherine was talking about this took Claire completely aback. She wondered if she could be that detached talking about her own death.

"Oh, they could put me on a machine, but that would only postpone the inevitable—drag it out for everyone else. In the end, the end would be the same. I've told them absolutely no machines."

"Have you had last rites and all that?" she asked.

"Yes—for what it's worth," Katherine said. "And I hope it's worth a lot, by the way. I think I'm more scared of that part. The dying will only last a little while. What comes after—well, who knows how long that lasts."

Never having been a devoutly religious person, Claire couldn't offer much help in that area. So changing the subject, she said, "I talked to

Paul Levine a couple of nights ago, and he said that you had told every-one that you were going to be out of here on election night. Did the weakness part of the symptoms just hit all of a sudden?"

"Well, the end-stages do move pretty fast they tell me—and I've ob-served some of it first hand," Katherine told her. "But that statement was just a combination of bravado and denial. I thought I could just grit my teeth and will myself through it. I ended up on the floor, half under the bed for trying. I cracked one of my just-healing ribs and have a bruise on my hip that looks like Texas—shape *and* size! So much for the power of mind over body."

Claire shook her head in amazement and admiration at the strength that this woman continued to have. Wondering about the strength of those around her, Claire asked, "Who else knew about this? —before now, I mean."

"Not many," she replied. "My doctor, of course, but he was sworn to absolute secrecy. Richard naturally, and my mother. And that's about it. We didn't tell Melissa until I got in here from Boston. That's when the symptoms started to set in."

Suddenly, a thought occurred to Claire. "Oh my God!" she said. "This is why you wanted that shopping spree in Newburyport, isn't it? It was your last ..." Claire hesitated before finishing the sentence.

"Go ahead," Katherine said. "You can say it. My last chance. My last chance to kick up my heels—my last chance to just be a person, not a ce-lebrity—my last chance to *flirt*," she said with a wiggle of her eyebrows. "And I want to thank you for that—for all of it. That was the best going-away present I could possibly have gotten."

Referring to it as a "going-away present" hit Claire harder than she was sure Katherine had intended, and blinking away tears, she replied, "I'm glad that you asked me to do it, Katherine. If I'd only known ..."

"What?" Katherine said. "You'd have done something different? You did exactly what I wanted—everything was perfect. I mean that." She thought for a moment then added, "You know what part I liked best?"

Claire just shook her head, as too many memories of that day streamed through her mind.

"That mocha cake! Weird, huh? For some reason, that memory just hangs in my head. If there's a bakery in heaven, I know they have mocha cakes!"

Claire laughed as a tear ran down her cheek.

"Okay, now it's my turn," Katherine said. "I'll ask—you answer. Tell me about the investigation—I don't think I'm going get to read the final report. Richard told me that my would-be assassin is dead, but did you find out why he wanted to kill me, yet?"

Claire hesitated just an instant before replying, "From what we've gathered so far," she began, "it looks like it could have been in reprisal for supposedly blasphemous remarks you made four years ago in an interview in a woman's magazine. You remember that flap about shopping malls in the West Bank and women running Islam?"

"Yes, I do," Katherine replied. "I got a little too witty for my own—for *Richard's* good that time. A lessoned learned." She looked into Claire's eyes for a long moment before continuing. "You hesitated before answering Claire, and there was something in your voice. You're not convinced about this, are you?"

"Not really, no," Claire answered, this time without hesitation. "Something just doesn't feel right about the whole thing."

"Your *voice*?" Katherine asked.

"I guess," Claire replied. "But my other senses, too. The whole thing—the attempt on your life just seems way too complex for such a—a *nothing* motive.

"I mean, big deal, some low-level Islamic church lawyer says that a comment you made in a magazine four years ago—then apologized for—is blasphemous. That's worth all the time, money, organization, and risk that went into this attempt to kill you? It doesn't add up.

"Maybe if you were Salman Rushdie it would make sense. That fatwa was issued by an Ayatollah, and there was a two-and-a-half million dollar reward to be collected. It appears that whoever set all this in motion—and I don't believe Dunham was acting alone—it appears that they didn't even want public credit for it—just a reward in heaven. No. Something is wrong—I just know it."

"Well, I for one have a lot of faith in your instincts—your *voice*," Katherine replied, "but what do the others think? Mr. Gants, Paul Levine, my husband. Do they share your reservations?"

"I don't think they agree," she said remembering the debate in the Oval Office as if it were from a dream. "But if I recall correctly, it seems like they were more concerned about how it would all look on Election Day, rather than what the truth is."

"That's a little harsh," Katherine said, mostly in defense of her husband. "I'm sure they're as interested in the truth as you are. Richard would never ..."

"No. I didn't mean the President," Claire interrupted her, as her recollection of the conversation sharpened in her mind. "General Lindenthal—from Israel. He's the one who said there were two truths—one public and one private. I think he's the one who has my *voice* screaming the loudest."

"Well, if the motive isn't this fatwa thing," Katherine said, "then do you have any other ideas?"

There was a heartbeat's hesitation before Claire answered, "Not really," but Katherine picked up on it. "You're not leveling with me, Claire," she said. "What about swaying the election? Wasn't that your pet theory to begin with?"

Recalling what the President had said about Katherine's reaction to that idea, Claire had intentionally avoided that topic. "I didn't think you'd ..." Claire began and stopped. "I mean, from what the President said, I thought ..."

"That the subject would upset me?" Katherine finished for her again. "Well it does—but not so much that I'm going to all of a sudden die because it comes up. I'm interested in why you think there's more validity to that theory than the fatwa motive. I don't recall that there's any hard evidence for the election-swaying theory."

Katherine was clearly becoming agitated, and Claire didn't want that. "No. You're right," Claire agreed, wanting to put the issue away. "There really is no evidence to speak of. It's more of a—a *hypothesis* than a theory, I guess. Just an after-the-fact observation, because that's what the *effect* was. But no, there's no proof that someone *intended* for that to be the effect."

Katherine looked at Claire for a long while without speaking. Claire could see that there was something on her mind.

"Claire," she said finally, "I'm going to ask you to do something for me, something that I know will go against your grain, but I'm going to ask anyway—mostly as a friend—but also as an American."

Claire had an idea what was coming, and she knew she wouldn't be able to say, no.

"Claire," Katherine went on, "I want you to please just go along with Richard's plan from now until the election. Please? Just go along with the preliminary report idea, and don't stir up a lot of questions that don't have answers anyway.

"We're going to win this election, that's an almost sure bet. Nobody but the dumbest die-hard Republicans think Evans has a chance anymore. I'm not asking you to lie, Claire. I just want you to go along—just for a few days. Please?"

Claire just looked at her for what seemed a long time. A few minutes ago, Katherine had seemed so scared and vulnerable, wondering about the afterlife, and now she was focused on her husband's campaign again, as if it was the most important thing in the world. Claire had an idea that the latter was a front, much like her "Dragon Lady" façade, but who, she wondered, did Katherine want the pretense to fool? The world or herself?

"Katherine," Claire said, "I will make you this solemn promise: I will do what you're asking, and I'll even help write the preliminary report.

"And then, when the election is over, I am going to make it my personal Holy Grail to find the real truth. Whatever it is, however long it takes me, and even if I have to do it alone, I promise you that I will find out who did this to you, and why. You have my personal word on that!"

"Thank you, Claire," Katherine said. "But I don't want you to turn into some crackpot conspiracy nut over this. In a week or two it's not going to matter, anymore. The truth is supposed to set you free, not take prisoners."

"It'll matter to me," Claire said. "Because *you* matter to me."

Katherine extended her left arm, inviting Claire for a hug, and when they broke the embrace, each of them pulled a tissue from the box on the nightstand and dried their eyes. "You'll come by and see me again, won't you?" Katherine asked.

"Every day," Claire replied. "Is there anything I can bring you?"

Katherine began to say, "Not really," then stopped, and with a chuckle said, "Yeah—a mocha cake. I am *so* tired of Jell-O!"

Chapter 61

Saturday, November 1
Washington, DC

S aturday morning found Claire, Gants, Levine, and Diane Stevens, huddled in Levine's office in the Secret Service building. It was eight o'clock, and they had announced a special news conference for eleven, which gave them three hours to figure out exactly what they wanted to say about the preliminary findings of the task force, and how to say it. And perhaps more importantly, they had to figure out what they didn't want to say, and how *not* to say that.

At first, Claire had been uncomfortable with Diane's involvement in what was supposed to be a non-political exercise. But as the meeting went on, Claire realized that Diane wasn't trying to swing the statement in any political direction, but was rather offering the wisdom of her considerable experience to help with phrasing, so that nothing that the other three decided to talk about would come back to bite them.

Because there would be a question and answer period after Claire's statement, Diane suggested phrasing of certain topics that intentionally left significant information out. The idea was not to try to hide anything, but to lead the reporters to ask the questions that Claire wanted, and was prepared to answer. Diane also led a mock question and answer period with Claire, advising her on how best to handle the awkward questions that they knew would be asked.

At eleven o'clock, Claire was standing at the podium in the Service's media room, feeling well prepared, but still a bit apprehensive. This "media manipulation" stuff was not something that she had done before, and she was concerned that someone might see through her act, and call her on it.

"Good morning," she said on the cue from the director. "I have a brief prepared announcement to read, after which I will take questions."

Though she knew the next few sentences by heart, she looked down at the sheet in front of her and read as if the copy had just been handed to her.

"At approximately three forty-five Friday morning, in the city of Ramallah in the West Bank, the person known as Frances Dunham, who was wanted in connection with the attempted assassination of Katherine McClure, was shot and killed during a raid on a suspected terrorist safe house.

"The raid was carried out by Israeli Special Forces with the knowledge and cooperation of the CIA and the US Secret Service.

"Five men and two women were taken into custody during the raid and are currently being held on charges unrelated to the assassination attempt. They are being detained in a maximum-security facility at an undisclosed location."

Looking up from her paper, she said, "That is the end of the prepared statement. I'll be happy to take your questions, now."

Nearly every hand in the room shot up.

The question and answer period went on for twenty minutes, during which time Claire remained at the top of her form, fielding every question articulately and with a confident voice.

Thanks in large part to Diane's coaching, she was able to spoon-feed the media exactly the information that she, Levine, and Gants had decided they wanted them to have at this point.

"Have you established a motive for why these terrorists wanted to kill the First Lady?" one reporter had asked. "It would seem that a terrorist organization would rather kill a president, than a president's wife."

"All I can tell you about a motive," Claire answered, "is that the subject is being vigorously investigated. We were able to obtain certain information as a result of Friday morning's raid that is currently being processed by multiple agencies. But until we have additional information we're not going to speculate. So, you'll just have to be patient."

Claire herself had crafted that response, in order to set up the "leak" that would take place a couple hours after her press conference was over.

At eleven twenty-eight, the director gave Claire the hand signal to "rap it up," and as she walked from the stage she was surprised to feel what could only be described as *disappointment* that the briefing was over. Two weeks ago, she couldn't *wait* for them to end. It seemed that Katherine had been right—she *was* becoming a spotlight junky.

Working in do-not-disturb mode, Claire and Levine spent the next nine hours hammering out drafts of the preliminary report and sending them through encrypted e-mail to the President, the Attorney General, and to Gants.

At around twenty past ten, Saturday night, they finally all agreed on the language and content of the report, which Levine then sent to Margaret for final formatting and printing. Before midnight, the report was released to all of the wire services and networks, and was e-mailed to every member of Congress.

Listening to the car radio on her way home, Claire caught the eleven o'clock news on which the lead story was the unconfirmed report about a possible motive for the attempt on Katherine McClure's life. Though Claire knew the facts behind the "leak", this was the first time she was hearing what had actually been fed to the media.

A female reporter with a super-serious tone in her voice announced that an unnamed source within the Executive Task Force—speaking on condition of anonymity—had told CNN news earlier in the day, that investigators both in DC and in the Middle East were placing "great significance" on a report that the First Lady may have been the target of an Islamic religious fatwa, or order-of-execution, for a blasphemous remark made more than four years previously, during her husband's first presidential campaign.

"The fatwa," the reporter said, "is apparently similar to the one ordering the death of British novelist Salman Rushdie for writing *The Satanic Verses* in 1989, and may carry with it a substantial monetary reward. The reward for Rushdie's death reached two-and-a-half million dollars and has never been collected. It has been speculated that the Rushdie assassination fund could potentially be used for this and possibly other fatwas, as well."

Claire wondered how much of that claptrap—to use her father's expression—had been leaked that way, and how much of it was embellishment by the reporter. Not that it really mattered, Claire thought, but it would be nice if *someone* in the town respected the truth.

When Claire got home she found her answering machine blinking, indicating that she had three messages. The first was from her mother.

"I know how busy you are dear, with all your traveling and your news briefings and all," the recorded voice said. "But sometime in the next couple days, if you could give me a call, okay? Nothing important. I just wanted to chat. Bye bye, Honey. You take care of yourself. I love you."

Claire smiled, knowing that the translation to all that was, "Why am I hearing what you've been up to from the TV? Call your mother!"

The next message, left just after nine, was from Dave. "I know you're busy, so I didn't want to call your cell," he said. "I'll try you again later. Hope everything's going well. Bye for now. Oh, I caught your news briefing; you're getting better at that stuff all the time! Talk to you later—bye."

The third message was also from Dave, having been recorded just five minutes earlier. "Wow, you're really burning the midnight oil," he said. "I hope nothing too serious is happening. Call me when you get in, okay? It doesn't matter what time it is. I'm off tomorrow, so I don't have to get up early. Bye."

Claire was dialing Dave's number before the message was done playing.

"Hi there, Night Owl," he said, answering on the second ring. "How are you?"

"Not too shabby," she replied. "My boss gave me tomorrow off, too, so we can talk all night."

"Well, what do you know?" he replied. "I guess our *voices* do talk to each other."

"What do you mean?" she asked, but with a good feeling about it.

"My *voice* told me to make plane reservations, and I listened," he said. "Six-ten shuttle to Reagan."

"Really?" she said, not even trying to hide her excitement. "You're not teasing me are you?" Then something occurred to her. "Wait a minute ... you said you didn't have to get up in the morning. To catch that flight out of Logan, you'd have to get up about 3:00. You *are* teasing me, you brat!"

"Delta flight 5340. I can give you the confirmation number if you want," he replied. "If I had told you in my message that I had to get up at the crack of dawn, would you have called me back so late? I needed to talk to you to make sure you weren't going off on another international adventure or something."

"No more adventures," she said. "Not for awhile anyway. But I *will* be at the airport. I'll be waiting for you at the security gate. I'll be the one with the big smile!"

Thirty minutes later, after numerous reminders of how early he had to get up, Claire finally convinced him to say good night by warning him, "You better not get down here, and fall asleep on me!" She had almost set the phone in its cradle when she suddenly thought of something. "Wait, wait! Don't hang up!" she blurted into the phone. "Are you still there?"

"Yeah. I'm still here," he said. "What'd you forget?"

"I need you to do me a real important favor ..." she began. "You know where the Agawam Diner is in Rowley, don't you?"

Chapter 62

Sunday, November 2
Washington, DC

Claire was at the Delta terminal at Reagan National at six-fifty Sunday morning to meet Dave's seven forty-three flight. Remembering how she had gotten stuck in the traffic from a rollover accident driving back from the NSA, she was taking no chances; there was no way that she was not going to be there when he arrived!

When he came out through security, Dave set his carry-on down and with an ear to ear smile that matched hers, he wrapped his arms around her and held her tight. In that instant, everything that had gone on in the last few days—the last two *weeks*—vanished. There was only right now ... and right now was wonderful!

He put his hands gently on the sides of her face, leaned down, and lightly kissed her lips.

"Get a room!" a passerby commented, and they broke their kiss with a laugh.

"That's jealousy talking," Dave said as he picked up his bag with one hand, and took Claire's hand in the other. "You notice that *he's* leaving the airport alone. So, what have you got planned for our day off?" he asked as they walked across the parking lot to her Jeep.

"There's an arts and craft fair on the Mall, that I thought might be fun," she said. "There's bands, and shows, and food. All sorts of stuff. How does that sound?"

"Sounds great," he said. "But I'm pretty easy. Anywhere with you will be great."

"You're so sweet!" she said as she gave him a kiss on the cheek and unlocked his door. "Oh, speaking of sweet, were you able to do that favor for me?"

He held up his carry-on and said, "Ask and ye shall receive."

"Great!" she said, climbing in behind the wheel. "We need to make one stop before going to the Mall then."

Thirty minutes later, they were making their way through the security checkpoint at George Washington Hospital.

When they entered Katherine's room, she was sitting up in bed, and looking remarkably well. She was reading something, and with a bit of difficulty, she was making notes on it. It was a draft of her husband's acceptance speech, and despite her declining muscle control, she was determined to polish it up.

"I brought something for you," Claire said with a big smile when Katherine looked up.

Katherine made a show of looking Dave up and down, and said with a raised eyebrow, "Yes, you certainly did. But now I feel terrible ... I didn't get *you* anything."

Claire laughed, more from the joy that Katherine was still able to joke, than at the joke itself, and Dave blushed slightly at being "ogled" by the wife of the President of the United States.

"Down girl!" Claire said with a smile. "He's spoken for! Katherine McClure, this is David Perkins. David, Katherine."

Katherine extended her good arm to shake his hand. "Please, excuse the left hand," she said, "the right isn't quite up to par, yet."

"It's a pleasure to meet you, ma'am," he said. "How *is* the arm? Will you be getting out soon?"

"I would have," she lied. "But I took a fall getting out of this stupid bed the other day, and I hurt my thigh bone. A hairline fracture. I've got a bruise the shape, and about the size of Texas on my hip, and the doctors won't even let me stand next to my husband when he wins the election Tuesday night. I'm going to be stuck in a wheelchair!"

Claire had wondered what story they were going to come up with for why Katherine, after two weeks of recovering, was still not ambulatory. Very smooth, she thought. It had Diane Stevens written all over it.

"Well, maybe this will help you get over how mean the doctors are being to you," Claire said unzipping, and reaching into Dave's carry-on. She took out a squat eight-inch square box tied with string, and handed it to Katherine.

Katherine pulled the string off the box, and slowly lifted the lid. She looked up at Claire with an ear-to-ear smile and wetness in her eyes. Two mocha cakes sat in the box, slightly misshapen from their journey, but otherwise just like the ones she and Claire had had in Newburyport.

"Where'd you get them?" Katherine asked. "I've never seen them around here." Then it clicked, and she looked at Dave, and teased, "You flew all the way down from Newburyport just to bring me mocha cakes? Well, aren't you sweet?" Then she glanced at Claire, and with a mischievous grin, added, "Or did you come down to have some dessert of your own?"

This time it was Claire who blushed.

It was after ten by the time Dave and Claire made it to the Mall, and nearly five in the evening when they arrived back at Claire's apartment.

Dave said that he wanted to complete that dinner that they had started a week ago, so he had brought a change of clothes suitable for a nice restaurant.

Although they were not in a private penthouse with a view of the city lights, Claire had a wonderful time at dinner, sharing *voice* stories with Dave, and getting to know each other as well as could be expected in a public place.

Afterwards, as Dave unlocked and opened her front door for her, he asked, "So, you ever think about moving back north?" It was a subject that both of them were thinking about—and avoiding.

She thought for a moment before answering. Not about the answer— she *knew* what that was—but about what the answer was going to sound like to Dave. Finally, in a quiet tone, she said, "Not really. I like it here. I like my job."

There was a little pause while Dave thought about the ramifications of *his* answer, and then he said simply, almost resignedly, "Me, too."

Claire felt that feeling in her nose that she knew would eventually lead to tears, and she fought it back with all of her might. Knowing that she couldn't look into his eyes and still speak without her voice cracking, she pretended to check her answering machine, and said, "So where does that leave us?"

He walked up behind her, and put his hands gently on her shoulders. He turned her around to face him, then cupped his fingers under her chin, and gently turned her head up toward his.

In the dim light he could just make out the glint of wetness in her eyes. He leaned down and lightly touched his lips to hers. He gave her three such kisses then he said softly, "I know this seems awfully fast, but I believe I love you, Claire. I have never met anyone like you, and now that I have, I don't want to even *look*, anymore."

Her eyes filled completely then, and a crooked smile broke across her face. "You think our *voices* are trying to tell us something?" she said. " 'Cause I feel the same way."

He kissed her again, and then said, "I *hope* it's our *voices*. They seem to have a pretty good track record for getting things right." He kissed the tip of her nose, and added, "So, does your *voice* have any thoughts on how to make this thing work? I'm certainly open to suggestions."

Chapter 63

Monday, November 3
Washington, DC

When Claire awoke on Monday morning, she propped herself up on one elbow, and looked at the person asleep beside her. She had never felt this way about a man before, and the fact that she had known him for such a short time, only made it that much more amazing. She thought about his words from the previous night, about figuring out a way to make their relationship work. Last night, that didn't include leaving her job. This morning, she didn't see *anything* as being off the table.

Unlike Dave, Claire did not have Monday off. So, after breakfast, they drove together to Service headquarters, and after a long have-a-wonderful-day kiss, Claire let Dave take the Jeep, while she went to work.

His flight back to Boston left Reagan at two-twenty in the afternoon (the six-fifty flight was full), so the plan was to drive to the airport together, have a quick lunch, and a long good bye. Passersby, be damned!

Claire tried to make the hours go faster by burying herself in work. She had a meeting with Levine and Gants to discuss the format of the final report, and then she sequestered herself in her office, and began sorting and compiling her notes.

The tactic worked. She was unaware that it was quarter to twelve until Margaret called her to announce that a young man was at the front desk waiting for her.

After lunch at one of the fast-food places in the airport, Dave and Claire stood in front of the security checkpoint, arms around each other, neither of them wanting to let go.

Finally, with the line growing, Dave leaned forward and gave her a passionate kiss. "Did I mention that I love you?" he asked.

She chuckled and replied with a big smile, "Yeah, I think you did mention that—in words and deeds, actually."

"Well, just in case it should slip your mind sometime, I got you a reminder." From his pocket he produced a ring with a narrow band of gold, and a single heart-shaped ruby. As he held it out to her, he said, "Will you be my sweetheart?"

It was the most corny and most wonderful thing any guy had ever said to her.

"Yes!" she replied enthusiastically, holding out her right hand for him to slip the ring on.

When she held it up to admire, she had a hard time focusing on it through the wetness in her eyes. She threw her arms around him and gave him a kiss that rocked him to his toes!

A half-hour later, Claire was back at headquarters, passing by Margaret's desk.

"Thanks for covering for me," Claire whispered conspiratorially as she slipped out of her jacket.

She was just past the desk, when Margaret said, "Wait a minute! Wait a minute! Get back here! That wasn't on your finger when you left! Let me see that!"

With a huge smile, Claire extended her hand so Margaret could see her ring.

"I guess it means we're going steady," Claire said. With a thoughtful grin, she added, "No one's ever given me a ring before ..."

"For what it's worth," Margaret said, "I think he's a keeper!"

Claire laughed and said, "Yeah, so do I!"

It took a concerted effort for Claire to get back into outlining the report, but she did finally manage to shift gears and get focused, once again.

Although the task force's final report wouldn't be released for probably a couple of months, Claire didn't want to put it off at all. She knew there would be many drafts that they would have to go through before it was published.

But she also wanted to sort through the facts and lay them out to see if she could get a handle on her "something's-wrong" feeling.

After printing out a copy of the case outline that was on her whiteboard, she erased it and began making a new outline that included only the relevant facts, as she now knew them, in chronological order.

She sat down and kicked her feet up onto her guest chair, facing the board. She had just begun scanning the notes when her phone buzzed. She recalled with a combination of amusement and dismay, that this is what happened the last time she tried to do this.

"You still want to be in on the First Lady's security detail tomorrow?" Levine asked her.

"Of course!" Claire answered.

"Well, head down to the briefing room, Gants is ready to go over schedules and assignments," he replied.

Claire printed a hard-copy of her whiteboard notes, stuck it in her purse, and headed out the door.

On her way downstairs, Claire's mood swung abruptly from her positive, getting-things-accomplished feeling, to a deep melancholy, as it struck her that this might well be the last security detail that Katherine McClure would ever require.

Chapter 64

Tuesday, November 4, Election Day
Washington, DC

B y six-thirty, Tuesday morning, Claire was on her way to the hospital. When she got to Katherine's room, the First Lady had just been transferred into a wheelchair by two male orderlies. With her mother and her daughter at her sides, she was wheeled to the elevator by Aaron Powell, who had been assigned as head of the detail.

Twenty-five minutes later, the entourage arrived at the White House.

Not surprisingly, the atmosphere inside the White House was upbeat as one pundit after another predicted a stunning victory for Richard McClure. Although the exit-poll numbers wouldn't be "officially" released until the polls had closed in California, at eight in the evening, there was not the slightest doubt in anyone's mind (even Senator Evans') that Richard McClure was going to be reelected.

Since the First Lady and her entourage never left the White House once they arrived, the security detail had little to do until the First Family appeared before the press and invited well-wishers.

Even then, with every person there having gone through security, the agents weren't exactly "on edge". They all knew that this would be the itinerary, of course, so they were prepared for a long day. More than once, Gants had told Claire that she didn't need to be there, but Claire *wanted* to be there—for Katherine.

Claire only managed to get a few minutes alone with Katherine during the day, but during that time, they chatted like old friends. Claire showed Katherine her ring and Katherine gave her a congratulatory kiss on the cheek along with her admonition to not let him get away!

As Jimmy Carter had done in 1980, when Ronald Reagan's landslide victory became obvious hours before the west coast polls had closed, Senator Evans graciously conceded the election to President McClure by telephone call, before nine-thirty, DC time.

Shortly thereafter, with Katherine seated in her wheelchair on one side of him and Melissa standing on the other, Richard McClure gave the final acceptance speech of his political career.

By ten-thirty, Katherine was exhausted and ready for bed. During the week, a quasi hospital room had been set up in the White House, so that once she got home, she wouldn't have to leave again.

As soon as her two attendants, her nurse, and her primary doctor got her settled in, the First Lady's special security detail was dismissed.

Although the White House victory party continued for hours, Claire didn't feel the least bit celebratory, and decided to head home.

Claire knew, as did only a handful of people at the White House, that this was the last election celebration that Katherine McClure would ever see. That thought made Claire very sad, but at the same time, she was glad that Katherine had gotten to see it. Two weeks ago that wasn't a sure bet.

By the time Claire got a ride back to the hospital to pick up her Jeep, and then made it home, she was in a particularly glum mood. Although it was after midnight when she got in, she decided to call Dave, feeling sure that just his voice would lift her out of the funk she was in.

Shucking her jacket, and slipping the automatic from her belt, she plopped down on her bed, and unbuckled the snub-nose from her ankle. She reached over and picked up her nightstand phone and was surprised to feel a folded slip of paper taped to the underside of the handset.

In hand-written block letters it read, "DIMTILY?", with the initials "DP" signed in the corner in cursive. "Dimtily?" she pronounced the odd word out loud. But the word didn't *sound* any more familiar than it *looked*.

It was obvious that Dave had left it there yesterday. He had had her key ring all day, and plenty of time. The mystery was why had he hidden it there, and what did it mean? Was it in some other language? Was it an acronym for something?

Just the thought that he was playing some little game with her changed her mood at once. She found herself smiling as she stared at the slip, running possibilities through her head. Her mind easily drifted from the puzzle to how much she liked him. Was it really love? She thought so. She *hoped* so! She turned her hand over and admired her ring for the millionth time. Then it clicked! It was what he had said just before he gave her the ring! "Did I Mention That I Love You?" D.I.M.T.I.L.Y!

She dialed his number, and when he answered, she said, "Yes, you did! And I love you, too!"

Chapter 65

Friday, November 7
Washington, DC

For Claire, the days that followed the election were filled mainly with working on the final report, visiting Katherine on her way home, and talking with Dave at night. It actually felt good to have a routine again, Claire thought.

The visits with Katherine were difficult, because each day she was visibly weaker than the day before, and Claire knew that she was watching an inexorable countdown to a very sad end. Each time that she said good night to Katherine she wasn't sure if it would be the final time. Each time that she gave her a hug, she could feel the difference in Katherine's body. Surprising, though, Katherine's mind never faltered. She remained as sharp and as quick-witted as ever, and it was only those easy friend-to-friend conversations that kept Claire from complete despair over the ordeal that Katherine was going through. And each visit only served to strengthen Claire's resolve to find the truth.

By the time Friday rolled around, Claire had gone over her fact-list so many different ways that she was beginning to doubt her *voice*. If there was something wrong there, she sure couldn't see it. The only fact still not verified was the fatwa, and that changed at three-fifteen in the afternoon, when Claire got a call from Avi.

"We finally got confirmation that the fatwa that al-Abassi talked about is real," Avi told her. "The mufti who made the edict was in Pakistan, not the West Bank. That's why it took us so long to find him. Even after the fatwa became public, nobody around *here* seemed to know anything about it. Apparently, Hamoudi and this mufti were both traveling, and crossed paths in Egypt. That's when Hamoudi asked him to rule on that magazine article."

Claire's first reaction to the news was elation that the last piece of the puzzle had finally been fit into place, but immediately, her suspicion of well-timed good fortune kicked in, fueled, at least in part, by her underlying distrust of Avi.

"How did you end up finding this mufti in Pakistan?" Claire asked keeping any tone of challenge out of her voice. If Avi knew that she was suspicious of her, the communication might stop all together. "What made you look there?"

"al-Abassi remembered his last name; Qadri," Avi said. "Not a terribly uncommon Islamic name, but at least it gave us a place to start. Once we found him, we had a journalist who's on the CIA payroll interview him, and he verified what al-Abassi had told us."

"Did he say when the fatwa was issued?" Claire asked.

"January 8th, this year," Avi replied. "Just about ten months ago."

"That's what, more than three years after the article came out?" Claire said. "Why did he wait so long? Surely there were other clerics he could have asked."

"Maybe he only came across the article ten months ago," Avi suggested. "It's pretty unlikely that he has a subscription to a woman's magazine."

"Or, maybe it's just a convenient smokescreen," Claire replied. "Can you give me the name of your journalist? I'd like to talk to him if you don't mind."

"Sure," Avi said. "His name is Jalaal Rishi. He's a freelance. You got a pen? Here's his number."

After hanging up from Avi, Claire did a quick time zone calculation, and as much as she wanted to talk to Mr. Rishi, she figured that one o'clock in the morning would not be a good time to introduce herself.

Going to her whiteboard, she added this new information to her list of facts. Standing back to see if anything else needed to be updated, something began to show itself. She took a marker, and put an asterisk in front of certain items.

The items that she had marked were all pieces of information that had come from al-Abassi and that had little or no corroborative evidence behind them; they were simply recollections of events that he had witnessed or overheard. The possible exception was the fatwa, and Claire wasn't one-hundred percent sure on that.

Another thing that Claire noticed was that if all of the marked items were removed from the list, there was no longer any link between Dunham and the Hamoudis, which meant there was no link to the fatwa. If there was no link to the fatwa, there was no motive. Claire decided that she wanted to know a lot more about the man that Avi called Samer al-Abassi.

But who, aside from Avi, could tell her anything about him? Was he on the CIA payroll? The Israeli's Shin Bet payroll? Both? Was he part of whatever connection that Avi and Colonel Yousif had? She thought about calling Leo Bond, over at the CIA, but then rejected that idea. If she asked him anything about al-Abassi, it would surely get back to Avi, and Claire didn't want to tip her hand.

She picked up her phone and hit one of the speed dial numbers.

"Gants here," came the answer from the other end.

Claire briefly explained what she had picked up on, and that she wanted to find out more about Avi's operative. But she wanted to do so in a way that wouldn't raise alarms—possibly *false* alarms.

"Let me make a couple calls in the morning," Gants said. "In the meantime, you should come over here to the White House. I was just about to call you. Katherine isn't doing very well."

Chapter 66

Friday, November 7
Washington, DC

When Claire arrived at Katherine's White House hospital room, the mood both in the corridor and inside the room was somber, to say the least.

The President was there, of course, as were Helen and Melissa, and it was obvious that all of them had been crying.

Making her way to Katherine's bedside, Claire found her friend lying so still and so quiet, that if it hadn't been for the lines on the monitor tracing her heartbeat, Claire might have thought that she was too late.

Believing that Katherine was asleep, Claire tried to fight back her tears as she whispered, "Good-bye, Katherine. God bless and keep you, my friend. I'm going to miss you, but I'm sure glad I got to know you. Thank you for allowing me into your life." With tears running down her cheeks, Claire turned away, and wiped her eyes with the heels of her hands.

Then, from behind her, she heard a soft voice whisper, "Thanks for coming, Claire."

Claire turned to see Katherine looking up her through very tired looking eyes and wearing a weak, but unmistakable grin. "Come down here," she said, "I want to tell you something."

Claire leaned close and cocked her ear toward Katherine's mouth.

"Is anyone else listening?" Katherine asked.

Claire looked around, and answered curiously, "No. Why?"

"I want to tell you two things," Katherine said so softly that Claire had to strain to catch the words. "The first is; don't let Dave get away—marry his ass as soon as you can—you two are perfect together."

As Katherine struggled to get more breath, Claire smiled and whispered in reply, "I wish he were here, so you could tell *him*."

Taking very short breaths, Katherine managed to force out in a halting manner, "The other thing—is that—you must believe—Carol. Please—for me ..."

Claire wasn't sure that she had heard her correctly—she didn't *know* any Carol.

"Believe Carol?" Claire repeated. "Who is Carol?" She turned her ear toward Katherine's mouth to catch the answer.

But Katherine didn't answer.

When Claire turned to look at Katherine again, she was startled to see her head craned back, and her eyes rolled grotesquely up into their sockets. Her mouth strained open, desperate for a gulp of air that her lungs could no longer pull in.

Claire recoiled in shock as Katherine's body began to twitch and convulse as random panic signals were fired from her brain to the muscles over which she had lost all voluntary control.

Claire backed quickly away from the bed as the President and Katherine's mother and daughter came forward.

Claire had moved expecting the doctor and nurse to rush in, but then she remembered Katherine's do-not-resuscitate order.

For the next full minute—an eternity to everyone in the room, they all watched helplessly as Katherine struggled—futilely—grotesquely—to cling to life. Finally, with a paradoxical mixture of relief and sorrow they heard the monitor issue its flat-line alarm, and Katherine was gone.

"Good-bye, Katherine," Claire whispered one last time. With tears running down her cheeks she made her way out of the room.

Chapter 67

Friday, November 7
Washington, DC

The White House press corps had, of course, known that something was wrong by all of the comings and goings of people who were not White House regulars. But so well guarded had been Katherine's secret, that no one had managed to even speculate correctly about the reason.

Twenty minutes after Katherine had passed away, Denise Stevens called a special news briefing and read a prepared statement, after which, she said, there would be no questions.

"At four oh-three this afternoon," she read, "First Lady, Katherine McClure succumbed to a long-term medical condition. Her husband, her daughter, and her mother were with her when she passed away peacefully, as were a number of other family members, and close friends. At six o'clock this evening, eastern time, the President plans to address the nation regarding the sudden passing of his wife. I'm sure that you will all join with me in expressing your deepest sympathy to Mrs. McClure's family and friends."

Every hand in the room shot up and questions were shouted out, but Diane left the podium and the room without another word.

At six o'clock, a solemn President McClure, wearing a black suit jacket over a white shirt, and a black tie, addressed the nation from behind his Oval Office desk.

"I want to begin this message with an apology to the citizens of America and to all of the people around the world who loved and admired my wife, Katherine. I am sure that her sudden passing comes as a shock to all of you, especially coming so shortly after her survival of an assassination attempt just three weeks ago.

"Approximately one year ago, Katherine was diagnosed with a terminal degenerative brain disease. For personal reasons, she did not want the diagnosis made public then, and her physicians and I honored her wish.

"For many months my wife fought the progress of the disease through prayer, experimental medical treatment, and sheer willpower. She was determined that she would be at my side on election night this year, just as she had been throughout all the years of our marriage. And through her strength, and the grace of God, she was there with me.

"Her reason for steadfastly—some might say selfishly—refusing to allow her condition to be made public was not an act of denial, but simply a wish for privacy in a very public life.

"Throughout the years, as a politician's wife and as First Lady of the United States, Katherine had gladly accepted the fishbowl existence that is part and parcel of that life, but in the end, she made the very personal decision that this last—this final struggle should not be a public one.

"I am going to miss my wife, my companion, my best friend, very much, as I am sure all of her family and her many friends will. On their behalf, I thank you all for your thoughts and prayers, and your wishes of condolences.

"Good night, and may God bless."

With that, the camera faded to black.

For the next two days Katherine McClure's flower-surrounded casket lay in state in the Capitol rotunda as thousands of mourners filed quietly past, paying their last respects to a person that few of them had ever seen in real life, but who had still become a *part* of their lives.

Gants told Claire to take the next couple of days off, and despite the fact that she protested that she was fine and that she'd rather be working, he was insistent.

Although she took the time off, physically, she never stopped *thinking* about the case, or about the promise that she had made to Katherine to find the whole truth behind her shooting.

Two thoughts dominated Claire's mind all weekend. First, of course, was why had Frances Dunham tried to kill Katherine? The fatwa motive just wasn't holding water as far as Claire was concerned.

Unfortunately, there was little that she could do to answer that question from home, and since the case no longer held emergency status, and since it was the weekend, she couldn't even get other departments to do any research for her. Besides, it was really Gants' cooperation that she needed at the moment. She needed to find our more about Samer al-Abassi.

The second question was what had Katherine meant when she had said, "You must believe Carol"?

Who was Carol, and why did Claire need to believe her? Believe her about what?

Claire had known a couple of Carols in the past, one in high school, and one in college at NAU. She found it pretty unlikely, however, that Katherine could ever have met either one of them, or that they would know something that Claire would need to be persuaded to believe.

Did it have something to do with Dave? After all, he was the subject of the first piece of advice that Katherine had given her.

She called Dave, and asked if he knew any Carols. He said that his mother's name was Carol, as was his first steady girlfriend's in high school. His mother had passed away several years ago, and he had no idea what might have become of his old girlfriend. Claire considered it a dead end.

So, what else could it be? Claire knew that Katherine liked 60's and 70's music, and remembered her half singing, half humming a Carole King song when they were in Newburyport—but which one was it?

She got on the Internet and did a search for Carole King songs. Could that song or some other title have been what Katherine was alluding to?

Claire was surprised at how many King songs there were! Scanning the list, she spotted several titles with which she was familiar, including the one that Katherine had been singing, *You've Got A Friend*.

With some imagination, that song *could* conceivably contain a message that Katherine wanted to give to Claire. But why in the world would she be so cryptic?

On a whim, Claire did a search for the works of Louis Carroll, which included, *Alice's Adventures In Wonderland*, and *Through The Looking Glass*, but she found that avenue even less likely than her Carole King idea.

Perhaps Claire had misunderstood Katherine. After all, she *had* been struggling to even whisper. Maybe she hadn't said, "believe Carol" at all. But what then?

She went on-line and used a rhyming dictionary to find words that she might have mistaken for "believe". Bereave? Relieve? Aleve? Maybe it wasn't "must believe"—maybe it was "disbelieve". All of those words might have been possible, but they didn't make any more sense than what she thought she heard in the first place. She did a rhyming search for "Carol", and came up with even worse possibilities there.

As sad as it was to think about, Claire had to admit that it was possible that Katherine's last few words to her didn't mean anything at all—at least not to anyone but Katherine. Claire remembered her father's last few hours, and how he had talked about people that no one knew, and had said things that were just gibberish.

Still, Claire wasn't giving up on "must believe Carol," at least not yet. But she did decide to let it slip into the back of her mind for awhile. Maybe her subconscious would come up with something.

In the meantime, she pulled from her purse the folded sheet of paper that was a hard-copy printout of her office whiteboard. When she had printed it the previous Monday, just before Gants' briefing on Katherine's security detail, she really hadn't known why. Now, as she sat in her living room, on forced leave from the office and separated from the original list of notes, she could keep working on the case. *Chalk up another one for the voice*, she said to herself.

Chapter 68

On Monday morning, the funeral services for Katherine McClure were held at the Washington National Cathedral, after which the six-mile funeral procession made its way past the White House, across the Mall, around the Lincoln Memorial, and finally across the Potomac to Arlington National Cemetery.

Security for the graveside service was extraordinary and daunting, but Claire was not part of the detail. The President had asked her to be with Katherine's family and friends, knowing that Katherine would want it that way.

Claire graciously—and tearfully—accepted, but when the President asked her if she thought she might like to say a few words during the service, she humbly declined, saying that she was sure there were much more eloquent speakers who knew his wife far better than she did.

Katherine was not the first First Lady to die in the White House. In fact she was the third, following Letitia Tyler and Caroline Harrison. Nor was she the first First Lady to be buried in Arlington. Both Helen Taft's and Jacqueline Kennedy's final resting places were there beside their husbands. Katherine McClure *did* make history, however, by being the first First Lady to *precede* her husband to Arlington National Cemetery.

Following the service, Claire was invited to attend a private reception at Helen's temporary residence in Virginia, a sprawling English Tudor estate, complete with helipad, on which Marine One sat.

While she was honored to have been invited to the reception, she felt decidedly out of place there, knowing almost none of the McClure's family and friends, or the political elite on a conversation basis. So, as it turned out, she found herself mingling more with the on-duty Secret Service personnel than the invited guests.

Eventually, she asked Mark Wells, the agent in charge of the parked limousines, to let her know when one was called up to head back to DC, so she could try to hitch a ride.

An hour later, the Vice President and the Attorney General called for a car, and Claire was able to get a ride back to the White House where her Jeep was parked.

As Claire reached the steps to her apartment, all she had on her mind was calling Dave as soon as she got inside. He had suggested coming down to be with her, and now she found herself regretting that she had declined his sweet offer.

"Excuse me. Miss Bradley?" a man's voice came from behind her, just as she started up the steps. The voice startled her, both because she was lost in thought, but also because she had not seen anyone on the sidewalk. Where had he been?

She wasn't sure exactly why, but her self-defense instincts kicked in at the sound of his voice, and she turned to face him while inconspicuously slipping her hand into her shoulder bag, and wrapping her fingers around the small .22 caliber "purse-piece" that she had carried, even though technically not on duty during the funeral.

"Sorry, I didn't mean to startle you," the man said, as he slowly lifted his hands from his pockets and turned his palms toward Claire, showing her that his hands were empty. He pointed toward her pocketbook and added, "There's no need for that, believe me."

Her hand still on her gun, she made a quick assessment of the mustached stranger in front of her.

He was probably in his mid to late fifties, and well attired in an expensive topcoat over an equally expensive suit. His shirt appeared to be silk, as did his tie. His shoes were expensive and well shined. His hair was thinning, but neatly trimmed. He was about six feet tall and perhaps 15 pounds over his ideal weight—but he carried it well.

In New York he would have been taken for a banker or a lawyer—here in DC, he could have been either of those, or a senator, or a diplomat.

Although he didn't *look* the least bit threatening, Claire's voice was telling her that there was something dangerous about this man.

"Do we know each other?" she asked.

"No," he said. "I don't believe we've ever met, Miss Bradley. I'm here at the request of a mutual friend. Katherine McClure. She told me that she would make sure that you were expecting me. My name is Leland Carroll."

Carroll! Could that be it? "May I ask how Katherine addressed you?" Claire asked him. "Did she call you Leland? Lee?"

"She always addressed me by my last name," he replied. "But that's a long story." Then Claire's odd question suddenly made sense. "Did she tell you to expect someone named Carol, and you were expecting a woman?"

"Something like that," Claire said, still on her guard. "Do you have some message that you're supposed to deliver to me?"

"Would you mind taking a ride with me?" he asked. "What this is about is a rather private matter and I'd feel more comfortable discussing it as we drive. It's harder for people to eavesdrop if you're moving."

"Who would be eavesdropping?" Claire asked, looking around for any surveillance cars. "What's this about?"

"Probably no one," he replied with a shrug. "Just call it occupational paranoia."

"And what would that occupation be?" Claire pressed.

"I'll explain all of that, Miss Bradley," he said, "but not here."

"Okay, but I'll drive," she said. "And you won't mind if I pat you down first, will you?"

"Not at all," he answered. "But I assure you I have no reason to be carrying a weapon. You won't mind taking my car, will you? Yours is a bit conspicuous. Very easy to follow."

They walked up the street to his dime-a-dozen white Toyota, and she did a quick, but thorough check of his person before she slid in behind the wheel. Before she unlocked his door, she popped the glove compartment, and felt under the passenger seat. No weapons.

"East or west?" Claire asked him as they pulled away from the curb.

"Your choice," he replied. "Just so long as we're not being followed. I assume you know how to spot and how to lose a tail?"

She glanced at him curiously as she did a U-turn across the street, and said, "You really *are* paranoid, aren't you? Why is that?"

"Twenty-five years with the CIA will do that to a person," he answered.

"The CIA, huh?" she said, thinking immediately of Avi and the distrust there. "So what is it about the CIA that Katherine wanted you to tell me, that couldn't be uttered in public?"

"It's not about the CIA, Miss Bradley," he replied. "It's about Katherine. I'm going to tell you some things about your friend that you're going to find difficult to believe at first. When she mentioned my name, did she tell you that I'd know the truth, or to put your trust in me? Anything like that? She was supposed to."

"She said something about believing Carol," Claire said, giving him a wary glance, "but I didn't know what she meant—and she didn't get a chance to explain."

"Ah," he said, "I can see why you weren't expecting me then. That's a little cryptic even for a puzzle-solver like you."

She looked at him wondering what else he knew about her. If he really was a friend of Katherine's, and she had sent him, had Katherine told him everything she knew about her? And if so, why?

"The reason that it was important that she told you to expect me," he said, "that she told you to believe me, is that she knew that your instincts, your emotion, even your logic would tell you *not* to believe what I have to say.

"Now, before I tell you about Katherine, the first thing you need to understand is my motive for being here—I am *not* here because I want to be. I'm here talking to you because Katherine was emphatic that you know these things. I tried to talk her out of this."

"Why didn't she tell me herself then?" Claire asked while making a right turn from the left lane and watching her mirror to see if anyone followed.

"I asked her the same thing," he said. "She said it was because she could never get enough privacy in the hospital or in her room at the White House. Frankly though, I think she was scared to tell you herself. She had a tremendous amount of respect for you, Miss Bradley, and she truly cherished your friendship—I think she was afraid of losing that— afraid of what you'd think of her."

Claire shook her head uncomprehendingly. "What could she have been so scared to tell me when she was alive, that is so important for me to know now? Did she have an affair with Dave Perkins or something? What?"

He took a breath, and said, "Katherine went to her grave knowing exactly who was behind the attempt to kill her, Miss Bradley. She knew exactly who it was … because it was she."

With a skeptical look that she didn't try in the least to hide, she said,

"What's your game, Mr. Carroll? Why would you tell me something so absurd? Is this more CIA smoke, or what? What the hell have you people done?"

"I did warn you that you wouldn't believe me," he said. "And it has nothing, whatever, to do with the CIA. What I'm talking about is a completely private matter, between Katherine and me. I was a part of this with her, almost from day-one. If I hadn't been, I suspect that my reaction would be much the same as yours; I wouldn't believe it either."

"I see," said Claire, cynically. "While you're confessing to being part of a conspiracy to kill the First Lady—just a *minor* player, I'm sure—you're also telling me that the intended victim was also the mastermind—that it wasn't an assassination attempt—it was a suicide attempt."

"Aside from me being a minor player, Miss Bradley, you have it correct," he told her.

"And just why might the wife of the President have wanted to kill herself?" Claire pressed with the same cynical tone.

"You were at her bedside when she died, Miss Bradley, and I understand that it was not a pretty picture—not to watch, and certainly not to go through. That's a *large* part of the reason," he said. "Katherine was an amazingly strong, almost fearless woman, but the prospect of a long suffering death scared hell out of her. I'm surprised that she never talked with you about that."

Claire was a long way from being convinced, but her resolute *disbelief* was wavering. "What do you mean, 'That's a large part of the reason.'?" she asked. "What's the rest?"

"I'll answer that with a question," he said. "What happened immediately after Katherine was shot—regarding her husband's campaign, I mean."

Claire thought for a moment, and then realized what he was getting at. "Oh, bullshit!" she said. "You want me to believe that Katherine McClure arranged to have herself shot to boost her husband's ratings in the polls? Jesus! Is that really the best you can come up with? How did you last twenty-five years in the CIA if you can't lie better than that?"

"Sometimes the truth is harder to accept than a convenient lie," he replied. "Wasn't it your own theory that the motive behind this might have been someone trying to sway the election?"

"Yes," she snapped. "But not the frigging *victim*, for Christ's sake! That's crazy! Even if Katherine was afraid to die from her disease and decided to take her own life, you want me to believe that rather than just taking a bunch of sleeping pills, that she cooked up this elaborate scheme to have herself *assassinated* so that her husband could get a sympathy vote as a by-product? Well, I happen to know, Mr. Carroll, that a sympathy vote from her death is the *last* thing that Katherine wanted! That's why her illness was kept a secret! She didn't *want* Richard to win just because she was dying; she was afraid that it would taint the election, even his presidency."

"You're partially right," he said calmly. "And that's actually another part of the whole story. You're much closer to the truth than you think, Miss Bradley. When Katherine went to Newburyport with you, she had known for almost a year that she was going to be dead some time around the election. A month before or a month after was the time frame they gave her.

"If she died *before* the election, the sympathy vote would have been pretty high, but from the limited research we could do, it didn't look like it would lock-up the election. The Evans people could probably deal with it."

"You *polled* people on who they'd vote for if the First Lady died of some brain disease just before the election?" Claire said in astonishment.

"No," he replied. "We didn't take a poll. That wouldn't look real good when she suddenly *did* die, now would it? No, we ran demographic computer models using psych profiles. It's surprising how sophisticated those things are these days."

Claire looked at him, trying to figure out that if all this was true, how he could be so cold, so *detached* about it.

"The other problem," he went on with the same matter-of-factness, "was *when* she was going to die.

"If she announced, shortly *before* the election, that she was sick and dying, Evans' people would have ripped into that as being the most crass kind of political opportunism. Oh, they'd have expressed sympathy all right, but they'd also make sure that the media asked why it wasn't until a few weeks before Election Day that the McClures bothered to mention it. It had a very good chance of backfiring—tainting the election, as you say."

"According to the computer," Claire said mocking him.

"According to political logic and almost fifty years of research data."

"I'm sorry," Claire said with a dismissive wave. "This is more manure than my Grampa used to put on his strawberries! You're telling me that your *demographic analysis* said that if Katherine died of natural causes, it might hurt her husband's reelection bid, but that if she was *assassinated*, that he'd be a shoo-in? Come on—nobody would knowingly sit in front of a gun, patiently waiting to be shot because some computer model said it would get her husband elected President! Why are you telling me this crap?"

"It's not crap, Miss Bradley. *You* jumped in front of a bullet for Katherine. At least you thought you did—it amounts to the same thing. You were prepared to sacrifice your life, and as you've said yourself, *you* were only doing your job."

She glared at him. This was the second time he'd twisted her own words into his argument. "That was different and you know it!" she said. "That was a reflex action—not planned suicide!"

"True," he replied calmly. "But let's say there'd been a standoff situation and you knew that a sniper had a gun trained on Katherine. You would still have put yourself between the sniper and her, wouldn't you? Even after having time to think about the consequences of your actions."

"That's a lame analogy," Claire shot back. "Risking one's life—even sacrificing it to save someone else's is hardly the same thing as arranging to have yourself shot to get your husband elected President!"

"You keep losing sight of the fact that for all intents and purposes, Katherine was already dead," he replied. "She was not *sacrificing* her life for anything—it was already being taken from her and there wasn't a damned thing she could do about it. What she did—or *wanted* to do— was to ensure that her death would serve some purpose."

"Having your death serve some purpose is donating your organs," Claire snapped back, "not creating some elaborate international conspiracy to sway a presidential election! Speaking of which, are you also telling me that her husband didn't have a problem with all this?"

"The President doesn't know anything about it. He would *never* have gone along with it!"

"Katherine didn't think he had a right to know the sacrifice that his wife was willing to make for him?" Claire insisted.

"A *right* to know?" Leland replied. "That's not a right, that's a burden—a *sentence*. If he'd known beforehand, he certainly wouldn't have let her go through with it. And if he knew now, how could he function knowing that his wife had deceived him like that—had deceived the American people—and that maybe it's the only reason that he's even in the White House a second time. He'd resign. If you know him at all, you know that's what he'd do. The whole thing would have been for nothing."

"Okay, just so I have this clear," Claire said sarcastically, "you're saying that Katherine knew that she was going to die, so she figured she might as well do her husband a favor at the same time? I'm on my way to the morgue, dear. Can I get you anything? —another four years in the White House, maybe? I don't buy that for a second, Mr. Carroll. I may not have known Katherine for a long time, but I know better than that!"

"Again, Miss Bradley, you're closer to the truth than you know," he replied patiently. "She *didn't* do it for Richard. If she was going to do something for Richard, she'd have talked him *out* of running a second time, just like Lady Bird Johnson did with LBJ. That job will suck everything out of a person. Katherine saw that better than anyone.

"As hard as it might be for you to comprehend, she did it for you and me—for the American people—for the world, for that matter.

"Look at the legislation that sat on the table waiting to see who won this election." He counted the items on his fingers as he said, "A health-care bill that will actually make a difference because it includes equitable controls on insurance companies *and* hospitals; a European trade policy that doesn't give away the store; a domestic oil program that protects the environment, promotes alternative energy sources while still producing affordable oil and makes us oil-independent for the first time since World War II. There's a China policy that addresses China's impact on the world economy and human rights; and a Middle East policy that for the first time since Jimmy Carter, has an actual chance of helping the situation over there, not just the economies of a few favored nations."

"Oh, come on!" Claire shot back. "Like the world was going to come to an end if Richard McClure didn't get reelected? I don't see Katherine McClure cooking up this diabolical plot for a few pieces of legislation."

"Then you *didn't* know her very well," he replied. "I've never known anyone who could become more passionately committed to a cause. When we were in college together—she, Richard, and myself—we were all pretty politically active. There was a group of eight or ten of us who thought we knew how to finally straighten out the country," he said, musing about their naiveté. "Pretty much like every generation before us thought. We were always active about something; writing letters, protesting, having rallies.

"But it was Katherine who was the gutsy one in our bunch, the risk taker. If the police were coming at us in riot gear, she was in the front row, throwing their tear gas canisters back at them. If there was a sit-in or protest rally anywhere within a hundred miles, she'd hitchhike to get there. There was one time in the summer of our senior year, that she nearly got a riot started by impersonating an FBI agent, and getting the local cops to go out and break up a rally we were having. Of course, she also alerted the local news channels to the fact that the "pigs" were planning to *bust some radical heads* in the town square, so the whole thing was caught on tape, including Richard being arrested while he was peacefully speaking to the crowd. It was publicity we couldn't have bought even if we *had* money. We ended up paying some small fine for parading without a permit, or some bunk, but if they had figured out that it was Katherine who had started the whole thing by impersonating an FBI agent, she'd *still* be in Leavenworth. Remember, that was right after Hoover had died, and the man *running* the FBI was a hand-picked Nixon man, *and* it was during the height of Nixon's paranoia."

Claire had actually heard that story before. It was during her and Katherine's night of conversation after their shopping adventure. It had been amusing, then. Now, it was painfully sad.

"But you see," Carroll went on, "that's the kind of limb she'd climb out on for a cause she believed in. She knew the consequences if she was caught, but she went ahead and did it anyway, because she believed in the end result. And she did it alone, so none of the rest of us would be implicated if she got caught. She never even told us what she'd done until years later. She didn't do it for the glory—she did it because she felt it was the right thing to do. That's the Katherine McClure that we're talking about here."

Claire's resolve was wavering a bit more, but she was still not convinced. There was more to the Katherine that she knew than politics.

"Okay. She's a fanatic when it comes to a cause. But she's also a dedicated mother, a devoted wife, and a daughter with a loving mother. You're saying that she's so committed to her cause that she didn't care that her mother, her daughter, and her husband were going to actually see her head get blown off? Katherine and I had a couple of conversations about Melissa, Mr. Carroll—I don't believe she could do that to her."

Leland nodded his head, understanding her point, if not agreeing with it.

"First of all, she was *emphatic* that the shot that killed her not be a head-shot. She was aware of the gruesome nature of that kind of thing, and she also knew that it was too easy to miss the head. Snipers almost always go for a chest-shot, if possible. That's what *she* wanted."

Claire looked at him through squinted eyes, her skepticism back in full force. "You're telling me now, that she dictated this thing even down to exactly where to have this hired assassin shoot her?"

Carroll paused before answering, knowing what Claire's reaction was going to be.

"Technically speaking, Miss Bradley—and I know you're a stickler for the technicalities—Katherine shot herself. *She* actually pulled the trigger, in a manner of speaking. Admittedly, there's a pretty fine-line here, but she didn't want anyone else to bear that burden."

Claire started to say something, but Carroll held up his hand to stop her. "Let me get back to your other question, and then we can talk about this, okay?

"You talked about the trauma that Melissa, that the family, would go through if Katherine died by a sniper's bullet. Well, think about what they just went through—what *you* went through—watching Katherine die the way she did.

"When *your* mother goes, Miss Bradley, do you want it to be so quick that it's virtually painless, or would you rather sit next to her day after day in the hospital, watching her dissolve into a vegetable, and then see her gasping, tongue swelling, straining to get just one more breath of air, and finally to suffocate before your very eyes?"

Claire just gave him a contemptuous look as the image of Katherine's death replayed in her mind.

"I'm sorry for being so graphic, Miss Bradley, but that's the whole point, don't you see?" he said. "She knew that she was going to die; there was no escaping that, and she honestly believed that a quick, even shocking, death was going to be better for all concerned—including herself. She didn't want to suffer either, you know.

"But as well as it being quick for her and all concerned, she felt that having somebody to blame for her death would make accepting it easier—at least for Melissa. I don't know that I believe that myself, but it's what *she* believed."

Claire didn't reply right away. She was trying to put herself in Katherine's position, and she thought she was beginning to understand what she must have gone through. Claire was remembering Katherine's crying and her talk about Melissa in the motel room that night. It all made a lot more sense now.

She also recalled Katherine's words when she first reached her on the stage. "Jesus, Claire, it hurts so much!" she had cried, as if the pain was the thing that surprised her, not getting shot in the first place.

Claire's resistance to this incredulous tale was eroding little by little, but she still had her doubts. "Okay," Claire said finally, and with obvious skepticism, "tell me how she allegedly shot herself."

"Well, I don't know all the particulars of how it was set up," he said, "in fact most of what I do know about this came from your reports about all the stuff they found in the hospital. I didn't even know that's where the shot would come from. Neither did Katherine. I can't speak for her knowledge of such things, but I knew that the hospital was too far away for a sniper shot. I expected it to come from one of the houses on the hillside.

"Anyway, she basically fired the gun by answering the cell phone in her pocket. That much I knew about; that the gun would be rigged to fire by remote control. From what you and the FBI have gathered, apparently when the gun went through its automatic tracking and was aimed on her chest, the computer sent a call to her cell phone. All she had to do was hit the 'Talk' key to answer the call, and the gun would go off. To tell you the honest truth," he added, thoughtfully, "I didn't really think she could go through with it—I don't know that I could have."

Claire looked at him with a self-satisfied smirk. "You've finally gone a lie too far, Mr. Carroll. I happen to know that *that's* a load of crap!" Claire felt good that she had finally found the hole in his fabrication. "I know, because I personally took her cell phone out of her jacket pocket after we got her to the hospital, and the last call received on that phone was a call from *me*! And I sure as hell didn't shoot her!"

Leland thought for a few moments before answering. Finally he said, "I'm wondering why I'm going to such great lengths to convince you of something that I'd prefer that you not know in the first place." He looked upward, and said, "I hope you appreciate this, Katie. I hope you're putting in a good word for me up there." He looked at Claire, and said, "I believe that if you think about it, you'll find that there could be multiple explanations for that."

She gave him a sidelong glance, and said, "Like what? My phone number was hijacked?"

"That would be one explanation."

She was being facetious, but she realized that that probably *could* be done with the right equipment. She hadn't noticed what the date on the call had been; there'd been no reason to, then. She decided to call his bluff. 'Except that the date on the call was from the day before she was shot."

"Assuming that you know that to be a fact, then I guess you'll need another explanation, won't you?"

"What? A second phone?" Claire said. "I told you; I'm the one who took the phone out of her pocket, and there was only one."

"When did you say you removed it from her pocket?"

"At the hos ..." Claire paused, suddenly realizing that there had many others around Katherine from the time they picked her up off the stage until all of her clothes were cut off in the ER. Claire had only been in control of her jacket, and only for part of the time. Damn! "Well, if there was a second phone, where did it go?" She didn't really expect him to tell her, but nothing else came to mind.

"You're the one who suggested a second phone," Leland replied. "You tell me."

Claire just glared at him as she thought back to that morning. In her mind, she was seeing Katherine with her right hand in her pocket just before the shot, but she wasn't sure if that was reality or if it was her memory filling in blanks for her. If Carroll was telling the truth, the phone would have to have been removed before Claire got into the ambulance.

Either of the EMTs could have done it—or could they? Perhaps not. She tried to recall if either or both of them were ever alone with her. Even in the back of the ambulance, the President was with her, and according to Carroll, the President wasn't involved. And *that*, she believed.

Who else was there? —close enough to get the phone out of Katherine's pocket? From the time she was lying on the stage with Katherine, who did she see? There was Burger, Powell, and Gants, and then the two EMTs showed up. There were two other agents there, too. They were carrying the stretcher. She couldn't picture who they were, though.

She began to replay the scene in her mind.

Katherine was lying on her right side until they rolled her onto the stretcher, and then Claire had stayed right with her, blocking that side against another shot. Then what?

Once they got off stage, the EMT cut away her bra, and kept her from bleeding by putting his hand over the wound. Then the two agents—Samuels and Hall, that's who they were! —they carried the stretcher to the ambulance, with the EMT right beside Katherine.

Then in her mind's eye she saw something that gave her an ominous, hollow feeling in her chest. Gants had leaned over Katherine—from her right side—and had given her a hug.

Claire recalled thinking at the time that that was a bit odd, but so much else was going on that she never thought about it again—until now. Could Gants have pickpocketed the phone during that hug? *Gants?*

Claire made a turn into a gas station, and then back out onto the street in the opposite direction. As she performed the maneuver, she asked, "How in the world did she—or you—ever get James Gants to go along with this?" She asked the question as if Gants' involvement was a given, and only his reasoning was in question. "I'd have thought you would have had a better chance of getting the President on board, than Mr. Gants."

"Trust me, Miss Bradley, you'll be far better off if you don't try to speculate about who might or might not have been involved. And I'm certainly not going to confirm any guesses you make—nor am I likely to be *tricked* into confirming your guesses.

"All Katherine intended for you to know is that she herself was responsible for what happened to her. She and nobody else. Look at it this way, Miss Bradley; the only two conspirators in this who had anything to do with the actual shooting are dead. You watched Dunham get shot, and you identified the body yourself. And Katherine, the person who came up with the whole plan, and who actually pulled the trigger—well, you were there when she died, too. What more can you ask for in the way of justice?"

"So, what about the people in Ramallah," Claire queried, "they had nothing to do with this? They're just innocent scapegoats that you set up to divert attention?"

"Good God, Miss Bradley!" he replied. "Those people are anything but innocent! They may not have been involved in *this*, but the crimes they *are* guilty of are far worse! And no. I didn't set them up. Any setting-up was Dunham's doing.

"Your Dunham, the Israeli's Teacher," Carroll explained, "was suspected to have undergone plastic surgery several times before this. Even the Mossad didn't know what he looked like, for sure. And it is my understanding, through usually reliable sources, that he intended to retire after this operation. I assume that's why he let his face be seen as Dunham, and then got the plastic surgery. I would bet that he set up the Hamoudis to give your investigation a place to focus. I guess he didn't think you'd make the connection so fast. He probably thought that he'd be long gone, and completely unidentifiable, before you swooped down on his scapegoats."

"And that's your idea of justice? If the suspects are dead, close the case? Do you expect that now that you've told me all this, that I'll just accept it and back off of any further digging? What proof can you give me of *any* of this?"

"I don't *have* any proof, Miss Bradley," he replied. "That's exactly why I finally agreed to Katherine's request to tell you—because *you* wouldn't be able to prove it either. But if you *were* to pursue this, where do you think it would go? Who would you want to see your mighty sword of justice slay?"

"You and Townsend, for starters," she replied. "Gants, if he's involved."

"That's twice that you've thrown Gants' name out," Carroll said, "I thought that you and he were pretty close. But apparently," he added in a mocking tone, "your loyalties lie more with the abstract notion of the truth than with flesh and blood. But, okay, let's say that he is involved. Prove it." Claire shot him a contemptuous glance, but he ignored it and went on. "Townsend?" he said. "If he was involved in this in some way, you'd have to find him to bring him to justice—which, unless he wanted you to, you wouldn't—and then there'd be that thorny issue of proof, again.

"And what evidence do you believe you have against me? Even if you were able to recall this conversation word-for-word, and transcribe it as soon as you got home, it would just be your word against mine that this meeting ever even took place. And I'll guarantee that any shred of corroborating evidence that you might be able to come up with regarding Katherine's death, or even this car ride, for that matter, I'll have an alibi for. If I needed to, I could prove beyond any doubt that I'm sitting in a hotel bar on the beach in San Diego, right now."

Claire was in such a state of conflict that she found herself almost wishing that he *was* in a bar in San Diego, and this whole conversation was not taking place.

"But let's say that you *do* get me," he said in a hypothetical tone. "Somehow, you manage to convince, first the Attorney General, and then a jury, of my involvement in this, and you get a conviction. What, exactly, would I be convicted of? Attempted assisted suicide?"

"Conspiracy to commit murder comes to mind," Claire said.

"Okay, fine," Carroll agreed. "What's that going to get me? Ten years? Twenty? Life? What about the fallout? You claim to be concerned about Melissa and Helen. What do you think the truth would do to them? And like I said before, Richard would resign if he knew what Katherine had done. But even if he didn't *resign*, his Presidency would be politically castrated. I don't know if such a thing is possible, but they might even call for a new election. Undoubtedly, the Republicans would be howling for impeachment.

"So, the very things that Katherine wanted to accomplish in dying, you'd undo—and for what? To satisfy your personal definition of justice? To prove to the world that you're more right than everyone else, maybe? Or is it so you can say that you played by the rules no matter what the outcome? That you're Miss High-and-Mighty—above all the politics and weaknesses of mere mortals? That you ..."

"You've made your point!" she snapped. "But if there's no evidence out there for any of what you've just told me, why should you care if I spend the rest of my life investigating this thing?"

"Frankly, I *don't* care," he said smugly. "But Katherine did. She had tremendous respect for you, Miss Bradley. Your abilities, your morals, your convictions. She told me that she was sorry that she had brought you into her security detail. Not just because she was afraid of you finding out the truth—which she believed you are capable of—but because she felt she was betraying your trust. She felt terrible about that.

"When you told her in the hospital that you were going to make this your personal crusade—that you'd never give up until you found the truth, she knew, then, that she had to *tell* you the truth. She could see this being like the Kennedy assassination, still not completely put to rest decades later. She didn't want that for you *or* the country."

"You could have arranged for me to have an 'accident'," she replied.

"This isn't a movie, Miss Bradley. Nobody's going to push you in front of a subway because you know too much. This is Washington DC—birthplace of deniability."

She drove in silence for a while, running everything back and forth in her head. Finally she said, "So, I'm supposed to believe you, to *trust* you even after you've apparently double-crossed Dunham? How do I know you're not double-crossing Katherine, too? Twenty-five years in the CIA—that's got to come pretty easy by now,"

"What makes you think I double-crossed Dunham?" he asked.

"*Somebody* set him up," she said. "I don't believe that his death was an accident."

"And you think that I arranged to have the Israeli army shoot him? I wish I *had* that kind of pull."

"It wouldn't take the whole army," she replied, "just Colonel Yousif. Repayment of a favor from your CIA days, maybe. Or maybe just cash."

Leland laughed. "Moshe Yousif would put a bullet in *my* head before he'd do something like that for me. Hell, I think he'd put one in his *own* head first! Don't get me wrong; he's *capable* of doing something like you suggest, just not for me. He and I had a run-in some years ago, in which I came out on top. There's been no love lost between us since then. I assure you that whatever happened over there, whatever the reason might be that Dunham was killed—accident or assassination—I had nothing to do with it.

"The story that you released to the media about the shooting being a self-defense *accident*, of sorts, is very plausible," Leland said. "I can see that happening. On the other hand, there are probably a fair number of people, agencies, and governments who would rather see Dunham dead, than on trial in the US. In all honesty, I'm not exactly mourning his passing myself. It's a loose end I no longer have to worry about. But, I didn't *arrange* his passing."

"Speaking of arranging," Claire said, "how was all this paid for? A contract to kill the First Lady of the United States can't be cheap. And I'm pretty sure Katherine wouldn't have put it on her Visa."

"Nor were any government funds involved," he said, if that's what you're implying. "The taxpayers of America did not finance the assassination attempt on their own First Lady.

"In my line of work, there are monies we refer to as *appropriated funds*," Leland went on. "This is money that comes into our hands as a by-product of some operation. It might be cash that we come across when we make a raid somewhere. It could be a bank account or safe-deposit box left behind by a fleeing or dead enemy operative. It might even be money from a drug or arms deal that was part of a sting operation. The point is that it's money that doesn't show up on any CIA books. It's rarely even talked about—one of those don't ask, don't tell things.

"If Ollie North, for instance, had had access to *appropriated funds* rather than having to use accounted-for arms-sales profits for the whole Iran/Contra mess during the Reagan administration, it would have been a lot *less* messy.

"Anyway, over the course of my career, I managed to salt away a fair share of these funds. They paid for a lot of very black operations over the years. Necessary evils, as it were. Things that Congress, even the various Presidents, were better off not knowing about.

"Since none of these funds ever officially existed—and there is certainly no accounting of them—when I retired, I turned a good deal of the money over to my replacement—sort of seed money, to get his own network going.

"But some of the funds stayed under my control—part of the unofficial retirement package, you might say. That's where the money came from."

If that was true, Claire thought—and it didn't seem the least bit far-fetched—then she had been right to suspect al-Abassi. The Hamoudi/Dunham money-conversation would never have taken place. What else was al-Abassi lying about?

"Then it was *you* who bought the Dynametric gun," she said.

"Through Townsend?"

"You're fishing again, Miss Bradley," he replied with a hint of amusement in his voice. "But the truth is that I didn't know that such a gun existed until you reported it on TV. As for Townsend ..." Carroll shrugged. "I know *of* him, but we've never actually met. We traveled in different circles. If he had anything to do with acquiring the gun, it must have been for Dunham directly."

"So what *did* you do in this conspiracy?" Claire asked bluntly. "Just supply untraceable funds?"

"I did the same thing that I did through most of my career," he told her, "I arranged things. Katherine certainly didn't have the necessary contacts for something like this—aside from me, of course. In fact, I'm the only contact she had throughout the whole project. Very purposely, she didn't even know *if* anyone else was involved—though I'm sure she suspected that I couldn't do something like this by myself.

"She didn't know of Dunham, and Dunham didn't know that Katherine was part of the plot, except that she was the target. He thought that *I* would be using the cell phone to fire the shot."

Again, Claire simply drove in silence, trying to weave connections between all these pieces. She finally decided that she was not going to be able to do it in her head. She was going to have to sit down with her notes and lay it all out. Maybe then it would make sense.

"So what is it that you're expecting from me?" she asked, finally posing the question that had been on her mind since the start of this conversation. "A promise that I'll keep all this to myself? A pledge on Katherine's memory that I'll take this to my grave?"

"Not really," he answered. "I'm not expecting anything. Katherine wanted you to know the truth, and I've delivered it. What you do with it is out of my hands—and certainly out of Katherine's."

"And if I choose to pursue these leads that you've given me," Claire said, "I suppose you'll just go the way of Mr. Townsend. Drop out of sight and live off your *appropriated funds* somewhere?"

"That's always an option, of course," he answered. "But I kind of like the life I'm leading. I don't really want to go off somewhere and start a new one. That's not as easy as it might seem—even for someone in my profession. No. I believe I'd just take my chances—just as you'd be doing."

"What's that supposed to mean?" she asked. "I thought you said you weren't into arranging accidents."

"Oh, nothing so dramatic, Miss Bradley" he said with a dismissive chuckle. "But possibly even more effective. Like I said before, it would come down to your word against mine, and unfortunately, all you'd have on your side would be the truth. That'll give you a nice warm feeling, but it's no match for cold, vicious, deceit.

"Don't take this the wrong way, Miss Bradley—I don't mean it to sound like a threat—but if you were to pursue this—pursue me, and by extension, Katherine—it would be your credibility that would be the casualty.

"Not only would I have an alibi," he went on, "for any shred of evidence you could possibly come up with, but I'd be out in front of you feeding and leaking all sorts of bogus information to the media about how and why you're trying to destroy the late First Lady's memory because she was such a tyrant to you and because you're looking for an eight-figure book and movie deal. I'm sure I could even get a sexual scandal in there somehow. You'd have to spend all your time defending yourself against *lies*, rather than exposing the truth."

"Gee," Claire replied wryly, "for something that wasn't supposed to sound like a threat, that seems downright hostile."

"I only want you to know how the game will play out, Miss Bradley," he replied. "I hope it doesn't come to that, and I'm sure that Katherine felt that way, too. She'd hate to see you taken down like that—even for as noble a cause as the truth."

Without really planning to, Claire found that she had driven in a large circle and was now just a couple blocks north of her own street.

A minute later she pulled up in front of her building, and double-parked. She shifted the transmission into park, and turned in her seat to face him. "Well," she said, "you've certainly given me a lot to think about, haven't you, Mr. Carroll? How should I get in touch with you if I have any other questions?"

"If there are any other questions, Miss Bradley, ask them now," he said. "When you get out of the car, this topic is concluded and—nothing personal—I hope never to see you again."

"Don't you want an answer as to whether I plan on pursuing this? Pursuing *you*?" she asked.

"Surprise me," he said.

She looked at him trying to determine whether that was supposed to be a challenge or if it was just a show of arrogance.

They both got out, and as Claire went to the sidewalk, Carroll circled the car and got in behind the wheel. He checked traffic over his left shoulder, and then pulled out without even another glance at Claire.

As he pulled away, she made a mental note of his license plate. She didn't figure it would get her much, but she'd run a trace on it anyway. She wanted to do a lot of checking on the mysterious Mr. Leland Carroll.

She climbed the steps and entered her apartment. She closed and locked her front door, and then just leaned against it, her head swimming with all that Mr. Carroll had just told her. Was his story really possible? He certainly made it sound *plausible*. But if it *was* a ruse, why? Who was protected if the investigation shifted focus to Katherine? Not Dunham; he was dead. Carroll himself? That didn't make sense; his name had never even come up before. He wasn't a suspect until he made himself one.

Absently, Claire began going through the motions of being home as her mind continued to churn the bizarre story that she had just heard. She hung her jacket in the closet, and then began transferring the contents from her "formal" purse back into her everyday one.

As she removed the small pistol, she noticed a tiny red glow inside the purse.

"Oh, my God ..." she said out loud as she took her voice recorder in her hand and stared at the illuminated "record" light.

She hadn't even though about it being in there, but as she had reached into her purse for her gun when the well-dressed stranger had first approached her on the steps, she must have hit the "record" button. It wasn't the first time that that had happened, and she kept meaning to get a different recorder, because she kept ending up with dead batteries and long worthless recordings. Until right then, she'd have chalked up her not getting a new one to procrastination, but now she wondered if it had been her *voice* that had made her drag her feet.

Holding her breath, she pressed the button to get to the beginning of the recording, and then pressed "play."

The voices were muffled, but recognizable. She fast-forwarded to where they were talking in the car. She had to turn the volume up all the way to hear Carroll's side of the conversation, but she *could* make it out.

She skipped ahead stopping and listening to different passages. She was able to understand what he was saying, but she had the advantage of having just heard it, live. She was sure that digital enhancement would make it clear enough for others to understand.

The question was, did she want others to hear it? If everything that Carroll had just told her was true—if Katherine really *had* been behind her own shooting—did Claire really want to make that public?

How many of the ramifications that Carroll had talked about

would come to pass?

McClure's presidency might not be castrated, as he said, but it would certainly be weakened. Maybe to a point where he *would* resign.

Certainly Helen and Melissa would be devastated by the revelation.

It would turn a nicely healing American wound into another festering scandal. And she had no doubt that Carroll had not been bluffing about going on the attack if she broke the story.

Not that she was afraid of him. Not that she could be dissuaded from what she knew was right by his threat of a disinformation campaign—not with the recording that she held in her hand. But what good would such a crusade do? Who or what would it serve?

Dunham was already dead. Whether by accident or execution, the result was the same. No further justice could be exacted from him. And while the so-called coconspirators from Ramallah might only be scapegoats in the conspiracy, exposing the truth would not win them their freedom. Israel had them for their own reasons, and they were not about to let them go just because the US said they were innocent of *this* crime.

Standing alone in her kitchen, feeling as if there was a ten-ton weight on her shoulders, Claire found herself wishing that Dave was there. Not that she could confide all this to him, she just felt a desperate need to be held right then.

She put her pistol and the recorder in her gun vault, took off all of her clothes, and crawled into bed. She picked up the phone, dialed Dave's number, and prayed that he'd answer.

On the second ring he said, "Hi sweetie. How are you doing?" Knowing she had just come from Katherine's funeral, he expected that she might be a bit depressed.

To his surprise she said, "I'm naked, I'm in bed, and I want you here!"

There was something in her voice, however, that was anything but frisky, despite her playful words. "Are you okay, Claire?" he said, the concern obvious in his tone.

"Not really," she managed before she began to cry.

Chapter 69

Tuesday, November 11
Washington, DC

Just talking with Dave the night before had calmed her a great deal. She couldn't talk about what was actually bothering her, of course; the conflict that was raging in her head between right and wrong; good and evil; truth and lies.

But even when they didn't speak at all and she just laid there holding the phone, just knowing he was on the other end comforted her. Unfortunately, it was a feeling of serenity that didn't last long after they had said good night.

She had never really gotten into a deep sleep all night, and turned her alarm off before it buzzed. She was in the office before most of the others arrived, and began trying to satisfy herself as to whether Leland Carroll had been telling the truth the day before.

The first thing she did was to log into the Virginia DMV web site and do a search on the white Toyota's license plate. She was a little surprised—even disappointed—to find it was registered to a Leland Royce Carroll with an address in Arlington, VA. He would have known that she'd check, and if he was living that much in the open, any digging that she could do without the CIA's cooperation wouldn't be very helpful.

Next, she logged onto Google, and did a search to find out where

Katherine McClure had gone to college.

Having found the school and the years that she was there, Claire was next able to pull up an on-line copy of Katherine's yearbook. There, along with photos of Katherine and Richard, she found a photo of Leland Carroll. He had a good deal more hair and no mustache, but it was undeniably him.

Under his photo were listed his activities, which included the debate team, drama club, and intramural judo, in which he held a black belt. He was also a member of the non-school-affiliated Young Democrats of America.

She scrolled through a series of photos and found one of the debate team. She immediately picked out Richard, and then found Carroll, but she didn't see Katherine in the group. She was about to jump to Katherine's school bio, to see if she had been on the team, too, when another member of the group caught her eye.

Was that who she thought it was? He had a mop of hair and a full beard and mustache, but there was something in the eyes. She jumped to the senior photos and scrolled down. Sure enough, there he was; James Winthrop Gants.

It would never occurred to her that Gants might have gone to school with Richard and Katherine. He seemed much older. She wondered if he had been part of Katherine's, Richard's, and Carroll's clique, back then—and how close he was to them, now.

As unsettling as that revelation was, Claire kept her focus on trying to think of other ways that she could verify who Carroll said he was—specifically his CIA connections—without raising flags by going through official channels. Disappointingly, nothing came to mind, and she felt an irksome sureness that Carroll had known that.

Before leaving her apartment for work, Claire had replayed the recording of the conversation from beginning to end—twice. She was looking for some flaw, some hole that would prove—or at least *suggest*, that he wasn't telling the truth about Katherine. She could find none.

As disconcerting as it was, she had to admit that all of Carroll's allegations fit together as well or better with what she knew to be facts, as anything the task force had generated.

But she wasn't ready to concede, yet. She logged onto the task force data-bank, and pulled up the video of the shooting. She did a fast-forward through the first part, and then switched to slow motion as Katherine sat back down after her husband's applause. Watching Katherine's movements with Carroll's allegations in mind, a knot grew in

Claire's stomach as her every action fit perfectly into place.

Once seated, Katherine had sat bolt upright and as still as a statue. Watching the replay more closely than she ever had before, Claire thought she could see Katherine jump slightly, a few seconds after she took her seat, and just before she slipped her right hand into her jacket pocket. If Carroll's story was true, and Katherine knew exactly what was going to happen in the next few moments, Claire could easily imagine that Katherine would have been startled by the sudden vibrating of the phone in her pocket.

It seemed like a very long time to Claire, that Katherine just sat there not moving a muscle after she put her hand in her pocket. If she really did know what she had just done by answering the phone, it must have been an *eternity* to Katherine! An eternity to think about the decision she had made, and with no means of stopping it.

Then, with suddenness even in slow motion, Katherine slammed back in her seat and her head rocked back.

Claire stopped the player at that point, and exited the program. There was no need to watch any more—she'd seen what she needed to see.

While Katherine's actions didn't prove that Carroll had been telling the truth, they certainly showed that his story was *plausible*. Then it occurred to Claire that it was also plausible that Carroll had studied the video and had fabricated the suicide story to fit Katherine's actions. Damn! Why couldn't any of this have a *definitive* answer?

The more she thought about it, the closer she found herself to the edge of accepting Carroll's story—to accepting that Katherine McClure could actually have done what he had told her. Katherine's strength, her convictions, her dedication, her will power ... they all fit. As did the chain of events and all of the circumstances that Claire knew about.

The one part of the whole puzzle that she had the hardest time accepting was Gants' involvement. While Carroll had never confirmed her accusation that Gants was involved, after seeing that the phone had been in Katherine's right pocket, Claire felt even more sure that Gants not only *could* have removed it, but that doing so would explain his oddly-timed hug of Katherine.

Her problem was that she just couldn't believe that Gants could deliberately be involved in such a thing! It was so completely out of character for the man that she knew and respected.

Not only would he have conspired to commit murder, he would have knowingly put hundreds of spectators at risk if panic had broken out—as it easily could have—and he would have put himself in a position of having to lie to the President, and perjure himself to Congress during the inevitable investigation. Worst of all, he would have to have stood there, knowing and watching as a woman that he'd known for years—a personal friend—a person for whom he would sacrifice his own life to protect, was shot to death.

Those things were incomprehensible to Claire. She had liked and admired Gants from the first day they met. His integrity, his unwavering commitment to doing things the right way, his distaste for good-old-boy politics, his refusal to back down from what he believed in, his ability to accomplish any task that came his way, all made him as much a role model and mentor for her as her father had been—and those were large shoes to fill. That bond made it very difficult for her to accept his involvement. Yet there seemed to be so much evidence.

Evidence, she thought *What exactly was the evidence?* Flipping open her notebook, she began making a list of Gants' possible involvement—the so-called *evidence* against him.

- Personally oversaw all security details at Newburyport.
- Was at my side when K was shot.
    - To stop me from interceding?
    - To get to K first, to get the phone?
- First words at scene were, "Where's she shot?"
    - How did he know she was shot? Could have been heart attack.
- Did not want to take her to the better hospital in Boston.
- Took immediate charge of on-site investigation.
- Led search team to hospital.
    - How did he know gun was in hospital? Even Carroll didn't think that possible.
- Present in NH when Ramallah phone number was discovered.
    - Who suggested looking inside shredder for scraps of paper?
    - Why was Gants even there?
- CIA contacts.
    - Avi; Leo Bond.
    - Carroll? Townsend?
- Was against trip to Israel.
    - Knew of Dunham's pending "execution"?
    - I would be too close to the truth?
- Offered to look into al-Abassi.

- o   To warn Avi about my suspicions?
- o   Still no report!
- Proponent of pre-election preliminary report.
  - o   To put the matter to rest, quickly?
- Proponent of fatwa-motive.
- Very vocal against election-swaying theory. (Too vocal?)

Claire leaned back and looked the list up and down.

Jesus! she thought. *Talk about a preponderance of evidence!*

Granted, it was all circumstantial, and there was no single item that could get someone convicted of conspiracy, but taken together it was certainly more than she'd want to defend *herself* against.

She thought about that for a moment. She then went back through the list with another suspect in mind, and she began to see a chilling pattern.

On another sheet she constructing a new list—one with *her* under suspicion of aiding Katherine rather than Gants. The lists weren't identical, but there were unsettling similarities.

- Spent day and night before shooting with K in Newburyport.
  - o   Not on any planned agenda.
- Closest person to K before shot.
- Announced "Shots fired" before anyone heard a shot.
- First person to K after shot.
- Access to K's cell phone after shooting.
  - o   Sole possession of K's jacket with cell phone.
- In charge of all information released to public.
- Heavily involved in all aspects of investigation.
  - o   Frequent meetings with K.
  - o   Numerous wrong avenues & dead ends pursued.
  - o   Personally stopped Ramallah phone number from being sent to data base.
- CIA contacts.
  - o   Avi; Leo Bond; Townsend; Carroll.
- On-site when Dunham killed.
  - o   Personally took prints from body.
  - o   Personally gathered evidence to implicate Hamoudi *et al.*
- Coauthor of pre-election preliminary report.
- Coauthor of final report.

So much for circumstantial evidence! she said to herself. *There's more evidence that says I was involved in a conspiracy, than Gants!*

She felt a feeling of relief that she could conceivably explain away the so-called evidence against Gants as mere coincidence—the same as she could the evidence against herself. She was relieved, but not very re-assured.

Claire had never been more conflicted about anything in her life. If she accepted what Carroll had told her as the truth—and she was leaning heavily in that direction—then what should she do?

Should she stand by her moral conviction that regardless of its possible unpleasantness, the truth should never be compromised? If Carroll was telling the truth, then Katherine had made her choice of her own free will, knowing full well the possible consequences.

Why should it be put on Claire's shoulders to keep the truth hidden? Why should she carry the burden of *furthering* the pack of lies by helping to write a fictitious final report? If Katherine's image in the minds of the American people was tarnished, if her husband's presidency was tainted, if Leland Carroll didn't get to enjoy his retirement, those things were Katherine's fault, not Claire's!

On the other hand … what about the people who really *were* innocent? Melissa and Helen, specifically, but maybe even Gants.

Once this door was opened, whether he was actually involved or not, others would look at Gants' actions the same way that she had. He might never be charged with a crime of any kind, but the media wouldn't let a little thing like that stop them. His career would be over whether he had had anything to do with the plot or not.

And what about the President? If he really didn't know, what would he do when he found out that his wife had tried her best—and had apparently succeeded—in *rigging the election*? Would he really resign? Claire believed that he probably would. What would that do to the country? Nothing good, that's for sure.

Once again, she found herself no closer to knowing what the right thing to do was. She felt very small and alone.

There was only one person whose advice she could imagine seeking about something like this—and he was gone. She never missed her father more than right then.

She sat there in her office thinking for a long time, before she finally decided what she should do ... what she *needed* to do. She turned to her computer, and began typing.

Chapter 70

Tuesday, November 11
Washington, DC

Fifteen minutes later she was in her Jeep and heading for the White House. After passing through security, she made her way to Gants' office, where his secretary announced her, and he invited her in.

"Good morning, Mr. Gants," she said as she closed the door behind her.

Gesturing toward a chair, Gants said, "What's going on? Why the closed door?"

She took a seat, and without preamble she handed him the folded sheet of paper that she slipped from her jacket pocket.

"What's this?" he asked as he unfolded it.

"Please read it, sir," she said, "then we can talk about it."

He read what she had written very carefully, and then looked up at her and said, "You can't be serious!"

"Sir," she began, "I understand how this would come as a shock, but believe me, I've put a lot of thought into this, and ..."

"I don't care how much thought you've put into it, Special Agent Bradley," he said, cutting her off. "This is bull! What could possibly possess you to come to this kind of conclusion? You've been under tremendous stress lately, and I have to question your ability to have really thought this out. I am not going to accept your resignation—period."

"You don't understand, Mr. Gants," she said. "It's not the stress; it's what *caused* the stress. I just can't take the politics any more."

"*Can't take the politics*?" he repeated. "Well, you sure chose an odd line of work for a person who doesn't like to be around politics."

"That's not what I mean, sir," she replied. "What Presidents, Senators with presidential aspirations, even what First Ladies do as part of their jobs really doesn't bother me. Well, not *professionally* anyway.

"The politics I'm talking about is what's been going on in and around this investigation since day-one. Despite the President's assurances that the task force would be politics-free, it's been anything but. From the very beginning, starting with my appointment to be spokesperson—what amounted to the campaign's poster-hero—every decision has had a political underpinning."

"You've just now had this sudden epiphany about how this town works?" he challenged. "Why didn't you bring this up earlier?"

"I've asked myself the same question," she said. "I guess I thought I could stay above it—be the one person who could defy the politics, and keep the whole thing on the straight and narrow. My epiphany has been to realize how naïve that was."

Gants looked her in the eyes for a long moment before replying, "I'm not buying it, Claire. You're *not* that naïve. You've known from the beginning that there would be political ground to be gained—or lost—from this investigation. If this political manipulation bothered you so much, why wait until now to bring it up? You could have raised this issue with me at any time. Why let it boil until you feel you have to resign over it? Especially *after* the fact?"

She thought one more time about what she was about to say. "There are a few reasons, I guess," she said finally. "I couldn't bring myself to walk away from this earlier, because I felt a sense of obligation to Katherine. Maybe it was guilt because I was right there when she got shot and didn't stop it. Maybe I felt that I needed to redeem myself because I *couldn't* stop it. I don't know—I just felt that I'd let her down and needed to make that up to her.

"As to why I didn't raise a flag earlier," she said, "in the beginning, I guess I was afraid that opening the political issue would simply distract everyone from the investigation and nothing would get done while everyone played cover-your-ass. Again, I guess I thought I could stay ahead of it."

"You didn't have to throw the door wide open, Claire. You could have talked to me about it. If there was a problem—if the President, First Lady or anyone else was getting in the way, I'd have roadblocked them right away, you know that," he told her.

Claire didn't reply immediately, she just looked at him. Her thoughts were obvious in her eyes.

"I see ..." he said slowly. "You *didn't* know that. Did you see me as *part* of the problem?" His tone was one of surprise, with just a hint of hurt behind it.

"No, no. Well ... I don't know—maybe, I guess. I'm sorry, Mr. Gants. I don't know *what* to think anymore. In the beginning, I thought we were going after the person or persons who tried to kill the President, and who shot Katherine, and that's all I needed—that was my total focus. Damn the politics! Full speed ahead!

"I thought I could actually use the position as spokesperson to advantage. I thought that by being the one in the public eye, I'd have the last word if I thought anyone was trying to manipulate things. Then Katherine started in with her photo op stuff. I balked at that and got nowhere. Then there was the Israel trip. Talk about political!

"But the last straw, I guess, was that meeting in the Oval Office when I got yanked back from Israel. Nobody cared what the truth *was*, they just wanted to make sure that it didn't get in the way of their own little objectives. Looking back now, I was so fed up at that point, that I think I'd have quit right there if I hadn't been hit with the news about Katherine dying.

"What about *you*?" she said, turning the subject around. "How do *you* keep functioning, knowing what you do about all this? You'd known Katherine for a lot longer than I did—how do you reconcile her shooting being used to win an election?"

She watched his eyes closely for any sign of surprise at the question—any indication that he knew there was a deeper meaning behind her carefully chosen words. She saw none—not even an involuntary blink. Either he really didn't know what she was alluding to, or he was one hell of a cool actor.

"I don't know," he replied, picking up her letter of resignation. "Maybe I keep functioning because I've been around this stuff so long. Maybe too long. I guess I've just grown calloused to it—for good or bad.

"But this isn't about me," he went on. "I understand how you might be feeling right now, but I'm not convinced that a little time won't change that. You can have a hell of a career with the Service, Claire. I can see you setting in this chair, one day. I don't want to see you toss that away."

"Thank you, sir," she said. "But I'm afraid my mind's made up. I don't think sleeping on it is going to change anything."

"Well, Special Agent Bradley, *my* mind is made up too," he replied. Then with a grin, he added, "And I don't think it's a good idea for you and me to tangle over who can be more stubborn. So here's the deal. I'll *keep* your letter of resignation, but I won't *accept* it. I'm just going to put it in your personnel file, for now. As you point out in here, you have four weeks of paid leave coming, and I think you should take it. Lord knows you've earned it.

"But then I'm going to put you on unpaid administrative leave for the following eleven months. If you change your mind at any time during the next year, Claire, give me a call, and I'll have you back on active duty in no time. Deal?"

She couldn't help but be touched by his gesture and his confidence in her. It struck her as the kind of solution that her father would have come up with.

"I don't think I'll be changing my mind, Mr. Gants, but thank you for giving me the opportunity." Rising, she extended her hand, and said, "You've got a deal. Shall I leave my weapon and shield with you?"

"Nope," Gants replied flatly. "You don't cease to be a law enforcement officer just because you're on vacation. You can turn them in, if it comes to that, in four weeks—after we talk again."

They walked to the door, and with a hint of moisture building in her eyes, she opened her arms. Gants stepped forward, and they embraced each other. "You take care of yourself," Gants said.

"I will." Claire replied. "You too." Then she added, "Tell Burger and Powell that my leaving is all their fault—I just couldn't stand working them any more."

Gants chuckled and said that he would. When they broke their embrace, each extended their hand to return what they had pickpocketed.

They each held the other's cell phone.

Claire looked into Gants' eyes. Was he telling her something? —or was it just coincidence?

His eyes gave away nothing. She was pretty sure she was happier for that.

Chapter 71

Tuesday, November 11
Plum Island, Newbury, MA

I t was a little before four in the afternoon when Dave Perkins pulled his pickup truck into the driveway in front of his small frame house on Plum Island. On the street in front was a maroon Ford sedan. He didn't recognize the car, but he had an idea why it might be parked there.

He unlocked the front door and went in, hoping that he was going to find Claire—that it was her rental car out front. He had told her where he kept a spare key hidden and had invited her to make herself at home if she was ever up north and he wasn't around.

The house was empty, however, and exactly as he had left it when he went on duty that morning. With one notable exception. His black Labrador retriever, Max, was not there.

Dave walked to the picture window that looked out across the sandy beach and the dark waters of the Atlantic Ocean. There, where the sea met the shore, walked a solitary figure, bundled against the cold November wind. A big black dog walked beside the figure.

Dave stepped out onto his back porch and made his way down the steps onto the sand. At the first creek of the door, Max abandoned his walking partner, and bounded across the sand to greet his master. To-

384

gether they made their way back to the shoreline.

A smile spread across Claire's face as Dave approached and Max bounded back and forth between them.

The face that peeked out from between the woolen scarf thrown several times around her neck, and the heavy knit cap pulled low and over her ears, was absolutely adorable in Dave's eyes. "This is a pleasant surprise," he said above the noise of the surf. "Is everything okay?"

She nodded her head as she reached out a mittened hand to take his. They walked along in silence for a while, just listening to the waves crashing against the shore and the gulls squawking their protest as Max ran ahead, chasing them from his beach.

"You know," Claire said at last, "I'd almost forgotten how this place can put me at ease. How a little bit of the world just disappears with each step in the sand." She stopped and turned toward him. "Yeah. Everything's okay," she said. "I think everything is going to be just fine."

She wrapped her arms around him, and held him as tightly as she could with her heavy jacket and mittened hands, and buried her face into his shoulder. Above the noise of the crashing waves and the cold wind, she said, "God, I've missed you!" She turned her face up towards his and he kissed her passionately, pulling her tightly to himself.

When their lips parted, she looked into his eyes and said, "Did I mention that I love you?"

Epilogue

As Claire was flying above the Atlantic on her way back to Washington from Israel, Henri Marchaund's computer announced that he had received a new e-mail.

He opened it and read it to himself. Then, shaking his head and making little "tsk, tsk" sounds, he said to the other man in the room, "This is not good news, I'm afraid. My condolences on your grievous loss, *mon ami*, but my friend in Israel has just confirmed that you are dead—positively identified by the American woman, Bradley, and confirmed by the Shin Bet."

François DeCarlo, a.k.a. Frances Dunham, a.k.a. The Teacher, lifted his eye from the lens of Henri's telescope, and replied solemnly, "A distressing loss indeed. But, I guess it's just something I'm going to have to live with, no?" The two men chuckled and rose their glasses of sherry to each other. "To you," François said. "The *maestro*!"

*****

It had been François who had initiated the chain of events that the two men were now toasting. Over the years, François had become a very regular client of Henri's, and also a close friend. So, it was naturally to Henri that François turned with his special request. He wanted to retire. And since the only way to truly retire from the business that François was in—and to have people stop hunting you—was to be confirmed dead, the two began working on just such a plan. But François' enemies were a wary bunch. Finding a body floating in the Mediterranean with François' identity papers would convince very few. The authorities had no fingerprints that they could conclusively say were François', and because of numerous plastic surgeries, they weren't even sure what he looked like. A month after François' decision to retire, while he and Henri were still formulating a workable plan, another of Henri's long-time clients unknowingly became *part* of the plan.

Moshe Yousif, whose children were grown, and whose wife had died the previous year, decided to sell his house, and move into a condo in Tel Aviv. In doing so, he had to get rid of the odd weapon in the sealed container that had been buried in his back yard for years. Although Yousif had never tried to fire the gun, he had read the hand-written manual that he had recovered with it, and knew that it was a cumbersome weapon, to say the least. In the years that he had had it in his possession, Yousif had never come up with a target against whom it would be practical. The gun was an interesting curiosity, but of no realistic value to Yousif. His friend, Henri, however, might enjoy having it, if only for its uniqueness.

The day before he contacted Henri about the gun, Yousif had been in an intelligence meeting where The Teacher's name had come up several times. He decided, then, what his price to Henri would be for the gun; information that would allow him to capture or kill The Teacher.

The third major player in Henri's grand ensemble was Leland Carroll, who, it turned out, was the catalyst that allowed the whole plan to work. When Leland contacted Henri and said that he wanted to arrange the assassination of the First Lady of the United States, Henri was surprised, to put it mildly. But when Leland responded by saying simply that it was a personal matter, Henri let the matter drop. He was sure there was more to it than settling some personal grudge, but Henri was the hallmark of discretion; he asked no questions and he didn't judge ... especially when he was handed a golden opportunity. He immediately contacted François.

Since the security surrounding the President and his wife was always extraordinary, the means to kill her would have to be even more so. After Henri learned, well in advance, through Leland, that the President planned to speak in the open-air Newburyport High football stadium, he passed the information on to François, who reconnoitered the area. When he reported back to Henri that there were a number of good sniper points, but that they would all, undoubtedly, be sealed off, or at least be closely monitored, he asked Henri, only half jokingly, what he thought about using a shoulder-launched missile from the hospital that was two miles up the hill. Henri explained that the hit needed to be "surgical"; only the target was to die. And it was of the utmost importance that the President not be harmed. It then occurred to Henri that this might be the perfect opportunity to use the fascinating new weapon he had recently acquired from Yousif. On top of it being practical, Henri loved the irony. Henri knew, through Yousif, that the CIA had built—and then lost—the gun in the eighties, and now it was to be used to kill their own First Lady, and it was an ex-CIA operative who was arranging the hit. Although Leland didn't know that the CIA gun would be used for the assassination, Henri wondered how well insulated Leland was. Once the gun's origin hit the fan, he might find that he needed a very deep hole in which to hide. But that was not Henri's concern. Leland had been in the game long enough to know what he was getting into. Henri was sure that he would have some type of cover in place. François' exit-strategy, however, *was* Henri's concern.

In the months prior to François' employment at the St. Jacques Hospital as Frances Dunham, Henri had gone to great lengths to find a lookalike double for François in his *persona* of Dunham. The double hadn't needed to be a twin, since he, like François, was going to undergo plastic surgery. The critical issue that was required of the double was that the distance between the eyes be nearly identical. Photo comparisons of Dunham alive and dead would be inevitable, and incorrect eye spacing would be a dead giveaway. The surgery, rather than making the imposter look like Dunham, would, instead, make him look like Dunham *after* he had undergone surgery to alter his appearance.

Henri had found a suitable surrogate in the person of small-time dope dealer in Barcelona.

One of Henri's people, posing as an agent for the Mossad, had tapped into the man's greed, and had easily recruited him to become a mole for a single operation in which he would set up a Palestinian terrorist for assassination. After the job was successfully completed, the man would receive $250,000 and a new identity.

The tricky part of the plan was to make sure that the authorities could positively identify the body of the look-alike as that of Dunham-after-plastic-surgery. The most certain way to do that would be through fingerprints or DNA, but such evidence would have to be on something that the stand-in had touched, bitten, or bled on, *and* that could then be transported to the St. Jacques for "discovery". The problem was that it would have to look like it had been left accidentally, even though Dunham had been meticulous about not leaving any evidence on the computer or gun.

The solution came to François when he realized that he needed a new pair of lever-action wire strippers, because the set he was using wasn't cutting cleanly, requiring two strokes to pull the insulation instead of the normal one. He had nearly thrown them out when he noticed that the end of each stripped wire had a unique mark in the insulation that matched a small defect in the gripping jaws of the strippers.

When he was done assembling the computer and gun, using those strippers, François sent them to Henri along with duplicates of the other tools in Dunham's tool belt. He instructed Henri to have the look-alike use the tools for bomb-making or some such activity that would seem logical in the situation.

The tools were then returned to François, who, on his last day at the hospital, left the imposter's set, and took the set that he had been using as Dunham with him. It was hoped, and proved correct, that the authorities would assume that since Dunham never took her tools home with her, she had simply neglected to do so on her last day before the shooting. Or, perhaps she had left them intentionally so as not to arouse suspicion when she left. After all, the authorities theorized, Dunham would believe that there would be nothing in the tool belt to connect her to the gun.

François had no doubt that the authorities would dust all of Dunham's tools for fingerprints. But he could only hope that they would notice the marks on the wires and make the connection to the strippers.

Since François had not known then—nor did he know now—about the part which Avi Geller, prompted by Henri, would eventually play in his "death," he took it upon himself to point the authorities in the direction of the house in Ramallah by leaving a trail of telephone calls from the hospital to his safe-house in Seabrook. There, he had replaced one of the toilet seats with one that had been used by his double, and wiped it down to remove any trace of its use, carefully "neglecting" to wipe the underside. He also, painstakingly, planted a scrap of paper with a partial telephone number on it inside a shredder.

Concerned that the trail to the safe-house might not be discovered in a timely enough manner for it to be of use, however, François had backed-up his plan by calling Claire as Larry Douglas, and letting her trace the call to the Seabrook house. François also knew that such a call, warning her off the trail of Frankie Dunham would have exactly the opposite effect on a person of Bradley's character. Her addition to Henri's ensemble had been one of pure luck, but François wanted to take full advantage of it. If she could be manipulated, through Henri's contacts and simple guile, to be there as a witness to François' death and to identify the body, the credibility of the whole charade would be increased tenfold. In a poll taken two days before the election, Claire had been named the most trustworthy person on television.

Unfortunately, even though François could *lead them to the water*, he had no means by which to tip the authorities that they should disassemble the shredder once they "discovered" the Seabrook safe-house. He had to put his faith in the competence of the agencies involved. Always a huge risk.

Henri, however, had no such faith in the competency of government agencies. So, without François even knowing, he initiated his own plan to direct the authorities to Ramallah. That plan included calling in a favor, one of hundreds owed to him by clients all over the world, from Charlie Townsend. Henri had Charlie contact Claire and plant the seeds that the assassination may have come out of the Middle East, and that she should contact Avi Geller. It was pure coincidence—or, as Claire might speculate; *voices* talking—that Charlie happened to know the history of the gun. That fact was unknown to Henri. Henri then provided Avi with the photograph in which Dunham-in-beard had been digitally edited into an Israeli surveillance photo taken in front of the house in Ramallah.

But Henri's web of connections in the plot went further yet.

Henri had been instrumental in getting Avi's operative, Samer al-Abassi, accepted into the Hamoudi cell, so he knew as much about what was going on in Ramallah as Avi did. And it was that connection to Avi and al-Abassi, and also to Moshe Yousif that allowed Henri to fit so many pieces of Leland Carroll's "Weaver" project together—and to be sure that his old friend, François, ended up "dead" at the end of it.

Moshe Yousif's ties to Henri were long-standing, but unlike most of Henri's customers, who were simple criminals, Yousif's motives were far more altruistic than greedy—altruistic in *his* mind, at any rate. Moshe Yousif was a patriotic Israeli whose only vision of whether actions were right or wrong was whether or not the result benefited the state of Israel.

After the wheels of Weaver were set in motion, Henri contacted Yousif with an updated proposal regarding the information about The Teacher that Henri had agreed to supply. Henri wished for Yousif to personally guarantee that The Teacher would be killed rather than be taken prisoner. Henri explained that the reason for the order of execution was to settle a personal matter, but Yousif didn't really believe him. Nor did he care. The Teacher was better dead than alive, regardless of the reason.

During his training for the "operation", François's double had been told by his "Mossad" handlers that when Colonel Yousif's raid took place, that he needed to be out back and light a cigarette. The cigarette would be the identifying signal that he was one of the hit-squad and was not to be harmed as the Israeli commandos stormed the house.

The double was told that a member of the raiding party would give a signal at which time he should draw his pistol and move toward that person, away from the house. He should hold the gun down, in a non-threatening manner, but should make sure it was visible. That would be a second signal, but would also give him a cover-story if someone from the house saw him walking out into the darkness. He should say that he was going to investigate a noise.

Henri's faux-Mossad agents, who were training the double, found it hard to believe that anyone could be that gullible and survive as a criminal past the age of about twelve. But there he was—living proof that the human gene-pool needed a lot more chlorine.

Claire's suspicions about al-Abassi had been absolutely correct. al-Abassi was indeed central to Henri's whole game plan. Without knowing it, he was not only working for Henri and Avi, but also for Yousif and Leland Carroll, and by extension, for the First Lady of the United States.

As part of the web of lies that would point the blame for the assassination at the Hamoudis, Henri, unknown to Avi, had had al-Abassi plant the notebooks in the house and then tell her about his "discovery." al-Abassi had *not* known about the booby trapped file cabinet, however, and it was likely only his *own* "voice" that had him put the books into the *bottom* drawer, and not the top.

al-Abassi was also used by Henri to introduce, "into the record," other bits of critical information, such as the fatwa against the First Lady. And while the fatwa was technically genuine, it had been a product of Henri's Muslim contacts, not Hamoudi. Hamoudi, as he claimed during his interrogation, never knew a thing about it.

And the back-of-the-truck conversation that al-Abassi had supposedly overheard, in which Hamoudi and Dunham had talked about the President's wife, had never taken place at all. Nor had the backdoor debate during which al-Abassi had reported to have heard Hamoudi and Dunham arguing about Dunham's payment schedule.

al-Abassi was also enlisted to pass information to Avi that she would then pass on to Claire as if the bits were genuine revelations, and not part of Henri's master plan.

*****

All in all, Leland Carroll's "Weaver project" had been the most complex venture that Henri had ever had his fingers in. In terms of the number and level of the people who were involved; in terms of the logistics; in terms of the timing and the coordination not just between people, but between government agencies; and even in terms of risk, it was unlike anything he had ever done before—or would likely ever do again. And it gave him the utmost satisfaction when he thought about how smoothly it had all come off. "Weaver" was indeed, his *pièce de résistance*.

*****

Richard McClure spent the next four years trying, with better than average success, to fulfill his campaign promises. Though he endured his share of battles both in the media and in Congress, his approval ratings remained consistently higher than any other non-wartime president. Upon leaving office, he retired for about a year, during which he nearly went nuts from boredom, and finally accepted a professorship teaching politics at his and Katherine's *alma mata*. He is currently working on a memoir of his life with Katherine.

Claire Bradley returned to Washington after her four week leave, but only to turn in her weapon and her Secret Service identification. She moved in with Dave Perkins and after her resignation was final, she took a job as a fraudulent-claims analyst with a major insurance company in Boston. She has begun writing a mystery novel in her spare time, and teaches a free self-defense judo class two nights a week.

Dave Perkins was promoted to sergeant with the Newburyport Police Department and began the college courses necessary to advance to lieutenant and higher. On the one-year anniversary of their dinner at Dave's uncle's, Dave proposed to Claire. She accepted, but the couple has yet to set a date for the wedding.

Leland Carroll, in the years that followed, performed the occasional odd job for Henri Marchaund and also took on a few very discreet, very black operations for his former employers at the CIA. As retirement goes, Leland's is fulfilling and comfortable. He has never had contact with Claire again.

Samer al-Abassi was convicted, as planned, of being an accessory-after-the-fact in a single terror bombing where no deaths had occurred. He was sentenced to 12 months in prison where he was killed by fellow inmates suspicious of his light sentence as compared to the Hamoudi's and Hamshari's life sentences. His body was found in the prison showers with a bar of soap jammed down his throat. Prison authorities were sure they knew who had murdered Samer, but were not able to produce any evidence to allow them to prosecute them. Within a month, two of those inmates were dead themselves. One had hanged himself and the other had met with an unfortunate choking accident—both with the assistance of people working for Henri Marchaund. Henri had considered Samer to be a very valuable asset and was most cross when he heard about his death.

François "Frances Dunham" DeCarlo had planned meticulously for his life-after-death. He had salted away plenty of money in accounts all over the world; he had a complete new identity, including Australian citizenship; and he had purchased a small horse ranch just south of Canberra.

Staring out through Henri's telescope on that day that he found out he was dead, however, caused him to re-think the rancher's life. Watching the sailing and power yachts plying the Mediterranean coast he made an instant change in plans. A week later his ranch was for sale and he had made a down payment on an 82-foot ketch. (A cash purchase—which he could easily have afforded—might have drawn attention that François didn't want.) One condition of the sale was that the current owner stay on long enough to teach Frank to handle the boat. Always a fast learner, Frank was running the boat smoothly and, along with the former owner and a crew of two, had made a complete loop of the Mediterranean within four months. Two years later he had his captain's license from the Spanish Coast Guard and had begun taking on charters. It was not uncommon after that, for Henri to focus his telescope on a smiling and waving Frank as he guided his seaborne home along the Cartagena coast—very often with sun-worshiping young men and women on the teak decks.

James Gants retired from the Secret Service at the end of Richard McClure's second term, with Paul Levine taking his place. Though it is a secret and a burden he will take to his grave, Gants was, indeed, involved in the conspiracy to assassinate Katherine McClure. His involvement was out of love for her, however, not political idealism.

In college, Gants had developed a one-sided crush on Katherine, and although she considered Gants a very dear friend, she had her romantic sights set on Richard. Katherine and Richard's relationship, in the beginning, however, had a few rocky patches, and during one of their fights, Katherine had turned to Gants for consolation, which culminated in their sleeping together. They agreed, the morning after—although Gants was lying through his teeth—that the sex had been an unfortunate mistake, and neither of them ever told anyone or talked about it again.

After graduation, they went their separate ways, and had no contact with each other until Richard was assigned a Secret Service detail during his first run for the Presidency.

During their school years, Leland was well aware of Gants' unrequited love for Katherine, and he strongly suspected (although he never knew, for sure) that Gants had been intimate with Katherine on at least one occasion. It was that knowledge, and playing on that suspicion that allowed him to recruit Gants into the web.

Recruiting foreign agents had been Leland's specialty for years with the CIA, but it still took several months of delicate influence, rekindling Gants' feelings for Katherine, before Leland felt that he could even let Gants in on the secret of Katherine's terminal illness. Convincing him not to interfere with Katherine's "suicide" plan took more time, still. And getting him to actively participate by retrieving her cell phone was the most daunting part of all. The most emphatic condition that Gants made to Leland was that Katherine not know that he was involved. It was a gift to her for which he wanted no recognition.

The morning of the shooting, Gants began having second thoughts about watching Katherine die, and he actually hoped that Claire and her enigmatic *voice* might, somehow, stop the whole thing.

In his retirement, Gants continues to conduct training seminars, and frequently lectures at the Secret Service Academy. He has accepted Claire's request that he give her away at her wedding.

The End

Acknowledgements

I would like to thank the following people for their contributions to this book:

Jennifer Blaisdell for the cover design.
Shar Edwards for final editing.
Robert Blaisdell for advice on legal content.
Jim Wilcox for technical assistance regarding ballistics.
Matt Curtain for technical assistance regarding software and encryption.

Printed in the United States
200407BV00005B/10-36/A

9 781432 715700